A Mercedes sedan coming down the street toward the bank suddenly left the traffic lane and jumped onto the sidewalk. Its horn blared. People scrambled out of its way. A few stunned pedestrians fell into the street to escape. The sedan had a clear path to the bank.

Jesse watched as the Mercedes slowed, a rear door opened and then closed. Then the automobile thumped back onto the road and hurtled by their table and up the street.

Jesse could see what looked like a bundle on the sidewalk outside the bank's front entrance. He leaped to his feet and looked harder. Lilli rose and half turned. Every eye on the street was caught by the bundle.

Jesse grabbed Lilli's hand across the table for a moment, "Get across the street, Lilli," he said, "and watch the bank and the alley. We're in the middle of a goddamn war!"

THE
QUINTANA INHERITANCE

a novel by

Elliot Tokson

FAWCETT GOLD MEDAL • NEW YORK

To the brothers Al and Ken

THE QUINTANA INHERITANCE

Copyright © 1980 Elliot Tokson

Published by Fawcett Gold Medal Books, a unit of CBS Publications, the Consumer Publishing Division of CBS Inc.

ISBN: 0-449-14354-6

Printed in the United States of America

First Fawcett Gold Medal printing: August 1980

10 9 8 7 6 5 4 3 2 1

Part 1

Chapter 1

Michael Quinn laid aside his Premier Winchester and the oily rag he had been using to wipe it and, looking up, asked the chauffeur, Frank, to turn off on 68 and drive over to Crane's Beach.

Then he picked up the engraved shotgun and continued to run the cloth lovingly over the finely chiseled scrollwork, wiping away the moisture of invisible fingerprints, caressing the gold inlays of bear, stag, Canadian goose, and ringtail pheasant. He carefully removed every trace of fouling from the breech and chamber that had accumulated from the day's hunt up in Georgetown, north of Boston.

Sitting next to him, Joseph Quinn was cleaning his own favorite Purdy gun with as much care and affection as Michael was taking with the Winchester. Purdys and Winchesters. Shotguns were one of the few subjects Michael and Joseph ever disagreed about.

Soon their black Cadillac limousine was moving across the parking zone at Crane's Beach toward the famous bone-white sand dunes patched with sharp sea grass. It was Crane's as the aging, handsome Quinn brothers loved her best—deserted. Refreshment stand, comfort stations, and first-aid house boarded up, the only residents were a few hungry gulls circling the sands or pecking among the dunes.

Before the limousine came to a halt near a dune, Joseph Quinn gave in to a nagging in his brain and looked back. As he did so, a blue Ford pick-up truck with two men inside swung into the parking area after them.

Frank coasted the Cadillac to a stop at the front of a high dune, resting its bumper against the low heavy barrier that prevented vehicles from climbing onto the sand. The motor was already dead. A gull on the dune stood on one leg and eyed them.

Suddenly, twisting further in his seat and still watching through the rear window, Joseph shouted, "Jesus Christ, Michael, they're coming right for us!"

The Ford pick-up had rolled slowly across the parking lot toward another dune. But as soon as the Cadillac halted, the truck suddenly speeded up, then skidded to a stop and crashed into the limousine's bumper, blocking it from movement. A cloud of dust rose so that Joseph could not see who was in the truck.

"Get us out of here, Frank, ram them!" Michael Quinn yelled at the chauffeur. He reached down, broke open his Winchester, and had shoved two shells into the chambers when he heard the explosions outside.

The motor of the Cadillac came alive with a roar, but Michael couldn't see that Frank had fallen half over the wheel. The glass divider between the front and rear seats had changed into an opaque web of tiny cracks. The horn of the Cadillac was blaring.

On his side of the limousine, the window was down and Michael could see a man swinging a short carbine toward the rear seat. Unexpectedly, two more shots rang out from the opposite direction. Glass poured in on him as the glass partition inside the car was fractured into a million pieces.

Michael could feel the impact of slugs striking into the rear seat next to him. He heard Joseph.

"Shit, Michael, what a way for us to go!"

Michael tried to figure out whether there was gladness in those words or despair. They had faced death often over the years, in their fighter planes, in their saddles, and, yes, in the back seats of cars, too. And they had talked plenty about it, because it helped. But that was long ago.

Now Michael could not decide whether Joseph was complaining or rejoicing. There was too much noise to think. And there was a funny dampness under his shirt. The effort he was making to lift his Winchester and swing it toward the window took all of his concentration. The Winchester had never felt so heavy. He couldn't understand it. He had bought it partly for its lightness. It was getting heavier by the minute. He had to get the man on his left.

Joseph felt the first hit in his left shoulder, the second in his left arm. His body pressed backwards into the seat under the impacts. Somehow he managed to load his Purdy.

When Joseph shouted to Michael about what a way to go, there was no fear in his voice, no complaint. Death had sat on his shoulder often enough to give him little discomfort now. But the pain was harder to take. The first lines of its travel streaked from his left side into his face and twisted his mouth. But it stopped there. He felt relieved. The flesh was numb. Hope rose suddenly in his chest, and left quickly as his brain assessed the situation. But the fear never came. *It was the dogfight over the Marne all over again, the massacre at Deraa, the attack on the bridge in the Riff Mountains.* And they had survived those!

Joseph instinctively raised his Purdy toward the window, but he had no room to draw the silver bead above the muzzle onto the man out there who was shooting holes into him.

He squeezed the front trigger anyway. The light birdshot dissolved the right side of the windshield and removed what was left of the window in the right front door. Before he could squeeze the second trigger, he heard a roar from his side and he heard Michael laughing.

"That scared the bastard," Michael chuckled.

The gunfire outside was crackling from both sides of the Cadillac. The horn was still blaring but was fading rapidly beyond the dunes. Michael and Joseph were listening to it as though it were *the scramble alarm on the flying field of the Escadrille Lafayette. The Hun were buzzing in. Boeckle and Goering and the Baron. The Circus was here. The red triplanes were in sight. They were running for their Nieuports, and the horn behind was fading, growing dimmer and dimmer as they approached their aircraft and their engines warming up until finally the scramble horn gave way completely to the roar of the powerful Gnomes. And then they were off, in a few feet, into the air, climbing, climbing, Michael on Joseph's left. Always on the left.*

The jacketed bullets from the carbines tore into and through them, ripping up the leather seats, fanning the blood and flesh everywhere. The pain flowed back into both of them, stinging them alive like wasp stings surging and then growing distant as the wasps buzzed off. *The triplanes, with empty guns, streaked away.*

The impact of slug after slug toppled Joseph toward the center of the seat, where he faintly sensed Michael's body, still jerking, Joseph thinking, still on my left, always protecting my left. With one last effort he squeezed the second trigger and smiled somewhere in his mind as he thought he had hit something other than air and the car.

He tried to say something to Michael. His lips moved and he tried to say, "It's a hell of a way to go, Michael, but it's been good," and he would have sworn Michael answered him and said, "It has, Joe, hasn't it? And didn't I tell you—we *are* going with our boots on! Together. Together. Tog—"

Before the third "together" passed over the last pulsation of his brain, the horn stopped blowing, the pain went, and the quiet came.

Chapter 2

The timing was awkward. The harsh ring of Jesse Quinn's telephone upset the atmosphere of the moment and spoiled his equilibrium.

He was about to make the essential move to change his relationship with the lovely girl sitting next to him on the sofa from a pleasant social friendship, recently made, into a more intimate one. Jesse had met Sherry three weeks earlier at the Longview Tennis Club, where she split four sets with him and attacked Ike's golf administration at the same time. Since then he had seen her three or four times casually, kissed her twice, and now, in the middle of their third kiss, was unhooking her bra under her sweater and had one hook to go.

Jesse had learned at the age of fifteen that when a girl allowed him her bare breast, she would give him whatever else he could think of afterwards. The pattern had never changed, except that with grown-up girls it moved even faster.

At twenty-nine, Jesse was darkly good-looking, with an angular face, dark, warm eyes, black hair, and firm but sensuous lips. Only his excessively high cheekbones that gave his face a faintly Eastern flavor kept him from that handsome all-American look.

He was wealthy and expensively educated, Sherry could see that easily enough—from the car he drove, the tennis club he belonged to, and the original Monets and Picassos on the wall in front of her. His speech was obviously Boston Ivy-League.

"I know you play tennis," she had said when he had begun to undo her clothes. "What else do you do?" To be silent at that moment, she thought, would have been obscene.

"I ski," he said softly. "I can sail the family ketch by myself if I have to. You'll like the boat."

He kissed her ear. What he did not tell her was that he could shoot any kind of weapon as well as most men and fly almost any plane, single or twin engined, better. He also rode dressage, and he could acquit himself quite well on a polo field. Sherry knew that

10

he worked five days a week in the family business, but to reveal all his talents to her would have made him sound like a playboy.

She had already seen him display all the social graces that should attend money and education, including a healthy share of intelligence. When he had taken her out to dine, he was as at home ordering in Italian as he was in English, and she knew he spoke Spanish fluently. On their date in a French restaurant, he did not have to ask the waiter to translate the menu.

What more could a woman want?

Evidently something else.

At first Sherry did not know what. Neither did Jesse.

He could not keep a woman very long. His affairs lasted a year, perhaps two, and it was usually the women who did the walking. Not in anger or bitterness, nor in physical dissatisfaction, but often in sadness and always in amity. He was invariably good to them, but he never really cared when it ended. It was the not caring that bothered him.

This time he was with a girl who was not very rich or well connected, and that was a change. Neither of those things mattered, because he was excessively both. She was brighter than he was, though, and he was bright enough to have gotten through Harvard, *magna*. She had almost convinced him that Stevenson would have been better for the country than Ike and that Korea had been a tragedy. He had shrugged at that and never told her that he had been there. He disliked talking of his war service except with people who had shared it and could understand, people like his father and his uncle Joseph.

Sherry had a dark, fresh look without actually being beautiful, but her figure was good, although it was too full for modeling. He liked that too, but he liked better the way she talked and thought. And he could tell from the way she was kissing him now how good the lovemaking was going to be. To frost it all, she was Jewish, and Jewish was not what Jesse's women usually were.

He paused for a moment. "We're going to have a beautiful friendship, aren't we?" he whispered.

"I didn't know you went in for euphemisms," she said, smiling.

"I don't," he said, and he knew that she was not going to mean anything important to him. Sherry knew it, too.

That was the problem. The girls always knew, sooner or later, that they were not going to be very vital to him. They gave him their friendship first, and then their bodies as well, and he never abused either. He always made them feel more than just a lay, and they *were* more, but not enough more. They always had a good time, in the bedroom and out of it. But everything stopped at friendship. No commitment, no exclusiveness. Sometimes they would hang on for a year or a little longer. And when the sex ended, the friendship continued.

To Jesse, women seemed so much generally alike that he let them drift when they wanted to. There were no sharp breaks. They parted the way light parts at the end of day, into twilight and then into night. For a long time he didn't know anything was wrong. But now, at twenty-nine, he was beginning to suffer short spells of self-doubt. For a while he thought he might prefer the camaraderie of men. He was happiest with Uncle Joe and his own father when the three were alone. But that was not enough. He liked women, he was easy and comfortable with them. And he had no trouble finding them.

The trouble was that he had not met a woman whose company he could say he would miss if he did not see her for a week. That was the way he measured his feelings. Would he miss her if he could not see her for a week? The answer had not yet been "yes."

Except for Lilli.

But she was his sister and did not count. Cousin rather, although he thought of her as a sister, so closely had they been brought up in the same house in Beverly. Just the four of them: his father, Uncle Joe, Lilli, and he.

He had missed Lilli when they did not see one another for a week. During the wars, when he had flown in Europe and then in Korea, he had missed Lilli most of all.

He had to remind himself sometimes that she was not any woman, that she was his sister. He trained himself successfully to crowd her out of his mind when she intruded. He thought of other things—his flying record, his kills, the lost men who did not come back from a strike over Germany, the English girls who betrayed their Tommies with him at nineteen. He thought about anything but Lilli, because she was his sister.

Not that he hadn't really tried with other women. He *had* married. It was expected. Not by his father or uncle, but by the world of the North Shore. Leslie had everything Sherry had and much more. Better looks, better schooling (Switzerland and Radcliffe), a figure that could be a model's, all the money she could ever spend, and a nice old Beverly Farms address, and she knew all the right people connected with addresses like hers.

12

The marriage had problems from the beginning. They cared for each other, were tender when it mattered, and behaved kindly without trying. But Leslie always complained she found him remote when she wanted him near, always found him holding back when she wanted him to let go, never felt he was all hers or ever would be. Leslie realized that she could never be all his, because he did not want her that way.

And she was right. Jesse never denied it.

Their separation and divorce came within two years of their marriage. One morning over coffee Leslie quietly said that he cared more for cousin Lilli than he did for her. That afternoon he had gone back on active duty in the Air Force for jet training to fly in Korea. She divorced him two months later and called him in Tokyo to give him the news.

Sherry, too, had sensed that Jesse had a lock on his feelings. At first she had thought it shyness, but within a few hours after meeting him she knew the reserve went deeper. Too bad, she had thought. She had studied his face over the tennis net and sighed. He would never be for her—too good-looking in a fine, almost Yankee way, chin cleft and all, dark hair, dark eyes.

Right now, knowing him better, she thought him Spanish or something farther east, certainly not Yankee blue blood. What a catch he would have been! So gentle, too, and slow. But she would never break that cool reserve of his or rid herself of that discomforting idea she had that an important part of him was somewhere else. Still, here she was, letting him undo her bra and finding it impossible to keep from trembling as his fingers deftly caressed her breast.

When the telephone rang a few feet away, Sherry gasped a tiny "oh" of disappointment at its first jangle. Jesse touched his fingers to his lips and then to hers as though it would stop and go away if they were quiet. It did not. It rang and rang and rang. He leaned over and picked up the receiver.

"Hello. . . . Yes, Tom. . . . Say that again, Tom. . . . What? . . ." Jesse's dark face lost its handsomeness. His brows furrowed so deeply the eyebrows were pushed toward the bridge of his nose, where two long parallel lines appeared and separated them. The skin along his cheeks stretched tight over the high sharp bones and his dark eyes seemed to have sunk deep into his head. The knuckles on the hand gripping the telephone whitened.

"Dad *and* Uncle Joe? Are you absolutely sure?" His voice had shaken for the first three or four words, but the control was back.

13

"Edna took the call, then?.... Both of them?.... Did you check back to get it straight?.... Give me his name..."

He found a pen in his coat and started to write on the telephone pad. "Give it to me again." He wrote a name: *Lieutenant H. Wilkinson, State Police barracks, Georgetown*. Then he wrote a number. "Could there have been a mistake?.... Frank, too?.... What were they doing at Crane's Beach? Weren't you and the dogs with them?.... All right, Tom. Take care of things there. I'll get Lilli and we'll go right out there. Ipswich Hospital. Tom, keep it quiet until I see you, if you can.... How's Edna taking it?... Stay with her."

He replaced the receiver mechanically and stared numbly toward a window, seeing nothing of Louisburg Square, which it overlooked. Consciously he transformed the image in his mind into reality, digesting the words, internalizing them until a terrible buzzing in his head blocked them, the tears still too deep to come, the discipline too strong to express his feelings to a stranger, and thankful that the strange girl sitting there, stunned, held back her questions. When he did cry it would be alone—with the thoughts of his father, his uncle Joseph, his old friend Frank. Even Lilli would not see him cry. He would cry as he had cried when he was nineteen on a hidden airfield in Sussex, silently, the tears hardly coming from his eyes, crying for the friends shot down over Liège, Cologne, Stuttgart. By the time of Korea, the tear ducts had dried up; the mood had changed and no one cried for anyone. He had not cried since Sussex.

A few minutes passed as he sat there. Finally Sherry reached out a hand to his arm.

"What is it, Jesse?" Her voice was half-frightened.

Jesse blinked his eyes a few times. His lips were drawn tight across his teeth.

"Can I call a taxi for you? It's my father. He's dead. And my uncle too."

"Oh, God, I'm sorry." Her face went white. She stared at him with big green eyes that were filling with water. She struggled to get the words out. "Is there anything...?"

"No, nothing," said Jesse, interrupting her and reaching for the phone again. "Can you get yourself home? I'm going out right away and I have to pick up my cousin Lilli."

The girl was already slipping into a pale blue woolen coat. She swung a bag over her shoulder, kissed him briefly on his cheek,

14

squeezing him around the shoulders as she did, and whispered in a broken voice.

"I'll be all right. I'll get a taxi over on Charles ... Jesse ... call if you want me."

"Thanks," he said and started to dial a number.

He heard the apartment door open and close quietly as his call began to ring.

Chapter 3

Lilli Quinn was lying naked on her back next to her fiancé when the telephone near the bed rang. A light sheet covered them. They were sharing an English Oval cigarette. James Wainwright lay with his arms akimbo and his hands clasped behind his head. Lilli's head rested on his bicep, her mop of black hair spread out over his arm and shoulder. She held the cigarette, inhaled deeply herself, and then raised the cigarette to his lips.

The telephone rang again.

Her fiancé made a face. She nodded and murmured, "The hell with it."

They had lain motionless since they had finished making love. Lilli was weary. Today was Wednesday. It was the day that Jim took off from work, and they spent all afternoon in his apartment. Midday sex was always avid, experimental, and tiring. At college she had learned the palindrome "sex at noon taxes," and it turned out to be true, either way you read it.

Jim was her first and only lover. He had taken her virginity. He was skillful and loving and taught Lilli everything he knew about sex. She thought he was undeniably good at the whole business. It should have been ideal. And yet . . .

The telephone stopped ringing.

Even now, at this moment of drowsy pleasure, there was the reservation.

Jim was James Wainwright III, a State Street lawyer and junior partner in one of the most prestigious law firms in Boston, founded by his great grandfather over a hundred years ago. In Boston society, Jim Wainwright of Harvard, Yale Law School, Marblehead Yacht Club, Manchester Polo Grounds, was one of the finest catches of the day.

And Lilli Quinn, daughter of Joseph Quinn of Quinn Corporation and Quinn Foundation International, had caught him.

Jim was Harvard like her brother Jesse—cousin Jesse, that is, but more like a brother than anything else. (They had taken baths together right up until the time he was ten and she was seven,

16

when their housekeeper Edna noticed once that Jesse, getting excited, looked too much like a grown man to be sharing the tub with young Lilli.)

Jesse had not known Jim at Harvard and had only met him a few years ago at the Harvard Club, and later introduced him to Lilli.

When Jim had found her a virgin at twenty-four, he was stunned. She almost couldn't believe it herself. There certainly had been opportunities to lose it—Christ! the fellows tried hard enough. But something bottled up inside her had always made her quit before it happened.

It was the Quinn men, she used to think, her daddy, Uncle Michael, Jesse, along with herself, who made up a ring not to be broken by a fifth link. As long as she kept herself intact, the Quinn chain would remain unbroken. To break it through her body would be a betrayal of the family.

Then Jim came along and she talked with Jesse about it. The talk was difficult, leaving much unsaid. Afterwards she had gone right to Jim with Jesse's words in her mind.

"It's time to break it up a bit, Lilli," Jesse had said, looking past her. "Time for the woman in you to come out. We really aren't four men, you know, not until you bring the fourth one into it. There's no ring that hasn't been broken before. What about my marriage?"

She thought Jesse's sad speech was what he had to say, not what he wanted to say. But she believed he was right.

She had gone directly into Jim's bed. And shortly after, he proposed. Other girls who had everything she had and more had held hopes for Jim. Yet Lilli didn't enjoy her triumph.

She was aware of the envious looks of her colleagues at the Boston Museum of Fine Art, where she worked in the French Impressionist collection. She accepted the best wishes from the mothers and daughters at their Beverly Farms country club. She read the lengthy articles on her engagement in the *Globe* and the *New York Times* that her old classmates from Wellesley would be certain to read—they all gave Lilli just enough satisfaction to bolster her intention to go through with the marriage and make the most of it.

Make the most of it.... Words like those made it sound as though there were drawbacks to the marriage. Lilli knew of none, except— She struggled against the thought, but finally she had to examine her feelings for her handsome, blond-haired fiancé.

Was it really love? How could she find out? When she had gone to Jesse about it, he had shaken his head and turned away. It was something she would have to work out alone.

"You helped me get into his bed," she had pleaded. "Help me now." She grasped him by his arms.

"That was different, Lilli. It was time. You weren't going to be a nun, were you?" He turned his head away and she released him. "Marrying him is different. I'm not going to help you into that."

Then she had gone to her daddy, and Joseph had listened, as he had so often in the past, with sympathy and love, and waited for her to talk through the tangles until she could see how to work things out for herself. It had always worked for them and it was what she had come to expect. This time she almost got more. Almost.

They had talked in his bedroom the same night she had gotten no help from Jesse. After a while she came around to a conclusion.

"I think Jim's right for me, Daddy, don't you? And then again, I'm not sure. I know he is as right as anyone could be. I know that here"—she touched her forehead with a finger—"but I don't feel it here." And she laid a fist over her heart. "Shouldn't I feel it here, too?" Her voice was touched with anguish.

"Yes," Joseph said quietly, his deep gray eyes studying her face. He reached his arms forward and held Lilli close to him and spoke over her shoulder. "I felt that way for your mother, Lilli, with my head and my heart—and I never felt it for anyone else."

"Did she feel the same way?"

Joseph remained silent for a moment, slipping away into the same enigmatic manner he always adopted when the subject came up. "We were talking about you and Jim, honey." He stepped back from her. "It isn't Jesse, is it?" he asked suddenly.

Lilli's eyes flashed to his. "I don't know. I think he'd be happy to see me married to Jim."

"Honey. I think we'd all be happy to see you do what makes you happy, whatever it is. You come first. You've always come first."

So the engagement continued, but Lilli's feelings remained the same mixture of warm involvement afflicted by doubts, and neither was getting stronger.

It was at times like this afternoon, half slumbering next to Jim's slim hard body, drifting in that delicious mood of post-coitus *tristesse*, the sting of her own desires so sweetly pulled,

18

smoking a rich cigarette—that her doubts should have gone. Instead, Lilli felt more confused than ever.

She drew on the cigarette and let the smoke out slowly. The telephone rang again.

"Jim, you'd better answer it this time," Lilli said sleepily. "Whoever it is knows you're here and just isn't going to go away." She stirred on his arm. "We've got to get ready anyway if we don't want to keep my Quinn men waiting for dinner."

She rolled her head off his arm onto a pillow to let him reach the telephone.

"Hello . . . Hello, Jesse. Sure, she's right here. Did you call a little while ago? . . . Sorry." He handed Lilli the telephone. "He wants you, naturally. Do you tell him everything you do and everywhere you go?" Jim spoke playfully. "He sure as heck knew you were here." He lay back on his pillow and took her cigarette.

Lilli balanced the phone on her ear and spoke with her head half buried in the pillow. If her muffled voice gave her position away, she only half-consciously cared. Jesse knew what she did Wednesday afternoons.

"Hello, Jesse . . . Why? Has our dinner date changed? The hunt sharpened everyone's hunger, huh?" Her voice was sleepy, her face still flush on the clear cheek from the sex. She listened. Her head came off the pillow, her face showing she had come awake a little concerned. "Yes, I can be ready by the time you get here. Ten minutes. But why?"

She sat up straight, the sheet falling away from her upper body, her dark brown eyes a bit wider. Her hair came down onto her shoulders. Jim reached up and cupped her small tight right breast. She laid her hand on top of his. She talked back into the phone as though Jesse were right there facing her.

"I don't like the sound of your voice, Jesse. What's wrong? Tell me now, right now. . . . No, not when you see me, right now." Her voice had risen.

Lilli listened as though she were transfixed. Her mouth came open, her hand left Jim's and came up clenched, white knuckles pressed against her lips. A terrible groan broke from her throat.

She leaped to her feet at the side of the bed, breaking away from Jim's caress.

"Oh, no, Jesse, say it's not true. Please, God, please! Oh, no!" she wailed.

Her slim body bent forward as though a great pain had struck

19

her middle. Her body shook, her skin crawled with gooseflesh. Her face had gone sickly pale. She took a deep, shuddering breath before she could speak again.

"I'm all right, Jesse. . . . I just can't get hold of it." Her mind had clouded in a thick fog. Her eyesight was blurred, her body reeling.

Jim had moved quickly from the bed and supported Lilli by her arms. Suddenly, her knees became unhinged under a great weight set on her shoulders, and she dropped onto the bed in a sitting position, her body caved inwards. She held the phone tightly to her ear and listened to Jesse, hardly aware of Jim kneeling at her feet. Her legs jumped up and down nervously.

Jesse's words began to pull her together. The weight that had pressed her downwards began to lift enough to ease the pressure in her chest and let her breathe. She sat straighter as she heard his soothing voice, until she finally regained her poise and had control of herself. Her legs stopped dancing, and when she spoke, the quiver was gone from her voice.

Before she hung up, Jim asked to speak to her cousin.

A small frown crossed her face and then passed as she said, "There's no need for that, Jim." She replaced the receiver in its cradle. Her hand was steady as though it were not her own. The confusion in Jim's face made her voice shake again as she spoke.

"I've got to go someplace with Jesse. My father and his father have both been killed."

"Oh, God!" Jim paled around his eyes and mouth. He grasped Lilli's hands folded in her lap.

"We'll go together," he said tenderly, getting up and rummaging in the pile of clothing heaped on a nearby chair.

Lilli watched the muscles ripple in his limbs and back as he moved. She traced the clear curve of his boyish buttocks as he bent. Then, as he turned to face her, putting on his shorts, she focused on the curled blond hair on his chest and pelvis. The fog suddenly cleared from her head as though lifted by a breeze. Her mind was surprisingly lucid. It was not Jim and his blond hair that she really wanted.

"No, Jim," she said firmly, picking her underwear and stockings from the chair. "This is something I'll do alone. It concerns Jesse and me. Alone. You don't belong."

Listening to the quiet hum of the tiny mahogany elevator taking her down to the street, Lilli wondered why she had been so harsh.

Chapter 4

Lilli arrived on the sidewalk just as a black Jaguar drew up to the curb. Jesse, leaner and more drawn than she had ever seen him, climbed out, leaving the motor running, and came around to her.

For a moment Lilli stared dazedly into his grim face, trying to find words to comfort him, knowing that Jesse sought to provide the same relief for her. On the phone he had said things about the Quinn family and the Quinn solidarity to strengthen her, but now no words came from either of them. His eyes were dry and sunken, hers were wet and swelling.

He held out his arms and Lilli broke into sobs and fell against him, the top of her dark hair just grazing his chin. Her defenses collapsed. She cried freely. Her shoulders shook violently and her anguished sobs cut into his body.

Suspecting that his call might have caught Lilli in the middle of an embrace, Jesse was oversensitive to her womanliness. He stroked her head gently, and she was his kid sister again.

Her sobs continued. A few tears appeared in his own eyes, but they did not reach his cheeks. Yet he cried inside as hurtfully as she cried openly. The Quinn cousins were crying for their dead fathers, for each other, for themselves.

People walking on Beacon glanced at them discreetly and hurried by, embarrassed. Lilli finally looked up at Jim's apartment on the fourth floor. She could make out a face staring down. She took a deep trembling breath to control her tears and then crouched to get into the Jaguar. Jesse got behind the wheel and sent the sleek low machine roaring off into the traffic.

As they drove across Boston, they spoke very little and mentioned their fathers only once. But they thought of little else, except each other. Sitting with their arms almost touching, crowded in the compact Jaguar, each was sharply aware of the other. There was nothing else to think of now but their fathers and themselves.

Jesse remembered the small celebration Michael and Joseph

21

had given him when he received his fighter pilot's wings in 1944 before he reached his twentieth birthday. The three of them were in uniform—two colonels and a second lieutenant—and they had toasted each other warmly in a small bar and eaten the finest steaks in Tampa. Then they had taken turns talking on the phone to Lilli, who was braving it alone up north with Frank and Edna in the Beverly house.

Watching his father and Uncle Joe joke with Lilli over the telephone, hearing their words of love, and then sitting across from them for the last time before they shipped off to separate air bases—he to England and they to Africa—he was more deeply struck than ever by how much alike the two men were. Their colonel uniforms, marked identically with eagles and the same Air Corps insignia, only increased the effect. Michael and Joseph together and so much alike. But that was the way it had always been. The Quinn brothers agreed on almost everything.

Jesse had never heard them argue over a business matter, and they had talked business freely at home. In November they always voted as dyed-in-the-wool Boston Democrats and were openly proud of it. They had raised Lilli and him from infancy in the same marvelous house, following the same rule of paternal permissiveness warmed by deep affection—and without the help of wives. Lilli's and Jesse's mothers had been dead for years. There were no memories of them. The Quinn brothers had been silent about their early lives.

Michael and Joseph simply thought the same way about that, just as they did about business, politics, child-rearing, women worth dating, even baseball (they both loved the Red Sox and Ted "the Kid" Williams). And there was a deeper harmony between them that was too uncanny for Jesse to recognize until he grew older. Their friends said that they were closer than Damon and Pythias, than Sears and Roebuck, even than Smith and Wesson. He once heard someone say it was unnatural, as though a single spirit invested both bodies. And what irritated some of their smaller-minded acquaintances was that, in spite of all the years of their close association, running the same businesses, living in the same home, they really had never stopped liking each other.

Lilli, too, sitting almost physically numb, was thinking of how much alike her father and Uncle Michael were. And yet their characters were so strikingly distinct. Joseph was quiet, steady, and thoughtful; Michael tense, demonstrative, extroverted. She could not force her mind to the image of them—dead. She thought

22

of them as she had seen them last—at dinner the evening before, filled with plans, looking forward to their first day this season in the fields up in Georgetown, betting who would take the first bird and talking of the new dog their handler Tom was putting into the field with them. It was man talk, and she loved it, had grown up with it, knew little else that she cared for as much.

Dead?

They couldn't be dead. For the first time in her adult life Lilli felt the need for a mother. But there was no woman there.

Neither brother had remarried or had ever brought a woman into their house, though both had dated often. Aside from Edna, Frank's wife, there had been no special female in Lilli's life. And Lilli, three years younger than Jesse, had been the only woman in his, acting like a sister or a mother when he needed one or the other. As they grew up they talked secretly of their mothers and made up some stories about who they might have been and what they had been like. But they had learned not to ask anything more from either father. Questions brought only pained looks from the Quinn men, or blank enigmatic stares.

Now Jesse and Lilli had only each other—and that would be enough to get them through what lay ahead. Jesse had repeated that over and over on the phone, and Lilli knew it was true.

Several times Lilli laid a soft, smooth, trembling hand on Jesse's when he rested it on the stick shift. Twice she asked the same question and he answered her patiently, as though she hadn't asked before.

"I don't know what happened. The police called first and then came out to the house, found Tom, and told him they were shot. I don't know why or how. But whatever took place, we can't let go of the fact that we have each other to count on. Right?"

Jesse forced a smile. He was offering her the encouragement of a big brother, and she took it. She nodded and smiled back, chewing her lips. Jesse noticed only Lilli's strength when he looked at her sturdy features—the long, well-shaped nose, the prominent cheekbones, the dark skin drawn tight over the bone, the dark eyes, tired but no longer dazed or afraid as they had been outside her fiancé's apartment. The tenacity of the Quinns had returned to his sister's face. There would be no hysterics at the hospital.

Outside the small brick, slate-roofed building in Ipswich there were three gray-and-blue state police cars, two local police cars, a police ambulance, and two cars with press cards on their windshields. Inside, the building was in chaos. State police moved around talking with men in plain clothes, excited nurses and morbidly calm doctors conferred with local officers and with each other, and press people were on every telephone in sight.

When Jesse and Lilli walked in, several reporters tried to find out who they were. Jesse pushed them aside and spoke to a state trooper who was right behind them. The trooper was a tall, heavily built man with kind eyes and a paternal expression unsuited to the threatening uniform he wore with its polished badges and the heavy gun at his side.

"I'm Wilkinson," he said. "I spoke to your man in Beverly. I'm glad you made—"

He was interrupted by the reporters who had stopped Jesse when they walked in. They had returned full force, firing questions and snapping flash pictures.

"Mr. Quinn, can you tell us why your fathers were at the beach this time of year?"

"Who were their enemies? Do you have any suspicions?"

"What was their real business, Miss Quinn? Are you going to take over the corporation, Mr. Quinn? You're vice-president, aren't you?"

Spreading a pair of long arms, Wilkinson physically swept the reporters away and made them stand across the room with a blunt threat to have them thrown out. He sauntered back. The cameras continued to flash.

"You have all our sympathies. Miss Quinn, Mr. Quinn. Would you come with me now? We don't want to make any mistakes."

That was the extent of Wilkinson's diplomacy. Walking down the well-lit hospital corridor, which smelled strongly of harsh antiseptic, they listened to their footsteps squeak rhythmically on a dark rubber-tiled floor until Wilkinson led them into a small white room.

The trooper gave them no warning. He simply showed them into the room where, on three stainless-steel tables, three bodies lay covered by sheets.

Wilkinson asked Lilli and Jesse to look at the faces of the men and tell him who they were. If he expected hysterics and this was his way of hardening himself to them, he was wrong. Jesse had warned Lilli what would happen. He said he could do it alone, that she could wait outside. But she would not. Though exhausted, she continued with the identification. She was not just any woman, she reminded herself, she was a Quinn. And she would behave like one.

Jesse held Lilli tightly, strengthening her and himself as well.

The lieutenant, his pipe clenched between his teeth, quickly turned down the sheets one at a time to reveal the faces.

Michael's and Joseph's faces were unmarked. But there had been no time to remove the grimace of pain that twisted their mouths. There was still a bloodstain on Michael's cheek where some doctor or orderly had been careless. They looked like two old men who had not died easily. And there was worse. Frank's face was almost unrecognizable. One side was gone and the top of his head was a soggy mess.

Lilli almost gagged. She had prepared herself to kiss her father, but she couldn't at first. She was frozen to the spot.

Jesse did the talking. Lilli nodded as he spoke their names.

"Yes, that's Joseph Quinn, my uncle. This is Michael Quinn, my father. That's Frank Delaney, their chauffeur. Worked for them twenty years, like another father to us. He used to drive us to Crane's Beach before the war, before we could drive ourselves. We all went there. It was the family's favorite beach."

"I see," said Wilkinson. His pipe had gone dead, and he pushed it into a shirt pocket.

Lilli stepped away from Jesse and freed his arm from her shoulder. She took a few steps and bent over her father's body, resting herself on him, holding his face between her hands. She kissed his cold cheek. Then she went to Michael and did the same thing. Her eyes were dry. She looked achingly at the smashed face of Frank, shook her head at whatever was in her mind, and went back to Jesse. Her face was drained of color.

"The only reason," Jesse was saying as he watched Lilli say good-bye, "they could have had for driving out to Crane's was a sentimental one. They had been bird shooting in Georgetown. I don't think they have been to that beach in years."

The state trooper covered the bodies again.

As they left the room, Wilkinson talked. "We found their shotguns. We'll keep them a while, give you a receipt for them. Never saw any so beautiful. When your fathers finished a hunt, would they leave empties in their guns until they got home? I mean the last two, would they leave them put?"

Jesse's head tilted.

"No, we always broke the guns open. The empties would have been ejected."

"Well," muttered Wilkinson in the corridor, "there were empties in them in the car. I think they got some shots off at their killers. That's gumption. Come on with me, will you. I'd like to show you something."

As they walked down the hall, Jesse put his arm around Lilli's shoulder. He spoke to the state trooper. "If they had any chance at all, they would not have died without putting up some fight. That was their style. But my father was a romantic too, getting more sentimental every year, wasn't he, Lilli? He would have been the one to want to stop there at the beach just for a look. On a whim, a spur-of-the-moment thing. They were planning to meet us for dinner in Boston. Their killing wasn't planned for Crane's Beach."

"That fits our theory," said Wilkinson. "There were two sets of tracks in the parking lot. One belonged to your fathers' Cadillac. The killers tailed them in there. Two of them did the shooting. We found empties from two different rifles."

The noise of voices grew louder as reporters came down the corridor.

"In here, please. We'll get rid of those vultures before you leave."

Wilkinson opened a door to a small office where three plainclothes detectives from the state investigator's office and the county sheriff's office were gathered around a desk. He introduced Jesse and Lilli to them.

"They'll be working together on the investigation."

One of the plainclothesmen, named Reilly, picked something from the desk and handed it Jesse. It was a piece of tattered cloth about an inch wide and three inches long.

"This is a tough time, I know," Reilly began, "but we'd like to ask you and your sister a few questions. Is that all right?"

They nodded and did not bother to correct his mistake.

"Will you both look at that piece of cloth. We think it might come from the lapel of a man's suit. It could have been shot off the coat of one of the killers if your fathers did get off a shot at them. That means we could be looking for a wounded man. I hope we are. But look at what is on the cloth, will you?"

Jesse fingered the cloth carefully. Stuck into the material was a battered piece of red metal the size of a thumbnail. It was a piece of circle or the blade of a sickle or a quarter moon. Part of the red metal disc had been broken away and there was obviously more to the design.

Jesse handed it to Lilli, who examined it closely.

"Does it mean anything to either of you?" asked Reilly.

Lilli shook her head.

"Nothing," said Jesse.

"O.K.," said Reilly. "We'll see what the lab can tell us."

The talk turned to motives—robbery, business rivals, rackets. Jesse and Lilli could give them little help. Robbery was ruled out. The men's wallets were found untouched on their clothing and they were still wearing their watches. The expensive guns had been left behind.

"No rackets," Jesse said firmly when that question turned up. "You'll find that out soon enough. Call Carmichael in the district attorney's office in Boston. You know him?"

The three plainclothesmen and Wilkinson nodded and grunted.

"It looks like a gangland killing," Jesse said, "but you'll be wasting time on that. One thing I'm sure of—it wasn't that."

The talk continued for fifteen minutes but nothing new came out. More plainclothes policemen were coming and going all the time. The hospital lobby was getting crowded. Some reporters slipped past the guards into the office and barraged Jesse and Lilli with questions. Wilkinson had them ushered out.

When Wilkinson's questions grew increasingly unproductive, Jesse got to his feet and helped Lilli up. He spoke quietly. "We're not helping you very much with this. For a while we'll be staying in Beverly, at the family home, Route 127, number 471. You can reach us there. Is that all right?"

Lieutenant Wilkinson questioned the plainclothesmen with his kindly eyes. Reilly nodded. The two others left the room.

Lilli followed them out. The state trooper touched Jesse's shoulder to hold him back for a moment. He dropped his raspy voice to a half-whisper.

"You'll want their bodies, Mr. Quinn. We'll be finished with them by morning." This was his way of being tactful. "This was a rotten thing. We'll damn well try to find the people who did it. I'm sorry for you and your sister. I mean your cousin, right? I'm sorry for both of you."

He gave Jesse his hand for the first time. It was firm and dry.

"One more thing, Mr. Quinn. Will you be careful? You and Miss Quinn. If this was a grudge killing, you may be in danger yourselves. Would you care to carry a weapon? I can fix it."

27

"I have a license," Jesse said. "Thanks."

Jesse went out to Lilli, thinking of cemeteries and funeral arrangements, things he had seldom thought of before—even during the wars. In the family circle there had been little talk of death or dying. The three men had seen enough of both not to talk of them in front of Lilli. For the four Quinns it was living that mattered.

There were wills with the family lawyers, of course, and Jesse knew their contents. Four years with the Quinn Corporation, even though broken up by two served in Korea, had prepared him to take over the business. He could manage that. But he knew nothing of grave plots or the wishes their fathers had concerning them. After all, Michael and Joseph were only in their sixties, in fine health, with many plans for the future. They had chosen by silent agreement not to talk of dying, and the subject had been avoided, except on one occasion.

The four of them were flying from a private field on the North Shore to Logan Airport in a company-owned twin-engine Bonanza. Jesse was at the controls, Lilli was sitting beside him, and Michael and Joseph were in the rear seats. On their way they passed over a small cemetery in Marblehead lying on a hillside overlooking the sea and shaded by two or three great oaks.

"Now there's a place to settle down in," said Michael lightly. "What a view!"

"Is there a family plot anywhere?" asked Lilli idly. Michael had broken the taboo or she would never have asked the question.

"Now, now, honey," laughed Michael, leaning forward and massaging his niece's neck under her long dark hair, "you know the demons of the sky don't like that kind of talk. Your daddy and I respect them. I'm sorry I brought this up."

"Oh, Uncle Michael, you and Daddy and your superstitions." But Lilli had already decided to drop the subject.

Surprisingly, in a voice that sounded somewhat unfamiliar, Joseph said, "Whoever survives this wonderful circle of four will make the arrangements. I assure you, Michael and I won't mind whatever you do, will we, Michael?"

From that time on, as though honoring that superstition about the sky demons, the family didn't discuss the subject again. Now it really was up to Jesse and Lilli. It was going to be a bad time for them both, and worsened by events they could not control, the least of which was the arrival of cold, drizzly weather that hung over the New England coast straight through the funeral.

Chapter 5

The next morning, which dawned bleak and wet, was spent trying to reach friends, comforting Frank's wife Edna, and keeping a small swarm of reporters off the estate. One of the morning dailies hinted too strongly at the "gangland" angle of the murders, and Jesse asked his lawyers to threaten a libel suit.

Jim came by and Lilli sent him away after they talked alone a few minutes. She explained nothing to Jesse. He did not ask.

Bad as it all was, the dreary morning, at least, brought no surprises.

The afternoon, however, yielded a shock almost as severe as the killings.

Ed Watson brought it. He was a senior partner in the law firm that handled most of the affairs of the Quinn Corporation, and he was a close personal friend of the Quinn brothers. A short, balding but brilliant man, Watson knew most of what there was to know about the Quinns, or thought he did.

He came to the Quinns' eighteenth-century white brick mansion that afternoon bearing a sealed letter for Lilli. He found her and Jesse in the downstairs library discussing funeral arrangements with a large, gloomy-looking man with pasty white skin and in a morbid black suit. Watson came in without knocking. His face was somber and lined with deep shadows under his eyes. He looked grim. But so did everybody else.

Lilli, wearing a dark gray tailored suit, with her hair pulled back tightly behind her head and no makeup to hide the red-eyed grief in her face, greeted Ed Watson with a kiss on the cheek. Jesse was also dressed in a gray suit. When Lilli was back at his side he put an arm around her shoulder. It was becoming his standard gesture to express how conscious he was of his responsibilities for her. They were standing before tall French windows that looked out across three acres of grounds sloping off to the rippled Atlantic, just visible under the heavy gray mist.

"We knew you'd come, Ed," Lilli said warmly. She smiled briefly.

Watson took Jesse's hand in a tight clasp and ignored the mortician. "From what I've heard downtown, your fathers went the way they would have wanted to go—fighting. It's not much consolation for anybody, but it's some."

There came an unspoken moment of sympathy that passed from Watson to the young Quinns. Then, without wasting any more time, Ed Watson gravely opened a worn leather case he carried and took out a large yellow envelope.

"I don't know what's in here, Lilli, but your father gave this to me twenty years ago. It's been lying around in my personal safe where he wanted me to keep it so that I'd see it every week at least. That way it would never be forgotten. Even the color of the envelope he picked was to remind me of the inscription on it and who it belonged to. Read it."

He passed the envelope to Lilli and then, taking the mortician politely by the arm, led him toward the door. "Would you mind waiting out there for now, sir. They'll be with you as soon as possible."

The inscription on the envelope was in Joseph's hand. It said: "To be opened immediately upon my death if I survive Michael. If Michael survives me, to be opened at his discretion. To be opened in either case only in the presence of Lilli and Jesse Quinn."

Lilli hesitated. Jesse said, "Go ahead, Lilli." He handed her an ivory-handled letter opener. She slit the envelope at one end and shook out two sheets of foolscap and two smaller pieces of parchment paper that looked like deeds. She stepped closer to Jesse and let him hold one end of the foolscap so that they could read it together. Joseph's hand was bold and flowing.

September 1933

My dearest little girl of four,

Uncle Michael and I do not expect you and Jesse to understand this that I am going to tell you. Let it be enough that we have our own reasons for what we are doing. When you are grown up—and I hope you will be an old woman before you have to read this—you may not need to ask why. Still, if you did, I don't know whether we could really tell you. Human nature is a mystery.

Well, my little girl, here it is—at least part of it.

30

First, Michael and I are really Michael Quintana and Joseph Quintana. Not Quinn. Not such a big thing.

Second, Michael and I are not really brothers, though we should have been as you'll see. We are not of the same family, not of the same city, not even of the same religion.

But you *are* my real daughter, flesh and blood, and Jesse the true son of Michael. We play no games with you on that account.

Michael and I did not even know each other until 1914— I was twenty-three, he was twenty—when we met at a small airfield in Revere where we were both learning to fly. Can you imagine how we felt to discover that by a sheer stroke of fate we both had the same last name, and not a very common one. Somewhere in our past both our families lived in Spain, though his was Catholic and mine was Jewish, and that hardly mattered.

We became fast friends. Natural brothers could not have been closer than we grew to each other. We flew together in France in 1917 and 1918. When you and Jesse are older we will tell you more of that part. Yes, your fathers were not just fuddy-duddy businessmen all their lives.

The pilots in the squadron thought of us as brothers, treated us as brothers. Someone dubbed us the Quintana Brother Aces. The idea had its advantages. The commanders kept us together, gave us the best planes, the same missions, and the same leaves.

Michael and I became brothers because we wanted to, and we swore to stay that way. Even now a partnership of brothers is proving an asset in our business. We hope the two of you will be as close to one another as we have been. You are like brother and sister already, and Michael and I take pleasure in that.

To the third point of this letter: It is my wish that I be buried as privately as possible in the little Jewish cemetery of Chevreth-Thilim in Everett. The records there will show the graves of two Quintanas buried along the north fence. A third plot is nearby for me. The deed for the plot is in this letter.

One can never forget his deepest roots. Michael and I believe that. Across from that fence, very close by, Michael will be buried in the Holy Cross Cemetery that lies there.

The deed to his plot is also in this letter. If he outlives me and you are reading this, he will corroborate all of this.

   You and Jesse will be brought up as his father and I wish it—with ties to no church. Someday, if you need a church or a synogogue, you will find one for yourselves.

Your loving father,
JOSEPH QUINN
and
UNCLE MICHAEL

P.S. Michael is signing this to let you know he approves.

   As Lilli read silently, her hands shook. Jesse had kept his left arm around her back, feeling the tremors moving through her body like weak electric shocks. With his other hand he tried to steady the letter. But the foolscap crackled away. Finally they finished reading the two sheets and Lilli let Jesse have them. Her arms dropped to her side. The blood rushed to her head. For a moment the dizziness was bad. Jesse steadied her. His own face was scored with bewilderment. The cleft in his chin was sharper, his eyes deeper, his cheekbones more prominent. He reread the letter.

   "Is this true, Ed?" Lilli asked, taking a short step toward her father's lawyer and long-time friend. "Is it true?"

   "I don't know what it says, Lilli," said Watson, shaking his head. "If it's a will, it's a new one to me. I've got their wills back in the office. I thought they could wait. You and Jesse know pretty much what's in them."

   When he had read the two pages of foolscap himself, Ed shook his head again, harder. "They had me fooled. I don't know what to say. They never did talk much about their families, did they?"

   "Nothing about our mothers," said Jesse quietly. His eyes grew distant. "Joseph was the only one who ever mentioned an uncle or his own father. Never my father. I always thought Joseph was speaking for them both, and he said very little."

   Watson agreed. "You're right. They never talked about their wives. I asked once, years ago. I didn't get a straight answer, only the feeling that it was a subject I'd be better off not bringing up again."

   Lilli's face was a study in disbelief. The flush had drained away. Her eyes had a strange, glazed look, her lips slightly parted and dry. As she gazed up at Jesse, she felt numb, as though she had drunk too much. When she spoke, her voice sounded alien to her, as though she were listening to someone else.

"Jesse, if it's true . . . we're not cousins, or brother and sister, we're nothing. . . . Oh, Christ!" Lilli pressed her hand to her forehead as though some terrible pain had struck.

Ed Watson moved his gaze from one Quinn to the other and knew enough to leave. He started for the door, and stopped with his hand on the knob. He spoke to Lilli.

"It won't be difficult to run all this down in the city halls around Boston." He realized that the next thing he intended to say might be wrong, but he said it anyway. "Whatever we find—brothers or not—it won't change a thing as far as the corporation goes—or the foundation. They're tied together neatly to protect the Quinn family, whether the four of you were a legal family or not. You're both indisputably the sole owners of the whole enterprise. Here's your father's letter, Lilli. You'll want it. I'll keep the deeds and work out the arrangements with that man out there."

"You go on home, Ed," Jesse said. "It's for us to do, not you."

"I guess it is," said Watson. He handed Jesse the papers.

As soon as Watson left, Lilli lit a cigarette, kicked off her shoes, and sat down on a couch with her legs drawn up under her. A faint flush now lay along her neck up into her face.

Neither she nor Jesse spoke. For the two of them it was like being in the room with a stranger they knew a great deal about but were afraid to meet in the flesh.

She turned her eyes to the old portraits on the wall of her father and Michael Quinn, not her uncle, but still her uncle. Her father's was an adventurer's face, Lilli thought, filled with knowing and good times. He had a high broad forehead, dark gray experienced eyes, a strong jaw, thick dark hair that had gone gray in recent years, a nose—was there a trace of a Semitic curve to the nose? Or was that her imagination? She had never noticed one before. Was she reading into the face features she now thought should be there? She had once thought of the portrait as that of a classic Boston patrician. Joseph had posed for the artist in brown tweed slacks, a dark flannel shirt, and a brown fringed-suede hunting jacket cut with large pockets and fitted with sleeve loops where shotshells were showing.

As she sat there in silence, it was wrenching to believe that she would never again see that face break into the deep comforting smile that had always softened any problems she brought to him.

It was the face of a man who never lost his temper. But that, too, was reading into it what she already knew.

She shifted her gaze to Uncle Michael. He was easier-going than her father. Never called Mike, but always Michael. There was the dark complexion and hair, the shorter, sharper nose, the eyes almost black but still like Joseph's. The chin was strong and cleft. If they had claimed the same parents, their looks would not contradict them.

And there was Jesse, alive and warm, comforting to the ache in her heart, standing near the cold fireplace, not far from his father's picture, appearing taller than ever, even as he slouched at the marble mantel. They called it the Quinn slouch. Michael and Joseph had it, too. They said it was the fighter pilot's pose—natural and fluid—it let a man blend his body into the plane and go with it—or the other way around. Ramrods, Michael had once said, did not belong in fighter cockpits.

Jesse. Her eyes brooded over him. She thought that Jesse resembled Joseph more than he resembled Michael—around the eyes, the hairline that tended toward a widow's peak, the mouth with the fuller lower lip, the narrow, long upper one. Yet Jesse was not Joseph's, he was Michael's.

He was not her brother. Not her cousin. Just a man she had grown up with. No blood bond, no blood barriers. She shivered at the thought.

She caught his eyes unwittingly, but instead of feeling more cribbed, she sensed a release from a tiny stifling pressure deep within her. She wanted to talk.

Jesse saw the change in Lilli's expression, and he feared what she might say. His feelings were already too tangled and uncertain to handle another complication. Lilli had always had what they jokingly called a crush on him, and she had never outgrown it. He had forbidden himself to think about Lilli and found other women.

Lilli understood his signal but she spoke anyway. Her voice was strained and hoarse.

"The guilt, Jesse . . ." she stammered. "Do you remember in this library we once talked about guilt when we were too young to know what guilt was? You were seventeen and I had just turned fourteen—it was my birthday party—and there had been some wine we sneaked in. You were leaving for the service. We almost lost our heads that day. If we had known then that we were nothing to each other, the guilt would have been different, easier, maybe none. Do you remember?"

For a moment Jesse's face lost its grimness. He lit two cigarettes and handed one to Lilli.

"How could I forget? You wanted to wrestle, to pin your big brother. We were lucky I was more frightened than you." He almost smiled. "That day has been hanging over both of us, Lilli, and it's still there between us—in spite of what we've just found out. You've been my sister from the beginning—and you'll always come first with me, but it will still be as my sister. We can't wipe out twenty-five years with a stroke of a pen. I don't know if I'll ever be able to wipe it out. I've tried to keep that afternoon out of my head ever since then and it still haunts me."

Lilli had not kept that day out of her mind at all. It was as vivid as yesterday.

Chapter 6

Jesse was wrong about that afternoon eleven years and two wars ago—wrong as Lilli remembered it. Wrestling had had nothing to do with what happened on that mid-December day in 1943. She inhaled her cigarette smoke deeply and thought back over the years.

It had begun as a late-afternoon party for friends from school and the clubs.

Jesse was going into the Air Corps in a few weeks when he reached eighteen. The party was partly for that and partly for Lilli's fourteenth birthday. It began at four in the afternoon and lasted until midnight. Dinner was served at seven.

Lilli's girl friends ranged between fourteen and sixteen and their boyfriends a year or two older.

There were the usual activities, dancing to the records of Harry James, "One O'Clock, Two O'Clock Jump," and the rhythms of Gene Krupa, "You Hear the Bugle Blowin'," "Drum Boogie," and a stack of others. There were pool and ping-pong matches in the game room and ice skating on a large frozen pond on the grounds and hot chocolate around the fire. It was a warm and cozy party.

The dinner was dandy. Daddy and Uncle Michael, who were in the Air Corps again at a base in the South, had arranged in advance for turkeys and all the trimmings to be in the coolers. The war had not starved the American people or even pinched them yet very much. Frank and his wife Edna were running the Quinn household and were the chaperones for the evening.

After dinner, in the middle of the evening, Lilli and Jesse invited everyone to a splash in the indoor pool. With their winter-white skins and pale faces, the kids looked strange in their bathing suits. But to Lilli they looked marvelous. The young men were all handsome, strong in the shoulder, athletes. All future officers in the service. The girls showed off slim, flat stomachs, budding shapely bosoms, rounded rears—all except Tessie Cornwall and Sue Kramer, who were more developed in the chest.

An hour after the splashy dive-in, the search began for bath towels. A dozen stacked in the pool lockers were not enough. The young guests began to share them.

"Come on, Jesse," Lilli laughed, shaking her long hair free after snapping off her rubber bathing cap. Her black one-piece suit clung damply to her skin, and gooseflesh covered her thin arms and legs. "We can find some more towels upstairs. Be right back, everybody. Stay wet."

She grabbed Jesse by the hand and forced him away from the girls he was talking to. They were all older than Lilli by at least a year, and she saw the difference in their fuller bodies, all of them tempting Jesse, who was the handsomest man in the house at that moment—in Lilli's eyes. Especially in his brief black swim trunks that showed so much of him when she dared to look.

Oh, she was going to miss him!

On the second floor, Jesse and Lilli padded softly down the long carpeted hallway toward a linen closet at the end. Lilli's room was directly to the right of it.

"Do you hear something?" she asked Jesse in a whisper as she began to pick towels off the shelves and pile them onto his arms. "Listen."

Sounds like squealing mice came from Lilli's room. When Lilli and Jesse paused to listen, the mice stopped playing and voices drifted through the door.

"Shhh," said Lilli. "Who do you think is in there? I'll bet it's Jessica or Terry. They're very fast, you know."

Almost childishly, Lilli brushed up against Jesse to let him know she knew about things.

"Cut it out, Lilli," Jesse said above the towels filling his arms. He meant about what she was saying. He ignored what she had done. "Let's go back down. The kids are waiting for these."

"Not on your life. Someone's using my room. That's all right with me. But I want to know who. And how far they're going. You do, too."

Quietly she eased the door open, slid her hand along the wall to her right, and flipped on the switch. She sucked in her breath.

Big white buttocks above a pair of heavily haired legs heaved and tossed on her bed. Beneath the hairy legs and flanking them, two slim white legs were raised, bent at the knee and fluttering in unison with the buttocks. Two soggy bathing suits lay on the rug at the foot of the bed.

"Oh, Jesus Christ!" yelled a voice. "It's only you, Lilli. You scared the living daylights out of me."

It was Tessie Cornwall. Her pretty face, with a kind of naughty-girl smirk on it, peeked over the shoulder of the boy on top of her. Her blond hair appeared like a halo.

"It's Tessie," Lilli whispered to Jesse, who had crowded her in the doorway and was staring wide-eyed at the naked bodies rocking on the bed. "And she's not even fourteen yet. Jesus, Jesse, look at them!"

Lilli's long thin legs shook beneath her.

The boy on the bed kept moving his body, grumbling into his own shoulder. "Get the hell out of here, Lilli, will you. Get the hell out. Please."

"God, is that you, Russ?" Jesse asked.

"Oh, Jesse, you there, too?" It was Russ Halston, who played left halfback to Jesse's right and had scored the most points for Beverly High on the football field, and the most for himself in the back seat of his Ford convertible.

Russ pushed himself up and twisted around without letting go of Tessie underneath. "Christ, Jesse, if you can't get something from your cousin Lilli, come on in here and shut the door. Sweet Tessie's promised it to all the guys going into the service, haven't you, Tessie?" He moved his body in long wicked strokes, giving Lilli a view of what she had not seen before.

"You rotten rat, Russ. I said that only as a joke. But if Jesse wants to, Lilli, you wouldn't tell anybody."

Lilli struck the light switch off and pushed against Jesse to get him out into the hall. She shut the door hard behind her.

"Jesse, say you wouldn't. Say you wouldn't do that with Tessie, like Russ. No love, no feeling—say you wouldn't." She was gripping his arms and pressing herself against the bundle of towels he was carrying, pressing to get her breast against his arms. Her body was shaking from excitement and God knew what else. She fought hard to keep him from feeling how it was carrying on, beyond her control.

"I wouldn't, Lilli," Jesse said, thinking that he probably would—as the picture of Tessie spread-eagled on the bed flashed across his mind. "I really wouldn't."

"Oh, Jesse," Lilli cried, and the words came spilling out without any help from her, "you know how I feel about you. I've never said it out loud, but you've known all along, how I've

38

always felt. You're more than a brother to me, Jesse. I love you. I'll prove it."

She crushed against the towels and kissed him on the mouth. Jesse was bewildered. Lilli's confession was not big news, but it came so unexpectedly and at a bad time. She was right, he had known how she felt all along, but now he felt almost helpless to stop her. The party, the girls, the wine he had drunk, the war, the memory of Russ and Tessie—they sapped his will to flee. He would see how far she would go—she knew he was still more her brother than her cousin. Lilli was a virgin and only fourteen, she wouldn't go as far as Tessie, that was certain. It would all end harmlessly. He gave in.

She took him by the hand across the hall to her father's room and opened the door. She held the door open and did not turn on the light. The room was darkly visible from the hallway light.

It was a spacious room, twice or three times the size of Lilli's, but it contained much less furniture. There was a big old oak-framed bed in the middle of one wall. On another wall was a glass case holding some rifles and shotguns. Bookshelves and a few photographs of Jesse and Lilli were on the others. The dark floors were bare except for an old woolen-fringed rug at the bed's side. Near the headboard of the bed, on a small low table, there was a big dark blue revolver under a glass bell jar. Its grips were smooth, polished, light-grained wood. She had looked at it often but her daddy had never let her touch it. In Uncle Michael's room down the hall, also under a thick bell jar, was a twin revolver to this one, except on Uncle Michael's the wooden grips were darker and had fifteen small, even cuts on one handle. She had counted them.

Once when she was much younger she had woken in the middle of the night and sneaked downstairs into the library to find Uncle Michael and Daddy there sitting in their easy chairs, drinking whiskey and smoking cigars and talking quietly. On a low table at their knees were the two big revolvers, naked and in the open. It was eerie to hear their murmurs and watch them pick up a gun and handle it and put it down again. She had sneaked back upstairs to bed and never asked a question of either one.

The only other curious thing in her father's room was a blown-up newspaper photograph of a bearded man's face with a serious, almost sorrowful expression on it. The picture was framed in dark wood and hung opposite the bed. Her father had never told her whom that face belonged to. "Just a face I happened to like," he used to say. But she suspected that the man in the photograph had meant much more to him.

She took the towels from Jesse's arms and dropped them on a chair. She led him to the bed without closing the door behind her.

"What do you think you're doing?" Jesse asked nervously.

"I want you to see something, Jesse. In here. Just sit there."

Embarrassed and uncomfortable in his damp bathing suit, Jesse sat gingerly on the edge of the bed and crossed his legs. He could not believe he was letting this happen. He was getting excited. His bathing suit bulged—from the sight of Russ and Tessie, from his own near-nakedness, from Lilli's excitement. He watched her cross the room in the light from the doorway. Thin. But not that thin. Admit it. Lilli was exciting him—his cousin, his sister really, not Tessie. What the hell was he doing? His mind jumped but his body stayed on the bed.

The door closed. Lilli waited only for as long as she needed. Then, without a second's hesitation or a second thought, she flicked the wall switch. A soft yellow light came on near the bed. Its glow barely reached the door where she stood. She was naked, her bathing suit at her feet. She held her hands by her side and fought the impulse to cover herself with them. She watched Jesse looking.

Jesse jumped to his feet. He could not stay. Lilli had suddenly gone crazy. But he did not move from the side of the bed. He could not draw his eyes away from her long thin body, her small untouched breasts, her belly, so flat it formed a slight hollow between her hip bones, the faint fine dark hair shaping a perfect triangle at her pelvis. Skinny, but just about to bloom.

His mind raced, trying to grasp what was happening. Here was Lilli offering herself. But she was his sister. His cousin rather, but she might as well have been his sister. Jesse stood paralyzed.

Before he could say something to her, Lilli was at his side, her arms around him, her breasts pressed against his chest, kissing him, forcing her tongue between his lips.

It was easy to let himself forget who she was. She was a naked girl, lovely and there. He had been with a few girls before, one for almost a year. He knew what to do, or thought he did.

Lilli let him. Anything Jesse wanted. She was determined to give him her virginity. She felt his hand rubbing her body roughly. It didn't matter. She made herself more accessible and suddenly felt his hand down there, rubbing too hard, hurting. Then his finger was inside, sliding in and out. Nothing hurt any more. She thought she was in heaven. It was true what her friends had sworn. Doing it with someone you loved was heaven. She wanted to do it. All of it.

She tugged at Jesse's bathing suit, but he twisted away. She started to rub his stomach, and when his back arched, she pushed her hand inside and held him.

"Oh, Jesse, Jesse, I love you," she said. "I love you, Jesse." What else was a fourteen-year-old able to say?

That had been her error, she thought later. It was a mistake to call his name, to speak at all. It made him conscious of who she was. With a sudden groan of agony, and then, calling out her name—"Lilli, Lilli, Lilli"—Jesse yanked at her hand inside his swim suit. Lilli held onto him as he started to roll away from her. She moved her hand in an awkward jerking motion, rolling with him, not letting go, feeling the tears beginning to come, desperately wanting him to stay, to love her. She held him tighter, felt his hand on top of hers, trying to free himself from her grasp. Her sobs became louder and the tears rolled down her cheeks. Then she felt his body stiffen, his hand relaxed on hers, and a slick oily wetness covered her fingers. Her hand slid smoothly on his penis until he gripped her wrist hard to make her stop.

He turned away from her, moaned softly, and sat up. His face was glowing yet drawn. His shoulders shook but he did not cry. For a moment he seemed like a little boy that needed comfort. But then he faced her and he was big brother again.

"Oh, God, Lilli! Please. We can't, don't you see. You're my baby sister. You don't know what you're doing. For Chrissakes, Lilli! It's like incest. How could we ever face Michael and Joseph?"

Instinctively he reached for her again, to comfort her as the tears were wetting her cheeks. But he caught himself, as his mind focused on her nakedness. She was not moving to get her suit.

He took a hand from her lap. "I love you, too, Lilli. But this is not for us. We were crazy just now, but we can't let it happen again. We both know that, don't we. Three weeks and I'll be gone. Let's promise not to let this happen, Lilli."

She saw him blurred through tear-filled eyes, thinking that the whole world had collapsed. She dropped her eyes and blinked the tears away to clear her vision.

"Promise, Lilli. When we grow up we'll find the right people.

41

And we'll have something between us that will be different and maybe better than anything else. Will you promise?"

"I promise," said Lilli calmly. But what she was promising was never to stop loving him more than anyone else in the world, forever and forever.

That was the way Lilli remembered that night. She dropped her cigarette into an ashtray and went up to Jesse. She took his face into her hands. She wanted to tell him he was lying to himself, that she had known, ever since she was old enough to know what the look meant, that he had regarded her as a woman.

But the moment was wrong, and she lost her nerve to speak. The effects of a long night of fitful sleep and nightmare had upset her judgment. Yet she had to say something, she refused to be dishonest.

"You can go on seeing me as your kid sister, Jesse," she said in a faintly hoarse voice, "but you can't be a brother to me any longer. I don't think I can make that work."

"Hey," he broke out, his teeth clenched, his eyes hot, "what are we talking about, Lilli? Our fathers have been shot to pieces, not even in their graves, and we're talking about this?"

When she blanched, his voice softened. "No more talking now, Okay?"

Her voice was firmer. "A step at a time, Jesse. Isn't that what Daddy would say? That's the way it'll be."

Lilli gave Jesse a light sisterly kiss on the lips as they went out to finish the funeral arrangements, but for the first time in their lives they seemed strangers to one another.

Chapter 7

Two days later early on the morning of the funeral, Ed Watson appeared at the Quinn mansion. He looked only slightly less grim than when the Quinns had last seen him. He showed Lilli and Jesse copies of separate birth certificates of their fathers.

Joseph Quintana had been born to Rafael and Deborah Quintana in 1891 in the city of Malden. Michael Quintana, son of Carlos and Charlotte Quintana, had been born in 1894 in the neighboring city of Somerville. Carlos and Charlotte had had three other children in Somerville—all girls. No record of any other children born to Rafael and Deborah turned up in the search.

Watson had also located some World War II military records and had them flown up from McGuire Air Force Base in New Jersey.

In their Air Corps enlistment papers, taken out on the same day in January of '42, the Quinns had named each other as brothers. For their background, all that they had recorded was their experience as pilots in the American squadron in France before America entered the Great War. The squadron was the same Rickenbacker had flown in—the Escadrille Lafayette.

Strangely, there existed no record of the Quinns' having ever joined the American Army Air Corps when the United States finally did come into World War I. In 1918 they had been transferred as a team but the documents did not reveal where or for what purpose. From 1918 to 1932 there were no entries made by either Quinn as to where they were or what they were doing.

Ed's visit settled the matter of Jesse and Lilli's relationship. But it revealed another incredible enigma about Michael and Joseph. The ordinary world of the young Quinns had gone out of orbit. The shock of the change was acute. They knew that their lives could not go on as usual.

"We'll take things in order," Jesse said. "The past will have to wait. The murders come first. We want to find out why and who, Ed. That's got to be done. Have you heard anything from Wilkinson?"

"The pressure is on everyone, Jesse. They've got a dozen full-time ranking detectives on the case. And I've been in touch with a private agency that can do things the police may not want to do. It'll be a thorough job any way you look at it."

"And the business? How are they taking it in Boston?"

"Everything will be set for you to take over whenever you return. A lot of people wanted to come today, but I think they understand. Things are in good shape there. Michael and Joseph were meticulous."

Lilli had been brooding thoughtfully. She looked up suddenly and said, "Jesse, I can't go on at the museum. And the doctoral work seems so unimportant now. I'm going to go in and work for a while at the foundation." Her voice sounded raspy.

"They'd like to have you," said Watson. "I've spoken to Edison and he even suggested something like that. But isn't it too soon to make decisions like this now? In a week or two you may feel different."

"I'll go back to the routine then, if that happens. But the family business—it's Jesse's and mine now. He's going to run the corporation. I'd like to spend some time at the foundation. It's what you might call 'carrying on,' isn't it?"

Ed Watson nodded his head and gave her a swift hug and left the library to attend to some final matters before the funeral.

When he was gone, Lilli said, "Jesse, I can't stop thinking about those blank years. We were born during that time and we really don't know where. Where were they and what were they doing? Why didn't they tell us anything about themselves?"

"The earliest memory I have," said Jesse, his eyes narrowing, "and I don't think I've ever told you about it—was flying somewhere in the open with the wind rushing into my face and making it hard for me to breathe. I don't remember how young I was, but Dad was holding me. When there's time, Lilli, we'll dig into that past. When these other matters are settled."

The talk went on as they watched the clock move slowly toward the time they were to leave for the funeral. Jesse finally suggested putting off the whole subject for a while.

"We'll have to let this go for now, Lilli. It's going to take a long investigation by people with special talents to dig into the past and dredge up all those years, when we don't even know where to begin. It's too much for us now."

Lilli disagreed. "But if the past could be told, we might know why they were killed, Jesse."

Jesse shrugged. "It's time to go." He held out his hand to her and she took it.

Later that morning, Joseph and Michael Quinn, born Quintana, were buried just as they wanted to be, simply and in private. But not unnoticed. All of the Boston papers carried at least one full column of obituary with pictures, and the stories of the murders were still on page one. But strangely, it was a *Wall Street Journal* newsman with close Boston connections who gave the most complete picture of the Quinn brothers and the considerable business empire they had built.

From their whiskey-running days in the early thirties to their multiple business interests in the fifties, he had assembled most of the significant details. He called his story "The American Dream."

The Quinn brothers had appeared on the American business scene in 1930, flying whiskey into the country from Canada in their own Fokker Trimotor. But their whiskey-running days were short, and long before repeal they switched to legitimate freight and called their airline Quinnair Freight. They flew their Trimotor themselves all over the East Coast, eighteen hours a day, sometimes longer, seven days a week, carefully selecting their customers for growth and consistency. In a year they added another plane and another pilot. And then three planes and six pilots during the second year. Then came the automobile agencies, Cadillac-Olds primarily, managed by Quinn people, profit sharing—and that was revolutionary, but it worked and business boomed—while the country starved. When repeal did come, they got into the liquor business, stores in Charlestown and Somerville, and soon a chain growing like weed throughout New England, and restaurants in every large city, catering to the rich. Finally the big investments were made—the wide tracts of real estate on Cape Cod, the buildings block by block in Back Bay, and the oceanfront properties along the coasts of Massachusetts and New Hampshire. Except for their holdings in the horse and dog tracks in Revere, which might brush occasionally against some shady money, their investments were clean and profitable.

Their success was phenomenal. Everything they tried in business turned sweet, but it wasn't the Midas touch. The Quinn brothers were tough, hard businessmen with a sense of fairness and a flair for finding the best places and the right people to manage them. Even their absence during the war when they served

45

as bomber-squadron commanders in Europe did not slow the growth of their corporation.

From rum-running to the Quinn Corporation and the Quinn Foundation, Michael and Joseph Quinn were partners. Not a bad example of the American Dream, the reporter concluded. But the dream had ended so tragically with the Quinns' brutal and mysterious slaying.

The burials were held one after the other, twenty-five feet apart, separated by a high wire-mesh fence. The ceremonies were sparse and secular. Jesse and Lilli agreed that their fathers wanted no eulogies. Two friends, one at each grave, spoke a few hopeful words about the future. They were meant to be comforting, but they were not.

Nor was the weather any comfort. Before the brief remarks were over, a heavy drizzle fell on the small group of mourners, who stood first at one grave site in hats or yarmulkes and then, under large black umbrellas, filed slowly along a path through a small opening in the fence to the second grave. Joseph was buried first. Then Michael.

Lilli and Jesse stood hand in hand by each grave, under a single umbrella. Lilli wore a small, dark hat pulled tight to one side of her head, almost unnoticeable against her black hair. She wept silently through both ceremonies. Jesse, in a dark suit, remained taut and composed. They both kept their heads up and watched the caskets disappear into the ground.

A half-dozen other people, close friends of the dead men, stood at each grave a few feet from the Quinns. Tom Singleton, the dog handler and estate handyman, stood by Lilli. Edna, the cook, was near Jesse. She had insisted on coming, though her own husband was being buried tomorrow fifteen miles away in Saugus. Jesse and Lilli would be there with her.

Private detectives outside the cemeteries kept away crowds of reporters who had followed the double funeral procession.

Jim Wainwright was not there. He had come out to see Lilli again, the day before. They had talked privately for an hour. When he left he went to see Jesse. The two men had shaken hands warmly.

"I'm deeply sorry about all this," Jim had said.

"Thanks, Jim. I know you are."

"I think Lilli is taking it well, don't you?"

Jesse nodded. "She's a family trooper, if that's what you mean."

"She doesn't seem hysterical, but I think it's over between us. For a long time I've felt something was wrong. This thing about her being part Jewish doesn't make a difference to me, but she won't believe that."

"She told you that?"

"Yes."

"Give her time," said Jesse.

"Good-bye, Jesse. Good luck. I'm really sorry."

"So am I," Jesse replied, but he was not certain just how sorry he was.

A week after the funeral, the engagement between Jim and Lilli was officially broken. On the same day, broken just as completely were the resolutions that Lilli and Jesse had made to organize their immediate future. A complication of such urgency developed that Lilli and Jesse had to drop everything else to consider it immediately. And when they did, they found themselves being led right into those missing years in their fathers' lives.

Chapter 8

The complication arose within the Quinn Foundation International, an organization established in the tradition of the Rockefeller Foundation, the Ford Foundation, and the Mellon Fund. It was more modest than any of these and therefore less renowned, but it was still quite substantial, skimming rich amounts of money from the top of the heavy profits the Quinn Corporation piled up each year.

The Quinn Foundation, however, was structured in sharp contrast to the corporation that fed it. The key feature of the Quinn Corporation, aside from its whopping success, was its diversity. It owned fourteen different businesses, controlled the major shares of ten others, and had healthy investments in a half-dozen more.

The foundation, however, was different. It was designed as a single-barreled philanthropy. Its assets went exclusively into medical care and research. It supported free hospitals and clinics worldwide, offered scholarships to promising medical students, and gave direct grants to research men and laboratories it considered worthy.

National boundaries were ignored by its managers in accordance with original Quinn directives. Throughout the medical world the foundation was known as the Maecenas of Hippocrates, the patron saint of the physician. If a hospital or a doctor needed a hundred thousand dollars—or a million, on occasion—he could be assured that an application to the foundation would be carefully considered.

The foundation offices, through which flowed applications and funds, were on the upper floors of a row house on fashionable Newbury Street in Boston amid expensive shops and chic restaurants. The foundation, though conservative in its management, could not help but acquire a quiet chicness from the neighborhood.

A week after the funeral, Jesse and Lilli were in one of the quietly decorated, polished offices of the foundation with a short, gray-haired thin-chinned man named Paul Edison. Edison was the foundation's senior accountant. He was a formal, starchy man and an unerring accountant, a Harvard MBA and a CPA.

The three people were gathered around a large antique mahogany desk on top of which sat an old ivory French telephone with pendulous mouth and ear pieces, a spotless green blotter, an onyx inkwell, some gleaming black pens, and a stack of twenty-four ledgers, dated from 1931 to 1954.

A twenty-fifth ledger, much smaller than the others, about five inches by seven, and bound completely in soft brown kidskin, lay open by itself near Paul Edison's hand.

Edison's generally inexpressive face was lined with anxiety. Fingering the small ledger, he spoke to it rather than to the Quinns.

"I've never seen this before today, and I would not have seen it if you hadn't ordered Mr. J. Quinn's safe opened." He always distinguished the Quinns by prefacing the name with the initial. "But at last it explains a terrible difficulty I have had with your fathers for a long time. Look at these sums."

He pointed a small trim finger to figures next to a series of dates for the complete year 1953. There were twelve dates, one date for each month, always the fifth, and one figure for each date. The twelve figures ranged from a low of $75,000 to a high of $132,000.

At the top of the page, handwritten, was the word *"Transferred."*

"That's over a million dollars there," said Edison, running his finger down the column. Lilli came closer and bent. "And look at 1952." He turned the page back crisply. "Just a little under a million, I'd say roughly." He seemed to be struck by something. "Let me check some other amounts." He turned a few pages, made some more mental calculations.

"What is it?" Lilli asked, shifting her glance from Jesse to Edison. "It's my father's handwriting, I'm sure of that. He made his fours that way, with a single stroke."

She moved aside to give Jesse room to examine the ledger. Lilli looked much better than she had a week ago. In that short time her skin had regained its healthy, polished tone. The shadows were gone from under her eyes and her voice had regained its clear timbre. Her black hair, combed out to her shoulders, gleamed in the sunlight pouring through the window. It had a clean delicate scent to it and sprang into a trembling motion away from her neck when she moved her head.

49

"One more page and I'll have it," said Edison. He thumbed through it to the page dated 1939, 5 January. He tapped the date. "That's about the time I came here to the foundation. At the end of the year when we got our financial report from Boston First, it was my responsibility to corroborate the sums granted by the foundation with the figures of monies transferred from the bank. The first year I was here I spoke with your father, Miss Quinn, about a sum transferred out of the foundation's account at the Boston First, for which I had no record of the recipient. The amount was marked on the bank statement as 'Miscellaneous.' I distinctly remember the figure. It was nothing to sneeze at or brush away simply as 'Miscellaneous'—not $205,000. Now look at this."

He showed Lilli and Jesse the figures for 1939 in the small ledger. "They add up, I think—let me see . . . to $205,000. In this little private ledger, your father was keeping his own accounts of the flow of money he designated 'Miscellaneous.'"

Jesse resisted a frown and kept his casualness. He sat down and picked up the leather ledger and turned over some pages.

"What did Uncle Joe say when you asked him about it?"

"At that time," Edison said, in a voice that meant he knew his job, "and for the next few years, when the same 'Miscellaneous' item appeared on the yearly accounting sheet from the bank, I thought fit to ask him where the money was going. I needed to know so that it could be properly deducted from tax-susceptible income. Each year he answered me the same way—Who the hell did I think I was? Excuse me, Miss Quinn, he talked that way sometimes, with a laugh, but it did not bother me. Well, he asked me why I had to know as much about his business as he did. Then he would smile strangely or stare out that window and tell me to ignore it, not to count it as a deductible from the corporation's profits. The taxes on that money would be paid. I once mentioned the matter to Mr. M. Quinn. He agreed with his brother that I keep my nose out of business they considered private. He used to laugh, too, when he spoke that way. Of course, they had the right to do whatever they wanted with the foundation's assets. If they wanted to siphon some money into a private charity of theirs, they could. They did.

"The money went every year—even during the war. I used to send the reports to Mr. J. Quinn overseas wherever he was stationed. And look here . . ." He bent and turned some pages as

50

Jesse held the ledger. "The entries for the forties are complete. They knew where the money was going, but I didn't."

Jesse had been handling the small ledger, flipping the pages quickly, examining the inside covers, front and back, more carefully, retracing his search. Finally he closed the book and looked up. Two narrow vertical furrows stood above the bridge of his nose.

"Mr. Edison, have you heard of the Aleph hyphen Palestine Fund?"

The question came as though Jesse had plucked a name from the air. Lilli tilted her head to look at him, her eyes slightly widened and puzzled.

Edison shook his head. "Aleph-Palestine? No."

"What hat did that come out of, Jesse?" Lilli asked. She moved a chair and half sat on its arm.

"Think again, Mr. Edison. The Aleph-Palestine Fund," Jesse repeated more intently. His dark eyes were bright and intense. "Here, look at this. In ink, at the bottom of the inside leather flap. Right here. It's not easy to make out."

Edison took the ledger to the window overlooking Newbury Street and held it tilted under the bright sunlight. He squinted for a few seconds, then put on a pair of horn-rimmed glasses and peered at the ledger again.

"'Aleph-Palestine Fund—3/5/31.'" His voice was excited. "That's the date of the first transfer of funds!" He turned to the first page. "A little over four thousand dollars."

Lilli took up the ledger next and went through the pages, one at a time, continuing through the empty pages at the end. Jesse watched her deftly separate each page, including the ones stuck together by time.

"What about those sums of money, Mr. Edison?" Jesse asked. "Look here."

Lilli paused in her own search to let Edison copy down the sums for 1953, and then she continued examining the pages, listening to Jesse as her eyes scanned each blank sheet for something else that might have been overlooked.

Jesse was saying, "The numbers vary quite a bit from month to month, don't they? And look how odd the amounts are themselves. $103,200, $115,500, $87,700. Isn't the whole thing strange?" The vertical lines in Jesse's brow gave him a rather handsome, sardonic expression.

Edison's face brightened suddenly as though he had been struck by an unusual idea. He pulled out one of the larger ledgers and reviewed the figures on one of its pages, writing down a few numbers next to the numbers he had copied from the small ledger. Finally he closed the ledger and looked a little pleased with himself. He continued to compare the figures.

"Odd amounts, certainly, Mr. Quinn. But not really strange, I think. Each of these sums transferred to the Aleph-Palestine Fund, whatever that is, represents a full ten percent of the total assets of the foundation on that particular day—divided by twelve, I'd say. By the end of the year, then, the Palestine Fund would be pulling out ten percent of the yearly assets of the Foundation. Ten million dollars of assets, for example, would offer the Aleph-Palestine Fund a million dollars that year, transferred at a rate of something under a hundred thousand dollars a month. That's what has been happening."

"Here's where it is going," said Lilli in a voice rising in surprise. "Look at this." She held up a thin scrap of yellowing paper that had been torn from a larger sheet. "It was stuck in between two pages near the back here."

On the scrap of paper were the words: *"Barclay's Bank, 18 St. George Street, Jerusalem."* Underneath, something had been completely inked out. It could have been another address.

Jesse straightened his long legs, got up, and began to pace from one window to the next.

"Jerusalem," he muttered. Something tried to click in the back of his mind but couldn't.

"It's almost incredible," he said aloud, and stopped next to Lilli's chair.

"Incredible, yes," said Edison. He placed the ledger on the desk and laid a finger on it. "But not impossible or illegal." He stood up and faced the two Quinns. "Well, Miss Quinn, Mr. Quinn. What do you wish to do about it?"

Jesse looked questioningly at Lilli. He waited for her to speak first. She said, "It's like a pet secret charity of Dad's, Jesse. I wonder if it's really a Jewish fund or another medical project that happens to be in Israel."

When she spoke the word "Jewish," she felt a curious quiver in the pit of her stomach that she could not define. She had not gotten used to the idea that she was Jewish, or at least part Jewish from her father. Lilli realized that all she knew about being Jewish was from the Bible course she had taken at Wellesley. This past eek she had not thought much about anything except her memries of the family. She thought that discovering Judaism would ave to wait. But now...?

Jesse pursed his lips thoughtfully and frowned.

"It's a lot of money to be pumping out to a question mark. Jeither one of them—Joe or Michael—was ever in Israel, unless ney were there during the war—and I don't think so—or during ne twenties, when the country was Palestine. I wonder how they ould know what was really happening to the money there."

Jesse tried again to remember something that had suddenly egun to bother him. To himself he began to murmur, "Aleph-Palestine Fund, Aleph-Palestine."

"Are you suggesting something, Jesse?" Lilli asked. She had airly well made up her own mind. She spoke to Edison. "Today s the first. We have four days to the next transfer of money to iis Aleph-Palestine Fund. It must be a substantial amount."

"Several hundred thousand dollars, if I'm right about that one welfth of ten percent," Edison said.

Jesse released the frown from his face and grew sympathetic. It's really your decision, Lilli," he said softly. "The foundation s in fine condition. It's not that it can't afford it. Yet..." And nere he stopped, to insure that the final choice was hers.

"'Yet' is right," said Lilli quickly, picking up his reservation, vhich strengthened her own. "We need time to find out what the Aleph Fund is, what purpose it serves, and who handles it. Daddy nd Uncle Michael knew, and we should, too, if we're going to eep it open." She moved off the arm of the chair and faced Edison. "Mr. Edison, will you make arrangements with the bank or somebody over there to help us. Someone at Barclay's must now where the money goes—I mean the name of a person or an nstitution, something more definite than the Aleph-Palestine Fund. We don't even know if we're helping Jews or Moslems or omebody else."

The vague nagging tugged at Jesse's brain again. Something Lilli had said disturbed him. *Moslem. Moslem.* He concentrated. Nothing.

"I can try," Edison was saying. "I'll get over to the bank this fternoon. It'll go better in person. We'll call Barclay's if we have o."

Jesse was hardly listening. He was forcing his mind to make connection. The Moslem banner? The black Kabala of Mohammed. Mecca? No, he was into a dead end.

Lilli was talking. "And call us as soon as you learn anything." Edison assured her he would, shook Lilli's hand, then Jesse's and left.

Outside, in the cool autumn morning air, Lilli stopped Jesse at the door of the Jaguar. "That was the right move, Jesse, wasn't it?"

Jesse could see in the steady gaze of her deep brown eyes that she was not unsure at all. He nodded anyway. "It was the right move, Lilli. It would have been my move."

"Good," she said. She smiled one of the few smiles she had been able to manage since the killings. After they were seated in the car, she said, "What do you think they were up to, Jesse?"

"Nothing very terrible, knowing them."

She stared thoughtfully at his profile, straight-lined and strong. After a while he felt her eyes on his face and glanced at her and smiled.

She said, "I wonder if there's a connection, Jesse."

"Between what?"

"The Aleph-Palestine Fund and the shooting."

Jesse shook his head. "I don't know."

Lilli watched the neat row houses on Commonwealth Avenue glide by. "I think I'm going to like working at the foundation."

"It'll be just right having two Quinns running everything. I think our people will like it. We could make a good team."

He glanced back at her and found her staring again.

"In the business world, Lilli, in the business world."

He laughed for the first time in a week.

Chapter 9

Jesse dropped Lilli off at the Boston Museum on Huntington Avenue to arrange for a leave of absence and went over to his own office in the Quinn Building on Boylston. There he attended meetings for three hours and forced himself to forget the Aleph-Palestine Fund and the murders of his father and uncle.

At one meeting he accepted some changes in retail advertising suggested by his publicity department and approved of two managerial requests for transfers. At another, he approved the terms of stock bonuses for the executives handling their automobile agencies and their liquor-store chain. At a final conference he was shown a bid a New York real estate broker had made on a piece of Quinn property in Greenwich, Connecticut, whose purchase Jesse had handled himself a year earlier. Jesse postponed deciding on the sale until a broader study had been made of the residential growth of the area. During the same meeting there were smaller problems about freight delays and liquor licenses that he handed over completely to his assistants. By the time he left the building the executive force of Quinn Corporation knew that the business was still in the strong hands of a Quinn.

Except for a very few people, no one had been told the truth about the relationship between the Quinn brothers. Jesse had persuaded Lilli and Ed Watson to agree that nothing would be said.

At five o'clock he called for Lilli outside the museum. He tried to ignore how quickly his eye had picked her dark-haired beauty out of the crowds milling around her.

She kissed him lightly on the cheek when she slid into her bucket seat. They headed out toward Beverly and stopped in Salem at a popular Chinese restaurant for wonton and roast pork made the way only Boston Chinese could make it, with light pink centers and beet-red edges. When the pork came, Jesse stared at the red layers of sliced meat. Lilli ate hungrily. He picked idly at the food, holding up a pork strip, studying it, putting it down, cutting it with his fork. The nagging was back in his head, the pieces of

55

puzzle still floating around haphazardly in his mind, only a few disconnected pieces.

Leaving through the restaurant's arched foyer, which was enameled in Chinese red, Jesse felt as though a ligament of nerve had snapped in his brain, and he suddenly made the connection that had frustrated him during the morning. He kept silent and mulled it over for several miles on their way home.

They crossed the straight narrow bridge over the small bay between Salem and Beverly where many pleasure boats were still in the water. A lone fishing trawler with one man in sight at the wheel was moving slowly out to sea, followed by a score of gulls swooping above his wake. For a swift moment Jesse was swept by a wave of longing to be aboard the vessel with Lilli, heading out for a long peaceful voyage to Nantucket, which by this time of year should be abandoned by the tourist.

At the end of the bridge, the road dipped and became rough, and Jesse's mood faded. Reality flowed back.

"Lilli, what's the dominant emblem of the Moslem world, some figure or shape that would stand for Mohammedanism? Something they'd put on a banner or sign?"

Lilli thought about it. "It's a scimitar, I think. Isn't it? Wait a minute. It's not a scimitar. It's a crescent, a crescent like an early moon—only it's red, I think, with a small star inside its arc. Why do you ask?"

"Just think." The engine broke into a throaty roar as he downshifted and accelerated through a bend that would put them onto the shore road.

"Oh, Christ!" She almost shouted the words. Her voice dropped and sounded strained. "The lapel insignia! It was a red crescent. And some of it was broken off. There could have been a star there, couldn't there have been? And now this thing about an Aleph-Palestine Fund, and Palestine was under the Moslems and then under the British during the twenties, and the Moslems and the Jews were there together." She clasped her hands tightly over her lap. "Do you think the men who killed Daddy and Uncle Michael were wearing Moslem red crescents? That there's a connection between Palestine and what happened here?"

Jesse stared at the road ahead.

"What do you make of the Aleph? It sounds like alpha, A. It might just be the letter A."

"It is, Jesse. I thought of something like that. I asked Bill Cohen at the museum. It is the letter A. In Hebrew. They gave

56

the fund a simple enough name, the A Fund. Do you think it has something to do with why they were . . . they're gone?"

"I won't know what to think," said Jesse, shifting up to get the Jaguar moving faster on the coast road to their home, "until we reach Wilkinson. Maybe they've done something with that pin."

Wilkinson was on duty when Jesse called. Over the phone the lieutenant spoke even more slowly than he did in person. But he surprised Jesse before Jesse could even ask his question.

"I was just about to call you, Mr. Quinn," he said haltingly. "Something came up I thought you'd like to know before it hits the papers tomorrow. It's about your father's killers. Goddamn strange, too. One of your fathers took one of the killers with him. We're pretty sure. You see, a body was washed up in Winthrop. It had shotgun wounds in the chest area. The shot is the same size your fathers were using—number eight. But the body is a dead end. Get this, will you. It had no head or hands or clothes. Just a naked torso and legs. Can you beat that? Gunshot wounds and no other marks. Coroner says the man was killed by a cord. Marks on what's left of his neck. Death due to asphyxiation. His friends strangled him and then took him apart to prevent identification and dumped him in the ocean. Not gangland style at all. Not around here."

Jesse mulled over the news before he spoke.

"Are you there, Mr. Quinn?"

"I'm here," Jesse said. "Just a little stunned by all this."

"I certainly can understand that," Wilkinson said. Then, taking a breath that Jesse could hear, he said, "There's more. We've found the vehicle that followed your fathers' Cadillac onto Crane's. It was a blue Ford pick-up truck, 1950, reported stolen a week before the killers used it. Winthrop police tagged it on a side street near the waterfront right after the body washed up. It had some blood on the front seat, and the tire treads match the casts we took on Crane's. It was the one the killers used, all right. We've gone over it for fingerprints without luck and we're checking every possible place your fathers might have stopped at between Georgetown and Crane's—gas stations, fruit stands, diners, everything—on the chance that someone might remember the Ford pick-up and who was in it. It's a long shot, but we're taking it. One other thing. We found a few cigarette butts on the floor. They weren't American. The lab identified the tobacco easily. It's a common Turkish blend not found much in this country but used widely in North Africa, the Middle East, and Europe. Does that mean anything to you?"

Jesse hesitated and then said, "No, it doesn't, but you've been busy, Lieutenant."

"I told you we were going all-out on this, Mr. Quinn."

"Have you found out anything about that piece of red pin you showed us?" Jesse asked finally. He almost held his breath.

"The lab says that it's made of copper with red enamel baked over it. And this one had traces of lead on it. We're positive enough to say that one of the killers was wearing it when he got hit by a shotgun blast. Other than that, no one can even guess yet what it was. Do you have an idea?"

"Not good enough to share it with you and foul up your own investigation," Jesse said.

"I know you've got private people on this, Mr. Quinn. That's your right. But are you working on it yourself?"

"No," Jesse said. "I don't think so."

"Good," Wilkinson said cheerfully. "Are you carrying a gun?"

Jesse thought of his service Colt Commander in his bedroom upstairs. Once a month he shot two or three boxes of ammunition through it, but he had not carried it since Korea.

"No, I'm not carrying anything."

Wilkinson grunted. Jesse couldn't tell whether he was pleased or disappointed. "Why do you ask?"

"I just wanted to remind you that carrying a piece doesn't make you a cop. Please, Mr. Quinn, if you come up with any ideas, call us."

"Don't worry, I will," Jesse promised. "And thanks for keeping me up to date."

He hung up without telling him about the Aleph-Palestine Fund. The red crescent of Islam, Turkish tobacco, the Aleph-Palestine Fund. He wanted more time to think about their connection before he went off sounding like a fool. Besides, Uncle Joe and his father had set up the A Fund in secret and kept it that way for over twenty years. He would keep it that way—for them, if that's what they wanted.

When he told Lilli what Wilkinson had just passed on to him, she grew excited. "What the hell is this all about, Jesse?"

"I don't know, Lilli, I can't even guess." He laid his hands on her shoulders. "But you're right about what you said the other day. We've got to find out more about this whole thing or we're

58

not going to be very happy with ourselves. The past isn't going to wait. I thought it might."

A few minutes later as they were sitting in the living room, smoking, drinking brandy, hardly talking, the phone rang. Lilli made Jesse stay where he was, comfortably sprawled out in a large easy chair. The phone was in an outer hall.

"Yes. . . . That important? It must be if you insist. We'll be home." She hung up, walked back into the living room, and dropped wearily onto a couch. Her face, which had been showing signs of relaxation, had grown serious again. Her dark brown eyes were troubled.

"That was Paul Edison. He said he has some unusual news for us. He doesn't like talking over telephones. He wants to come over right now—he doesn't live far from here, in Marblehead, about thirty minutes away."

"What did you tell him?" Jesse asked, warming his brandy by cupping his glass in his hands. The nineteenth-century register clock on the wall struck ten.

"I told him to come ahead. Jesse! Can you imagine it?" Her voice quivered with stress. "Unusual news! What the hell more unusual can happen to us?"

Chapter 10

Edison sipped at a Scotch and soda and placed it carefully on a coaster to avoid ringing the fine wood of the table. He had changed his suit and shirt.

"Here it is in brief," he said, "and it's a beauty." He laid an envelope and some notes on the table next to his drink. "The flow of money from the foundation to the Aleph-Palestine Fund in Jerusalem—and that *is* where it is going—cannot be stopped. Not very easily. And not by either one or both of you."

There was the expected moment of silence while the Quinns digested the latest development.

"Are you serious?" Lilli asked uncomprehendingly. She crossed her legs under the floor-length blue skirt she had changed into. A crisp white shirt buttoned at the cuffs and up the front to within three buttons of her neck completed the least somber outfit she had chosen since the funeral.

Jesse continued to smoke his Camel. He remained mutely skeptical although he knew Edison as a shrewd and brilliant accountant.

Edison's face showed tight lines around the corners of his mouth, deep hollows below his eyes, a slight oily glisten to his skin. He looked peaked.

When he felt the skepticism in Jesse's silence, he spoke in his starchiest voice deep from his narrow chest.

"I was never more serious, Miss Quinn. The facts are that your fathers—both of them are signators of the papers—have built up around the Aleph-Palestine Fund such a complex system of conditions that the fund can hardly be touched. The money is going to continue flowing to that bank in Jerusalem come Hades or high water"—he almost blushed at his own boldness—"unless we can get four signatures put on a kind of stop-payment order. Your fathers fixed it so that even by themselves they could not stop the money if they had wanted to. It's going to take the signatures of four people to do that."

Jesse had replaced his business suit with a pair of tan trousers, a brown Jaeger turtleneck sweater, and loafers. He looked like a *Life* cigarette advertisement, except for the slight bulge of a colt under his sweater on his left side. "All right," he said, reaching for a drink, "I believe it. Whose four signatures do we need?"

"That's the crux of the matter," said Edison, a little dramatically. "Two signatures have to be from the heads of the Quinn Foundation. Those would have been of Michael and Joseph themselves. Or their immediate heirs. That would be the two of you. You had already been born when the contracts were constructed. Your names are included in several passages."

"And the other two signatures?" asked Lilli. Jesse squashed his cigarette in an ashtray and waited for the answer.

Edison made a mouth and grunted with his lips tight before he spoke. Jesse had never known him to be so theatrical.

"Here's the weirdest part," Edison said. "The other two signatures will have to come from the two people who control the Aleph Fund in Jerusalem. By the way, aleph is the letter A in Hebrew."

Jesse and Lilli threw each other a look of approval.

"To cut the money off, to dissolve the A-Palestine Fund, you will have to get the consent of the people who have the use of it. Your fathers really wanted insurance that as long as those controlling the fund felt a need for it, nobody could interfere. The givers *and* the receivers have to agree to its demise."

Edison took a long sip at his drink as though the extravagance of what he had been saying had parched his throat.

"Well," he said, "is it unusual enough to have made me come right out here to tell you?"

"It's unusual, all right," said Jesse, "if you go in for understatement. It's goddamn bizarre to me. I'm glad you came over."

"I haven't got a copy of the whole document, but here's a summary of the main clauses." He handed Jesse the envelope lying on the table. Jesse gave it to Lilli. "I spoke with Richard Ferguson, vice-president in charge of special accounts at First National, and he spoke to his counterpart at Barclay's. Neither one has any idea of who gets the money. It's being handled almost like a Swiss numbered account. The money is transferred in New York City to Barclay's Bank, and the Jerusalem branch picks up the credit. Someone over there—the people running the Aleph Fund—get the withdrawals in cash. The acknowledgments with their initials are all kept in Jerusalem."

Jesse made the obvious suggestion, just to see how tight things really were. "What about closing down Quinn Foundation, transferring its assets to another charter, and then changing the recipients, omitting the Aleph-Palestine Fund? At least until we find out what it is."

"Listen, Mr. Quinn," said Edison, in a tone of self-satisfaction. "Richard and I discussed this for three solid hours. All the loopholes were blocked by your fathers' lawyers way back in '31. Including that one. I'm not a lawyer, but your own lawyers will tell you the same thing."

Jesse ran his hand through his hair like a comb. He got up and walked over to the cold fireplace, above which hung the portraits of the two Quinns. He raised his head and stared at his father. The handsome face that stared back, half smiling, open, now seemed that of almost a stranger. For the first time in his life Jesse felt that he hardly knew the man. He knew nothing about his family, his childhood, his early manhood, nothing about the woman he had married—Jesse's own mother. Jesse had asked nothing, assuming that his father had led an ordinary life and would have spoken of the extraordinary if there had been any. Thinking of the emptiness now brought a deep frown into Jesse's face.

Lilli came up behind him without touching.

"Does this mean we are going to Jerusalem, Jesse?" she asked.

He kept his eyes on the portrait and spoke half-mindedly to it. "I think it means that someone has to go there, and not just for the signatures of a pair of ghosts. It's the past, Lilli, that we have got to get hold of. The past more than the signatures. If we can get that uncovered, we may not need the others. Do you think?"

He turned to her.

Lilli nodded her head in short, swift movements, jouncing the dark hair on her shoulders. There were questions in her eyes. "I believe that, Jesse," she said.

He read what else she was saying to him without saying it. His eyes deepened and an eyebrow arched.

"Okay," he said. "We'll go together."

Chapter 11

A stray dog hidden in the lower alleys of Jerusalem's Arab Quarter pierced the chilly silence of the night with a series of sharp barks. The animal sounded as though it was calling to a mate lost somewhere in the city. Higher in the northern section of the quarter up the side of a hill, two chained Alsatians rose from their pad and answered the call of the stray and spoke almost angrily to its message.

For five steady minutes the Alsatians growled and barked alternately. When a light appeared in the villa the dogs were guarding, they ceased barking, but their growls remained deep and harsh.

A pair of large floodlights came on and threw their brightness across the front of the blue stucco building, illuminating the entire estate down to a high wire fence a hundred feet away. The dogs were caught by the light in the middle of the grounds at the ends of their long chains. They were oversized wolflike Alsatians with eyes that glowed yellow when they turned their heads at the sound behind them. In spite of the growls rumbling in their throats, the hair on the backs of their necks was not bristled.

A door opened near one end of the villa and two men came down the few steps onto the grass and cautiously went out to the perimeter of the floodlights' arc at the base of the fence. They were both carrying Uzi submachine guns that had been captured from the Israelis in a recent clash. At the sight of the men the two big dogs fell silent. Their tails wagged as they waited for the men to come back and give them their customary caresses. Down in the alleys of the lower city, the stray had given up calling for its mate and had gone away.

One of the men broke the silence and spoke softly in Arabic. "It was nothing. The dogs are just a little jittery."

Slinging their guns, they went over to the Alsatians and spoke to them and shook their necks roughly. The dogs wagged their tails harder, straining against their chains to jump up on the men,

63

and when they were deserted, they slinked back to the place where they had been lying close to the blue stucco building.

The guards went inside the low rambling building, killed the floodlights, and plunged the estate into darkness. They hung their guns on wooden pegs near the front door and returned to the room where the only light burned in the house. One of the men twisted a switch and the villa went completely dark again, as it had been when the stray dog first barked.

Before the eyes of the men adjusted to the darkness, a telephone rang. One guard snapped the light on. The other picked up the telephone. An operator announced in Arabic that a call was coming in from the East Coast of the United States. She gave the guard a name.

"Hold, please. He's sleeping. I will get his secretary."

A few minutes later he held the door open for a wavy-haired heavy-set man wearing light blue silk pajamas. The man rubbed his face roughly, as though to drive the sleep from his mind, and took the receiver that was held out to him. He ran a hand lightly over his head, and the hair, which had been only slightly mussed before, was suddenly in perfect place. After listening for a few moments to the receiver, he waved the guards out of the room.

"Yes, this is his secretary, Ahmud Darwish. Yes. We've met before. Yes. Ahmud. You can talk. . . . Yes. I can hear you. . . . Repeat that." He picked up a pencil and scribbled the message he was getting, repeating it to himself. "The young Americans are on their way. How are you certain? . . . You saw them yourself board the aircraft for . . . Where? . . . Paris and Tel Aviv. They may leave the plane in Paris, could they not?" He listened to the voice on the other end. "Yes, yes, I am certain you are right. They *are* coming here. Very good. The Holy One will be pleased. I wish to tell you he was very pleased with the transaction of that last business, and he mourns the loss we suffered. Allah's will. It is all well. There will be rewards when you return. . . . Allah's blessing on you, also, and on all of yours."

The secretary hung up the receiver and called the guards back in and left. At the end of the hallway, which cut almost through the full length of the villa, he knocked on a heavy ironclad door. He knocked and waited, and knocked again and waited. The villa was still and peaceful. The dogs outside were quiet. Ahmud Darwish did not like the dogs. He was always glad when he thought that he did not have to come near them and their hungry white jaws. The dogs were not his concern, thank Allah.

He rapped harder on the door. His master was a very sound sleeper. Finally there was a reply. When the door opened enough for him to slip through, he entered.

His visit lasted only five minutes, and when he left hurriedly for the room with the telephone, he knew precisely what his instructions were. He always did. Not that his master spoke bluntly, but he understood his master's will better than any man. Again he ordered the guards out of their room and put a call through to a man in the Arab Quarter not very far away.

When a sleep-ridden voice answered, Darwish spoke quickly and sharply. The sleep in his own voice had disappeared. The instructions he was passing on were as definite as those he had received from his master.

"The Americans from Boston have left for Jerusalem as the Holy One expected. He feels it would be unwise if they spoke to Mr. Sutherland before they spoke to him. As I understood him, I don't think he believes they have to meet Mr. Sutherland at all. Handle this, please, in any way you believe effective. So long as the Americans agree to meet our master and do not see Mr. Sutherland."

Ahmud Darwish hung up, quite confident that he had been understood.

Chapter 12

The morning sunlight shone like shards of gold on the roofto of Old Jerusalem. The unexpected beauty surprised Lilli. Yeste day, in the New City, she had seen barbed wire, barricades, a young Jews carrying submachine guns. They did not belong the scene she viewed now.

From her room in the posh King David Hotel, high on t rising slope above the rooftops, Old Jerusalem sprawled away staggered layers of flats broken up by shiny domes and slend minarets, displaying the history of centuries. The spires and fla reflected the oblique rays of the sun, and the clusters of gray sto and white marble were transformed into bright gold.

In the distant streets long-robed men crowded along the walk moving almost imperceptibly by shop fronts and market stalls. C the tops of buildings and on latticed balconies hanging out abo the streets, veiled women stood or knelt and scrutinized the li below.

Late yesterday afternoon, when the Quinns had been driv in from Tel Aviv, Lilli had been shown a Jerusalem which le her unprepared for this golden flow of Eastern life. She had se only a city of battered buildings and rusting hulks of trucks a armored cars standing where they had been disabled in the fightir six years before, a city of narrow streets crowded with nois strenuous people dressed in Western clothes, gorging on life th was still desperate. The sight of battlements in good repair ar unbroken barbed wire reminded her that peace had not really con to the city.

Yet in spite of the beating the city had taken, the people c both sides of the wire had withstood the assault and endure Nothing seemed new. The buildings and cobblestone streets, th sounds of people, the smells of food and spices, the distant gra hills—even the warm fresh air that flowed past her on her balcon seemed wafted in from the past.

In her hand Lilli held a pamphlet describing three thousar years of the endurance of Jerusalem. All the facts of its histor ointed to the single idea that the city was determined to outlast the efforts of generations to destroy her. Rulers changed, but the Jews remained. The Arabs had remained, too, she knew, but the pamphlet had been written by Jews for the Jewish tourists who stayed at the King David, having had the courage to come to Israel at all.

Lilli took no pride in her courage. She had come here with Jesse, knowing little at all about the land or its people or its plight. And not caring more than her humanity normally made her care for the plight of people anywhere, in Korea, Indonesia, India. Yet she was stricken by the thought that this was a city belonging in part to her, inherited from her father, who was Jewish, and from . . . She hesitated. Her mother? But if the city was somehow partly hers, she did not belong to the city. She did not *feel* Jewish.

She glanced at her watch. It was nine o'clock and she had not dressed yet. Jesse would be downstairs in the dining room at nine-thirty for breakfast. She had a few minutes more to enjoy the startling view of the Old City in the morning sun.

She opened the pamphlet to a silhouette map of the Old City seen from the Kind David. The most famous landmarks were clearly numbered and outlined—the Dome of the Rock, the Church of the Holy Scepter, the Jewish Quarter, the Jaffa Gate, and the Wailing Wall.

The Wailing Wall, she read, was the surviving western wall of the Second Temple, destroyed two thousand years ago. Lilli had heard of the Wall somewhere, but couldn't place it. She felt like an alien. What did any of these places, these people or their history mean to her? She would have felt more at home in Athens or Rome or Paris.

Yet these places, lying out there like so many links to the past, must have meant much to the people she came from, her Jewish forebears (the word sounded strange as she thought it), to the people out there right now, and to her father. Especially to her father. Or why had he created and managed the Aleph-Palestine Fund so secretly?

Lilli stared moodily out at the golden city, her dressing gown carelessly untied, her body warmed by the sun striking through the open French windows, but her mind remained troubled.

She tried to think of something she could handle better. She thought of making love. She had not been touched since that awful afternoon in Jim's apartment three weeks ago. The memory was unbearable. She ran her hands over her breasts lightly and the down her body along the inside of her thighs. As she touche herself, she forgot completely the pain of that day.

She dragged a soft chair into the sunlight before the Frenc windows and sat on its edge, when suddenly there was a strang thud in the distance as though the earth had hiccupped. Standin up quickly and drawing her robe tightly around her, she saw thread of smoke curling upward above the glistening roofs of th Old City.

Her heart raced briefly. From her suitcase she took a small pai of old German binoculars and found the spiral of smoke. Wit the help of the map, she placed the smoke somewhere near th Zion Gate to the Old City. But she couldn't see what was burning As she peered through the lenses her hands shook and she felt tremor in her body. She lowered the field glasses. This time Lill knew why she was shivering. She had not prepared herself fo the violence in the city, not when it came this close, this unex pectedly.

Lilli dressed hurriedly in white linens and went down throug the grand lobby, past the dark-wainscoted bar, and into a spaciou dining room. It was crowded with men wearing open white shirt and women in light, unfashionable dresses. The conversation i the room had created a low, unintelligible, yet excited hum. Th people around her were animated. Jesse was already seated, bu he stood to greet her as soon as she appeared at the door. Jess didn't look very American, Lilli thought as she regarded him i his white linens and open-collared shirt.

"You look like a native, Jesse Quinn," she said, kissing hin on his cheek and concealing her nervousness. It had become he habit now to brush his face with her lips each morning. He ha not minded and now anticipated the exchange with a little pleasure It was a family kiss, soft and close-mouthed. He almost felt lik returning it each time, but he didn't. He stood motionless an accepted it.

"Let's eat outside," she suggested. She no longer felt nervous The atmosphere of excitement around her had stimulated an warmed her. She felt alive and hungry and wanted to be in th fresh air.

As Jesse escorted her through the lobby toward an outdoo sidewalk café on Julian's Way, she asked, "Did you hear the explosion a few minutes ago?"

"I heard it," Jesse replied flatly. He looked around for an empty table.

The café stretched along the walk for a good half the length of the hotel. The tables were small white wrought-iron affairs with metal tops. They were lined two abreast with four thin-cushioned matching chairs at each one. A colorful awning attached to the side of the hotel shaded the tables and made everyone comfortable. At each end of the awning, hanging high and well out over the street, were blue-and-white flags bearing the Star of David.

"It was a bomb, wasn't it?" asked Lilli.

"Yes, a good-sized one," Jesse remarked. "It sent the smoke high enough and the sound carried way up here. There's a table over there."

He helped her into a chair at an empty table on the edge of the walk just inside the shade of the awning. A waiter in a white coat headed over to them as soon as they were seated. Lilli lit a cigarette.

Coming toward the café from across Julian's Way was a well-dressed, dark-suited man in dark glasses. He was slim and distinguished-looking. He dodged nimbly through the street traffic until he was on their side of the street. The waiter in the white jacket was a few feet from their table when the well-dressed man in the dark suit stopped for a moment, scanned the crowd of people at their breakfasts, saw the Quinns, and started toward them. Behind him streams of old American and European cars flowed noisily by in both directions.

The waiter reached their table and smiled at Lilli. He handed Jesse a soiled white envelope and started to move away.

Jesse reached up and touched the waiter's arm to order breakfast, but the man jerked away nervously and paid him no attention. The dark-suited man was twenty feet away, coming along the walk toward them, raising his hand slightly as though he were ready to greet them.

The waiter hurried his step as he got closer to the dark-suited man. Jesse could see him pulling something from his pocket. As the dark-suited man passed, still intent on greeting Jesse, the waiter brushed up against him.

There were two muffled reports. The waiter dashed into the heavy street traffic. The man in the dark suit said nothing. He tried to follow the waiter with his hand outstretched as though a mistake had been made. He folded his arms across his chest, took

69

another step or two, and stumbled to his knees. Then he fell forward and turned partially on his side. His dark glasses were still in place.

Someone at a table near him screamed, a few men jumped up and ran to him. Jesse saw a man with a moustache reach into his coat and bring out a big automatic. Jesse suddenly became conscious of his own gun tucked into his waistband. He had decided at the last minute to bring the Colt Commander along to Israel and had packed it in his shaving bag. The tensions he felt in Jerusalem had prompted him to wear it. Now he hesitated. This was not his affair. Though the killer and the victim seemed to know them, he and Lilli were not in danger.

Across the street in front of the YMCA, an old green Chevrolet rumbled away from the curve and headed south along Julian's Way. It picked up some speed and suddenly skidded to a stop in the middle of the street, blocking the traffic behind it. Horns blared, but the Chevrolet stood still. The rear door was flung open. The waiter leaped into the car with his pistol clearly visible in his hand. As soon as the door slammed closed, the car lurched away and vanished down the street, leaving a dark, smelly funnel of smoke behind it.

The commotion that followed was brief. There was no chaos. People were hurrying to the side of the fallen man. Several men were in the street shouting after the Chevrolet. The man with the automatic had put it away and gone back to his breakfast, reacting to the killing much as Jesse had.

Jesse pushed the envelope the waiter-assassin had given him across to Lilli. "See what's in here, Lilli," he said. He walked over to the crowd that had gathered around the fallen man. Everybody was talking and gesturing, but Jesse understood nothing. From the shaking of some heads, he assumed the man was dead.

When Jesse returned to the table, Lilli had grown noticeably paler.

"I think he was coming over to our table," said Jesse, sitting down. "Well, he's dead now." His pulse was still racing.

"The Englishman from Barclay's who was supposed to meet us?" Lilli asked. She twisted around and watched someone throw a tablecloth over the body. Now a police gong sounded down the street. She felt a slight pounding in her head.

"It's nine forty-five," said Jesse. "He was supposed to be here fifteen minutes ago. We'll wait another ten minutes. If he doesn't get here, then I'd say that's him over there."

Lilli lit a cigarette. Her hands trembled. Two police cars, both VWs, and an old Buick ambulance arrived. The commotion, which had subsided, resumed as people crowded over to tell the police the story.

"What was in the envelope?" Jesse asked, noticing that it was not on the table.

Lilli opened her bag and handed him a sheet of light brown paper. "I don't know what to make of it, Jesse. But look at the red mark." She was still trembling.

In the upper left corner of the paper was the raised stamp of a red crescent. Inside its arc hung a white star. Next to it were some Arab words printed in script. Halfway down the sheet was a message in English, written in a careful hand. It said:

> Haj Amin el-Husseini, Mufti of Jerusalem, sends his greetings. The sample of his force is to impress you with his power. As he has known the Quintanas, so he wishes to know their children. You will hear from him again. Soon. For your own safety and success in Palestine, respond as he requests.
>
> EL-HUSSEINI.

Chapter 13

"Let's get out of here, Lilli," Jesse growled, crumpling the paper in his jacket pocket. "We're not going to get anything to eat here."

Lilli rose and Jesse took her arm protectively. People were on the move everywhere. No one had an appetite for breakfast. The tables were emptying. The waiters were gone. The man with the pistol had gone.

Jesse felt vulnerable. The deaths of Michael and Joseph had given him that feeling. He had never felt so helplessly exposed before. Flying combat, he always knew his enemy when he saw him. The sides were clearly drawn and openly marked. If he had the skill, he would survive. If he didn't . . . But this was different. Someone knew who Lilli and he were, and had known their fathers and killed them. And he had no idea who they were. He had to resist the impulse to look over his shoulder.

Three or four men nearby left the café with them. Jesse caught their eyes deliberately, one at a time. One or two stared back. The others averted their glance. Who were they? What were they doing there? How the devil could he tell? He shoved them out of his mind.

He led Lilli toward the street away from the police cars and ambulance. The body of the slain man had been wrapped in a light canvas sheet and was being carried toward the ambulance.

A few idle taxis were parked up the road. Jesse headed toward them.

"Who's the Mufti, Lilli?" Jesse asked. "Have you ever heard of him?"

She shook her head. "I'm not positive. A leader of the Moslems in Jerusalem, I think."

In a few minutes they were settled in an old but unbattered Ford taxi and on their way to Barclay's Bank. Lilli questioned the driver. He was a coarse-looking man in his forties, thick-nosed, squat-necked, deeply tanned.

"The Mufti?" snorted the driver through the short, wet cigar he smoked. "A bastard. Pure red-haired bastard, he is. He's been around for years. I can't recall not hearing of him, except in the early forties, and I've been here since thirty-three." He spoke a cockney English through his nose. "He's their bloody spiritual leader, although there's not much of the spirit in what he preaches. Runs a bunch of Arab thugs all over the place. They do what he tells them. You people Jewish?"

Taken off guard, Lilli almost said "no." She caught herself with her tongue on the roof of her mouth, then answered quietly, "Yes, I am." Jesse said nothing.

"Well, Husseini's his name. Suppose you never heard of him." The taxi passed by the French Consulate building. "Been the Mufti of Jerusalem since the 1920s. Any trouble we've had with the Arabs has come from him first, even the '48 war. That shooting back there"—he paused to strike a sulphur match with a dirty thumbnail and light his dead cigar—"was probably his work. It had his style. I seen it. Seen it more than once, too." He puffed noisily at the cigar.

"What's his style?" asked Jesse.

"Style? Yeah, they have a style," said the driver. "Swift, smooth, up close, and quiet. No upset until the shooting. Then—bang, bang. It frightens the hell out of his own people who might oppose him. He kills more of his own that way than ours. That one back there, powder burns on his clothes, if you got close enough to look. I seen you looking."

Jesse felt Lilli grip the back of his hand, her fingernails digging into his skin. He turned his hand and held hers. He glanced hopefully across the seat and was not surprised to find that she was tense but in complete control of herself.

"Who was he?" she asked, her voice a little husky but without a trace of trembling. She took her hand away from Jesse, lit a cigarette steadily, and took his hand back. Jesse gave it a slight squeeze. Lilli was turning out to be a soldier.

"Not an Israeli," the driver was saying. "Blessed be God, I overheard that. Not a tourist either. Not dressed like one." He turned his head and gave them a fast once-over that seemed to approve of what they were wearing. "A foreign businessman, I expect. I could've caught the bastards that did it if I'd been facing the other way."

They were cruising along a road lined with shops.

"Is there a restaurant over there? Pull over, will you." Jesse pointed over the driver's shoulder.

They ate breakfast in the small café on King David Road. At their invitation, the driver joined them. As they ate, he told stories of the '48 war, of the Arab encirclement of Jerusalem, the starvation of the people, and of the Jaffa Road the Jews had opened. "I drove a truck on that operation, and it was something. When my truck was hit, I was put onto a machine gun, and when I ran dry I lugged stretchers for the rest of the fight. They had us badly outnumbered and shot the bloody hell out of the convoy. We lost a lot of people that day, and food, too, and we killed a lot. When you came into the city you saw those burnt-out trucks, didn't you? We left them there to remind us of that fight. One of them was mine. I can show it to you sometime. The blood flowed, but we saved the city—at least this part of the city."

Jesse and Lilli listened and ate and brought the conversation back to the Mufti when they could.

The driver spoke bluntly. "Husseini has been the bloody worst anti-Zionist in the whole country. He's fought against Jews and Jewish immigration since the 1920s any way he could. He's still fighting when he can, the bastard. The British tried to arrest him in 1940, I think—yes, 1940—because he was supporting the Germans. But he slipped out of the country, got to Germany, and lived in Berlin as Hitler's guest through the whole war. Everybody knows that." He dunked his second roll into a cup of steaming coffee and took half of it in a single bite.

"And nothing happened to him after the war?" asked Lilli, watching his jaws work. Throughout the meal her attention had been fixed to his rough but cheerful face. It was the kind of face one had to look at long and grow to like, and Lilli already liked it. The driver's name was Simon.

Simon made a fist, opened it in a gesture of frustration. "I don't know what the bloody hell happened," he grumbled. "I heard the French—de Gaulle, it was in '47, had him—let him loose and he turned up back here—as strong as ever among the marketplace Arabs. I can show you where he lives, if you'd like to see it."

"Where he lives?" asked Jesse. "Everyone knows where he lives, and he's still around?" He thought of showing the driver the Mufti's letter and then decided against it.

Simon laughed with humor. "Easy, my friend. He's not that easy to get rid of. Wait. You will see." He soaked the second half of his roll in his coffee, devoured that, and drained the cup.

Back in the taxi, the leathery-faced Simon, no longer talkative,

74

hunched over his wheel and drove rapidly on the cobblestone streets through small squares, down single-car lanes, working his way back toward the Old City. Soon they found the streets blockaded by heavy rolls of barbed wire and guarded by young Israeli soldiers carrying the ubiquitous Uzi submachine gun slung from their shoulders.

Simon wheeled his taxi along a narrow road winding south around the great ancient wall protecting the Old City. Soon they were climbing into the sun along a road winding up Mount Zion, passing small stucco homes, old stone apartments, and a deserted mosque that had been caught in the Jewish sector when the armistice had been declared six years earlier.

Halfway to the top, passing David's Tomb, Simon pulled over and stopped. They stepped out into the road. The sun had grown warmer and a light haze of dust hung over the city.

"Way over there. See a spot of blue just beyond the great dome—a blue stucco house with a high fence around it. One 75-millimeter mortar shell would take it all down, the red-haired devil along with it. I could land one on top of him myself, from a place on the north side. Have all of the angles and trajectory worked out. But no mortar. Anyway, we aren't allowed to do it. Not yet. Would you like to tour the city? I know the beautiful place like my own face, every old line and curve in it, and the new lumps, too."

"Sightseeing is going to wait for tomorrow," said Jesse. "Can we make Barclay's now before it closes at noon?" He looked at his wristwatch. The driver looked at his own watch.

"We have the time. And you get a little sightseeing done anyway." He swung the taxi around to head back. As he drove away, he jerked his thumb toward the slope where the Mufti's blue stucco house baked under the sun, and said, "What do you think of that, him living so near and yet so far?"

Jesse and Lilli looked at each other and said nothing.

In fifteen minutes they were at Barclay's Bank, Jerusalem Branch, which, next to its front entrance, had a small brass sign with the bank's name darkly etched and the date 1878. They went inside to inquire for Sutherland, while the cab driver waited for them at the curb.

The bank was a spacious room with floor, walls, and ceiling planked in dark mahogany. A waist-high counter with glass above it divided the room between clients and clerks. Overhead, four wooden fans hung motionless in the warm air. They gave the room the look of an old established business.

Jesse and Lilli approached the delicate-looking man with fine, wispy blond hair who was standing behind the glass partition. When they asked for Mr. Sutherland, the man stuttered, then blubbered an apology and held back what Lilli thought was a rush of tears. In a voice that shook with a suppressed sob, the clerk called to another man sitting behind a large desk well to the rear in the director's section of the bank.

The second man seemed to roll away from his chair rather than to rise from it. He was so short that Lilli thought he was going to be a dwarf. But he was not misshapen, though as he came over to them he did look a little penguinlike in his dress and a little jerky in his movements.

When the short man rolled up to the counter, the tearful man bent and whispered to him. Then, with a handkerchief held to his eyes, the first man disappeared through a back door. Jesse ignored him and instead watched the little man reach out and open a door concealed in the partition. He bowled through the door and came up to Lilli and Jesse with both hands extended.

His face was grave, his voice subdued and manly. As he spoke, looking at Lilli, his eyes brightened. His English was impeccable, his accent refined. It was only his unimpressive size that had exiled him to one of Barclay's lesser branches in the world.

"Mr. Quinn." He clasped Jesse's hand, glancing enviously at his tall, well-proportioned form. "Miss Quinn." He took Lilli's left hand in a backward clasp into his own left hand and held both of them. "We have just heard about the murder of Mr. Sutherland. Awful, awful. We expected something—but not this." The way he held their hands and spoke, they couldn't tell whether he was offering his sympathy or seeking theirs. "John—Mr. Sutherland— has been here for over twenty years. He and George Powell there"—he pointed to the bathroom door—"have been good friends for the last ten. You must understand George's feelings."

The little man's voice quivered as he spoke. He introduced himself as Paul Martin, director of Barclay's. He had been expecting them. Lilli and Jesse extended their sympathies. Martin listened politely, but his eyes were fixed rather impolitely on Lilli's beauty. Then he led them through the open door in the partition, holding Lilli's elbow as he walked by her side, closed the door, and brought them to his desk. He offered Lilli the seat closer to his chair, from which he could get a complete view of her. Jesse took the remaining chair, opposite him across the desk. Jesse tried to distract Martin's eye from Lilli but couldn't.

Lilli knew that he was staring at her and was suddenly inspired to cross her legs over the knee to show him a long calf and a fine ankle. Her tan high-heeled shoes accented the nice line of the leg. Mr. Martin smiled at her sheepishly as though in appreciation of the view. If that made him more helpful, she was ready to go as high as a kneecap. Jesse held back a smile as he realized what was happening.

Before anyone spoke, the bank clerk named George emerged from the back, drawn and pale but composed enough to carry on his duties at the counter. Mr. Martin nodded to him once. George nodded back several times, as though he were agreeing to something they had just talked about, and then lowered his head over some books.

Jesse fished out of his pocket the crumpled note the assassin had given him and pushed it across the desk. Martin stretched half his body over the desk to reach it.

"Mr. Martin," Jesse started, "am I right in suspecting that Mr. Sutherland's death was connected with Miss Quinn's and my arrival in Jerusalem?"

Martin took his eyes off Lilli long enough to read the note. Then he looked back at Lilli.

"If this note is really from the Mufti of Jerusalem, Mr. Quinn, you would be quite right to believe that."

Chapter 14

The undersized Mr. Martin sat straight in his chair. Lilli observed that it had been shortened to bring his feet in touch with the ground. He reread the note from el-Husseini. Then he dropped the note onto his desk and unexpectedly became very businesslike.

He opened a rosewood box in front of him and offered his visitors Turkish cigarettes. They both accepted. As Jesse inhaled he thought of the cigarettes the killers of his father had smoked waiting to do their work. The smoke tasted unusually bitter. Martin pressed a button on the side of his desk, and a large overhead fan began to whirl, slowly dispersing the smoke and cooling the area.

When all three were smoking, Martin spoke for ten minutes without stopping, addressing Jesse almost entirely, occasionally turning back to Lilli to acknowledge her presence. Lilli did not mind. What Martin had to say was better absorbed without the annoying distraction of his wandering eyes. His voice was suave and his manner polished smooth.

"The management of the A Fund—that's what we've been calling it," he said, "has been no simple affair, even before the Mufti began to interfere. Only three of us here at Barclay's know or knew anything about it. Mr. Sutherland, George over there, and myself. Only Sutherland and I knew that the money was leaving the bank secretly and how it was being taken out. But only Sutherland knew where it was going. You see, he was the only one of us who had ever met your fathers personally. That was over twenty years ago, in Paris, at their invitation, long before I came here.

"When Sutherland returned from Paris, he brought the design of the Aleph-Palestine Fund with him—its function, its methods, and the names of the central parties. Everything had to be held in absolute confidentiality. The identities of the Palestinians getting the money Sutherland kept exclusively to himself. Those were his instructions."

When Martin explained this last reservation, his voice expressed his disapproval, but he stuck to the facts and made no judgments on the Quinns' orders.

"When I took over the management of the bank nine years ago," he said, allowing a touch of smugness to creep into his voice, "I made no changes, and the system has remained exactly as it was when your fathers established it. And that included Sutherland's sole possession of the second two names connected with the fund."

"But something happened to change everything. How did the man called the Mufti get into this?" Jesse's voice was hard and demanding.

Martin was not intimidated. He stared almost glassy-eyed at Jesse and repeated the Mufti's name. "El-Husseini. The Mufti. Yes, something did happen, certainly." He turned his attention to Lilli. "George told us the whole messy story right after it happened.

"Until a few months ago, the fund and everything and everybody connected with it existed in the same secrecy that it had been established in. And then George Powell got himself mixed up with a belly dancer in the Arab Quarter, not an unusual thing for a single man to do who has lived in Palestine for years. In some intimate moments with her, he boasted about a few of his business responsibilities, to acquire importance in her eyes—also not a terribly unexpected thing for a man of his unimportance to do. Among other things, he mentioned to the woman his connection with the mysterious A Fund and the American Quinn brothers who were financing it.

"Powell had forgotten all about his breach of confidence until the Arab woman invited him to a cocktail party where, in a friendly conversation, another man questioned him further about the fund and the Americans. Powell knew little more than what he had already bragged to the woman, but he did know the people who had more information. During the party, under the pressure of cajoling and teasing, he finally dropped names—Sutherland's and mine."

Shortly after the party, Sutherland was contacted by two men. They wanted to know where the money was going and how it was getting there. They offered him a bribe. He refused. They then threatened him and his family and announced that it was the Mufti himself who sought the information. Sutherland told them nothing, sent his family back to England, and began to carry a gun.

79

Last week he was warned that the young Quinns might be visiting Jerusalem and that he was not to see them if they did. He was being watched, but he refused to be frightened. The news of the murder of the Quinns had angered and saddened him, but he swore he was not afraid. He was not even sure that that was the Mufti's work.

"It might have been better if he had been afraid," concluded Martin.

"Why weren't our fathers informed immediately that something had gone wrong?" demanded Lilli.

Martin faltered for the first time. "We truly never thought it would go as far as it did. I suggested we send a wire to Boston when all this first happened, but Sutherland thought it was premature. And then it was suddenly too late. We didn't understand why the Mufti, of all people, was interested in the fund, unless it was for the money itself. But a great many people would be interested if they knew about it. Sutherland underestimated the Mufti's interest. It was more than the money. Until we learned of the deaths of your fathers, Sutherland believed nothing would happen, that the Mufti would drop the whole matter when he found we could not be intimidated. But just before the news of the murders in America reached here, Sutherland got a call telling him that the Mufti had destroyed the founders of the fund because they were his enemies and that he would destroy anybody who tried to prevent him from getting compensation for his injuries. That's what the caller said to Sutherland. 'Compensation for his injuries.'"

"Compensation for injuries?" Lilli asked, shifting her legs unconsciously. "What injuries?"

"I don't know," Martin said. "None of us could find out anything about it."

"And that's all there is?" asked Jesse.

"Not quite. Sutherland arranged to meet with the Mufti himself, but even then he learned nothing except that the injuries must have been inflicted in the distant past. There was no question what the compensation was to be—the money in the fund. Poor Sutherland. He paid for his shortsightedness."

Jesse scowled at the feeble attempt to lay everything on Sutherland, who couldn't deny it.

"With Sutherland dead, then, no one knows where the money is going when it leaves here?"

"I've made that point clear already, Mr. Quinn. It was your fathers' wish. I respected it."

"Well, how does it get out of here? You said you know that."

Martin explained. "Every week on Tuesday morning, an old Arab cleaning woman comes here before we open our doors. She spends a good part of the morning doing her work. On the first Monday of the month, in the late afternoon, Sutherland has been placing a bank draft for a designated amount of money, pounds sterling, into a used envelope and slipping the envelope unsealed into one of the bank's trash baskets. That one over there, to be exact." He pointed to a small wooden basket near another desk. "Yes, raise your eyebrows at that. But it wasn't so crazy. On Tuesday morning, the Arab woman empties the baskets into the barrels in the alley. But first she has to carry the baskets through a small hallway between the bank and the alley. Until last week I did not know whether the bank draft went into the old woman's pocket. When Sutherland got the warning from the Mufti's agents, he confided in me about what she does. The bank draft goes into her pocket or into a barrel outside. The old woman has been transporting the money herself to someone in Jerusalem. But Sutherland would not go so far as to say to whom."

Lilli's eyes shone with excitement as she listened. Her hands were folded together on her lap. She no longer cared if Martin undressed her with his banker's gray eyes.

"Is the money going to Jewish people?" she asked.

"I can't say that for certain, Miss Quinn," said Martin, giving her his attention again, his eyes dropping to her feet and rising quickly to her face.

"This is the first Monday of the month, Mr. Martin," Lilli said. She glanced at Jesse, recognized his agreement, and then looked at Martin.

"Yes, it is," Martin said, putting a blank, thoughtful stare into his face but fixing his sight on Lilli's small shapely breasts, modestly outlined through her linen dress. "The transfer of money has already come by teletype from London. The sum minus the usual commission will be placed in the trash as usual. I will do it myself."

"And you have no idea where this woman takes it?" Lilli asked once again, as though repetition would jar his memory.

"No, none. I did not care and do not care. The A Fund is good business for the bank. The commission is healthy. If you really

81

are bent on knowing where the money is going, I suppose you will be here tomorrow early to follow the woman. I don't see how that would be very difficult. She has been doing this business for years. She is old and unobservant."

Lilli uncrossed her legs and shifted her position. Martin seemed stirred by her movement. He leaned his small body away from his desk and toward her. He placed a small well-shaped hand on her knee in what he tried to make seem a fatherly pat and looked up into her face imploringly. Lilli did not move. Jesse started to say something but caught himself.

"But do not do this, Miss Quinn. I strongly beseech you not to follow this woman. You are so beautiful. . . . Excuse me, you must understand. You are good clients of this bank. What happened to your fathers . . . I do not want to be responsible for anything happening to you. You've seen Sutherland. Listen to me—in this country death is meted out too easily, from both sides. urge you and your cousin to go home. Find a way to close the fund, but go home. The Mufti is a determined and ruthless man."

"Determined to take the fund, you mean?" asked Jesse.

Martin took his hand from Lilli's knee and sat back in his chair, his hands holding both arms.

"I think he's more strongly resolved than ever."

"And he would give very much to find out what we've just learned. About how the money leaves here."

Martin knitted his brows, stood up, and locked his hands behind him. He looked smaller than before. A nervous expression crept into his face, first around the corners of his eyes, then across his mouth, as he flicked his tongue along his lips to moisten them.

"Yes, I believe he would. I would say he wants to get rid of the people the old woman meets and substitute his own agents That would hardly pose a big problem for him. The money comes in like manna from the sky, yes, that's how I would describe it No questions, no papers, just deposits. With a little proper maneuvering, it could become his. Yes, I suppose he would be very generous to anyone who helped him to it."

"If he did manage all this," said Lilli, "he would still need the correct initials of the people who are cashing the drafts. And that's something you could provide him with, isn't it?"

"Yes, Miss Quinn, I could. I will tell you something else. He has already begun trying to force me into this. Like Sutherland and poor Powell over there, I am caught in the middle."

Martin walked to her side. "I do not wish you to be hurt, Miss

82

Quinn. Either of you." He reached out and took her hand into both of his. She thought he was going to kiss it. "I am getting out myself. By the beginning of next week, I am taking a long vacation due me. I will not serve the Mufti. But I don't want to be dead like Sutherland either. Take my advice and leave also. Let the people getting the money worry about the Mufti."

Lilli rose and looked down at the little man sympathetically. Jesse was by her side.

Jesse said, "Use the trash can, Mr. Martin. As usual."

"If that's what you wish," Martin replied.

"Good luck," Lilli said, and meant it.

"Keep that wish for yourself my dear, you will need it as much as I." Before he released her, Martin bent stiffly and kissed the back of her hand. His lips were dry and hot.

Outside, walking toward Simon's cab, Lilli said, "A pretty sad man, don't you think."

"A dirty little man is more like it."

"Yes, he did have rather prying eyes, didn't he!"

When she saw that Jesse was serious, her own smile died on her lips.

Chapter 15

The Mufti contacted them again that evening during their dinner in the King David dining room. A telephone was brought to Jesse and Lilli's table. Jesse answered the call.

"Yes, this is Jesse Quinn.... Say that name again.... I don't know anyone by that name." He was rotating his martini glass by its stem, but stopped.

Lilli watched Jesse's face darken. His left eye half closed, his right eye opened wider as his brow lifted on that side. Twin vertical lines appeared above the bridge of his nose and the lines around his jaw tightened. He held up a hand to Lilli to stop her from asking the question he could see coming.

"No, no, I'm sorry. That's impossible. If this man wants to see me, tell him to come to my hotel and join me for a drink. I'll talk with him then....I see.... The answer is still no. I don't know him."

He placed the receiver in its cradle and beckoned to a waiter to remove the phone. As the waiter started away, Jesse stopped him and said, "Could that call come across the armistice lines from the Arab Quarter in the Old City?"

"Not possible," answered the waiter. "Since the '48 war, every form of communication between us and all Arab states has been cut off. No telephone, telegraph, radio, bus line, air service. No nothing, sir. Even a carrier pigeon would be stopped at the borders. The phone call, sir, came from Jerusalem, our side of the barbed wire."

"He wanted to see us," said Jesse when the waiter left. "This evening." He sipped his chilled martini.

"The Mufti?" asked Lilli, hardly able to believe it.

"Not himself, Lilli. One of his people." Jesse studied the menu for a minute. Then he put it down.

"At first he asked, and when I said no, he got a little excited and almost issued an order that we be at an address tonight from where we would be escorted to that villa in the Old City. There are obviously holes in the barbed wire somewhere." He finished his martini and left the small olive in the glass.

He looked at Lilli for a long while as she pretended to read the menu. She was braver and more beautiful than he had ever thought of her. And her bravery did not come from naïveté. Lilli could recognize trouble when it faced her, as it was facing them both right now. His feelings for her deepened, and his regret she was there grew.

She found him staring at her. "Remember what we said when we decided to come over here," she said firmly, reading the concern in his face. "No solicitous big-brother act. No protective stuff, Jesse. I'm going with you. I'm involved in every bit of this as deeply as you are." She paused before she added, "And I can shoot almost as well as you can, if it comes down to that."

"We're not going to be shooting anybody, Lilli," he said smiling. "We're not going near the Mufti's zone if we can help it. Order your dinner. The schnitzel looks good."

But while they ate, although Jesse kept his manner casual, he could not free his mind of the threat in the voice he had just heard. "The Mufti will be displeased if . . ."

Chapter 16

When Simon, the cab driver, picked them up at seven-fifteen the next morning, they told him in the cab they were not going on a tour of Jerusalem.

"We're going to follow a little old Arab woman this morning," said Lilli.

"What?" asked Simon, increduously. "You're joking old Simon along."

"No, we're not," said Lilli, blowing smoke from a fresh cigarette through her mouth and nose as she spoke. "There's an old Arab woman who will be leaving Barclay's some time this morning. We're going to let you follow her and we're going to follow you. That way no one will think we're following her. Isn't that simple?"

"I don't suppose I can ask you what it's all about?"

"Will you do it for us?" asked Jesse. "You can name your fee."

"Sure, I'll do it," said Simon cheerfully. "It sounds like fun."

It was early enough for the streets of Jerusalem to be fairly empty. They passed a few trucks loaded with foodstuffs heading toward markets or restaurants, but there were few cars moving and the sidewalks showed only early-morning workers on their way to their jobs and a scattering of long-robed Jews strolling home from morning prayers.

On King David Road they passed lines of idle, empty taxicabs parked along the curb. They crossed St. Vincent de Paul Square and turned into King Solomon Street. In the square at the end of King Solomon Street they started to make a turn left toward Barclay's.

A taxi coming from the opposite direction through the square turned sharply and cut across their path. Simon flung out a string of curses in Hebrew and twisted the wheel hard, jamming his cab roughly against the curb and stalling it. The other taxi skidded to a stop up against his front fender.

Two men got out of opposite sides of the car and raced toward the Quinns' cab. They were dressed like Israelis, light pants and jackets, open-necked white shirts, hatless. Their driver stayed behind the wheel.

Jesse saw no guns.

"I don't like it," growled Simon.

Jesse didn't take his eyes off the men walking toward them, nor did he touch the Colt on his right side. Hooking his thumb in his belt, he unlimbered his frame climbing out of the cab.

He stood much taller than the man coming toward him. He heard another string of curses coming from Simon. Without turning his head, he gave an order. "Stay in the car, Simon. Don't get out."

But the surly driver was already out of the door frame facing the young, smaller man who had run up on his side.

Simon said something to the man in Hebrew. The man answered back.

"They're not Israelis, Mr. Quinn. Watch them."

The man facing Jesse now had his hands thrust into his loose trouser pockets. Jesse saw the bulge of his gun.

"El-Husseini wishes to see you and your sister in there right now," snapped the man in good English. "You would not listen when I spoke with you on the telephone. Therefore you will have to come under the barrel of the Mufti's gun. Get in the other taxi."

The man near Simon on the opposite side of the car was jabbering Hebrew to Lilli.

Simon heard the name of the Mufti mentioned. He shouted angrily back at the man.

Jesse risked a glance over the hood of the taxi. The Mufti's young agent was drawing a pistol from his front pants pocket. With a sudden violent movement, Simon dodged to his right and brought the edge of his right hand hard across the throat of the man before his pistol had cleared the pocket. It was a strong backhand stroke like that of a seasoned tennis player, the arm scribing a straight rising line, the palm's edge striking the Adam's apple solidly.

The young Arab choked, his eyes bulged, his face turned purple. His hand came away from his pocket empty and reached for his throat together with his other hand. He gagged and fell to his knees gasping for oxygen. He made loud tearing sounds in his throat as he struggled to suck air through his crushed windpipe.

The man opposite Jesse leaped forward. His pistol was swinging at Jesse's head. Lilli screamed. Jesse dodged lightly to one side and drove his fist savagely into the Arab's midsection. Then he recovered his balance and clipped the man squarely on the tip of the jaw.

"Get back in the car!" Simon was yelling. "He's going to shoot!"

The third man in the other taxi was leaning out of the window aiming a pistol. Jesse was bending over the man he had punched to the ground and was gripping him by the lapels as the shot rang out. He dropped the Arab back to the ground and leaped into the rear seat just as Simon ground the gears brutally to get the taxi moving. A second shot clanked against the fender.

Simon gunned the motor and hurled his taxi backward until it struck the opposite curb, changed gears, and screeched off down the street where they had come from. He turned a corner and sped through three intersections, ignoring the lights; then he slowed, coasted down a deserted street, and stopped.

"You'd better get out here," he said over his shoulder. "You're four blocks from Barclay's. That way." He pointed to his left. "Get out now before the police catch up to us and make you a whole lot of trouble. You'll miss your old lady if they do. Go on."

"Jesse!" Lilli cried, noticing that Simon was holding his left shoulder with his right hand. "He's shot! He's bleeding! Look! Simon..." She laid a hand on his shoulder. Simon leaned forward. The back of his left shoulder was wet.

"I'll be all right. It's in the shoulder, not the chest. I'll get to a hospital myself. They'll fix me up. Now go on, will you. You can't come with me."

"Simon..." Lilli started to protest. "How can we...?"

"Go on, lady, please, I can take care of it. You two be careful. Good luck to the both of you."

Jesse dropped some bills on the seat next to Simon as he was getting out and held up his hand against Simon's protest. "This will pay the doctor," he said. "Thanks again."

"You bet," said Simon. His coarse, leathery face broke into a grin.

Jesse and Lilli walked toward the corner without turning back. As soon as they reached it they began to run. Jesse held Lilli's hand, helping her keep her balance on her high heels. They ran easily for two blocks without calling attention to themselves in the empty streets. They found a tiny alley, took it, crossed to another, wider street, took that. There were more people there. Shops were already open, cafés had lowered their awnings, waiters were setting up tables for breakfast customers. Jesse and Lilli walked. They passed a swarm of noisy young students and then a few short-bearded men wearing dark robes and wide fur hats. They kept walking. Lilli hooked an arm through Jesse's, he held it with his hand, and they looked like a beautiful young couple in love, out for a cool morning stroll in one of the oldest cities in the world. But they were breathing harder than casual strollers, and they thought they could still hear the sound of gunfire. There was nothing casual in their minds.

A few more blocks of walking and asking questions, always speaking French, brought them back to the road where Barclay's was located. Across the street from the bank and up a few doorways was a perfectly located sidewalk café serving breakfast. They found a table where they sat quietly for several minutes to catch their breath. They didn't talk about Simon. Lilli fought to keep Jesse from seeing her tremble. This was the first time she had ever been shot at. Sitting quietly now and thinking about it left her in a state of mild shock. She felt cold and numb. The warmth of the sun was remote.

It was still not eight o'clock when their waiter brought them their first cup of strong coffee. Lilli anxiously sipped the hot, thick liquid, looking for its warmth. She lit a cigarette. Jesse, who had sat to face the bank, announced that Paul Martin had just arrived in a taxi and was going inside. George Powell was not with him.

A few minutes later, watching the street in the other direction, Lilli refused to give in to her feelings, and said in a firm voice, "Here she comes, Jesse. This has got to be her."

A slight, bent figure in a long, dirty white cloak swayed along the walk across the street, passed opposite their table, and continued on. The woman wore the *burkha*, the veil covering the lower half of her face, and a head shawl that concealed almost the rest of it. Only her eyes showed. She carried a limp cloth shopping bag over her shoulder.

Jesse turned his head as she passed and watched her, head slightly bowed, eyes on the walk before her, moving slowly with a side-to-side swing up the street. She stopped at the bank, pressed a button. The door opened a crack, swung farther open, and she disappeared through it.

"She's in there, all right," Jesse said. "Now we wait."

89

Chapter 17

Fifteen minutes passed. Lilli had been silent and troubled, smoking too nervously and crushing out her cigarettes a little too hard. A police car passed with its alarm going. She flinched and smiled weakly at Jesse.

When Lilli's hand resting on the table began to shake her cup of coffee, Jesse took the cup from her and gripped her palm. His eyes, however, kept shifting back to the bank and the alley next to it.

Whenever he moved in his chair, she began to stir. "No, don't get excited, nothing's happening up there yet. She's still inside. Just keep looking at me. That's it." He squeezed her hand and kept it clasped tightly. "Don't think about what happened back there, Lilli. Simon'll be all right. He knew what he was doing. He knew who the men were."

Jesse fished inside his shirt pocket and took out a small red object between two fingers, held it up for a moment before her face, and dropped it on the table near her hand. "Look at it, Lilli. This is the kind of people they were. I pulled it from the lapel of the man near me."

Lilli picked it up gingerly.

"Oh, God, Jesse." It was a red enameled badge about a half-inch long, shaped in the form of a crescent. A tiny star was raised and painted white within its arc. "He was one of them. Maybe he was the other one who was there at Crane's."

For a brief moment he took his eyes from the bank and fastened them on hers. "Well, if he wasn't, he belongs to the same organization who did it. That pin stared me in the face as soon as I got out of the car." Jesse looked across at the bank again and continued talking. "It wasn't easy to keep from killing him, right there as he was on the ground. I never felt like that before, Lilli, even when I was flying. We flew to stay alive, most of us. There were a few real killers in the squadron who enjoyed it. I could never understand them. But I do now, a little." Jesse rubbed the bruised knuckles of his right hand.

Lilli covered his left hand with hers.

They sat for an hour. Neither risked leaving the table even for a few minutes. The waiters were too busy to bother them. The air grew warmer but remained pleasant. They moved to another table to stay out of the sun that was creeping onto Lilli's back. She had gone hatless this morning rather than wear the conspicuous floppy wide-brimmed sun hat she had packed in her wardrobe. It was not the thing to wear while trying to follow someone. When she had spoken of it, Jesse had smiled approvingly. His appreciation of her good sense was growing all the time, and as he sat observing the traffic into and out of the bank, he was never for a moment unconscious of her presence a few feet away.

Another slow, strained hour passed. They ordered food from the kitchen, tasted it, had it taken away. The sound of spoken Hebrew grew steadily louder around them. The café grew crowded and steamy under the awning that had been lowered and then the crowd thinned out. The street traffic was heavier.

Shortly after ten o'clock, as their restlessness became harder to control, a Mercedes sedan coming down the far side of the street toward the bank suddenly left the traffic lane and jumped onto the sidewalk with its right wheels and bore down. Its horn blared. People scrambled out of its way. A few stunned pedestrians fell into the street to escape. The sedan had a clear path to the bank, riding with its left wheels in the road, its right wheels on the walk. There were no street lamps blocking its way.

Jesse watched as the Mercedes slowed, a rear door opened and then closed. He could make that out. Then the automobile thumped back onto the road, jouncing badly, and hurtled by their table up the street. The driver was alone up front and one man was visible in the rear. They both wore light-colored soft hats.

Jesse could see what looked like a bundle on the sidewalk outside the bank's front entrance. He leaped to his feet and looked harder. Lilli rose and half turned. Every eye on the street was caught by the bundle.

Jesse touched Lilli's arm across the table to get her attention. "Get across the street, Lilli, right opposite us, and watch the bank and the alley. We're in the middle of a goddamn war!"

People began to head up toward the bank.

Jesse crossed over diagonally. He got close enough to see that the bundle was the body of a hooded man, trussed hands behind, legs pulled up backwards and ankles tied to wrists. It did not take

91

much looking to see that the man's torso was riddled with holes. It took a second and even a third glance to realize that the man's pants and underpants were missing. So were his genitals. A dried-up mess was all they had left of him.

A young woman came up next to Jesse, squeezed forward, looked, and then threw up on the sidewalk.

The police had arrived and were beginning to drive the crowd back. One officer threw a coat over the man's lower body. Another yanked the black hood from his head. There were the genitals, grotesquely fixed in the dead man's face. A groan went up from the crowd and the hood was quickly pulled back on.

Paul Martin had been standing squarely in the doorway to the bank, the body of the murdered man almost at his feet. When the hood came off, Martin sobbed aloud, threw both of his hands over his face, and raced back inside.

The man on the sidewalk was tearful George Powell—the man, Jesse was thinking, whose weakness for an Arab woman had led the Mufti to the Quinns and started the whole chain of trouble.

Lilli was suddenly beside him, touching his arm.

"Look, she's leaving. She's using this whole commotion to slip away."

The Arab woman in the shabby cloak and veil was hovering on the other side of the crowd at the entrance of the alley. Through an opening between the corner of the building and the people in front of her, she peeped at the body quickly, then drew her head shawl further across her face and glided swiftly away. Over her right shoulder she was carrying the empty cloth shopping bag.

Jesse started to maneuver around the crowd until he realized Lilli was not behind him. He spun around and suffered an anxious moment before he spotted her. She was frozen to the place where she had found him. Her eyes were widened on the dead man.

Someone had uncovered the body again and thrown the coat on the walk.

Jesse had to jostle several people to get to her and then took her roughly by the arm. She was still unaware of him.

"Lilli, snap out of it," he whispered harshly into her ear. "If we lose her now, we lose her for good. Do you understand? It'll be over. Come on." He started to pull gently against her resistance.

He tugged harder at her arm until he got her off balance and she felt her legs under her. He steadied her, looking into her face, his eyes burning, his jaw clenched.

"Oh, Christ, Jesse, is that what they do? Is that what they did to...to..." She couldn't force herself to finish the thought.

"No, they didn't," he said, in a voice that suggested he really knew. "That kind of butchering is done to frighten the living. They're after Martin, and I hope the little man has the stomach to stand them off for another few days."

He placed an arm around her back and they picked up their pace in the direction the old Arab woman had taken. Lilli clung to Jesse's arm, feeling weak and sick, needing him more than she could imagine he would ever need her. They walked side by side, Jesse bending forward close to her face to be certain she was all right and at the same time trying to catch sight of the Arab woman.

When they got out of the circle of people the police were dispersing, Jesse spotted the old woman. She was moving slowly, her body swaying slightly from side to side in the easy rhythmical fashion of her people.

"This is it, Lilli," Jesse said with a hint of excitement in his voice. "That old Arab should be taking us straight to the home of the A Fund. Maybe someone there can tell us about the Quintana brothers."

Lilli barely heard him. At the moment she was thinking how good Jesse's arm felt around her shoulders, his fingers protectively pressing the flesh on her upper arm. She was considering how happy she could be even if their mission to Jerusalem failed. If only they could somehow find each other. What does all this matter, she thought, all this blood, this horror, the money? I'd be happy if only we could find each other, Jesse.

Chapter 18

Wherever the old Arab woman was going, they soon realized she was not going straight there—she was in no hurry. Somewhere on her person was a Barclay bank draft for over a hundred thousand dollars, and she swayed along the crowded streets as though she were a window shopper and had not a single care in the world. Jesse wondered if she knew what it was she was carrying.

She kept to the main roads through heavy shopping districts where the sidewalks and streets were jammed with people in Western clothes, men in slacks and shirts and women in dresses and heels, their legs bare. She shuffled openly in the middle of the sidewalk, so much slower than everyone else that she forced people to flow around her the way a stream does with an obstacle standing in the way of its current. Her unhurried gait made her so conspicuous as to be almost incredible. Everyone took notice of her. Either through her own ignorance or a cunning subtlety, she was making herself appear the least likely person to be a link in a secret chain. She was far too obvious to arouse the suspicion of the subtle Arab mind.

At times she detoured from the main roads into the market-places where open stalls displayed mounds of ruby tomatoes and heavy peaches, trays of breads and pastries, and fresh meat, fish, and chicken packed on ice. In these places the smell of fish monopolized the air. She made some small purchases here and there—a piece of fruit, a half a bread, a bunch of dates—stuffed them into her cloth bag, and moved off. Slowly the bag grew fatter and heavier and her pace more labored and halting. She paused to rest and bought an orangeade from an ice-cream truck near a small park and, surrounded by tanned, long-legged children in shorts, sat on a curb to nurse it. Then, throwing the empty carton into the gutter, she moved off again.

She was easy to follow but very hard not to give up on. Jesse would have quit on her after a few blocks if he had not been told she was the transport for the money. After an hour of agony, meandering around the city, he began to have doubts about Martin. Had the little man told the truth? Was this harmless-looking old woman really carrying the money? If she was the real carrier, whoever was employing her had carried the secrecy of the contract to its almost perfect limit.

He wondered how Lilli was holding up, somewhere behind him. They were following the Arab woman in tandem as they had planned to do with Simon. Several times, when the old woman crossed her own trail, Jesse resisted the temptation to shrug his shoulders and lift his hands to signal Lilli his own doubts. He struggled to be patient. They would have to wait the old woman out. They had changed positions twice, hoping to avoid the attention of any third person who might also be following her. Since they had left the vicinity of the bank, however, he had spotted no one who looked suspicious, and the old Arab herself was as oblivious of them as she seemed to be of everyone else in the world.

They were only vaguely aware of the flow of life around them, too. They heard the noisy voices of people buying and bargaining, brushed against their bodies in crowded places, saw the synagogues, theaters, food shops. But they took note of little and would remember less. Their concentration was on the ragged link in the A Fund they could not afford to lose sight of. And they never did. The bent figure of the Arab woman was always in the sight of one or the other. Inexperienced as they were at this sort of thing, they never had cause for alarm; they worked together well, even to the point of improvising a system of signals from the leader to the trailer which direction was to be taken next.

Jesse could feel the trail leading steadily northward through the city toward the residential suburbs. The old woman's route kept the sun on his right shoulder when he walked out of the shade, and it was still before noon. She was moving north. The buildings changed from commercial to residential. Row after row of concrete apartment houses took over the landscape.

Another half an hour finally brought the game to an end in a middle-class neighborhood that a few years before had been a battleground. The scars from the war were still visible. Many of the buildings were pockmarked, and one that had been completely gutted by fire was just undergoing restoration. Another still stood in untouched ruins. The men working on the renovation were cheerful and noisy. In the street the few people around were friendly and prosperous-looking. They smiled and followed Jesse's striking form with their eyes, and when Lilli came along two or three men greeted her and she smiled back and repeated their greeting, "Shalom." It was friendly flirtation. She found it hard to believe what she had heard from Simon, that so many of them kept machine guns in their homes.

The old woman stopped at a five-story narrow apartment building at least three or four decades old. The stone had been mostly white once and had gone chalky gray. The long, narrow front windows were set into lead casements, and the small balconies on each upper floor were rimmed by high wrought-iron-latticed railings. There were similar apartment buildings across the street and a few smaller brick and stone houses scattered around with little open gardens in front.

Jesse was half a block behind the old Arab woman when she shuffled up the steps of the building. He quickened his pace, then slowed to give her time to get inside just as he reached the bottom of the steps. He waited until Lilli could see where he was going and then he went up into the vestibule.

Inside he found a narrow stairway and a small glass caged elevator. Directly ahead was a door to the street-floor flat. The old Arab woman had rejected the stairs and chosen the elevator. Jesse could hear the hum. Above the door of the elevator were five tiny bulbs. As he watched, the third one from the bottom went on, stayed lit, and blinked off. To the left of the elevators, a directory in Hebrew listed five names.

The door behind Jesse opened and closed. Lilli came up close, flushed and excited, and embraced his arm and pressed her body against him. The weakness she had felt at the sight of the mutilated man was gone. Shadowing the old woman through the roads and byways of Jerusalem had intensified her sense of adventure to the pitch raised by the morning attack of the Mufti. Growing up, she had never considered herself particularly adventurous. The excitement of the museum job had always been sufficient for her intellectual needs, the quiet thrill of the hunt with her three Quinn men had met her physical ones. But now the danger and strangeness of what was going on in this bloodstained pearl of a city, holding Jesse and measuring his change toward her, had touched her more deeply than she could have imagined possible, had excited a nerve inside her almost to her groin and given her a sensation faintly like an orgasm and nearly as fulfilling. She was feeling happier about herself than she had for months.

Almost breathlessly, Lilli asked, "What floor, Jesse? Did you get the floor?"

Jesse nodded. He pressed the elevator button. He watched the five bulbs. There were loud clicks and whirrs and a deep clank. Lilli was staring at the bulbs, too. The third light from the bottom winked on and out.

Waiting for the elevator, Jesse could feel Lilli's body tight against his, a woman's body of firm yet soft stomach, of a hard round hip and shaped, yielding breasts. The perfume released by her warm perspiration was in his nostrils. For the first time since that crazy birthday party eleven years ago he was forgetting the "sister" in Lilli and feeling the woman.

A few moments later the bottom light glowed and the humming stopped.

When the elevator whirred back up to the third floor, Jesse opened the brass accordion gate and faced a heavy dark wooden door blocking the exit. He tried the small brass handle. The door did not budge. There was a small brass knocker mounted high on the door. That meant there was no hallway or foyer on the other side. The door gave entrance to the apartment itself. He applied three soft raps to the knocker, holding the accordion gate open with his foot.

There was no answer. Lilli moved nervously beside him. He made a quizzical face at her to show he was not concerned. Then he winked and rapped on the knocker again.

A bolt could be heard sliding in its cannelure. Then came a voice muffled by the door. He tried the handle again. It clicked downward and the door swung inward. He kept Lilli behind him. As he walked into a well-furnished room, he saw the old Arab woman, still wearing her *burkha,* standing near a table where her black sack was crumbled empty. Piled next to it were all the purchases she had made on her slow tedious trek across the city.

A long, worn-looking manila envelope lay in front of a triangle of oranges.

Beyond the table poised in a doorway to another room was an attractive, silvery-haired woman in her fifties, of medium build and height, wearing a modern Western-styled dress that had little flair or color by American standards. The woman's arms were round and strong and her hands slender but sinewy. Jesse couldn't help but notice those parts of her because, cradled in those arms

97

about waist high and held knowingly by those hands, was a new, compact, nasty-looking submachine gun that he recognized as an Israeli-made Uzi.

Chapter 19

The two guards at the blue villa had their hands full that morning quieting the dogs. There was so much unusual activity on the estate that the animals were badly aroused and difficult. All morning they snarled and lunged at the strange men who trooped past them a few feet beyond the end of their chains into the villa, and then, some minutes later, passed them on their way out.

Once the dogs even attacked the well-dressed secretary with the wavy hair who lived at the villa and whom they had been trained to ignore. In the fury of arousal, they failed to distinguish him when he walked some strangers back to their car and on his return to the villa incautiously stepped inside the arc scribed by their chains. Only the instant reaction of one of the dogs' trainers, who reached the chains and dragged the animals away, saved the man from a mauling. He reentered the villa trembling and cursing himself and the dogs.

Before noon the same man, dressed immaculately in silk suit, shirt, and tie, stood again in front of the villa staring thoughtfully across the grounds. Again the dogs, who failed to recognize him, leaped up howling and snapping and straining against their chains.

Another man, wearing a long robe folded diagonally across his chest and a tall strange hat, appeared at his side and watched the fury of the dogs. On his lips there was a smile, not of amusement but of understanding. He watched for a few seconds and then calmly walked toward them, keeping his left hand at his side and his right hand down in front of him, its back toward the dogs' jaws. His stride was awkward and stiff, as though his ankles were shackled together by a short chain. He spoke soothingly and approached the dogs without showing a sign of fear. Their snarls changed to whimpers, and when he touched their muzzles and ran his hands softly along the tops of their heads and down their necks, the whimpers faded. The animals finally stood silent, quivering but still. The man stooped somewhat stiffly, as though he was buckled into a corset, and examined the dogs' necks.

He beckoned to one of the guards who had charge of the animals.

"Their necks are being rubbed raw from the chains," said the man in the hat. He was red-bearded and spoke with a casualness that is normally used to observe that the coffee is too sweet. "Take them to their kennels. They won't be needed until this evening."

Then, with a smile still on his lips, he turned, walked back mincingly into the villa with his secretary at his heels, and disappeared behind the steel-clad door at the end of the hallway.

Ahmud Darwish stayed with the Mufti for ten minutes, listening to his master speak in the same quietly modulated voice he never changed. During that time, three new men arrived and waited down the hall with the two guards. When the secretary finally emerged, he was white-faced and shaken.

He found the new arrivals waiting nervously for their orders. One of the men had a bruise on his jaw and a torn lapel on his coat. Another held his head awkwardly, as though he was wearing a neck brace. If he lived long enough to see a doctor, he would actually need one. A small vertebra on the left side of the back of his neck was cracked where Simon had hit him a few hours earlier.

Ahmud Darwish, the Mufti's secretary, spoke. "You're lucky he does not wish to see you after you failed him this morning. I have just borne most of his scorn for you myself." There was deep exasperation in his voice. "He does not get excited at all, but just talks quietly with the smile on his lips. But you had better be successful before this day is over."

Darwish sat down and mopped his brow with a large handkerchief. With the handkerchief still in his hand, he glared into the eyes of the man with the bruised jaw.

"He wants the Quinn man and woman brought to him before this day is out. He wants the Jew, Lev, and his wife found and eliminated. If you absolutely have to, kill the Quinns as well, but you would make him happier to bring them here alive."

"It is impossible," said the young man with the bruised jaw, throwing his hands around angrily. "We can never find four people in the Jewish sector in a week. How can we do it in one afternoon? We will only be caught and arrested ourselves. You might as well kill us now."

The secretary stood up and folded his handkerchief back into his breast pocket. He spoke smugly. "Not impossible at all. You see, a man by the name of Powell died this morning. Partly

100

because he displeased him." He pointed in the general direction of the Mufti's room. "But before he died, Powell told us something about the old Arab woman who cleans at Barclay's."

The three men looked up startled.

"Yes, be surprised. One of you followed her from the bank not many weeks ago and gave up. You gave up too soon. She goes to the Levs."

He paused while the three men exchanged unhappy looks.

"Go back to the neighborhood where she was last seen," ordered Ahmud Darwish, "and begin looking there."

Chapter 20

For a long few minutes no one spoke. The outrageous weapon had stunned everyone into silence. A wooden clock ticked on a wall shelf. The bore of the machine gun was trained on Jesse's stomach, but the eyes of the woman were fixed on Lilli. He thought the woman paled slightly through the bone-deep tan in her face, but he could have been mistaken. He was not mistaken about the tremor in her left hand, gripping the forehand piece of the Uzi beneath the front sight and causing the muzzle to waver.

The muscles in Jesse's stomach twisted reflexively into knots, anticipating a barrage of bullets if the woman's right hand trembled a little too much on the trigger.

He said, "We're not here to hurt anyone."

Suddenly the trembling was gone, as though the sound of his voice had soothed her nerves. The silvery-haired woman inhaled deeply. She pulled her eyes off Lilli and swept them across Jesse's face, looking at him for the first time. She spoke briefly to the Arab woman in Hebrew or Arabic. Jesse could not tell which.

The old woman, who had swayed so lazily in the street, moved behind Lilli with unexpected quickness. She ran her hands over Lilli's dress, up and down her legs and between them. She took her purse and opened it, rummaged through it, and dropped the purse on a chair. Then she glided behind Jesse, never stepping between the barrel of the machine gun and either one of them. She found the Colt pistol, removed it carefully by the grip between two fingers, and searched him as she had Lilli. Her thin wrinkled fingers felt the cloth of his pants just hard enough to graze the skin and pick up a hidden weapon, were there another one on his body.

When she finished she moved Jesse's gun onto the table near the oranges and disappeared through a door in the wall opposite the elevator entrance.

The middle-aged woman with the machine gun spoke some words to Jesse. He shook his head. She had heard him speak

English, but she asked him in German who he was and what he wanted in her flat.

Before Lilli could reply, Jesse shook his head again and said, "We speak only English."

"You understood what I just said," said the woman in English. "But never mind." She hesitated as though uncertain which mood to adopt, then asked, "Who are you? And what are you doing here?" Her voice softened a bit as she spoke and she sounded more feminine. But the unmoving Uzi lost none of its ugliness.

"We'll tell you everything," said Jesse, trying to be casual and smile, "if you'll point your gun someplace else. It's making my stomach queasy, and it's a damn rotten way to greet your bene-factors."

A tiny shock seemed to run through the woman, but the ma-chine gun did not move. She did not look at Lilli.

"Who are you? I won't ask again. I can kill both of you right now—and your gun on the table will be good enough reason for the police."

Jesse laughed harshly. "Jerusalem, is this? How do you say it in Hebrew? With 'shalom' in it? It's the world's best piece of sarcasm, wouldn't you say? Peace, ha! Ever since we arrived in your city of peace we've had guns pointed at us or around us and going off."

"True, that is Jerusalem," said the silvery-haired woman de-fensively. "A city we never wanted that way." She had the greenest eyes Jesse had ever seen.

"Listen, Madam whoever you are," he almost growled, "we're here to find out what the A Fund is doing with the money our family has been feeding it, money like the cashier's check over there from Barclay's to the amount of $107,500 for the November installment."

The silvery-haired woman was visibly shocked now. Her full, shapely lips curled inside of her teeth, her eyes blazed wider, the green turning deep jade, the already firm jawline hardening into a straight edge as she bit down on her lips.

She looked across to Lilli, who had been waiting solemnly, expectantly, watching the older woman all the time, shaking inside from the nearness of the machine gun's muzzle pointing at Jesse and seeming to engulf her as well.

The older woman let the muzzle of the Uzi drop a few inches as though she sensed Lilli's fear. She moved her gaze over to the table at her side where the worn envelope lay unopened, its flap tucked inside, its contents exposed. She reached for the envelope with her left hand, ripped it open, and drew out the check. Her eyes picked out the pinpricked outline of the sum, and she held the check out as though she were offering it to Jesse. The Uzi rested against her hip, its muzzle pointing lower and away from Jesse.

"One hundred and seven thousand five hundred. So! Martin would know that. Sutherland, too, would have known it before he was killed. Either one of them could have told the Mufti. Even George Powell could have seen this, and he is already connected to el-Husseini."

She spoke without hesitating, but obvious uncertainty had crept into her accusation as though she was challenging them to deny it. The Uzi's muzzle was pointing at the floor by now.

Lilli spoke quietly. "We are not the Mufti's people, madam. We are from Boston and we are nobody's people but our own." Lilli's words did it.

The fire and distrust died in the woman's eyes and her face suddenly seemed gentle. She laid the submachine gun on the table against the oranges. She spoke tremulously as though almost afraid that she might be wrong.

"You are Joseph's daughter, then," she said. Tears were welling in her eyes. "You are Lilli. Yes, I can see that. And you are Jesse. Michael's boy."

Chapter 21

When Lilli nodded, the woman reached back and sank into a chair behind her, covering her eyes with one hand.

Lilli started forward. Jesse held his hand up.

"And you, madam? Who are you?"

The silvery-haired woman lifted her head. The tears were nearly gone. None had reached her cheeks. She used both hands to brush back her thick silvery hair, and then she straightened herself in her chair.

"Your fathers knew me as Anna Hirsch. For years I am Anna Hirsch Lev."

"Is that Anna of the A Fund, Mrs. Lev?" Lilli asked quickly.

Mrs. Lev appeared taken back by Lilli's beauty rather than her question. She caught herself staring. Blinking away the fixed gaze, she answered, "Anna of the A Fund? Yes, I think you might say they called it the A Fund for Anna. Not as any honor, of course, more as an acknowledgment. I knew your fathers well, both of them. But I take it they have never spoken of me." Her voice weakened as she said this and then grew stronger as she went on. "I see it in your faces. It is well they have not spoken of me."

Jesse motioned to Lilli to sit down. He took the chair opposite Mrs. Lev. Lilli took a chair closer to her.

"That's true, Mrs. Lev," said Jesse frankly. "They never mentioned you. You're a complete surprise to us. But so is this whole affair. When they set up this fund, however—and it's been set up so that it's almost impossible to interrupt or alter, you must know that—they *were* paying you some kind of tribute. For something you did or stood for. Or because they chose you to run the fund yourself. Would you tell us about yourself, Mrs. Lev, and our fathers and *why* they never spoke of you?"

Anna Lev had been unable to take her eyes from Lilli when she had come in, and now she avoided Lilli altogether and spoke to Jesse. "I heard what happened to your fathers last week, Jesse, Lilli—I would call you 'my children' if I dared—and for them I have shed a tear and more than a tear. I have been sitting *shiva* for them until today." She held up a hand to prevent an interruption. "I learned the news from people in your country. I heard also that they did not go without a struggle, fighting to the end." Her face lightened and she shook her head as though scolding unruly youngsters. "How very much like the Michael and Joseph I knew."

"You knew them that well?" Lilli asked, moving forward in her chair and forcing Mrs. Lev to look at her.

"Yes, I did." She did not avoid Lilli's eyes now. She folded her hands on her lap. "Before they died, you knew nothing about this fund. Now you want to know everything, I suppose, or perhaps you even want to close it, not knowing what it is. For one reason or the other you've come here to this country." She shook her head sadly. "And so you have discovered this apartment and found me and I was going to shoot you with our little brother here." She laid her hand on the barrel of the Uzi. "Not a very warm welcome, was it?"

"Too warm," said Jesse, trying to break through the tension. They all smiled briefly.

"I suppose that is Sutherland's work or Martin's," she said soberly. "But if they told you how to find us, others will find us, too. Martin will break. And the others will come who have been after us since Powell gave it all away." Her hand was still resting on the Uzi. "We will shoot them if they come."

"George Powell was murdered this morning," Jesse informed her. "They dropped his body in front of Martin's bank."

Anna's head jerked up. "What did he expect from them? He knew only a little and when they got that from him, they wanted more. Now they're after Martin."

"Why wasn't my father told about Powell?" asked Lilli.

Anna Hirsch Lev rose to her feet. "John Sutherland said he would take care of that. Perhaps I should have done it myself. But . . . enough. We will leave here soon, all of us. Together. No one connected with the fund is safe from the Mufti now. You two least of all, I'm afraid."

She headed for the kitchen.

"Mrs. Lev," said Jesse.

The silvery-haired woman turned. "Jesse, the story you want to hear from me cannot be told now. It will be told, I promise you, but it cannot be told now. This is not the time and it is not the place."

She went into the kitchen and put some coffee on. Jesse picked up his Colt and fixed it into its holster. Anna Hirsch Lev returned with cold sandwiches, fruit, and cakes, set them on a table, and went out to another room to make a telephone call. She spoke briefly and hung up. She returned with the coffee and poured three cups.

She sighed as she sat to join them. "You were not followed here. We are certain of that. We have the neighborhood watched carefully for the entire day on this Tuesday of the month."

They all ate with little appetite, the Quinns occasionally asking questions between bites. Anna ignored the questions or answered evasively. "Eat," she said. "The tales will come later."

Out of politeness they attacked the food until the sandwiches were gone, the coffeepot emptied, and the fruit passed around.

Anna's face was growing troubled again. Twice she went to the window and looked down to the street. Finally, as though she had made up her mind, she said, "I have a question, Jesse Quinn. Forgive me for bringing this up again. It is of some importance."

Jesse laid aside an orange he was peeling. Anna Lev touched his hand.

"Is anything known of who killed your fathers?" She laid a hand quickly on Lilli's arm. "Forgive me, my child."

Lilli almost drew her arm away, as though the painfully blunt question gave the woman no right to touch her. But in Anna Lev's face she saw the deeper pain it gave her for raising it. She held her arm where it lay, with the woman's strong yet slender hand on it.

Jesse produced the red pin shaped in a crescent with the white star on it and handed it to her. He quickly described how he had gotten the pin that morning, leaving out the part of the taxi driver Simon. Anna Lev closed her fist on the pin. Her face grew more grim. It was the same look of the woman who had held the Uzi a little while ago, prepared to fire it.

Jesse went on. "They found a piece of a pin just like that near the automobile my father and Uncle Joe died in. It came from the clothing of one of the men wounded during the attack." He described what happened to the wounded man.

"El-Husseini," said Anna Lev, speaking the name to no one. "All the way to America." She held the red crescent out to Jesse. "*Jihad Maquades*. Brothers in the holy war. It's a Moslem brotherhood. That's what it means. We've seen enough of them. It's the Mufti's group."

Jesse pressed the question once more. "If you know so much

about our fathers, Mrs. Lev, why are you stalling?" He tried to keep his voice temperate.

"You *are* impatient," she said. "I understand that. I am anxious, too, that you learn what you should know about them, about us, about yourselves. But I can tell you only part of a story. A large part, to be sure, but an incomplete part just the same, and not the earliest part. You will want to know the entire story, so we will wait for my husband Samuel to come."

Lilli's mouth went dry. She finished the last bit of her coffee and lit a cigarette.

Anna said, "Together Samuel and I can unfold a story that will teach you who your fathers really were before they became the rich businessmen you have grown up with. The fate of the A Fund lies with that story. You must hear it all."

Chapter 22

A coarse buzzer vibrated twice near the elevator door. It was an ugly jarring sound that was more of an alarm than an announcement. It buzzed once again. The elevator clanked.

"Samuel," announced Anna Lev. A smile of relief filled her face, showing her perfect teeth and dissolving the lines that had made her face grim. Jesse had thought her attractive before. Now he saw that she possessed the kind of mature beauty Lilli would have some day.

Anna Lev said, "The buzzer spares him from facing the Uzi." She laughed for the first time.

Samuel Lev turned out to be as mildly mannered and slightly built as his wife seemed aggressive and solid. His eyes were light blue, his face boyish despite the fine blond moustache he wore. He looked more suited to a chair at the Harvard Club in Boston than at a table with a Uzi casually resting on it. When he spoke, Jesse would have moved him from the Harvard Club to a lectern at Christ's College in Cambridge, where his British accent would have been quite in place.

Samuel kissed Anna affectionately on the mouth, and they spoke briefly in Hebrew. Then he introduced himself rather shyly to Jesse and Lilli.

"I told Anna to expect you sooner or later, but she refused to believe you would come yourselves. You came sooner than even I expected. May I say we do not point our guns at everyone." His smile was modest and genuine.

They waited while Samuel washed, ate some food Anna prepared for him, and made himself comfortable in an easy chair. As he stuffed a long-stemmed clay pipe with tobacco, he appeared to be appraising the Quinns calmly and to be happy with his findings. When he lit the pipe and it was drawing freely, he smiled. It was a smile that said he liked what he saw, and Jesse and Lilli understood the smile but wondered why they provoked it.

The smile was fleeting. Samuel found nothing to smile about in what he had to say.

"Your arrival in Jerusalem has certainly stirred up the Mufti," he said casually, as though they should have expected it would. "You've already seen the unpleasantness he creates. Sutherland—and Powell. Yes, Anna just told me. And I know how you've both suffered yourselves. So have we all."

"But why?" asked Lilli impatiently. "Before we came here we had never even heard of him." A rush of anger and frustration filled her voice and made her cheeks flame. She changed her seat close to Jesse on the couch, so that she could feel his body grazing hers and touch his hand if she wanted to. She needed the comfort of physical contact.

"But he had heard of you, my dear," Anna said heatedly, as though Lilli's frustration had made her more conscious of her own. "And he's a vindictive man with a bitter, passionate cause. Your fathers—and now you two, without knowing it—interfered with his plans. All these years he has bided his time—never forgetting—until George Powell told him where the Quintanas were and how they were still connected with us. And then he settled with them. And now his business is with you. With all of us."

110

Part 2

Chapter 1

Both Samuel and Anna had known Michael and Joseph well, and although Anna had known them longer and more intimately, Samuel knew their early history. His father was Sir Herbert Samuel—the first High Commissioner of Palestine appointed under British rule in 1920. Samuel had changed his own name to Lev years later.

During the first year of his appointment, Sir Herbert needed a special, rather irregular job done in Jerusalem, and someone special and irregular had to be sent there to do it. After a short, quiet search led by his son, he found two young mercenaries moldering in a British jail in Cairo, waiting for transfer to more permanent detention at Khartoum. The mercenaries were Michael and Joseph Quintana, fairly well known in certain high circles throughout North Africa and Palestine as daredevil pilots who would serve any flag for the right pay. They had been apprehended recently and found guilty of stealing a British warplane in Palestine two years earlier at the close of the war.

The Quintanas had some of the right qualifications for the job, but before Sir Herbert decided that they were completely right, he collected their military records that had come down with them from France during the war. In the spring of 1918, the Quintanas had been transferred to Allenby's army in Egypt. That staunch fighting commander-in-chief was then planning his final push to Jerusalem and Damascus to break the back of Turkish power in the Near East, and he needed good pilots to fly for his desert generals.

Because of Samuel Lev's knowledge of their war records and his own later involvement with the Quintanas themselves, he was able to relate to their children the early story of the American brothers from Boston.

France, April 1918

The sky over the front lines was just edging from black into leaden gray as they took off. The vast dead ground beneath them was blank and still. Troops on both sides of the wire slept in filth, exhausted, dead, or dying. The air on the ground stank of rot and gas. Anyone unfortunate enough to wake before the guns started could hear the rats ceaselessly at work on the bodies.

Three thousand feet up, it was another kind of war. The pilots were bathed, shaved, fresh and well fed. Their tunics were pressed, their jackets clean, their scarves gleaming white. They had breakfasted on ham, toast and jelly, fresh butter, good coffee. They had eaten as much as they wanted, taking as much time as they needed.

There was little urgency in their lives. They arranged their own hours. As long as they got up to meet and kill the enemy cleanly, face to face, flying skill challenging flying skill, aircraft competing against aircraft, their job was done.

They vied for records, not for missions. They all understood that the war in the sky had little to do with the war on the ground. What they could do in their aircraft changed no battle, shifted no power, altered nothing that could affect final victory.

They—the pilots—all knew their lives and deaths were a side-show to the war. But no one ever spoke that knowledge aloud.

They fought chivalric jousts. They scored their records carefully. They decorated their victors and saluted their dead. It almost did not matter which side the victor fought for. An ace was an ace. Both sides honored him. Von Richthofen and Boelcke. One hundred and twenty kills together over three years. The German aces. Everybody's heroes. Hawker and Chapman. One hundred and seven kills in three years. British and Canadian. Everybody's heroes. Beaucharis and Faucault. One hundred and three kills. Three years. French aces. Everybody's heroes.

Quintana and Quintana. They were different. American aces before America came into the war. Forty-seven kills in four months. Not widely known yet outside of the squadrons. But legendary already among the Germans who fought them.

Every squadron had its partnerships. Boelcke and Immelmann. Rogers and Corday. Guynemer and Brocard. Each man tied to the other as by an invisible umbilical cord, gambling his life on the reliability of his mate. Brother, cover my tail! Cover my tail! Got him! Got him! Thanks. Brother. *Danken Sie. Merci.*

The Quintanas had a difference. They *were* brothers. Everybody thought of them as brothers. Their requests for flights, for leaves, for patrol positions were granted to brothers. A mystique spread around them. They were indestructible if they flew together. They were charmed. They had met the Baron twice and Boelcke and Immelmann four times, and they had sent the Baron home once with a broken rudder and again with jammed guns. Immelmann had died. Boelcke had survived. And though the Quintanas' Nieuports were riddled, the brothers were untouched and they had brought their planes home still flying.

They were never separated. The French commander of the American volunteer group—the *Escadrille* Lafayette—swore that he would sooner break his own arm than break up that team. They were unbeatable. They were meant to fly cowl to tail and so they would. The demons of the air demanded it.

And yet in their official records there was nothing to prove they were brothers. Their names were the same, their birthplace the same—each had written Boston where it asked for home—but they had never designated each other as brothers. Spaces for the names of a relative or next of kin were empty.

They could have been brothers. Both had dark complexions, dark hair, medium builds. Joseph was slightly taller, hair more curled. Michael's hair was almost black, almost straight with a light wave in it. Joseph's eyes were a shade or two browner than the chestnut color of Michael's. They were Mediterranean types, obviously Spanish with a name like Quintana.

There were other distinctions. Joseph was temperate, soft spoken, more reserved, Michael more colorful, flamboyant, sometimes boisterous. But in the air they could not be told apart. They flew with equal aplomb, took the same kinds of chances, measured their margins of risk with equal care, stayed within two or three kills of each other's record, and brought their 28s home with about the same extent of damage.

They became known as the QBAs. The Quintana Brother Aces.

Which was the leader, the dominant one? Which the follower? Neither. Ask a dozen of their fellows—if you could find a dozen who stayed alive long enough to know them well, six would say Michael flew lead—in the air and on the ground. The other six would say Joseph.

114

Their commander, a fiery-spirited Parisian who fought hard to get them the best equipment, calling on the sky demons as his witness, swore they were each other, thinking alike, acting alike, sharing the same tastes—from fighting planes to women. They stuck with their Nieuports even when some Camels came in, and they had fervently courted a pair of lovely twins from Château-Thierry and gotten into a mess when they had decided to change off. That suggestion was Michael's. And Joseph loved it.

They were brothers, *mon dieu*, record or not, insisted their commander.

Coming home from that dawn patrol in late April, the Quintanas flew wingtip to wingtip. Again they passed over the bleak trenches burdened with their murky death and thanked themselves for being up there where their boots were dry and death came clean. Ten miles behind their lines they swooped down out of the rising sun onto their airfield and taxied their fighters into line with the others in front of their camouflaged hangers. One plane out of twelve had been lost.

Joseph and Michael peeled their leather helmets and goggles from their heads and shook hands before they headed for the recording room of their C.O. It was a custom never broken. The air was alive with the roar of planes from other groups flying in or taxiing on the ground. Before the Quintanas reached the low, ramshackle headquarters building, the last pilot revved his engine, cut the ignition, and the airfield was still.

"He wasn't there again," said Michael, puzzled. "Do you think somebody else got him?"

"We would have heard," said Joseph, shaking his head.

"Did you get that new Fokker with the red and orange striping? You were hitting him in the body but I lost sight of the two of you and then he was gone."

They were walking down a narrow dingy corridor on creaking wooden floors toward a closed door marked "C.O. Recording."

Joe wiped the grimy sweat from his face with a white handkerchief. His forehead was clean from his hairline down an inch or two and there were large white circles around his eyes.

"He went down. Turned over and into a wide spin. His aileron wires were gone, I think. He didn't make it. I don't know if there'll be corroboration."

"I'll corroborate."

"Like hell you will." He laughed.

"I'd like to see the Baron again," said Michael, slapping his leather helmet against his legs. "Damn it, Joe, doesn't he haunt you? I think I dream about him two or three times a week."

"We'll run into him in the next week or two," said Joseph. He started to turn the knob on the squadron commander's door. Other fliers were coming down the hall after them.

Michael laid a hand on his arm. "Let's taunt the demon gods. We'll put a bet on Richthofen's head. Twenty francs I get him. With a bet on him the gods will turn him up."

"You're on," Joseph said, with a low laugh, and walked through the low doorway into the office beyond.

Chapter 2

Neither of the Quintanas ever had a chance to collect on that bet. Fate dealt them a hand in a different game.

In the recording room, their commanding officer, an impassioned man, listened to their reports eagerly, congratulated them, and then reluctantly handed them an order that had just come down from Air Command Headquarters transferring them to British GHQ in Cairo—to be implemented at once. As the Quintanas were reading the orders, the C.O. pounded his fist on the table once and swore a string of oaths against those souls who were running the war.

Who was taking away his best aviators he did not know, but he cursed him anyway. Then he shook the hands of his Quintana Brother Aces, kissed them on the cheek as his personal way of decorating them, and left the room.

That evening the commanding officer threw them a party. He brought in the best wine, Rothschild '95, the finest food from the finest restaurant in the district—*boeuf bourguignon*, lobster Parisienne, fresh trout, and he hired three local violinists who knew all the sentimental songs of the aerodrome. The pilots ate, drank, toasted, and then sang the sentimental songs of unforgotten camaraderie until midnight.

The commander insisted, then, on ushering Joseph and Michael to their rooms, after the *au revoirs* were finished. There, waiting for them, sleepy-eyed but happy, were the twin sisters from Château-Thierry who had thrown them out when they had suggested swapping partners months ago. They smiled shyly at the Quintanas and kissed them, each choosing the one she had been with before.

The commander beamed. "A telephone call to the girls this afternoon—and all is well. They know you are leaving us for good and they have come to say farewell. *Au revoir*, my lucky boys, *au revoir*."

When the commander left, the young women broke into laughter, their shyness evaporated, they threw off their clothes and fell

117

back into the arms of their lovers. They all stayed together in Michael's room and drank and made love and exchanged partners and made judgments and kept score and slept soundly in each other's arms until the commander woke them in the morning to have the Quintanas driven to their train.

In Cairo they were to report to an Air Commander Barton for reassignment to Allenby's army, massing along the Palestinian coast south of Jaffa. When they arrived, a crusty old colonel named Bederline drove them through a heavy, damp heat to a dirt airfield on the east side of the city, pointed out two Bristol fighters, and handed them their papers.

"You Yanks are lucky. I don't know how you managed to get down here, but you *are* going to see where the action is. You'll have a field day against the Turks. No damn good as fliers you'll find them. I've read your records. Bloody good. And they are going to get better. But remember this. Those German kills over France or Germany did not make a bit of difference, now, did they. Not a bit to anybody but you—and the aviator you killed. You will find out that over the desert, shooting down the enemy will. You're going out assigned to Lawrence's bunch."

Michael looked interested. "You mean T. E. Lawrence and his Arabs?" The Quintanas had read of him on their trip down.

"Major Lawrence. That's the man. He's real, despite what the news people have made of him. He has asked Allenby for personal air support for his Arabs, and Allenby's given him two fighters, those Bristols over there, and two aviators. You. You'll have to train your own gunners from what you find out there." He gestured toward the east. "Come on back inside, chaps, have some tea, and I'll show you how to find Lawrence, if he's still where he said he was the last time he got in touch."

They started back toward an operations building. "By the way, that big Handley Page over there is going out with you to carry your supplies." He pointed to a ponderous twin-engine bomber looming high above the Bristols like some guardian protector. "Don't lose it on the way out, will you? It will be running back and forth between you and here for whatever you need. Within reason, of course. Petrol, ammunition, parts, bombs."

"Bombs?" Michael asked. "We'll be doing bombing? What the hell do you bomb in the desert?"

"Lawrence will find you something. Don't worry about that.

Feisty little bastard, he is. Big mouth and sarcastic. Especially to his superiors. You won't like him."

The old colonel would never know how right he was about one thought and how wrong about another.

Chapter 3

The following morning the Quintana brothers climbed into their two-seater Bristols and taxied around the airfield getting used to the aircraft. They were much larger than their Nieuports. Aside from the two pilots working on the Handley Page, they had the field to themselves. They revved up the engines, racing the planes along the ground, cut the engines and coasted almost to a stop, and then cut them back in. The great four-blade propellers slowed to a distinctive roar and then speeded into a silver blur.

Michael finally drew up alongside Joseph at one end of the field, gave him the conventional thumbs-up *I'm-going-upstairs* sign, and opened his Rolls engine to full throttle. The Bristol fairly lifted itself off the ground with little help from Michael. It rose easily, without a tumble, quickly climbing to five hundred, eight hundred, a thousand feet. The wing lift was marvelous, the engine purring effortlessly. Michael sensed no strain anywhere. He felt at home in the craft at once. It was as good as the Nieuport.

Over his shoulder he saw Joe climbing up behind him. He waved. Joe waved and gave him the sign. He thought the Bristol was lovely, too. Below on the field, four or five men had showed up to turn the engines on the Handley Page.

Suddenly Michael kicked his rudder, leaned into his stick, and brought the plane over, slipping in behind Joseph. He held Joseph's Bristol in the sights of his twin Vickers for little more than a second. But Joseph's reflexes were too sharply honed. He dropped his craft into a dive to the left, twisting it into an outside curve. He flung it straight along the ground and corkscrewed it back up to the right. Michael could barely stay with him. He anticipated one of Joe's maneuvers but came over a little too slow and never got his friend back into his gun sights.

Both aircraft flew through the dangerous patterns flawlessly. Not a quiver in the flying wires, a creak in the spars, or a shudder in the stick. The brothers had found themselves a pair of perfect mates.

Michael climbed back to eleven hundred feet. Below him Cairo was a sprawling city full of ancient walled mosques and separated fortresses, open courts, and spiky minarets stabbing upwards. But across the silvery Nile new buildings and metaled streets were pushing slowly out to the plains like a creeping tide. Michael regretted not having had time to prowl the city's streets, bistros, marketplaces—and the pyramids he could just see in the distant haze. He hoped he'd return someday before the city changed too much. At twenty-five he was already a sentimentalist with a tendency toward nostalgia.

When Cairo was far behind him, he reached up and squeezed the trigger bar of his guns. The twin Vickers clattered noisily in a short burst. A few minutes later he heard the distant chatter of Joseph's guns as he, too, tested them out. When they were side by side, they signaled each other, thumb and forefinger forming a circle. Guns functioning perfectly.

They now concentrated on finding Lawrence and the small airstrip he was supposed to have made for them by the simple procedure of having whole tribes of men walk over a piece of ground to pad it down. The Quintanas held their speed down so that the Handley Page, a few miles behind them, could keep them in sight.

They flew due east, over the Suez Canal, over the railhead at Beersheba, across the Dead Sea and the empty wastes of the desert, looking for the town of Azrak. Lawrence and his Arabs were somewhere to the east of that landmark. The old colonel had been a little indefinite about the exact location. Good pilots like the Quintanas would certainly find them. They could not go far, he assured them, and the Bristols had the ranging capacity.

Michael and Joseph had never flown over anything like this desert. The land was flat and empty and the visibility clear for miles. They had no trouble recognizing Azrak, which they distinguished from other villages they had seen by the oasis at its northern tip.

They did not have to find Lawrence at all. The Turks found him for them.

A few miles beyond Azrak they heard the bombing. It was coming from the northeast beyond a ridgeline of low craggy mountains. Soft, dull thuds floated up to them over the roar of their engines. They could feel the concussions pass their planes. They had felt those concussions and heard their dull sounds often enough to know they were coming from bombs and not from artillery, with its tandem explosives separated by even pauses of several seconds. What they heard now were light sounds coming in clusters of two or three or four at irregular intervals. Only bombs could make that sound.

Another minute's flying brought them up and over the ridge and looking down upon a great wadi. They saw the planes at once far below them. The scene was like a miniature spectacle staged for their viewing.

Lawrence's Arabs were camped in a settlement of black tents stretching out over a quarter mile. The tents were little larger than immobilized black ants, the men and animals scurrying about little more than mobile dots. The five Turkish airplanes swooping down and up were gnats striking a target and flying off, leaving the ground spotted with tiny shoots of earth, pricking upward and dissolving. The distance was too great to see the effects of the Turks' machine gunners.

Michael and Joseph looked around for the Handley Page. It was a small fly in the distance. They did not wait for it, but touched their helmets to each other almost at the same time indicating their agreement to attack. They had ten minutes flying time left on their fuel gauges—if the gauges were accurate. Some pilots would have run for it, hoping to get away unseen and put their planes down in the sand, risking the aircraft that way. It was a lot safer than running out of fuel in a dogfight. Others might have come down fast onto the flat strip of land stretching right among the tents, and climbed into the rear cockpit. They'd have a chance with the Lewis gun mounted there—not much of a chance, but a chance.

The Quintanas agreed on immediate attack. They sustained their height and flew east to come in with sunlight behind them and were able to identify their opponents before they were noticed. There were two old yellow-winged Albatrosses, a deadly little Eindekker, and two stubby Rolands painted in European camouflage greens. All of them were German aircraft that had been replaced in Europe by better designs.

The Turks were too busy riddling the tents and raking the camel herds to see the Quintanas coming. On their first dash into the Turkish group, the Quintanas each scored good disabling hits. One big old dusty-looking Albatross floated down in a swinging circle like a leaf falling from a high tree and crashed on its belly a quarter mile away. One of the Roland biplanes caught fire in its engine and nosedived into a dune.

The three remaining planes frantically tried to group into a formation to protect each other. They made a mess of it. Finding themselves under fire by enemy aircraft that were being thrown recklessly around the sky, attacking from the most unlikely positions, the Turkish pilots lost their nerve.

They scattered and fled. After his first pass, Joseph brought his Bristol back quickly and struck the second Albatross, riddling it from tail to cockpit, wounding the pilot but not destroying the plane. He flung his own plane over in a complete turn and fired two bursts at the Eindekker and missed. The Eindekker went into an Immelmann roll, expecting to come out on Joseph's tail. It was an old trick and the Quintanas were waiting for it.

As the Eindekker reached four o'clock in his loop, Michael was coming up toward him. The Turk passed slowly and cooperatively in front of his guns from cowl to tail. The Eindekker burst into smoke, its entire tail assembly broken away and dangling at the end of the fuselage. It did not come out of the loop but went into a tight spiral straight into the ground.

The second dumpy Roland had flown off over the high cliffs to the west. The Bristols were faster, but their gauges were reading empty.

The second Albatross was limping around the sky like a wounded bird. Joseph waved to Michael to finish him off and headed down toward the flat airstrip. His motor was beginning to sputter. He cut the ignition and glided silently around the entire encampment twice, each time dropping down toward the strip. He could hear above the whistling wind the wild yelling and crackling gunshots from the delirious Arabs below. An occasional bullet zinged close past his aircraft and he began to hope that irony had not caught up with him. It would be a lousy way to go.

The firing below increased, but the bullets kept their distance. Joseph brought the Bristol easily onto the ground and let it run to the end of the strip, where he kicked the rudder hard and spun the tail around, bringing the craft to a stop.

A few hundred feet above him, Michael approached the Albatross. He accepted the pilot's signal of a white handkerchief and followed him down. The Albatross landed at the end of the strip opposite Joseph's Bristol with Michael twenty-five yards behind him.

Arabs from everywhere, on foot, on horse, on camel, were rushing toward the three planes, which were now close together. The Albatross was hedged in between the Quintanas' Bristols, about thirty feet separating them on either side. Its engine was still idling as the pilot climbed down. He limped away a few feet saluted Michael with a touch to his cap and, underhanded, tossed something back into the cockpit of his Albatross, and continued to limp away.

All around, Arabs were cheering and shooting their rifles into the air. They reached Joseph first, swooping him off his feet and carrying him away on their shoulders. Michael was surrounded by beaming faces filled with grinning lips, broken teeth, grizzled and black beards. The torrential scream of voices hurt his ears.

As Michael was being lifted into the air, a sharp explosion cast a hush over the mob of frantic, startled warriors. The Albatross's top wing cracked into two as the fuselage burst into flames. The engine sagged and the spinning propeller struck the ground, flipping the whole aircraft onto its right wing. Another explosion tore into the stunned silence as a gas tank went, and the Albatross was lost in a wall of flames.

The enemy pilot was in a German flying suit. He was walking with difficulty toward Michael. The screaming among the Arabs had started again, and the shooting. It rose to a crescendo and began to subside. The crowds around Michael and Joseph seemed to be parting, but the Quintanas remained on the shoulders of the men who had raised them high.

A camel came through the parted crowds. Riding it was a scowling, light-skinned man with a thick Turkish-styled moustache. He trotted opposite the pilot about a hundred feet away. Then, with a shout, he ordered his camel forward. The animal moved into a walk, then into a trot, then, under the commands of his master, into a swift gallop, lowering its head into a line almost parallel to the ground. Man and animal raced down the strip.

The enemy pilot watched the rider and camel approach. He stood there frozen with fascination. When he saw the long saber appear in the rider's hand, he frantically reached for the closed holster at his side and with both hands fumbling, tried to get the flap open.

The sword caught him down across the shoulder, chest, and both arms, opening him up to his rib cage and bones. He did not make a sound as the camel shot by. He was dead on his feet.

Another deafening cheer was raised. And Michael and Joseph were carried away after the man on the camel.

A tremendous crowd of cheering Arabs, all armed, were gathred before a black tent larger than all the others and trimmed in silver.

Joseph and Michael were set down before three men standing in the opening of the tent. The man in the middle wore a dark robe, and a silver-and-gold-trimmed white headdress fell onto his shoulders. A golden-handled knife was protruding from his waistband. A smoothly trimmed beard and moustache, full lips, and moody eyes made his face sensuously handsome. Joseph recognized him from a Cairo newspaper picture. He was Prince Faisal, leader of the Arab forces friendly to the British.

The man on the left was the camel rider who had cut down the pilot in the German flying suit. He was an old, toothless, and scarred desert sheikh who followed wherever Faisal led. His burnoose was clearly dotted with small bloodstains. His cloak was dark gray, his headdress white with a black cord band. Around his waist he wore a wide leather cartridge belt packed with clips of ammunition. The sword he had just used was thrust through a second belt at his side. The blade had been wiped clean.

The man on the right also wore Arab clothing and a fancy headdress circled with golden ropes and decorated by four corner tufts of black fur, but he was not an Arab.

When Michael and Joseph were deposited before the tent, the man who was not an Arab took a step forward. His face was long and oval, his skin slightly freckled. He had a long crooked nose, brown eyes that brooded even as he smiled, and full curved lips like an archer's bow.

Joseph stepped forward and held out his hand. "I'm Joseph Quintana and this is my brother Michael. We were sent out here from Cairo to fly for a man named Lawrence."

"I'm Lawrence," he said and smiled as he held out his hand. His teeth were crooked. "And you *are* my pilots."

Chapter 4

And they were *his* pilots. Lawrence had them darting all ov
the desert around the city of Deraa twenty miles south of Da
mascus, hunting down Turkish patrols, studying railroad traffi
reporting on city fortifications. Week after week they flew cove
for his attacks on the railway, on the bridges north and south o
the city. They strafed and they bombed and they wrecked an
flew back the next day to find the damage repaired. Their bomb
were too light and there were Turkish aircraft in the area. The
could not overload the planes even though the Turkish aircra
fled when the twin Bristols appeared in the skies.

The short red-haired British colonel was determined to cu
the Turks' escape route north so that Allenby's army could smas
them. At night, Lawrence listened to the Quintanas' reports, tol
them what his plans were for the next day, and waited tensely fo
complaints that he was pushing them and their Bristols too far
He got none.

Joseph and Michael did not complain because they never hear
Lawrence complain, unless it was over a shortage of supplies o
bad markmanship from his Arabs. But the showy little man neve
complained about the heat or the rotten food or the dangers or th
sand. And neither did the Quintanas. The sand was the worst. .
sifted into just about everything including the canals in their bodie
no matter how carefully they were covered. Ears, nose, eyes
mouth, arse—when the wind blew they all got gritty. Joseph an
Michael finally asked for and were given Arab clothing to wea
when they weren't flying, but the clothing didn't help much.

They sought their Bristols like places of refuge. The air abov
the desert was clear and cool and free of sand. Sometimes the
were asked to take passengers. Then they would have to leav
behind the Arab machine gunners they had trained.

Lawrence frequently went up with them when he wasn't leadin
a raid. Prince Faisal, the man who had greeted them with Lawrenc
when they arrived, went up with them once. Lawrence's maste
and the pivot of the Arab forces, Prince Faisel, was the man wh

was supposed to become king of the Arab nations, the man who wanted his throne in Damascus. He was fearless when he flew. The morning he was to leave the camp for conferences in Cairo, he prince went up with Joseph.

When Joseph spotted a Turkish motor patrol, the prince motioned his urge to attack it. He had shot the Lewis gun on the ground for fun and he wanted to shoot it now in earnest.

Joseph wanted to tell him that it was not going to be like shooting fish in a barrel. The Turks had two armored half-tracks mounting aerial machine guns, and fifteen or twenty riflemen. And the Bristol was not carrying any bombs in its racks.

The prince insisted and Joseph made a low pass shooting up he patrol, scattering the riflemen, who did not fire back, and forcing the half-tracks to separate. But the Turkish machine gunners stayed by their guns and exchanged fire with them as they passed over.

Prince Faisal gestured for another attack. Joseph shrugged and banked the Bristol as he dove to the right after one of the half-tracks. Skillfully, he reversed his bank and passed the half-track on its opposite side before the gunner could bring his gun around. Joseph kept the Bristol level twenty-five feet above the ground, allowing the prince a perfect chance at the Turk. The prince did not muff it. With an unbroken long burst he caught the vehicle soundly, shooting the caterpillar treads off their wheels and killing he gunner. When Joseph turned in his seat to give him a sign, he prince was smiling.

That afternoon the prince invited the Quintanas to dine with him in his tent. Lawrence joined them and translated throughout he meal. For the most part the talk was about the attack that morning and the power of the aircraft in the desert.

When the end of the meal came, fresh wine was served. The prince preferred cool mint tea. He raised his glass in a toast and said, "To victory."

Lawrence soberly translated, and added, "To Damascus."

The prince smiled acknowledgingly and said, *"Inshallah!"* God be willing.

"Az m'vit leben." Joseph spoke the traditional phrase almost to himself, without knowing why he said it except that it came to his mind. "May we live to see it."

Faisal lowered his glass without touching it. "That is a Jewish phrase, Lieutenant Quintana. You are Jewish?"

Michael looked up startled. He scratched his head.

"Not very practicing, but not denying it either," said Joseph. His dark face looked deeply Semitic under the Arab headdress he was wearing.

Faisal raised his glass to him. "To cooperation between you people and my people, Jews and Arabs. We will need to help each other in dealing with the Turks and the French if we want our people to have a home here. And—" He cocked his head sideways, his eyes brightening to look at Lawrence. "—and with the British too, eh, Lawrence?"

After Lawrence translated Faisal's last remark, the four men in Arab dress, one Englishman and two Americans and the lone Arab, raised their glasses to each other and drank.

Chapter 5

Lawrence massacred the Turks of Deraa in early September. Joseph and Michael did their share of the killing from the air. But unlike other attacks they had made, this time they had the chance to see the blood up close.

The Turks in Deraa were cut off from their connections with Jerusalem when Lawrence's raiders, aided by Joseph's and Michael's Bristols, finally destroyed a rail bridge crossing a valley lying on the Jerusalem line. The Quintanas harassed the Turkish reinforcements, large units of mounted cavalry that were rushed to drive Lawrence and his dynamiters from the bridge. The Bristols scattered two large units of mounted cavalry and delayed them long enough, while the dynamiters completed their work.

The day after the bridge collapsed, the Turks burned their garrison at Deraa and two thousand bitter Turkish soldiers filed slowly and disorderly out of the city toward the north under low clouds of black smoke.

Lawrence's forces, heavily outnumbering them, moved around the city to take them on the flank on the plains before Damascus.

Michael and Joseph were flying without their gunners over the bedraggled Turkish column, just out of range of the desultory rifle shots that were aimed their way. Ten miles south they could see Lawrence's Arab camel corps circling Deraa. In a few hours, if Lawrence pushed the camels, he would be able to strike the enemy in the rear and on the right flank. The Turks were doomed. They would have to surrender or die.

Michael was exhilarated. Something big was brewing at last, a major battle that would decide something. When it was over, he and Joe could get into Deraa to see people other than the grimy Arabs they had been living with for three months. Women. As he thought about climbing into a clean bed with a woman who had washed recently, he got a little erection at two thousand feet.

Only two or three Arab sheikhs with Lawrence had brought women along, and no one else touched them and few even saw them. Lawrence prohibited the presence of any others. Sometimes

Arab warriors would ride off in the evening and return a day or two later, content to have visited their own villages in the area and seen their women. Michael and Joseph had had very little more than an occasional prostitute who had followed the camp, and they were almost as dirty and grimy as the men, and more dangerous. One night with one of these women was enough to make both Quintanas prefer abstinence.

Now Deraa would be safe. There would be women there and places to bathe in. A bath would be the first joy of the night, even before a woman. Michael wiggled his wings at Joseph in boyish exuberance and made a few gestures. Joseph, who was flying lazily fifty feet away, gestured back. Michael was more aggressive with women, but Joseph was right behind him.

They flew easily along the entire Turkish column, which was strung out more than a mile. Most of the Turks were on foot, but there was one company of mounted lancers riding in front. Joseph flew with his stick held tightly between his knees while he made notes in a log on the troop column's strength and armaments. When he reached the head of the column, he would fly back to Lawrence and drop the information in a steel cylinder.

As he soared over the advanced units of the Turks and was about to turn back, he saw a small village of tents and huts a half mile ahead, directly in the path of the column. Behind the huts were roped areas where herds of goats and sheep nibbled at sparse brown grass.

Small groups of peasants idled lazily in front of their tents and mud houses. At the head of the village were men and children and women holding their babies. They watched motionlessly as the Turkish column approached.

Joseph swooped low over the village and waved to a gang of children running naked among the animals out behind the village. The children shouted and pointed in glee. As his plane's shadow sped wiggling along the ground toward them, they waited until it touched them and then raced along in its shade to the rope fence.

At the rope they all stopped and waved, with the exception of one boy. That single slim naked figure took the rope in a single leap without breaking his stride. He followed the broad crosslike shadow across the sands straight toward the Turkish column.

As Joseph began his bank upward in case the Turks took target practice on him, he looked back and his sight was suddenly transfixed. The vomit started to rise in his throat.

The young naked Arab boy had slowed from his loping stride

to a hesitant trot. He had forgotten the shadow of the Bristol for the attraction of something else.

A lone Turkish lancer had broken from his column and was cantering easily toward him. The lance was straight up and down by the rider's side. The young boy continued to trot forward as though entranced by the lancer and his horse. As Joseph watched, the lancer slightly increased his speed, dropped his lance forward, and in a swift thrusting movement caught the child through the body and elevated his brown wriggling form high into the air. Arms and legs outstretched for a moment, the boy grabbed at the shaft in front of him and then slipped further down onto it. Several feet of lance appeared protruding from the child's back.

As if that were the awaited signal, the Turkish cavalry leaped forward and galloped toward the villagers, who were too stunned to move.

Out of the corner of his eye, Joseph saw Michael close by and waved and pointed down. He signaled again with two strong movements of his hand and, opening his throttle to its limit, flew east toward Lawrence's force. As he glanced back for a final look, his heart sank and again the urge to vomit struck him.

The Turks had caught the villagers frozen. From horseback the lancers were practicing their skills on everybody they could reach. Joseph thought he could hear the screams, although he knew it was only the wind ripping across his flying wires and the high whine of his Rolls engine.

Michael stayed behind hypnotized by the sight, as Joseph had been. The first units of foot soldiers had reached the village and were dragging people out of their huts. Michael dove three times and fired at the soldiers who were still outside the village. The stream of soldiers continued to flow forward as though the smell of blood had driven them mad. When Michael's guns went dry, he drifted above the village and watched helplessly.

No one was spared. People ran wildly to escape from one gang of soldiers only to fall into the hands of another. Old men were being hacked by swords, some women were bayoneted, others were thrown to the ground and raped. Lines of soldiers were forming behind bent figures. The bodies of children were being tossed around like dolls. Animals in the pens were slaughtered with the same frenzied abandon that comes from powerless anger and frustration, and the Turkish commanders were letting their troops vent those emotions on the entire village. No shots were fired. Everything was done with the blade.

Michael cursed that he had not taken a gunner. In his own frustration, he drew a long-barrelled Luger pistol he carried, equipped with a snail magazine, and dropped low to let off thirty shots at anything in a dingy yellow uniform. It did not matter whether he hit Turk or Arab, man or woman or child. He wanted to kill the butcher, but if he could not, it would be merciful to kill the victim. It was wild and desperate and he had no satisfaction even when he hit a Turk.

When the Luger locked open empty and his anger no longer blinded him to his helplessness, he flew back to Lawrence.

The Turkish column had done its job completely by the time Lawrence's Arabs reached the village. Not a being had been left alone. Not a man unmutilated, not a woman or girl spared rape, not an infant unimpaled, not an animal without its throat cut. The village was dead.

Overhead, watching as the Arabs silently entered the village, Michael and Joseph were thankful they could not smell the blood and smoke of death or hear the flies or the complaints of the camels bawling at the smell. The last straggling sector of the Turkish column had left the village only five minutes before.

Their Bristols refueled, their ammunition replenished, hand-picked rear machine-gunners strapped in their seats, Michael and Joseph circled slowly, waiting for Lawrence to react. The mass of Lawrence's camel corps was spread wide in an uneven line ten or fifteen deep across the entire northern side of the village and, like a single body, seemed to brood over the thin dusty line of Turks threading out across the plain, crawling slowly toward refuge in Damascus.

Startlingly, a lone man on camel broke away from the solid phalanx of Arabs and whipped his animal straight for the rear guard of the Turks. Michael, Joseph, and their gunners watched awestruck. The madman was launching a lone attack against the entire Turkish column.

Why was the whole mounted Arab force not attacking? Joseph repressed an impulse to strafe the tail of the column, to give the rider a chance. But Lawrence must have known what he was doing. Joseph dropped a few hundred feet.

As the rider dashed across the plain, man and animal rhythmically blended into one, a sword glittered upwards in his hand and the man's face was clear. At two hundred feet and sailing at seventy, Joseph recognized the sheikh who had cut down the pilot at Azrak and afterwards had stood at the side of Faisal and Lawrence, Talal el Hareidhen, sheikh of Tofas. The village below that the Turks had just murdered was his.

Lawrence was letting him ride to a death with honor. There was no possible life he could have after this. His death was swift and easier than those his people had suffered. His robes billowed out behind him, his camel ran close to the ground, his sword cut the air ahead. He charged like a fury of the desert, his dust trail rising behind him like a veil. He stayed in the saddle for a longer time than he should have. The Turkish bullets were riddling his body, smashing him to pieces, but he was still in his saddle when his camel went down dead under him, ten feet away from the last soldier in the column.

A Turkish soldier stared back at the massed camel corps of Lawrence, taking its first slow steps forward. He rose from his firing position, threw his rifle down, and lifted his hands above his head. Another Turk nearby followed, then another and another.

The Arab army had gone into a trot. Dozens of Turkish soldiers threw away their rifles and walked with arms raised toward the great wall of dust the camels were erecting.

A flare arched into the air from Lawrence's flare gun. It burst into a smoky red cloud and seemed to hang motionless before the propellers of the Bristols. Michael and Joseph knew the signal. The red rocket. No prisoners. They were to shoot at every moving target, to attack until their guns were empty and their bombs gone and return to their base for fuel and ammunition and attack again until there was nothing left.

One evening weeks ago around the fire, Lawrence had spoken to them about the red rocket. "I carry it in the bags as a symbol of power. But I do not expect ever to use it."

The Quintanas never thought he would. But there it was, arching now downwards, trailing a reddish banner of smoke, plummeting to the ground, a fading red mist dissolving as they flew into it.

For them it was a massacre with a difference. The horror was missing. Experience had hardened the nerves and numbed the nausea. The atrocity of the village had become its own immunization.

That day, for the Quintanas, anger and hate took the place of a red hand accustomed to wholesale bloodletting. They killed from the air without qualms. They both carried their best machine gunners. Joseph's gunner, Yosef ben Hussein, a cousin of Prince Faisal, was Lawrence's favorite dynamiter. When there was no

133

dynamiting to do, Yosef had begged to become a machine gunner. He became the best.

The two planes raked the column of Turks from one end to the other before the mounted Arabs struck it. They hit them with the Vickers going in and the Lewises coming out. Yosef had a field day. Ignoring the stragglers who had their arms raised in surrender, they went for the main body, hunting the lancers.

The first wave of howling Howeitat warriors swarmed over the stragglers, not wasting a bullet, as the Turks had not wasted one before.

From then on the Turks resisted. They understood the slaughter of the surrendering stragglers. No prisoners. They died at their guns or on the run. Those who ran, the Bristols chased back to the column, which was already disintegrating under the Arab onslaught. The Quintanas found a band of lancers and tore them to pieces, attacking simultaneously from two directions. They showered them with bullets and bombed them when they clustered for self-defense.

But the Turks were not cowards or weaklings. They were savage and tough. Hundreds turned and fought and took their good toll of Arabs. The band of lancers who had started it all wheeled and charged their attackers. Joseph and Michael struck them in a single murderous pass, but the survivors continued to resist until the last man was shot from his horse.

The pay was heavy when the score was tallied. Two thousand and thirty-seven Turks were dead. None captured. One hundred and forty-seven Arabs were killed or wounded. Lawrence would never give the final figures. Michael's trained gunner, Ali Ahmed, was dead from a rifle shot through the head. Michael had been wounded in the neck and shoulder but not severely enough to keep him from touring the field of slaughter with Joseph when they landed. The engine of Michael's Bristol was damaged beyond repair. Joseph suffered no more than a dirty shoulder and neck where Yosef, his gunner, had vomited on him from being thrown around so roughly during the pursuit of the lancers.

Yosef, apologetic and grinning cheerfully, insisted that Joseph and Michael walk over the ground where the battle had been fought. They did not walk very far. They could see the bodies everywhere, often heaped in piles where the Arabs had thrown them after searching for booty. But the Arabs had been busy doing other things besides searching the bodies.

A few hundred yards from where tents were being put up was

a huge crowd of silent Arabs, their rifles thrown carelessly over their shoulders or resting on the buttstocks. They were gathered around some object of interest. Occasionally they parted to let other Arabs through who, when they reached the inside of the circle, threw something down and then backed away to join the throng.

Yosef spoke the right words and a path opened for him and the Quintanas he was leading.

What they saw in the center of the throng Michael and Joseph would never forget and never talk of—except once, years later, when Michael was provoked to describe it to Samuel. It was a great soggy pyramid of what at first had the resemblance of hundreds of scrawny necks of chickens and bloody bulbous sacks of goose flesh. The mound was five or six feet long, three or four wide, and three feet high. It had been raised on an old faded tent cloth that extended six or more feet beyond the sides of the mound in every direction.

The Quintanas stared dumbfounded at the mound of flesh, unwilling to absorb the sight into their brains. Yosef said something aloud and a half-dozen Arabs nearby grunted in agreement. Suddenly an object sailed into the pile from somewhere to their left. Before it sank into the soaking mess, Joseph and Michael could no longer keep their doubts. The object was clearly a circumcised penis.

Sick to their stomachs, the Quintanas said nothing, held the gorge down in their throats, and struggled through the crowds to find Lawrence.

They found him pale and badly shaken from the massacres of the day. He held his sweat-soaked headdress in his left hand. His red hair stuck straight up, his lips were charred and caked with dirt, his clothes grimy. The strain in his face was terrible. The cartridge belt around his waist was empty, his hands blackened from extracting powder-burned empty cartridges from his Webley. He had seen them emerge from the Arabs crowded around their mound of flesh.

"They are savages, you know," he said, as they came up. "That's their cock-and-balls monument to victory. I don't really know if I can change them." Then, putting his hands on their shoulders, he said, "You Yanks have done us a job."

Michael looked him squarely in the eye and knew there was little sense in saying much more.

He said, "You've done some job yourself."

They shook hands hard.

To Joseph, Lawrence said, "We won't forget you boys were Jews in this with us. If we get Faisal on the throne in Damascus, he'll be good friends to your people. He already supports the Jews, you know—he's a friend of Weizmann—and it will be a good thing for you and my Arabs to have a Jewish and not a British Palestine."

Joseph shook his hand and did not know what Lawrence was talking about or who Weizmann was. "You're right," he said, pretending he understood. "We're all Semites, aren't we, Jews and Arabs."

Joseph looked comical and smelled bad from the dried vomit on his clothes. His face was black from the oil spray and powder residue of the Vickers except where his goggles had protected his eyes.

Lawrence broke into a smile that partly recognized Joseph's dilemma and partly thought he looked queer.

"It's the Balfour Declaration I'm speaking of. It gives your people a Palestine homeland, you know. Alfred Balfour wrote it up last year at Whitehall. We British are for it. Faisal is for it. But watch out. There'll be some who aren't."

He handed Michael a slip of paper. It was a message that the Handley Page had brought in during the battle. Allenby had taken Jerusalem and was pushing on to Damascus. Michael and Joseph were to fly to Allied headquarters in Jerusalem.

"I'm off to Damascus. Got to get my Arabs there before Allenby. For Faisal's throne, you know. I hate to lose you boys, but . . . Good-bye, Joseph. Good-bye, Michael."

Lawrence threw on his headdress carelessly and, with a little cocky swagger in his walk, strode off toward the tents where the booty taken from the Turks would be divided among the sheikhs.

That night in Deraa, Michael and Joseph got what they wanted. Not just women, but women washed, women clean, women smelling nice on sheets smelling fresh. They had had nothing like it since the twins of Château-Thierry.

They pooled their money and hired an entire floor of the best red-light house in the city, including the four girls who made their living on it. They had the best justification for the extravagance.

Dealing out death for three months on almost a daily schedule and escaping it, too often, by only a few thick hairs had affected them as it affects all men. It had magnified their natural urge to affirm their claim to life, the urge to sharpen their sense of living, their awareness of being. The daily presence of death had numbed it.

Flying itself provided a good sense of being alive, but in a different, incomplete way. Only in the completed singularly intense orgasm of sex, with its own kind of death and renewable life, was the need to feel alive really met. The embrace in the flesh of another person was, in the final run of things, the only act that would serve. The Quintanas had discovered the bizarre connection between death and sex while flying in Europe. When the smell of death grew too strong for a pilot, they noticed, he headed into the town nearest his airfield to find a girl.

To believe they were getting what they paid for, Michael and Joseph took the girls to the bathing quarter on the roof of the building, where they watched them bathe each other in large porcelain tubs under the moon and stars. One was around seventeen, two were a few years older, and the fourth had the face of a woman over fifty and the body of one much younger. When they were finished, they changed the water by means of an ingenious system of pulleys and great buckets hoisted up the side of the building. Then, after waiting for the water to warm up from the small burning braziers under the tubs, the Quintanas soaked in the scented, soapy water until they felt their skin begin to wrinkle at the fingers and the air grow cold enough to create a chill. Michael remembered the unforgettable feeling they each had, using thick Turkish toweling to wipe away the smell of Turkish blood from their bodies.

Afterwards, the girls—the older woman, who had been a prostitute for more than thirty-five of her fifty years, had never lost her girlishness—showed the Quintanas the time of their lives, including a crazy game they played first. Michael had laughingly described it as "musical chairs."

A musician was brought up, blindfolded, and asked to play on his *oud* and sing a melody. While he played, the girls, wearing veils and silks and cymbals, danced with their bellies around the Quintanas, who were sitting on cushioned stools. When the musicians stopped, whichever girl happened to be passing before either one dropped to her knees and caressed him in one way or another until the music resumed. The girls had finesse, except for the youngest, who was clumsy and rough and aggressive. She mistook vigor for pleasure and swiftness for sensuality.

The game grew frustrating, like a game of chance, the loser

137

drawing the youngster. The other prostitutes giggled a little and enjoyed themselves, until Michael and Joseph threw the musician out, chose two of the girls, and went off to separate rooms. They vied for the older woman, who had charm and sweetness as well as finesse, and they agreed that whoever won her had to take the youngster as well. They tossed a coin. Michael won.

For the rest of the night the Quintana Brother Aces flew a different kind of flight, climbing high and reaching more than once that feeling of being alive that the death of the village of Tofas and its two thousand mutilated murderers had depressed.

Chapter 6

5 November 1954

The Mufti's men who were selected to leave the cars and walk the streets to ask about the old Arab woman were perfect for the task. They spoke Hebrew like *sabras*, dressed in white shirts and tan slacks, carried Israeli papers, and knew the Jewish city as well as the Arab Quarter. But for religion and national allegiance, they were Israelis in every way.

There were three groups. Each took a separate block and reported to a car that cruised by them and waited at the end of the street. The three men spread out like a fan, starting from the marketplace where the old Arab woman had last been seen, and they moved north.

When they stopped someone on the street who might be local to ask about an old Arab woman, they aroused no suspicion. If questioned themselves, they had a story ready to explain their interest. The old woman was obviously a domestic, and since the war, with all the Arabs gone, domestic help was hard to find. Jewish girls would not clean. Who knows, perhaps that old woman might have a day free to help out a young housewife who had just given birth to twins. If they could only find the house where she went to work every Tuesday.

It wasn't long before the young Arabs began to pick up information. The very conspicuousness of the old woman that had so completely deceived them earlier had also made her memorable in the minds of the people who had noticed her. Even a local policeman remembered the old Arab woman. He had greeted her every Tuesday, including today, offered a guess of two or three streets where she might be heading.

With an hour or more of daylight left, the Arab agents had traced the old lady to within a quarter of a mile of the Levs' apartment.

Chapter 7

Samuel Lev packed his pipe for the third time. Jesse shifted in his seat and lit a cigarette for Lilli. Except for Samuel's voice, the room had been hushed. The ashtray in front of them had a small mound of butts. There were dirty glasses on the table and a half-empty pitcher of fruit juice. Only Lilli's glass remained untouched. She had sat through Samuel's tale as though she were in a dream.

Daddy and T. E. Lawrence. She could not get the words out of her mind. Lawrence of Arabia. "El-Aurens" was the way she had heard Lowell Thomas pronounce his name when he had lectured at Wellesley on the desert war of World War I. "El-Aurens." The Arabs could not say Lawrence. Thomas had spoken as though Lawrence and his bodyguard had beaten the entire Turkish forces in the Near East by themselves.

And at home neither her father nor Uncle Michael had ever mentioned him—even during the weekend she had told them of the Thomas lecture. Samuel's tale stunned her.

"My father and Uncle Michael really liked Lawrence, then?" she asked, half in disbelief.

"Yes," said Samuel, "they did. More than I've conveyed to you, actually."

"I read the book he wrote about the Arab revolt," said Lilli, speaking as though she were still in a trance. "I remember I didn't like it."

"You wouldn't," said Samuel. "The book exaggerated. He was more a desert wasp than a real threat to the Turks. That army he destroyed was already beaten. It had no effect on British plans. I was in Cairo at the time. I heard the talk. He annoyed the Turks, but with or without him, Allenby already had the Turks defeated. I saw Lawrence once from a distance at a party. I wasn't terribly impressed."

Anna smiled faintly at Samuel. She spoke to Lilli. "I saw him, too, and someone introduced us. He was cordial but not warm. Your fathers liked him quite a bit, though, and they had reason.

140

He treated them better than he did most people, actually made them his friends when he found out they were nobodies, two boys from Boston without family names or fancy education. They showed me how to like Lawrence a lot more than I did."

"I think I can like him now," said Lilli. "Daddy and Uncle Michael were not wrong about people very often. Were they, Jesse?"

She dropped her hand onto his. A thrill shot through her body. She was on the verge of acknowledging a Lilli different from the one she had thought herself two weeks ago. "Do you remember we laughed at Lawrence once, when I repeated some of the things Lowell Thomas said about him? Daddy and Uncle Michael didn't think I was very funny, but they said nothing. Do you remember that?"

"No, they didn't laugh, did they?" said Jesse. He closed his hand over hers. But Jesse had not been thinking as much about Lawrence as he was about Michael.

The story of the slaughter numbed Jesse's mind as he struggled to imagine his father's hand in it. It was not the horror of the killing that disturbed him. Slaughter had been his own work, too, but it had been safely distant. He had killed Messerschmidt pilots and JU-88 crews, and he had saved the B-19s and Lancasters for the slaughter of their targets. But he had never seen a man he had actually killed. Michael had walked among their bodies. It wasn't the horror that stunned him as much as his father's discretion in never having spoken of those times at all—as though they had never existed. Not even during that evening dinner when Lilli had spoken critically of Lawrence. The brothers had not repudiated her, not with a word or a look. The memories of that time were theirs alone. Having shared them once with Samuel and Anna, they had buried them for good. Not even their children would know.

The scenes faded hard from Jesse's mind as Anna served coffee. He felt moody, but his moodiness was touched with pride, and his pride surprised him.

There was nothing moody about Lilli. Her temples throbbed as the scenes continued to tumble through her mind. Her hand, still in Jesse's, was damp and cramped. Her mind floated. She had discovered a father she never knew. She already loved the quiet and caring man, who ran his business with the same fairness and concern as he ran his family. But aside from his hunting

141

weekends and his interest in flying his own Beechcraft, she had always seen him as a desk-bound businessman in a conservative suit. This was someone new hovering behind her eyes, making them shine with excitement.

Though Anna was not hearing the tale for the first time, her eyes, too, were bright and alive. At times she seemed to drift off on the vibrations of Samuel's voice, but Lilli knew she was listening keenly.

The afternoon had grown late as Samuel filled the room with scenes and bits of dialogue he could recall or imagine.

"Lawrence never did get Faisal on the throne," said Samuel, "and that set everybody back for years—Jews and Arabs alike."

"When our fathers got to Jerusalem, you and Anna met them?" asked Jesse.

"No," Anna replied, "I didn't meet Michael and Joseph until two years after the war."

She touched Samuel's hand. "Excuse me, my dear. I think it is time to eat, and then we must leave." She turned to Jesse. "We're leaving the city, all of us. There are things for you to see elsewhere."

Anna Lev rose a bit shakily from her chair. Lilli put an arm around her shoulders, surprised by her own forwardness. Anna trembled at her touch. Lilli said softly, "They must have meant much to you, Mrs. Lev."

"They did, Lilli, my dear girl, as much as anyone," said Anna.

"They meant as much to both of us," said Samuel, placing an affectionate arm around his wife. "We would not have heard all of this if Hannah had not been killed. Do you remember, Anna, the trouble we had with Michael then?"

"Who was Hannah?" asked Lilli. She was spreading butter on thick black bread. Jesse's head turned toward Samuel.

Before anyone answered, the telephone rang. Samuel picked it up. His face lost its composure at once, as though someone had swept its mildness away. He snapped questions in Hebrew and gave instructions. He had a brief argument that he seemed to win. When he hung up, the mild look of the professor was gone. In its place was the almost wolfish expression of a man who had been hunted and knew how to hunt. The transformation startled Lilli. Jesse's face clouded also, but he did not ask questions. Samuel spoke to Anna in clipped tones.

"Wrap that food up, Anna. There's no time to eat. That was Marcus. The Mufti's men have been talking to Martin again.

142

Martin called Marcus. They know about Adessa. They got George Powell to talk about her before he died." He turned to Jesse. "That's the woman whom you followed, who's been moving the money for us. She looks and lives like an Arab and was married to one for years, but she's one of us. They don't have this address yet, but they once followed her to this neighborhood and lost her. Now that they know what she's been doing, they've guessed we're around here somewhere." Samuel looked out of a window. "They're out there now, cruising the steets somewhere, asking questions—some of them speak Hebrew as well as we do—they're looking for someone who has seen her come here. She comes every week—like a cleaning woman. Visits with Anna for a while and leaves. They'll turn up this place soon. Marcus has spotted three or four groups of them."

"What about the police?" Jesse asked, thinking the question was reasonable. But Samuel waved it away with a hand and a shake of his head.

"The police would pick them up, maybe, and they'd be carrying well-hidden arms or none. And if they found none, there would be a big row about harassment. There are still a few old Hasids living in the Old City. Husseini would pay them some unpleas-antries if we touched his agents officially. We can't count on the police for this. Not yet." He spoke to Anna in English. "Marcus wanted to get rid of them another way. I said no. The occasion is not right. We'll have time to slip away before they find us."

Anna handed the Uzi to Samuel, who wrapped it loosely in some newspaper and placed it carefully in a heavy paper shopping bag with cord handles. The butt of the Uzi protruded innocently from the top of the bag. Anna took a small cheap suitcase from a closet and, going into the bedroom, packed it quickly.

"You *are* coming with us?" asked Samuel. Anna was back, watching the door of the elevator, avoiding Jesse's and Lilli's faces.

"I think it's obvious we are in this all together—with the Mufti," said Jesse, getting an approving nod from Lilli. "We came here for signatures, and the four signatures we need to touch the A Fund are available right here in this room. There's no one else. Shouldn't we get that fact out in the open and look at it?"

"That's correct," said Anna, taking her eyes off the elevator door and turning toward him. "We should. My signature, Sam-uel's, and your own two. You can have ours whenever you want them. And by now the Mufti must realize all this, too, and he

143

knows what he has got if he can get all of us. He would fairly well have the A Fund for himself, if he could persuade Martin to cooperate."

"And Martin, I am afraid, will," said Samuel. "He has weaknesses." He reached to call for the elevator, but before his finger touched the button, there was the click and clank of the elevator below them, and the light flashed at the bottom of the row. They heard the doors closing, then some more clicks, and the elevator started back up slowly.

With a deft motion, Samuel drew the Uzi from the newspapers and drew the bolt to arm it. He raised a hand to warn the others to be still. He crossed the room swiftly. Quietly he eased open the door to the narrow stairwell and stepped out and listened.

Jesse went out behind him, leaned into the darkened landing, and barely heard the light rapid pad of footsteps ascending. The narrow windowless stairwell acted as an echo chamber to make them audible.

Samuel was instantly back in the living room, speaking to Anna in Hebrew. Jesse had his Colt in his hand, but Samuel motioned for him to put it away. "Not yet."

Samuel watched the door as Anna pulled open a drawer in a small table near the elevator door, took out a long screwdriver and handed it to him, taking the Uzi in return. Then she hurried to the telephone, watching the rear door as she waited for the operator. She waved Jesse and Lilli back to a wall near the kitchen door that would keep them out of a line of fire from entrances to the apartment.

Samuel slid the edge of the screwdriver up and down in the joint between the elevator door and the wall, working the tip in gradually. Then with a quick thrust, as though he had found the right spot, he jammed the screwdriver in as hard as he could, forcing the door to give slightly. The whirring and clanking of the elevator stopped. The apartment grew quiet.

"They'll be stuck there for a long time," Samuel said, rushing past Jesse and Lilli to the other side of the room. Anna was talking to someone on the telephone rapidly. She nodded to Samuel, who was asking her a tacit question. Without stopping to speak, Samuel dragged the dining table across the room and wedged it under the knob of the rear door. It fit perfectly. Jesse thought he had practiced that maneuver before, as well as the trick with the screwdriver.

Lilli was half dazed by what was happening. She moved closer

144

to Jesse, who held his arms open for her. He folded her close to him inside his open suitcoat. Neither one spoke. For the second time that day Jesse let himself feel she was more than his "sister." And yet, though he was conscious of her high tight breasts and her firm curving stomach against his body, the perfume from her neck in his nostrils, he was thinking of how the Levs planned to get out of the apartment. Were they simply barricaded in, waiting for help? Would the Arabs really try to shoot their way in?

Jesse could hardly hear Lilli whispering almost frantically in his ear, over and over, "Jesse, oh, Jesse, I love you. I love you." Before he could say, "Not now, Lilli," Anna was beside them, hugging them together in her strong arms.

"We must go now quickly, my children. Now that they're in the building, there is no doubt they are armed. The police are on the way." She led them toward the kitchen. "Come. The police will be quiet but they may still attract more Mufti men here. We've got to leave before they arrive."

Samuel was already beckoning to them from the far side of the narrow kitchen. He opened a curtained door next to a low refrigerator and stepped out. A steep, narrow fire escape clung to the side of the building. Samuel, holding the Uzi again, waved them by. Anna went first, followed by Jesse, then Lilli. Samuel came last.

Their shoes thudded loudly on the iron grates as they rushed down toward the alley below. Jesse was surprised by Anna's agility. She took the steps quickly, hanging onto the railing and letting gravity draw her down, without once losing her balance. But Lilli was having trouble. Jesse could hear her cursing her heels that clattered on the metal and caught on the rungs several times, throwing her downwards against his back. Each time he braced hard until she recovered.

They made such a racket that a man on the second floor opened a door and looked at them passing and spoke angrily to Jesse, who ignored him. Samuel shouted an order and waved the Uzi in the air. The man ducked back inside and slammed the glass door shut.

When they reached the bottom, Samuel stepped inside the doorway leading to the rear stairs. He came right out.

"They're coming back down. Come on."

Samuel quickly checked the street before leaving the alley.

He ran across the few yards to the street, where a late 1940's Chrysler station wagon was parked ten feet away from the building. In front of the Chrysler was another automobile with a man

145

and woman in the front and a man and woman in the rear. Its motor was running. Up the block a big empty English sedan was parked. Nobody else was in sight.

Samuel opened the rear door of the Chrysler for the Quinns and signaled to the car in front. The car drove off furiously, screeching its tires taking the first turn.

Two new Mercedes police cars were driving up to the front entrance of the Levs' apartment house as Samuel Lev eased the big wagon down the street. He ordered Lilli and Jesse to keep out of sight. The rear seat had been folded down onto a platform, and Lilli and Jesse made themselves as comfortable as possible on the bare metal.

Before the Chrysler turned off the street, they could hear a series of popping sounds behind them as though someone had set off a string of firecrackers. Then the sound faded and all they could hear was the rumbling of the station wagon over very bumpy roads.

When they felt they could breathe a bit more easily, Samuel said, "There's a small settlement about forty miles from here where Anna and I live. We'd like you to see it. You'll find it much more interesting than our apartment." Then as an afterthought he added, "And much safer."

Chapter 8

Samuel's ruse worked, but not as completely as he wished. Two of the Mufti's cars fell for the red herring and went after the decoy car carrying the two men and women that had left the neighborhood rather conspicuously just before Samuel drove off. The three cars raced around Jerusalem up and down side streets for fifteen minutes without a shot being fired. Finally the Jewish driver led his pursuers down a side street where a roadblock had been prearranged and an ambush set up to drive the Arabs off. The police of Jerusalem were never involved.

Two of the Mufti's men were killed. The others escaped in one of the machines. From the Israeli point of view the result was not bad, considering the entire plan had been organized in fifteen minutes.

It was the third car that caused the trouble. It had drifted around the outskirts of the neighborhood, moving almost aimlessly up and down the streets waiting for the prey to be flushed.

But the prey spotted the hunter first. Samuel had waited until the streets had grown too dangerous to drive without lights before switching on his low beams. He turned them on a few blocks from the Gaza Road, just as a Humber appeared ahead of their Chrysler from the left, heading in the opposite direction. The Humber was a car known to be favored by the Mufti's agents, solid, compact, reliable.

The interior light of the Humber was on as well as its running lights. Inside, two men in the rear were hunched over the front seat talking with the passenger next to the driver and looking at a large sheet of paper that was probably a map.

As the two cars approached, Samuel reached for the high beam switch to turn his bright driving lights into the faces of the Mufti's men. The Humber rode higher than the Chrysler. The people on the floor behind him might be visible to someone who stretched high and looked hard.

It was a mistake. Samuel's hand accidentally struck the wrong switch in the dark and instead of the high beams coming on the low beams temporarily shorted out. The sudden darkening of the Chrysler alarmed the Arabs. Samuel could see them shouting and pointing at him.

As the two vehicles passed, Samuel pushed the Chrysler harder. Guns appeared in the windows of the Humber, but the Chrysler was too fast. In the rear-view mirror Samuel saw the driver swing the Humber around in a narrow U-turn, striking the curb and bouncing back onto the road.

He cursed in English. "Shit. Shit." And then he muttered in Hebrew.

"What's happened?" asked Jesse.

"Rotten luck," said Anna harshly. "Stay down, both of you. We're being followed. It's the Mufti's men. One car. Four men. Just rotten luck to run into them now. Stay down."

Samuel's foot was hard on the accelerator. The big Chrysler picked up speed slowly.

"I'm going to run for it," Samuel said. "Nothing's going to stop them now—people, traffic, police—they won't care who's around. Even if it's suicide for them, they'll follow Husseini's orders."

He swerved around a corner. The big wagon lurched clumsily over to one side. Anna fell sideways onto the seat unharmed. Lilli felt herself flung over roughly across the bare floor onto Jesse. Her knees and right elbow were scraped painfully. She stifled the groan she felt coming into her throat.

Jesse wrapped his arms around her and stretched his legs across the floor to the opposite side. He thrust hard until his body became a brace between his feet and shoulders. The Chrysler bounced brutally over the bad roads. A loose spare tire crashed against Jesse's hip. He held Lilli fast.

"Are you all right?" It was Samuel's voice, taut and low.

"We're all right," said Jesse, raising his voice to be heard over the engine. Then, "Can we crank the rear window down? I could get a burst off at them. What do you think?" He was using one foot now to brace himself while the other foot worked the heavy tire toward the opposite side of the wagon where he could pin it. One hand gripped the back of the front seat, the other held onto Lilli.

A deep rut bounced the tire free from his foot and brought it down heavily on his other ankle. He shoved it away and pinned it down again. The sharp pain in his ankle loosened his hold, and the two of them nearly were thrown against the front seat.

"We're coming to a better road," said Anna, leaning over the seat and touching Lilli's shoulder. "Can you climb over into the front?"

"I'll stay with Jesse," Lilli answered.

"Get in front, Lilli," Jesse said.

Samuel agreed. "We want you up here."

Lilli gave in. With Jesse's help she crawled over the backrest and tumbled down onto Anna. The two women, hugging each other, huddled down to keep their heads below the back rest.

A strange feeling of security fell over Lilli in the embrace of the older woman, as though she had found a good friend, one with whom an immediate sense of mutual trust had sprung into being. She felt almost invulnerable.

They were passing through a heavy commercial area of the city. Restaurants, stores, cinemas were all lit up. The walks were crowded. The vehicle traffic was light. They sped along, passing and ignoring signals from a lone policeman. Jesse started to speak, thinking of Lilli and Anna Lev, but he caught himself, and said nothing.

As they left the city district and cut through residential suburbs, the lights along the walks thinned out. Samuel handled the big station wagon expertly. He weaved around slower traffic and kept the Humber a half-block behind him.

"I think they're hanging back deliberately. Waiting for us to leave the city." He did not have to say the rest.

Jesse clenched his teeth. The men in the Humber would wait for a lonely stretch of unpoliced road before they tried an attack.

"Pass me the machine gun," Jesse yelled, thinking of the most obvious alternative. "I think I could stop them from here."

"Have you ever fired a Uzi? Or any submachine gun?" asked Samuel, glancing into the rear-view mirror.

"No," Jesse admitted, "but I could. It shouldn't be hard."

"It isn't, and I know you could," said Samuel, fixing his eyes on the dark road ahead. "But we don't want a shooting, Jesse. The risks are too great, and you and Lilli are not going to take them. None of us are, unless we absolutely have to. There's a small army patrol stationed a few miles down the road. They'll turn that Humber around, maybe even take those people into custody. The young fellows there won't mind shooting it up either. Hold on."

Samuel pushed the Chrysler to its limit. The buildings were farther apart now, and great patches of black opened up along the

149

road. Up ahead was a brightly lighted petrol station on their right, with a large spotlighted sign standing at the side of the road. Beyond that everything stood pitch-black, unbroken by the twinkle of a single light. They sped past the petrol station with the Chrysler's engine wide open. Three cars facing toward Jerusalem were waiting at the single pump. Jesse was sitting up, watching the road to the rear.

"God damn!" Jesse swore. "We're going to be all right. I think they're stopping, Samuel. Yes, they're slowing down. How the devil do you like that! They're stopping for gas."

Samuel began to laugh quietly as he looked again into the rear-view mirror. Anna and Lilli sat up and turned to look. The lights of the petrol station were dim in the distance and the road behind them was empty and dark.

"My God, Samuel!" Anna exclaimed. "This time the luck is with *us*. They're run out of gas! Is it to be believed?"

Samuel was still chuckling. "Perhaps they haven't run out yet, but they read Hebrew well. That sign back there, Jesse, at that petrol station, said it was the last fuel stop between here and Gaza, a good seventy miles. Thank God those gunmen weren't planning for the unexpected."

Lilli gave Anna a hug of relief and slipped her hand over the seat to clasp Jesse's. The handclasp meant more to her at that moment than a kiss.

Anna smiled to herself in the darkness as she sensed the two lovers reach for each other. She too reached for the hand of her mate, who still tightly gripped the steering wheel. That grateful man squeezed Anna's hand once and then hurtled the Chrysler deeper into the darkness of the desert away from the men of the Mufti and the city of Jerusalem.

Chapter 9

Two naked lightbulbs hanging a few hundred feet from each other barely revealed the low outline of buildings from the end of the dirt road. Nothing else existed for miles around. The Levs' real home was here. Jerusalem was a foster place. Beit Darras, one of the oldest kibbutzes in the country, was an isolated settlement of a half-dozen jerry-built dwellings that had been erected near an old single airstrip abandoned by the British decades earlier. Now the airstrip had an observation tower that looked like a grain silo, three long dirt runways in good repair, able to land a modern prop fighter, and four empty hangars equipped to service fighter aircraft. The land around the strip had been cultivated into rich farmland by the two generations of people who had lived there. But underneath the ground were capacious tanks of aviation fuel and inside several silos were aircraft munitions.

"It's a good producing farm," said Anna, as they drove down the sandy road toward the dark buildings. "But it is also an emergency airfield for our air force, if they should ever need one. Please God, never."

The trip from Jerusalem, once the Mufti's agents had been lost, took less than an hour. Samuel Lev knew the road well, and it was not yet nine o'clock when Anna, Lilli, Jesse, and he sat down to eat at a rough-hewn but smoothly worn table in one of the Quonset-style huts. The food was cold sandwiches, but the coffee was brewed fresh on a U.S. Army kerosene stove. Samuel got an oil heater going in the corner to drive out the cold desert air.

When they had finished eating and talking about their brushes with the Mufti, and cigarettes were lit over coffee cups, Jesse brought the conversation around to where he and Lilli wanted it.

"There's a lot more you can tell us about Uncle Joe and my father. We know that. Is that why we're here? This place has something to do with them."

Anna answered. "For now, let us say it is safer than Jerusalem. It is remote and it is guarded. But not far enough to be completely safe. Even America was not too far for the Mufti. Yes, there is no doubt in my mind that Husseini sent those men to kill your fathers. He still has enough power and he has the information."

She sipped her coffee.

"During the war, the Mufti was in Germany for five years supporting the fascists—especially in their hatred of Jews."

"We've heard that," Lilli said. "It struck us as . . . as weird."

"Weird, but true. When the war ended, he escaped from the French, who had caught him—or was let go to embarrass the British down here. And so he's back, still fighting his war against us. But old age will finally finish him."

"How we wish we could finish him ourselves—huh, Anna?" said Samuel. "How much we owe that old red-haired bloody dog." He took Anna's hand into his and stared into her bright green eyes.

Anna's eyes seemed to be staring beyond Samuel to some distant scene.

Impulsively, Lilli, who could see the unfocused look in Anna's face, touched her other hand.

"Tell us about him, then. Exactly how is he connected with us Quinns, with our fathers?"

Lilli's touch, more than her questions, brought Anna back to the room. "Yes, there is so much left to tell, and you will have to hear it all to understand why the Mufti killed Michael and Joseph after all these years."

Anna stood up. Her voice changed to a cooler tone. "But you were right, Jesse. We did not bring you to Beit Darras just to escape from Husseini's threat." She went to a window and looked out into the darkness. "This is one of our settlements. We run it for the Jewish Agency in Jerusalem, once called the Jewish Agency for Palestine. Today it exists still, but for political reasons it keeps itself in obscurity. It has only two purposes—immigration and land purchase. All of the money from the A Fund has gone to the Jewish Agency to buy land and the implements to farm it. And these"—she laid her hand on the Uzi submachine gun—"to keep it."

She faced the Quinns. "And there was good reason why land was so important. In 1919 and the 1920s we were promised a land of our own by the British, by the League of Nations. Weak promises, but promises, and it was all we had. There was, however, one overriding condition to the fulfillment of those promises. We had to create a large enough Jewish population to gain a majority over the Arabs in the land. That meant immigration. An increase through birth rate was impossible. Immigration became our life's work—Samuel's, mine, and for a while, even your fathers'. Although Michael was not Jewish, he worked alongside his found brother Joseph as though he were."

Anna paused as though she expected one of the Quinns to ask a question or make a comment. Neither did. She continued.

"But to bring people here we needed land that we owned. The Jew, who never owned land, never was permitted to own land anywhere, was to own land and cultivate it himself. We needed money desperately to buy land. Oh, there was plenty for sale—barren, sterile land, thousands of acres unused by its Arab owners. When we had money we bought. The Arabs sold gladly. When Michael and Joseph had to leave us, they never forgot. They sent us money and we went on buying."

"And today," asked Jesse, "is there land left to buy?"

"Oh, yes," Samuel said. "Large areas of it. Thousands of Arabs still live here on their own land, and there are many Christian settlements. Like anybody else, they sometimes put their land up for sale. The Agency buys it if it can. The land here in Beit Darras was bought from an old Arab to whom the British had given it after the first World War. Your fathers helped with that. Today Anna and I live here most of our time, and our children visit when they can. We have three. Two daughters and a son. Yehuda flies in the air force. Tova, the younger girl, is at the University studying physics, and Hannah, our older girl, is married and living on a kibbutz near the Syrian border, raising a family and guarding the border at the same time."

"You said Hannah had been killed," said Jesse.

"Our Hannah," said Anna, looking at Jesse, "is named for the woman who died."

Samuel handed Jesse a snapshot. Lilli glanced at it quickly, saw five smiling faces, and turned away. Jesse handed it back.

Lilli's face seemed to have fallen. She had been holding Anna's hand again and now let it go as though she realized she had been intruding into a ring of affection in which she had no share. She was uncertain of what she had been hoping for in her meeting with Anna Lev. A sinking sensation saddened her

Leaning against Jesse, she forced herself to smile. She hooked her arm through his, seeking the comfort of his brotherliness, and she found, instead, in his warm glance the deeper love that she had hoped for. Her feelings reversed themselves. Her heart began to soar.

153

As she gained confidence that she and Jesse would make it together, Lilli felt an urgency to get everything over with, to finish quickly what they had come for and go home. For the first time since they had left the States, she began to feel homesick for Beverly, for Boston, for Tom and the dogs, for normality and routine.

It was difficult to keep the impatience out of her voice. "You still haven't said how my father and uncle came into your lives." She swept her arm around. "Please, Mrs. Lev. You said you didn't meet them in Jerusalem when they went there after leaving Lawrence."

"That's true," replied Anna. There was just a touch of hurt in her eyes that made Lilli regret her tone. "I did not meet them then. I was only fifteen in 1918. I met your fathers two years later in Cairo. But what happened to them in the years between the Turks and Cairo is part of their story, too."

Chapter 10

Autumn, 1918

A month of loafing in Jerusalem was all that Michael and Joseph could take without complaining. They had been grounded by British commanders since they had come in from the desert. Allenby had no use for them, preferring to use English pilots for what little work was left. He had no doubt pulled them out of the desert to slow Lawrence's drive for Damascus. The British wanted to get there before the Arabs. But Lawrence beat them anyway.

Michael and Joseph requested transfers back to the European front. Denied. Too complicated at this stage of affairs to transfer them from English command to American. Besides, the war up there was going well. They were not needed. And perhaps their expertness in flying the desert terrain might be useful one day to the British. Not likely, the Quintanas thought.

They were trapped, but not desperate enough yet to disregard the rules.

For a few weeks they even welcomed their idleness. The October weather was perfect for drifting. The Quintanas sauntered around the city taking in the sights, visiting the great Moslem dome, the Western Wall, the Sepulchre of Christ, roaming through the Old City souks and famous gates.

They soaked in the ancient sounds and smells that hung thickly in the air of the city—the muezzin calling the faithful to worship from minarets, the Jews wrapped in prayer shawls rocking noisily before their Wailing Wall, the resonant bells of ancient churches, the incantations of the faithful, the incense of priests filing to sacraments, the food smells of the souks, the cries of hawkers and the whispers of whores peddling their wares.

In Jerusalem, God met men in many ways. It was difficult to judge whose city this babel was.

By the end of October, however, Michael and Joseph had had their fill of indulging their senses—although Michael said he could

155

suffer through another week of it, if he had to. Especially since he had found a young Jewish prostitute who entertained him with the twenty-nine prescriptions for lovers from the Arabic classic *The Perfumed Garden*. He invited Joseph to spend a few hours with her to confirm or repudiate his judgment that she was the finest woman either of them had ever been with. Joseph accepted and spent the better part of an afternoon with the young prostitute.

When he left, he suspected Michael and he were being slowly corrupted by the Holy City. His body was as lean and strong as ever, but right now he felt drained and flabby. It was an inner sensation that bothered him, a sponginess of the mind that struck him when there was nothing to anticipate for too long a time. He knew Michael was suffering from the same laxness. They thrived under tension.

Joseph wandered out of the Old City through the Jaffa Gate. He was wearing civilian clothes to avoid saluting the swarms of army personnel passing by, and spent his time idly stopping at market stalls to look at silver and gold trinkets, native cloth goods, and the usual brass and copper cookware. He picked up rings and bracelets and raised the hopes of shopkeepers only to put them down, and walk away with the cries of bargains in his ears. There was no girl he knew to give anything to. He drifted along, gazing into store windows where Western goods were displayed—tools, guns, clothing, footwear. His mind was restless.

Finally, he ambled into a small gun shop and bought two cartons of nine-millimeter parabellum cartridges. Both he and Michael were carrying Luger Parabellums. They could do some target shooting in the morning to pass away the time, kill a rabbit or two or take a desert jackal. Not very exciting but something to do.

Just before he started back for their rooms near the King David Hotel, Joseph passed an open lot crowded with old motor cars, trucks, ambulances—some just plain wrecks, some passable looking and perhaps running, and a very few in good condition. Almost every machine was an army castoff or salvaged casualty. Most were German-made vehicles that the Turks had lost to the British or to the Arabs during a retreat, or for which some Turkish guard had gotten a piece of silver or two for turning his back to let a smart thief lift.

Joseph wandered into the lot. An old Armenian, clean-shaven and well-dressed in Arab robes over a Western suit, spoke to him. Joseph shook his head and walked around the machines. Of the

156

hirty-odd vehicles spread around, most were not worth looking at for any reason, and Joseph had nothing in mind when he came in. The Armenian merchant stuck to his elbow and, in tolerable English, sang some moderate praises of each machine they passed, including the piles of junk. Joseph kept shaking his head and continued looking, not knowing what he was looking for.

But as soon as he saw the cycle, he knew what he wanted. And more than knowing that he wanted it, he realized what he wanted it for. It was a case of the machine dictating its purpose to the man.

"How much?" Joseph asked indifferently, as though he had asked only out of curiosity. He pointed with his thumb over his shoulder and was already walking on to look at something else.

What he had pointed at was a big Bavarian Motor Werken motorcycle painted the color of desert sand. It was perfect. Fixed to it was a spacious bullet-shaped sidecar carrying a sun cap over it. It was some damn good way of getting around the desert fast and comfortably. The tires were wide and deeply cleated, and the drive chain and most of the engine and gearing were cased against sand fouling. It had been used hard but it appeared indestructible.

The Armenian dealer easily pierced Joseph's pretense and drove a hard bargain. The price was high. As they wrangled, Joseph examined the rubber on the pneumatic tires and found them sound. Rubber under pressure, kept taut and used regularly, remained sound, wore slowly. The same rubber deflated, soft and idle, dried out, cracked, and became useless. He had been thinking the same thing about Michael and himself.

He finally had to give the dealer every English pound he possessed, and finished haggling by throwing in his silver American-made Waltham wristwatch.

Later, in a blast of noise, he drove up to the bleached white building where he and Michael had their rooms, took two flights of steps by twos, and found Michael on a small balcony staring dazzle-eyed down at the machine.

"Pack your razor and your toothbrush, Michael. We're going up to Damascus to see if Lawrence can use us for something."

Chapter 11

Lawrence could not.

They drove the hundred-odd miles from Jerusalem, eating dus and sand every foot of the way, to find Damascus a city of chaos The buildings were all there, untouched and looking like a city but nothing in it was working. Intertribal rivalry among the Arabs occupying it had created anarchy and disorder. Every system needed to run a city had broken down. Water, power, hygiene transport, police—every one of these departments had ceased to function. The British under Allenby, who had been standing idly by, were ready to pick up the pieces, reassert English power, and crush Lawrence's dream of Arab independence.

The short, hot-tempered Englishman who had led his Arabs there was frantic. When Joseph and Michael found him in the middle of a crowd of howling tribesmen, he was laughing hysterically. They drifted away without trying to reach him. Their timing was wrong.

On the following day the confusion lessened. Some lights were working and a few faucets had begun to gush water. The streets were being cleared of rubbish and people, and uniformed police were visible. The British were back in control.

When Michael and Joseph found Lawrence again, he was alone, walking disconsolately on the southern outskirts of the city. For the first time since they had met him, he was out of Arab dress and in his British tans with colonel's insignia and carrying a swagger stick.

He hardly seemed to know them when they drove up on their BMW machine. After a few moments of dismay, he shook their hands in embarrassment and avoided looking into their faces as though he feared their questions.

"Where did you find this?" he asked, fascinated by the motorcycle. "I must try it. May I?" He was caressing the body of the machine lovingly, running his hand over the handlebars, resting a palm on the smooth leather seat, squeezing the handbrake

ently, almost intimately. Joseph and Michael watched him dumbly.

Carefully, Lawrence mounted the saddle, kicked the motor live, and, still holding the swagger stick in one hand at the bars, drove the machine slowly around the Quintanas in sweeping circles growing larger and larger until his radius was a quarter of a mile. He stayed on the machine for fifteen minutes and then just as slowly tightened the circles until he was back by their side.

He dismounted, touched his swagger stick to his cap, and walked away.

Michael called after him. "Colonel Lawrence, can we help you in any way? We've come here to work for you. Is there something . . ."

Lawrence stopped and turned as though he had just remembered something. He had a faint smile on his face. "You Quintana brothers are all right. Go back to Jerusalem and don't let the British take Palestine away from your Jewish people. You see"—he pointed to the walls of Damascus over his shoulder without looking at them and laughed a little—"it's too late for my Arabs. Good-bye. Good luck."

He pivoted away again and strode toward a great gateway to his city. There was little spring left to his walk and a faint slouch in his posture.

"Christ," muttered Michael. "They've really beaten him. What about us?"

Joseph shrugged.

"I don't know. We didn't have his dreams. Let's go back to Jerusalem and wait for the goddamn war to end. Then we'll see. You drive. I'll sightsee."

They laughed humorlessly.

But during the monotonous hours crossing the barren sands back toward Jerusalem, the Quintanas succumbed to the throb of the cycle's engine and together drowsily constructed a fantasy. It was a fantasy with clearly defined borders but with very hazy details. They would stay in the Near East, and they would find a way to fly. These were the clearest points. The rest was murky. There was adventure in this land. The names were filled with it. Palestine, Syria, Egypt, Arabia, Cairo, Jerusalem, Suez. These places were going to be in turmoil. Oil, politics, colonization, trade. Someone, somewhere, would want a pair of pilots who could do what the Quintanas could and who were willing to do almost anything. All the brothers had to do was make it known that they were available. They would not go unnoticed.

Chapter 12

Three weeks later the war in Europe was over. Joseph and Michael celebrated in a plush dark English bar in Jerusalem's grand King David Hotel, sipping fine English whiskey., The room was a spacious open semicircular affair crowded with small tables and a high gleaming mahogany bar running along the curve of the entire inside wall. Great overhead fans whirled at high speed but they could not disperse the smoke and heat generated by the mob inside.

From bar to window and from door to door the place was packed with uniformed English officers and civilian-suited colonial administrators drawn from the ranks of the very important to the petty. Crowded among their beaming faces, filled with self-congratulation, were sleek foreign ministers in their most official regalia and rich businessmen looking for opportunities to get richer. And here and there, moving from one place to another, were the never-absent, half-seedy journalists, smiling and drinking and keeping their ears open for a good story.

The smell of victory was in the air and the excitement of spoils in the conversations. The talk flowed heavily about spheres of influence, mandates, colonies, trade rights, oil concessions, kingships, sheikhdoms, French rights, English rights, Arab rights. Occasionally someone dropped a remark about a "JNH," but no one picked it up for a discussion. The Quintanas understood it to mean Jewish National Homeland.

Joseph and Michael ignored the talk although they could not avoid knowing the subjects. When they heard Damascus mentioned and Lawrence's name dropped, they listened but heard nothing that they did not know.

In their pockets each had a separation paper issued from the American consulate in Cairo through the British air commander in Jerusalem. They were officially civilians, never having actually served with the air wing of the A.E.F. They also had one-way tickets to New York, by way of Cairo, Alexandria, and London,

161

and fifty pounds sterling each, which was given to them as separation bonus to see them home.

It was not much. And the future was uncertain. Surrounded by so much perspiring enthusiasm, the Quintanas could not help feeling subdued. Their fantasy had not yet materialized. But they were too young to become morose. Something would turn up that interested them. It always did.

They were not disappointed.

A small man in a white suit and red fez worked his way down the bar until he squeezed into the space between Michael's stool and the stool of the British captain next to it. He apologized humbly to the captain and then to Michael, and nodded to Joseph who had been watching him for ten minutes.

The man was a Levantine, probably an Egyptian or Syrian. He caught the attention of a bartender and ordered a sloe gin sling. When it came, he removed a finely tooled red-leather billfold from an inner breast pocket and, with a flourish that permitted Michael to see that the billfold was well padded with a sheaf of banknotes, laid a five-pounder on the bar.

He was half turned in Michael's direction, as he was forced to stand sideways at the bar. He saluted Michael with his glass before he drank, and Michael saluted back, finishing his whiskey.

The Levantine swallowed greedily at his drink, placed it on the bar, and lit a brown-papered cigarette in a short ivory holder.

The Levantine smiled a timid smile. "Please, sir, may I buy you and your brother a drink?"

Joseph nudged Michael's arm. Michael said, "Sure, why not Mr. . . ."

"Kader. Gamil el-Kader." He held up a hand, his arm bent close to his body. "And yours?"

Michael took his hand. It was boneless, soft and cold. "You already know ours."

"Oh, yes, that is true. I sometimes forget what I know. Quintana, Joseph and Michael. You men fly airplanes and you have none to fly right now. And you are—how do they say—unemployed at this time."

He could not get the bartender's attention.

"That's knowing a bit about us," said Joseph, who, because of the din, had to lean over Michael's shoulder to hear what the Levantine was saying.

"I am a newspaperman in Morocco, Spanish Morocco, the Melilla *Star*. Do you know where Melilla is?"

162

He waved again at a bartender.

"Hardly know where Spanish Morocco is," answered Joseph. Michael shook his head. "Along the Mediterranean somewhere in the northwest. Near Tangier?"

"Quite close enough, Mr. Quintana," Kader said unctuously. "Will it be possible to talk with both of you someplace privately? Not about newspapers. Could we do that? I have an offer to make to a couple of pilots who are not afraid of taking a risk for a very good profit. Would you care to hear it?" He tapped his cigarette and a long ash fell to the floor. Finally he caught a bartender's eye.

Joseph and Michael eyed him steadily.

"Good," said the Levantine. "Your silence is an acceptance. When can we talk?"

"Right now is always the best time," said Michael.

"Better and better," said the Levantine. "I am in room 510 right upstairs. Allow me to leave first. Then come up."

He gulped down the rest of his drink, picked up his change from the bar, and left. He never did buy them that drink.

Chapter 13

The Levantine's offer was interesting, all right. He made it immediately after Michael and Joseph settled down in his room, a few minutes after he got there.

The plan was reckless, lawless, and profitable. For the Quintanas, who were suffering boredom, the first two features were probably as persuasive as the third.

"We are going to steal an airplane from a British airfield, my friends," the Levantine announced with a big grin on his face. "To be more exact, you two are going to steal the airplane and I will assist you. Then you will fly it out of Palestine to a spacious meadow in the Riff Mountains of northern Morocco."

Michael could feel the excitement bubbling inside immediately. But, without batting an eye, he said, "That's pretty far."

"Two thousand miles."

"We're going to fly her empty all that way?" he quipped.

"No," the Levantine said nonchalantly, as though he were imitating Michael's poise. "You will carry a small cargo that I have accumulated these past few weeks."

The following afternoon, el-Kader, in a borrowed British Rover, drove the Quintanas from Jerusalem to the tents of some desert nomads a few miles from a small British airfield in southwestern Palestine. They spent the night in one of the tents reviewing the crazy plan.

The theft was planned for just before the sun broke the horizon. They traveled from the tents by horseback and camel. Four baggage camels heavily loaded with wooden crates came along. It did not take much imagination for the Quintanas to realize they were not carrying plows.

The airfield was an auxiliary unit in the process of being dismantled. It consisted of two open hangars, a small barracks, and a single brown grass runway. The place seemed deserted, but there was a light burning in the barracks.

On the field there were the shadows of four aircraft—a twin-engine bomber and three old Bristols. They were going for the bomber—a Handley Page biplane that turned out to be the same O/400 type that had serviced the Quintanas' Bristols in Azrak. Michael and Joseph had flown it together and separately, for the experience and fun of it when they were not flying their own fighters. They could have flown almost anything, but the earlier experience with the Handley made this job exceptionally easy. Except for starting the engines. They were positioned high between the two wings and they were tough to turn over. Michael had the plan for that.

According to the Levantine's Arabs, three or four fliers and mechanics were sleeping in the barracks at one end of the field. The Handley Page was parked a few hundred yards away at the other end. The lone guard, who was half asleep, was easily overpowered by the Arabs, bound and gagged. The Quintanas had insisted that no blood be shed.

In the dirty gray of daybreak, the Levantine supervised the loading of the crates, fastening them to empty bomb racks, squeezing them into the empty gunner cockpits. Michael found the fuel storage and filled the Handley Page tanks from large tins. Then he checked the four guns aboard, two mounted fixed Vickers and two Lewises on swivels. They were not loaded, but fastened to the fuselage near each gun were loaded drums of ammunition, over two dozen in all. The guns could be loaded in flight without difficulty.

Meanwhile Joseph was busy with a pair of wire cutters, removing essential wires in the control systems of the three Bristols.

Everyone was quick, efficient, and businesslike, doing his job and acting as though he were performing daily routines. When they finished, the tricky part began—Michael's plan to start the engines.

The Levantine stationed a camel at each wingtip. Attached to its saddle was a long coil of loose rope. Tied to the end of each rope was a thick strap of soft leather fashioned into a loop. Michael hooked the loops over the upper propeller blade of each engine. Arab riders mounted the camels. The Levantine and the other Arabs mounted their own animals and disappeared into the east, leaving only a third man behind, hidden in the sands a hundred yards from the barracks.

Now the Quintanas were ready to find out what this old Handley Page could do. Michael mounted into the open pilot's seat just below and in front of the upper wing. At Azrak he had flown the

165

twin-engine bomber more often than Joseph, and they had decided to let him fly it out now.

Joseph dragged the wooden blocks from in front of the airplane's wheels and climbed into the gunner's cockpit right behind Michael. He searched the landscape under the brightening sky until the third Arab stood up from his hiding place and waved his rifle.

He tapped Michael. "Let's go."

Michael turned on the magneto for both engines. He raised his hand above his head. The Arabs on their camels were set, their heads turned toward him. Michael dropped his hand sharply. The Arabs struck their camels with their prods and shouted. "Hut-hut. Hut-hut."

The animals moved. From a walk into a trot, from a trot into a gallop. The ropes uncoiled behind them as their hooves thudded on the hardened airstrip. They sped away from the aircraft in a line parallel to the wings.

Suddenly the rope on the left was off the ground, taut and straight. The propeller on the left snapped downward as the line reached its end and spun the engine. The engine coughed, sputtered, expelled a cloud of smoke, and then flowered out into a healthy roar. The engine on the right was already sputtering as the camel on that side had reached the end of its line and delivered the same thrust to its propeller. Within three seconds of each other, both engines were turning smoothly.

Michael eased the throttle down, slowed the engines, opened the throttle, then closed down a bit. The old Rolls engines were perfectly tuned. The big craft—its wings stretched out over a span of a hundred feet—was moving slowly down the airstrip. The wind was from behind them. Michael had difficulty making the turn at the end of the runway but managed to keep his wheels from drifting onto soft ground. They were almost on top of the barracks then. The wingtips were less than a dozen yards from the rooftop.

A figure in shorts appeared in the doorway and shouted. Then another figure appeared behind the first. A rifle cracked and the two figures scrambled back inside.

The takeoff was faultless. The tremendous wingspan and wide cord of the bomber created such a lift that the plane soared upward effortlessly without announcing a complaint anywhere. Not a tremor reached Michael at the controls. The ground fell away, the airfield and buildings shrunk to a fifth and then a tenth of their size. The sun showed itself above the horizon. A few miles to the east they saw the tents, toylike and isolated, where they had rendezvoused the night before.

The Quintanas did not shout or laugh or wave their arms or communicate with each other in any way to express the excitement they were feeling. Quietly and alone, they savored the joy of the feel of the aircraft, climbing easily, engines humming at medium throttle, winging toward a strange destination and a new purpose. The old familiar tension was back in their bodies and minds. They were alive again and glad of it.

Their pockets held maps and directions and names and letters of introductions to people they would have to meet, first at a refueling stop in Algeria and then at their final landing in Spanish Morocco. The tickets to home—through Cairo, Alexandria, London, and New York—were lying in a wastebasket in Jerusalem.

Chapter 14

What the Quintanas carried to a meadow in Morocco were cases of modern Mauser rifles and thousands of rounds of ammunition packed in brown cotton bandoliers. The rifles were not new, but they were in good condition. And the man who received them was well pleased.

In precise English, the man said, "I am Abd-el-Krim, chief of the Riffs."

He was a handsome man in his twenties with yellow-brown eyes, a very fair skin, and a short, neatly trimmed beard. Mounted on a white Arabian horse, his figure covered from head to stirrup in a white flowing burnoose, Abd-el-Krim was tall, erect, and spectral.

Having spoken those words, the Riffian chieftain waved his hand and a band of fierce-eyed, fair-skinned Berbers appeared from a grove of pines and began to unpack the cases and distribute the weapons and ammunition. Abd-el-Krim watched for a moment, examined several of the Mausers, and then invited Michael and Joseph to sit at his side on a richly woven red carpet in the shade of some great pines and drink hot tea flavored with crushed mint. It was a drink that the Quintanas were going to become habituated to during the next two years.

Michael and Joseph did not actually stay inside Morocco for the entire two years. They spent more than half that time outside of the country flying their stolen Handley Page to wherever el-Krim had friends or agents who could supply his needs for the rebellion he was leading against the Spanish.

Most of the time they flew to the small airstrip in Palestine from which they had originally stolen the craft. The British had abandoned the airstrip, and it had gone to seed, except for the landing strip, which the Levantine el-Kader kept in repair for them. They came to know that airstrip as well as they knew the meadow in the Riff Mountains.

To simplify their flights, the Quintanas modified the fuel system of the Handley Page so that they could fly nonstop from

Morocco to the deserted airstrip with no trouble. There were the British to worry about, of course, but by scheduling their flights across British territory at night, they were able to land unseen at dawn, fly out at dusk, and avoid the British completely.

The business was not exactly riskless, but that made the work attractive, and el-Krim paid them well in gold coin and sometimes a gold jewelry. They did not ask where any of it came from. As or the British, they never had an idea that their stolen Handley age was still flying, until much later.

Mostly the Quintanas flew in armaments—rifles, a few machine guns, small mortars, tons of ammunition. Mixed in with the ammunition were occasional cases of tea or chocolate or Near Eastern tobacco, delicacies for the hardened core of Riffian troops who lived and hid in the mountains with el-Krim. These were the men el-Krim led down into the lowlands between the Riff Mountains and the greater Atlas chain to strike at a column of Spanish troops searching for him, or to hit a military supply train heading to Fez, or to pillage an unhappy caravan that might be carrying goods useful to finance his rebellion.

Michael and Joseph had made one thing clear to el-Krim that first day in the meadow when they were working out an agreement about money and jobs over a cup of hot mint tea.

Joseph spoke of it first. He spoke slowly to be certain el-Krim understood him. "Mohammed Abd-el-Krim,"—he was not sure what one called a great tribal chieftain and called him by his whole name—"will you listen before we talk of this further. My brother and I agree to fly for you. We don't know fully what your cause is and we don't rightly care. You say you're fighting against the Spanish for your independence. That's all right with us. We're not idealists and we work for money and sometimes for the fun of it. But we won't fly for bandits and we won't do any killing for anyone. That Handley Page over there—that airplane—is now a transport airplane. It will carry cargo but we won't fight out of her."

El-Krim was unsmiling but not surly. He listened carefully, his brown intelligent eyes shifting from one Quintana to the other as though he were weighing which would be easier to persuade.

El-Krim always spoke softly. "You say, Señor Quintana, you do not care about the cause. But you do. You will not fly for the cause of plunder, but you will fly for the cause of freedom. That is something of a judgment. Now you will fly guns to us to kill

our enemies, yet you will not kill them yourselves if given th
chance? Killing directly or killing indirectly. There is a differ
ence?"

He paused and caught Joseph's eye and held it just short o
uneasiness. "Is it fear that falters you? I think not. Perhaps th
Spanish blood in your veins inhibits you from killing Spanish?"

"Neither of these matter, Mohammed Abd-el-Krim," said Jo
seph. "But we will not use the aircraft to bomb or strafe. The gun
aboard we will use if we are attacked. We will shoot in defense
but for no other purpose. Is this agreed?"

Abd-el-Krim leaned forward to Michael. "And this is you
sentiment, also, Señor? You share your brother's odd sense o
discrimination?"

"Yes," said Michael. "We're not very old, but we've see
enough killing in this last year or two to make us sick of it."

"If you stay here with me," said Abd-el-Krim, rising from th
red rug, Michael and Joseph rising with him, "I can not promis
you won't see more. We *are* at war with the Spanish."

"As long as we serve in your transport-and-supply group an
not out there in your front lines," repeated Michael.

Abd-el-Krim broke his face into a broad smile and extende
his hand to them.

"Good. Agreed. Come, you will meet my men and your com
rades. Already you have earned their respect and friendship whe
you brought your aircraft like a bird into our midst."

Abd-el-Krim turned out to be no crude mountain tribe *kaid*
He spoke Arabic, Berber, French, Spanish, and English. He wa
sophisticated. Michael understood much of this from their firs
talk. But they did not suspect how deep his refinement ran.

As the months passed and the Quintana transport, service, an
supply company succeeded spectacularly, Michael and Joseph ha
close and frequent business with him. Abd-el-Krim was a goo
host, a peaceful, positive man more like Joseph in temperamen
than like Michael.

He had been educated in Spanish schools and universities an
had served long enough in the Spanish colonial government i
Melilla to become disenchanted with the Spanish. He had trie
teaching school and finally put on the Berber hood and took t
the mountains to lead the fight against Spain.

He was a scholar and kept a small library in his hidden mountai
retreat. To Joseph and Michael he spoke often of the great Moorish
civilization in the Middle Ages that stretched across North Africa

nd covered southern Europe including all of Spain. When he poke of those glorious days, he subtly included details of the ewish well-being the Moors had nourished. He spoke of Jewish reedom and prosperity, of Jewish education and rights. He catlogued the contributions to the Moorish world of Jewish doctors, cholars, merchants, and travelers. He mentioned the famous Jewsh armorers to the courts of Moorish rulers like Yakoub el-Manour, conqueror of Spain. He spoke almost as though he thought Michael and Joseph were Jews and who could therefore be influenced by these facts.

Whatever el-Krim's motives were, the Quintanas slowly found hat they were flying for the Berbers not merely for pay but out f a vague sense of sympathy for their cause. For six months, however, as they had agreed, they did nothing besides flying upplies into Morocco, and spending idle time in French Rabat, or training to Fez or Casablanca. They dined well in good hotels, unbathed on the Atlantic, gambled occasionally in the casinos, and visited the fairest women they could find, European and naive, Jewish and Islamic, Christian and atheist. They had money, ight hearts, youth, and good looks. And a little mystery around heir eyes. They spoke little about what they did or where they ad been. And everyone welcomed them wherever they went.

Toward the end of the six months, el-Krim's stories of the Moorish past had taken their very slight effect. Slowly and shrewdly he brought Michael and Joseph deeper into the Riffian war. He invited them to move freely among his bands of warriors o witness their devotion to him, to hear them speak of battles ought down in the valleys and out on the plains. He translated heir stories. He encouraged the Quintanas to know his leaders. He showed them—as if by accident—the casualties he suffered, he wounded in their huts, the dead in graveyards scattered around he hills.

El-Krim's tactics now became obvious, but Michael and Joseph did not resist. And they were hardly surprised one morning when he called them to his large white and black tent pitched on a mountain ledge.

"I ask of you a favor," he said as they sipped mint tea and breakfasted on couscous and roast lamb.

"Ask a favor, *Kaid* el-Krim," said Joseph, "and you shall have t." He rinsed his mouth with tea to cut the strong flavor of the spiced lamb. "But do not ask us to kill. Agreed?"

The handsome yellow-brown eyes flashed and the white even teeth gleamed. "No killing, my friends. It is this."

He showed them a map, hand drawn on thick paper, of the valley on the other side of the ridges where they were camped. "Right here is a rail bridge. Spanish trains cross it with supplies to their garrisons here and here. We have tried to reach it ourselves but the garrison here has been too difficult to overcome. My casualties are growing. I must give up the bridge or..."

"We can bomb it," said Michael, laying aside his knife and fork. It was going to be Lawrence all over again. "You want the Handley Page to bomb it."

"Yes, my friends, and it can be done without losing life. The garrison is hundreds of yards from the bridge. On the bridge itself are only two guards at each end. They do not walk the bridge. At dawn from the east with the sun behind you, a bomb could be dropped right in the middle of the span and finish it. Not even one life will be lost. Of course, the Spanish will rebuild it, but it will take time. Time is what I would like to have."

He looked questioningly from one Quintana to the other.

"This is the favor I ask."

Joseph nodded first and the Quintanas did the favor for him.

They had no bombs, and so they blew the bridge crudely but effectively with a carefully fused case of dynamite hanging on a heavily knotted rope that they dragged across the span. As the rope tangled in the girders, Joseph cut it and the case was perfectly planted. It blew away the complete midsection of the span and left a gap a hundred feet wide. Not a man was hurt.

Michael and Joseph became greater heroes than ever to the Riffians, but they were not certain they liked it.

The second request for a favor came a few weeks later. This, too, was to be a bloodless job. El-Krim needed information about a garrison's strength. The surest way of determining it was to count the men at reveille or retreat when the full garrison appeared to salute its colors.

Michael and Joseph discussed the favor and decided to fly by at dusk rather than at dawn. Fifty miles from the garrison was a Spanish air base where fighters were stationed. It would be safer getting away in the dark than in the morning—and they had mastered night flying into and out of the meadow where their airplane was kept hidden.

Just before they started their engines, with the help of a dozen

172

men to twist the props, el-Krim handed Michael, who was flying observer, a bulky black object.

"God damn!" Michael swore. "Look at this. An aerial camera. We must have brought it in on our last trip from the Levantine."

El-Krim nodded without smiling. "We are not complete barbarians," he said.

Among the three of them they figured out how the mechanism operated.

On their approach to the Spanish fortress, which stood on a knoll overlooking a plain, Joseph had to fly the Handley Page low to catch the troop formations before they dispersed. For the final four hundred yards he kept her right on top of the ground, lower than the height of the garrison walls. When he was close enough to distinguish stone from stone, he eased back on the stick and felt the bomber respond. The wheels cleared the wall by a few yards and they were looking down into the startled upturned face of a sentinel.

Michael got two shots of the crammed parade grounds before the bullets began to sing around them. They had not heard that unfriendly sound since the day of the Turkish massacre with Lawrence. And neither of them welcomed it.

The bomber was hit six times, but they were lucky. Only the five or six sentinels on the walls had loaded weapons to fire at them. The plane would have looked like a sieve if the parade troops had been armed.

Later the film was developed by a villager who had lived in Melilla and worked on a Spanish newspaper when el-Krim was a teacher. The equipment for the job had come along with the camera.

After their return, Michael was dour. "Flying this kind of reconnaissance for him wasn't just a passing idea he had," he said, when he and Joseph were alone. "That fox was planning this for us a long time ago."

Joseph read Michael's unhappiness. "Don't worry, Michael, he's badly mistaken if he thinks we're going to do that kind of thing for him too often. The old H-P won't take it, anyway. We've run out of luck in her already. We're not going up again for that kind of job."

"I hope you're right," said Michael less gloomily.

But Joseph was not.

A few weeks later el-Krim took that same garrison after Michael and Joseph on a routine flight had spotted a large contingent of troops leaving it in a truck convoy. El-Krim divided his men, and attacked the convoy ten miles south of the garrison with one unit and took the garrison with the other.

Michael refused to take the Handley Page up to observe the action. "Do you think we could stand by if he got into trouble, Joe? We'd be in it up to our necks, killing a lot of Spaniards. I say no. We've done more than we said we would already—flying scout for him."

Joseph agreed. They needed a rest. The Handley Page was grounded for the future. El-Krim would have to construct a damn persuasive argument to get either one of them into the air for a long time.

Chapter 15

For several months, however, they continued to fly the old Handley Page—only as a supply machine. After the Riffs' victory over the convoy and the garrison, Michael had begun to feel morose. There had been much killing during those attacks.

"We had too much of a role in that, Joe. We were his eyes this time. We're going to be his hand one of these days. That's something we didn't want, did we?"

"That's right, Michael," Joseph said, trying to be earnest. "We're through with that."

Together they insisted that they give up all reconnaissance flights and resume their original agreement to fly supplies. They would not fly near combat. El-Krim gave them a reluctant consent and asked for no further favors. He knew well that Joseph, the quieter one, the deeper one, was warmer to his cause and could be swayed with some effort. But he was too shrewd to attempt to split the brothers. That would be a mistake and would lose both of them.

The new quietness in the Quintanas' lives came to an end one afternoon when a jubilant band of Riff warriors returned to one of el-Krim's safe villages with three slightly damaged Spanish lorries they had just taken. Along with the lorries was a collection of other booty including prisoners, mountain guns, and ammunition. It was a fine haul and the village erupted in celebration.

Michael was lounging in his hut when an excited Joseph ran in shouting, "Come on out and see what the demons of the sky have brought us."

Outside, men armed with knives were swarming over the lorries making short work of the canvas covers. Hundreds of soldiers and villagers crowded noisily around the vehicles.

On the raised porch of his wooden house el-Krim stood moodily watching the excitement. When Joseph and Michael emerged from their hut, he called them to his side. His manner changed when they came.

"What luck, eh! Do you think it's all there in the lorries?"

Stuffed into the big lorries lay the disassembled units of an aircraft. On one lorry bed was the entire fuselage and engine assembly without the propeller. The wings and propeller were on another lorry, and the stabilizer and rudder and a spare propeller and a variety of equipment including the Vickers machine guns were on the third.

Michael's eyes blazed brighter than Joseph had seen them for months. He whistled his excitement to himself, forgetting for the moment what he might be asked to do with the new plane if it could fly.

"It's a goddamn beautiful fighter, Joe! Look at the lines of that fuselage!"

"It looks all there," said Joseph.

When the excitement among the villagers and troops died away, Joseph and Michael had the lorries driven to a small field that offered sufficient room for a light plane to take off. There they set up living quarters and over the next three days supervised the aircraft's assembly.

They found a service and operational manual for the plane. El-Krim translated the Spanish himself as they went along. At the end of the third day it was ready to fly.

It was a single-seat fighter of late World War French design called the Spad 13. It was powered by the Spanish-Swiss engine, the Hispano-Suiza 200. Neither of the Quintanas had ever seen one. This aircraft had been camouflage-painted in browns and carried the red-and-yellow-bullseye insignia of Spain.

Michael and Joseph flipped a coin to decide who would fly her first. Joseph won. He flew her out flawlessly and kept her up for twenty minutes.

"You don't have to say a thing," shouted Michael over the idling engine as Joseph climbed down. "I watched every move."

"She flies as beautifully as she looks," Joseph yelled. He ducked low to get under the propwash and went over to stand by el-Krim. The Riff chieftain had been watching solemnly, his brow furrowed where it showed under his hood. He moved closer to Joseph until they were touching at the shoulder and arm. A friendship had taken shape between them that was missing with Michael. For the past few months, Michael had grown increasingly disenchanted with their situation. El-Krim remained friendly but favored Joseph.

"It is a good machine?" he asked.

"It is a very good machine, *Kaid* el-Krim," answered Joseph. "Watch Michael."

Michael put the Spad through sharper contortions than Joseph had. He threw the biplane fighter into inside and outside loops, outside spirals, straight dives, sharp climbs, and a fast corkscrew right over their heads.

When he landed, el-Krim invited them both to his house in the village for dinner.

Michael's enthusiasm for the Spad was even greater after he had flown it. But as he and Joseph walked through the dirt paths of the village in the late summer evening's coolness, Joseph deliberately dampened his friend's spirits to prepare him for what he expected to happen.

"We can't fly that Spad for supplies, you know," he said. "You know what she's built for, and he's not going to let it rot up in that field."

"Christ, you're right, Joe. He's going to ask us for another favor. Maybe we ought to just get the hell out of here. We've got a nice box full of gold back in our hut. Let's just get out."

"First, let's see what he wants. Then we'll decide."

For months Michael had recognized how strong Joseph's personal respect for el-Krim had grown. He had been puzzled by their affinity, not feeling himself the same attraction for the Berber leader that they had both felt for Lawrence. For Joseph's sake, though, he had accepted their difference and tried to find in el-Krim the qualities that had won Joseph's support. He had not been without some success—the man's warm intelligence, his concern for his people, his generosity, were attractive. And there had been occasional moments when Michael could not repress his admiration for the way the *kaid* led his men and bound them to the rebellion.

When Michael heard el-Krim's latest request after they had finished dinner, he looked across anxiously at Joseph, wondering what new strain was being exerted on their friendship. For, while Michael was already rejecting it, Joseph remained thoughtful, giving the request his full consideration.

The Riffian chieftain was planning a final assault on a great Spanish force that had been gathered to destroy him. "There is a way to draw the Spanish general into a trap and destroy him with a force one fifth the strength of his," said el-Krim confidently. "But for the ambush to be successful, I shall need both of the aircraft in the air." El-Krim raised his hand to anticipate Michael's protest. "I am only asking you to drive off any Spanish scouts that could expose my trap from the air. You will have to kill no one. Just keep their aircraft away until I spring the surprise. It is my final request of you. When this affair is over, if you wish to leave, you will do so with my blessing—and a more tangible payment surpassing anything you have received in the past. What do you say, Joseph? Will you support me this one time more? Michael, you will not let me down when I need you most."

Michael rose. His face was grim and strained. "We want to think about it privately, *Kaid* Abd-el-Krim. We've already vowed to each other we would not fight in this, but perhaps Joseph has something he'd like to tell me alone."

Back in their own hut, Joseph spoke frankly because frankness was one of the strengths of their friendship. "I'm not going to press you to go along, Michael, but this is something I'm going to do for him. It's a feeling I have that I owe him something. I think I can handle it alone in the Spad. We haven't seen a Spanish plane for months. They probably won't send one up now. You stay with the Handley Page until I get back and we'll fly out together. For good. What do you say?"

"Who the hell are you kidding, Joe? If you were going out there on horseback or something, I'd say go and good luck. But in the air? You need me up there. We need each other. Do you want the sky demons to find you alone? We're the QBAs, and that means flying together. You know damn well when you and I go, we're not going to go in some soft fleecy beds years apart. Oh, no, we're going to go together—and I bet we go wearing our boots. Listen, if the Spaniards send one plane they'll send four. No. I'll fly the Handley Page on your left. You'll owe me a favor. Some day I'll ask you to come along with me. And you won't say no. No matter what. Right?"

Joseph did not hide his relief. He smiled and threw an arm around Michael's shoulder. "Great. Agreed. We'll tell el-Krim tomorrow morning."

Michael's gesture lost nothing from the fact that the Spanish air force did not show up for the battle. Neither Quintana complained about missing combat. They soared at the highest altitude they could and still observe the movements of the troops on the ground. They watched the long line of the Spanish army contract and expand as it wriggled like a great serpent toward the mouth of the valley. As soon as the Berbers drew the noose around its neck, the body of the army writhed in strange convulsions and appeared to disintegrate. The snake lost its shape, and Joseph and Michael flew back to their meadow full throttle and refueled the Handley Page. They packed some provisions, and with the two small boxes of gold they had earned over the two years with el-Krim, they flew the big old bomber out of the Riff Mountains for the last time and headed east.

Four days later the news made its way around the world. A small handful of savage Riffs, following an even more barbaric leader named Mohammed Abd-el-Krim, had routed and destroyed a Spanish army tremendously superior in numbers. The plains between Anual and Melilla were littered with the rotting corpses of an army slain in flight. The head of its general, Fernandez Silvestre, now decorated the outside center tentpole of the Riffian leader. Spanish colonialism in North Africa—indeed, colonialism itself—had received a great setback.

The Quintanas did not see the news reports for over a week afterward. Prisoners in Cairo jails were not usually allowed newspapers, and British jailers were not disposed to treat them with consideration or kindness. The Quintanas found that out soon after they had been intercepted over Palestine by a British air patrol, forced down onto their own airstrip, and sent back to Egypt under arrest.

Only by luck did an English Cairo newspaper make its way into their cell, where they were awaiting trial for stealing government property, smuggling, possessing gold contraband, and violating a country's neutrality by flying an armed aircraft over it.

The morning that their appointed defense barrister left his newspaper in their cell, he informed them that, if found guilty, they faced ten years imprisonment, and the court was not known to incline toward clemency.

Chapter 16

Beit Darras—1954

It had grown late. But no one showed a sign of tiredness.

"Come," said Samuel Lev, rising toward the door. "Let us get some fresh air and stretch our legs outside. Huh, Anna?"

"Yes, I know what you mean. Why not."

It was a little after midnight.

Jesse, almost under compulsion to touch Lilli whenever he could without being awkward, circled her waist with his arm, and they went out into the cool, star-ridden night. The moon was down.

Samuel snapped on an outside light and called out softly into the dimness. Somewhere to their right in the direction of the road, a voice called back. Then up beyond the other buildings came another voice.

"We don't want to be mistaken for *fedayeen*—Arab infiltrators—in the dark," explained Samuel. "We lost one good man that way in the war. An American, in fact. Killed by his own sentry in the dark. Come, follow me."

With Anna at his side, he led Jesse and Lilli, who were walking arm in arm, out into the chilly air, across a grass field, onto a dirt landing strip, across it, and onto another one. He stopped there. The night was still except for the desert insects.

For a while they stargazed. Lilli murmured.

"Shhh," warned Samuel gently. "If you believed in spirits and listened hard, you might hear them. Anna and I have heard them."

"What do you mean?" asked Lilli, shivering and not certain that it was only the night air that chilled her.

Anna laughed briefly. "Only some foolishness that Samuel pretends. I humor him. There is nothing here."

"She's right, of course," Samuel said. "It is foolishness. We pretend we can hear their engines coming in or leaving. Michael and Joe's." His gaze swept the sky with a single motion of his head. "You know, it was right to this landing strip in the middle of nowhere that the Levantine brought them the night after he made his offer. And they flew here God knows how many times when they were with el-Krim and his Berbers."

Jesse and Lilli did know it, of course, but knowing it and feeling it were widely separated. Now they were feeling it. They listened hard, and the desert wasps hummed, and for a few brief moments they heard the sputtering drone of the Handley Page's idling engines as the great plane glided toward its landing.

Chapter 17

They stayed and listened until it was gone. It was a spell that was never meant to endure. Anna put it completely to rest.

"We all could use some tea."

"Hot minted tea," Jesse said.

"Exactly," said Anna.

Oddly, Samuel, who again had taken the lead across the airstrips, was heading toward the side of the Quonset hut instead of to the front door. Anna caught him.

"No, Samuel. It is late and cold. Tomorrow." She spoke to the Quinns. "There is something else. It can wait for the morning."

Inside, while they waited for the tea to brew, they enjoyed the light mint fragrance hanging in the room. Lilli's eyes were filled with tears as she inhaled the familiar scent. She shook her head to throw the dark waves of hair away from her face and brushed the tears from her cheeks with the fingertips of both hands. No one felt an embarrassment.

"Daddy and Uncle Michael never did give up that drink, I guess. That smell was in the house so often. Mint was always growing in the garden and stored for the winter in the pantry in airtight bottles. I've done it myself. At every dinner, tea and mint was served along with the coffee. Jesse and I take coffee but they always had the tea. Hot in the winter, hot or iced in the summer. They liked it both ways."

"We never had the luxury of ice," said Anna. "They took it hot the way it should be taken." The tea was ready. It was hot and spicy and took the chill from their bodies. They drank in an almost ceremonial silence.

Anna began to clear the dishes. Lilli was up helping her. "Time for sleep," Anna said. "Samuel has to be back in Jerusalem tomorrow. Oh, don't worry, he will be all right. Come, to bed. Everyone."

The Quonset hut had only three rooms, two bedrooms at opposite ends of the building and the sitting room-kitchen. Samuel said good night and went into one of the bedrooms. That left Anna to face Jesse and Lilli, who were standing close together, Jesse's arm still curved around Lilli's shoulders. Anna could not remember if he had ever taken it away, even while drinking their tea.

For a few moments there was an awkward silence. Through the open door to the empty bedroom close by, Jesse could see only a single bed.

He let go of Lilli and looked straight at her. "I'll sack out on this couch. Lilli, you take the bed." He saw her stiffen slightly.

She went into the bedroom and came right out.

"Jesse, you're not going to squeeze yourself onto that couch. Look."

She kicked off her shoes, flopped her body onto the couch, and stretched out. Her head touched one end and her feet the other. "This fits perfectly—for me. The bedroom's yours."

"She's right," said Anna. "The bed for you."

Anna disappeared into her own bedroom and brought back a pillow and heavy blanket and some pajamas. "Not very stylish," she said, and put everything on a chair. "Good night, Jesse." She came up to him. "May I?" He leaned down and she kissed his cheek.

Lilli watched and waited. Anna came to her. Lilli did not hesitate. The two women kissed warmly on the cheeks. Suddenly, Anna gripped Lilli hard by the arms and pressed against her. It was a swift embrace.

Tears again sprang to Lilli's eyes. She swallowed hard to keep back the thought that she was consciously unwilling to think because it brought the tears and with them the fear of disappointment.

Anna turned away and said good night and walked into her bedroom, closing the door behind her. It clicked softly and made the stillness of the room something personal, as though it belonged to the two people remaining there to be used as they wished.

Lilli found Jesse staring at her strangely. For the first time since they had come to Israel they were in a room alone. She went to him as soon as he moved and kissed him on the lips. It was a lover's kiss, her mouth slightly open, her tongue caressing his, her body tight against him.

Jesse shifted his eyes from her when the kiss ended. They were still pressed tightly against each other. She frightened him a little when she was aggressive like that, the way she had been the night of her birthday party. Of course everything was different—the old naïve little animalism, the innocent airs of girlhood were gone.

He could have made love to her long ago, even on that night when he had first touched her. Years later, he had sent her to be raised into womanhood by another man's body. How often he had thought about it with regret and then fooled himself into believing he felt none. Even recently he had caught himself looking at her with desire—over the dining room table in Beverly, in the museum where she worked, at the trap range.

He had always caught himself up short, for the phantom of the family tie never left his mind for long. Now there were no barriers at all separating them. And yet he was not sure that it was the time to complicate their lives, the place for him to confront the inhibitions she had never felt and he had felt only too strongly.

He said, "Did we ever imagine my father and yours like that, Lilli? They certainly had it in them. It's not incredible, is it? We just never really could see."

Lilli's voice was low. She was still pressing tightly. "We knew they were different from the others, Jesse. We're like them, aren't we? We are them."

"A little tamer," he said.

"Don't lock your door, Jesse."

Holding each other so close, they both had been aware of his hardness between them. And Jesse knew it had been there for a long, long time.

He kissed her again and released her and went into the bedroom alone and closed the door. In the far corner of the room a small shaded lamp glowed, casting a dim light half across the floor. He left it on, stripped to his shorts, and lay on the bed smoking. He did not wait long.

As he finished his cigarette, Lilli came in wearing her bra and panties. She stood above him by his bed, and slowly, hardly knowing whether she was suddenly stricken with shyness or a desire to tease him, she slipped into nakedness and did not move. He was looking at her as she had dreamed he would someday—her body now longer limbed, more curved, still dark from the summer's tan.

She leaned and kissed him, her breasts grazing his chest, her nipples hardened and, oh, so sensitive to the coarseness of his hair. And did not stop kissing him as she caressed his face, his arms, his chest, his thighs, his body, her hand inside his shorts stroking, cupping. And all the while she kissed him and felt herself stirring under the touch of his hands moving on her back, her buttocks, her thighs, her breasts, tiny orgasms began coming in

184

rapid succession like an endless string of milky pearls—even before his fingers reached her groin and slid inside her, she felt him slip off his underpants, and sensed his stark penis against her thigh. The massage of his hand inside her, gentle and loving, brought her slowly, slowly, and then ever so rapidly to the edge of that deepest of passionate chasms. Then, pausing to hover at the brink, Lilli felt herself lifted. He mounted as she spanned. Inside her mind so much love bursting in her, inside her body fast, thick panting, seething, drawing and withdrawing until she was tumbling into the chasm; her body shuddering, a thin cry in her throat, as in the high fever of a silvery death.

At the very end of her climax, Jesse, holding himself, holding himself . . . easy, easy, for her to finish, in his mind—"sister, not sist . . ."—felt he could hold himself no longer and drew away to save her from trouble. He should have reckoned with the love of Lilli. As he separated, she, knowing he had not completed, clasped tighter, thrust upwards with her hips, locked him by her legs and through her own strength, her body undulating under the weight of his, caught him fully, and destroyed his control. He rose stiffly above her, and with a low murmur sank downwards spurting, she coming once again under his passion.

"What about children, Lilli," he asked minutes later as they lay side by side smoking, her head on his arm, bodies touching their full length.

"I'm just at the end of my period, Jesse. We don't want children like this, I know that."

He reached over, touched himself with a finger and held it to where he could see a trace of blood.

Lilli said, "Just as though it were my first time, Jesse. It should have been you. Out of love."

"I know, Lilli, I know. But it will be me from now on, my beautiful love."

"Until I die, Jesse."

Chapter 18

Early in the morning Lilli woke to the unfamiliar sound of a tractor dragging a reaper across a wheat field. Young workers were following the machine, bundling the cuttings by hand. Stretching at the window contentedly, she watched them work for a few minutes. Though she had slept little, she felt refreshed. She yearned to see Jesse again, still sound asleep only a few feet away.

At breakfast, sitting opposite him, she hoped Anna and Samuel did not notice the difference in her. She thought her soul would clap its hands if she let it. When she had studied herself in the tiny bathroom mirror before breakfast, she imagined her cheeks were flushed, her eyes feverish. But she felt no illness or chill. She felt complete, for the first time in her life. But she did not want her happiness to show now, in front of Anna. Oh, the night had been too short.

Nothing seemed different about Jesse, she thought, as she ate her cereal and egg. Dark lover, comrade, brother. She wanted him as all of these. And father of her children, too.

She glanced up at Jesse again. Nothing shows except the dark gleam in his eye and the smile at his mouth. He loves and I love. Oh, if Daddy and Uncle Michael could only know.

The tea brought up the Quintanas again. Samuel served it hot and minty, and as they sipped, he said, "It was Abd-el-Krim who taught your fathers, and your fathers us, that taking it hot is the only way to fight the heat. I never agreed. It always made me hotter. I'll take mine cool."

"Abd-el-Krim," said Lilli. "Abd-el-Krim. It sounds so good to say his name. Was he a good man to have the Quintanas working for him?"

"Good, bad, it depends—as almost everything does," interrupted Anna, "whose side you are on."

"The Spanish hated him," said Samuel. "Later, the French, too, became his enemy. The Riffians loved him. And so did all the Arabs across North Africa, except those who were jealous of his success and power. The Mufti was one of his enemies. And still is."

"Is?" asked Jesse, finishing his tea and looking strangely at Samuel.

"Yes, el-Krim is still alive, living rather quietly in Cairo these days, occasionally making a speech against the French in Morocco. Hasn't seen his own country for thirty years. But in those days . . . I can tell you, it took a quarter of a million French and Spanish troops collaborating in a giant pincer movement to break his power. That was in '26, long after Michael and Joseph had left him. They left in '20."

"That's when I met them," said Anna. "But before you hear any more, Samuel must leave for Jerusalem. Come. We'll walk him to the automobile and stretch our legs."

Before leaving the room, Samuel removed an envelope from a worn leather briefcase, opened it and handed Jesse the bank draft made out to the Aleph-Palestine Fund.

"You'll want to keep this until you and Lilli decide what's to happen to the fund." He closed the briefcase and opened the door and waited for the others to move. A draft of cool air flowed into the room, chilling them.

Jesse stood hesitating with the check in his hand. His face reddened slightly. He disliked acting impulsively, and right then he felt a foolishly strong impulse to give the money back. He knew it was unwise. His thinking about the fund was unclear, and Lilli had to share in the decision.

Lilli sensed Jesse's predicament and came to his side. "We'd like to know about the fund," she said earnestly, "about Michael and Joseph's involvement especially, before we can pick up where they stopped. Can you understand that, Anna, Samuel?"

"That's the only way we would have it," Samuel said, stepping outside. "And that's why we want you to hold on to the money. When you have heard the whole story and gotten to know us better, we have hopes that the fund will survive."

They had all drifted outside now, at first a bit awkwardly, but now everybody had recovered some poise. Jesse had tucked the check into an inside pocket and cleared the air.

The Chrysler wagon was parked only a few feet from the door of the Quonset. It did not look like much of a walk to stretch one's legs. Lilli rather liked the faint air of mystery that Anna seemed to cultivate under the guise of getting a little exercise.

"This way," Anna said, walking past the Chrysler toward a road that ran by the hut and ended at the base of a small sandy knoll. "Come, Samuel and I would like to show you something before he leaves."

She trudged along the sandy road, a stocky woman, looking very much like what Lilli imagined all pioneer women must look like. Anna led them to the end of the road and onto the knoll, keeping to the right to bring them around the rise without having to climb the rough incline.

Lilli's shoes kept turning under her ankles, until she removed them and walked along in her stocking feet. Her feet burned on the sand, but she would not allow herself a complaint, and she would not put her shoes on.

Beyond the knoll, about a hundred feet away on flat ground, was a long open shed consisting of a flat corrugated-tin roof supported by a web of thin rusting bars and pipes. The shed was closed in on four sides, from the ground halfway to the low roof, by the same corrugated tin. Sand drifts had piled around the enclosed base, explaining why the lower enclosure had been placed there.

On the near side of the shed was an opening that Anna guided them through. No one had spoken at all in this walk.

As Jesse entered into the shade of the roof, a hot surge of emotion struck him, pounding at his temples. He barely heard Lilli's gasp as she sucked in her breath next to him. He stared at the huge crippled reddish skeleton that filled the shed from one end to the other like a dinosaur of the skies.

His eyes were narrowed and watery. He stood stark still and gazed. The throbbing in his head continued. Then he stepped up closer, past Samuel and Anna, to the frame of a huge ghostly bird.

"Jesse, what is it?" Lilli said in a low hoarse voice as though she felt herself in the presence of something sacred. She had been holding tightly onto his arm.

"It's what's left of their Handley Page," said Jesse, speaking softly, too, as though the ghosts of their fathers were sitting up there right now in the two places where the pilot and first gunner would sit and would not wish to be disturbed by the voices of the living.

The ribs and metal framework of the great aircraft showed through the tattered canvas hanging from its skeleton. Most of the fuselage stood stripped of covering. Its undercarriage had collapsed on one side and the long wings of the plane sagged toward the ground on that side. Its engines had been removed and the Lewis guns were gone. The entire tail assembly was exposed. For a once "fair lady" of the skies it was a sad sight.

"The Handley died when it landed here that last time," said Samuel. He too spoke low in respect for the spirits that haunted the old airplane. "A British patrol saw them coming in, arrested them when they landed, and left the plane here for the wind and the sand to ruin it for good."

Jesse walked around the gigantic, stark framework, trying to imagine what it was like to fly in it, touching the elevators and rudder, now stiff with light rust, running his hand along the control wires, which, surprisingly, were still in place, still taut, still waiting for a hand to work them.

Lilli watched him spellbound, but she remained at the side of the Levs. When Jesse stopped near the cockpits again, she went to him, and together, silently, they touched the reminder of the young daring men who had flown it. For some fleeting moments it was as though they had flown in the old wreck themselves.

Lilli had to say it. "Do you feel we've been up in it ourselves, Jesse?"

"It's strange that you should say it, Lilli, but I do."

Lilli nodded her head rapidly and bit her lip.

They left silently, taking another little piece of the past with them, leaving a little bit of themselves behind.

On the way to the station wagon, Samuel walked between Jesse and Lilli, hooking his arms into theirs. "The day they landed here wasn't the last time Michael and Joseph saw the Handley Page. They never flew it again, but they built that shed around it twenty-five years ago or more."

Jesse looked oddly at Samuel. He was about to say something and changed his mind.

Samuel continued. "Anna can tell you all about that. I've told the part I know as honestly as I could."

Samuel kissed Anna at the station wagon.

"I'll be back in early evening. Don't wait supper."

"Be careful, my dear," said Anna, holding his hand through the window.

Before he drove off, Jesse gave him the keys to their hotel rooms.

"If we're going to be here for a while, we could use some fresh clothes. We haven't changed in two days. And I'm beginning to feel it."

Samuel laughed briefly, one of the few times he had laughed since they met. Promising he would get their luggage and take care of their hotel, Samuel drove off before Jesse could press any money on him.

Anna persuaded them to change into some borrowed clothing while she washed their own and dried them in the hot afternoon sun. She dug out a few pair of shorts and shirts and sandals and then, almost reading their minds, left them alone, saying she had work to attend to on the settlement and would be back in twenty to thirty minutes.

In the bedroom, Jesse and Lilli could not stay apart. They shed their clothes the way children shed cares. Their bodies and hearts ached in a rare pain. The need to touch, embrace, kiss, make love was beyond what either one had ever felt. It was as though a slow white hot flame had been ignited somewhere in their minds, tempered by their long restraint and released as the phantom of incest that had long hung over them disappeared.

Alone they discovered a wonder they had not known existed, kissing and fondling each other's faces in their hands. Lilli stared into Jesse's eyes as though beams of light from his had met those from hers and prevented her gaze from turning aside. Then, wordlessly, sensing the exactly right moment, they made love.

When it was over and they were still lying close and joined, Lilli caressed Jesse's back with her fingertips. "Discovering them is like discovering us, isn't it, Jesse? Aren't we different from what we were yesterday? I feel different."

After a moment Jesse replied.

"You're what you always were, Lilli, only deeper. You've got all that your father gave you, that inside toughness I was always afraid of. Now I know how you come by that honestly. And, God, Lilli, I love it in you."

"Yes, you do, don't you," she laughed softly.

He laughed softly, too, kissed her, and moved away onto his back.

Jesse spoke to the ceiling. "I'm the one who has changed. I've found you. You knew what you wanted long ago. I suppose I knew too, but I couldn't admit it. That's what changed, Lilli."

Lilli's heart swelled. She was happy. Suddenly she sat up and said, "Oh, my God! Anna will be here any minute. We're a mess."

Chapter 19

Samuel felt tired from the shortage of sleep the night before, but he was able to drive the Chrysler hard toward Jerusalem. The time spent with the Quinns at the Handley Page had put him behind schedule for his first stop this morning. His mind was relaxed, however, and he expected no trouble, though he never let himself forget the Mufti to the point of carelessness. He whistled a melody from a Beethoven movement.

He was at ease with himself because he was pleased with the turn of events in the last twenty-four hours. Since the news had come of the deaths of the Quintanas, everybody had been living in the anxiety of uncertainty, not to speak of grief. Anna had suffered terribly. Now it looked as though the complications could be resolved and the wounds healed.

Jesse and Lilli had the stuff of their fathers. There was nothing spoiled about them. How Anna had joyed last night over the children! How she had cried in bed and wanted to be held and loved! For two hours they had stayed awake talking about Lilli and Jesse before he convinced her how badly they needed to sleep.

As the miles sped by on the road they had traveled over last night, Samuel dwelt on other pleasant thoughts. The Aleph-Palestine Fund was in good hands. He was pretty confident it would survive as the Quintanas wanted. That was what Anna and he had hoped for but had not counted on. And the Jewish Agency could quietly go on with its purchases from the uninterrupted flow of money. It would be good news to the people he was driving to see.

For a while he passed the time imagining the reaction of the Mufti to the news his henchmen had brought him of their failure. That would have been a scene to witness. Although the Mufti was known to keep his temper, his cool equilibrium was reputedly as murderous as another man's rage. Samuel envied no man who had to bring el-Husseini bad news.

As Samuel smiled inwardly over the last twenty-four hours, he approached the gasoline stop with the warning sign on the road and checked his gas gauge. It was low. He cut his speed and drew across the road and stopped before the pump. A small lorry had just left and was growing smaller in the distance. No one was around. Samuel touched his horn once. No one came out of the garage opposite the pump. The place looked deserted.

Samuel climbed out of the Chrysler and went inside. Sometimes the men who ran the station were busy with repairs, and then they just ignored the pump. There was more money in repairs, they told him once. It had happened before. He would have to cajole a bit or pump the fuel himself and leave the money on a table.

He called out into the bays that housed two automobiles. One machine was on the lift close to him. The other was parked over a pit. As he was about to call out for service again, he was looking at the machine on the other side of the one on the lift. It was a Humber.

Samuel quickly backed toward the door. He had to get to the Chrysler, to the Uzi on the floor in the front.

Just as he stepped back through the doorway, something struck him, a glancing blow across the right side of his head. His ear rang. For a bright second he thought he had bumped his head accidentally against a doorjamb. But then he smelled a sour, breath scorching the back of his neck. His arms were pinned to his side by a powerful bear hug. He felt himself dropping into darkness. Something rough like burlap was thrown over his head, completing the blackout. The last sensation he had was of being dragged across the ground, his body supported by hands under his armpits, his legs limp and bent somewhere underneath him.

Chapter 20

Anna was late. She did not return for over an hour. When she came in, Lilli could sense that something was wrong. As Anna did a wash, Lilli helped and chatted about the settlement, but she could not find out what the trouble was. By lunch time, Lilli decided she had imagined the change in Anna.

They ate a dairy lunch of cheeses, sour cream, cottage cheese, and fruits. They talked idly about the settlement and the dozens of others like it—planned or already established throughout the country. They were to be the backbone of Israel's border defenses, and the complete support of the Aleph Fund was essential to their success.

Anna talked mostly, Jesse and Lilli listened, asking a question here and there. Gradually, the subject turned back to Michael and Joseph.

"For nine years your fathers worked in the *kibbutzim* themselves. It was a life for them so different from what they had been doing in Morocco. Samuel told you they built that shed out there to preserve their old plane. To preserve in their own minds, too, the life they had had with people like el-Krim and Lawrence."

Jesse could no longer suppress a look of troubled surprise. It invaded his face so completely that both Anna and Lilli were startled.

"Jesse?" asked Lilli.

Jesse spoke to Anna. "Nine years, Anna? Nine years in Palestine from the time they met you?"

"Yes, Jesse, you are right. You *were* born here. Right here in Beit Darras. I was with your mother at the time. We all were."

A tremor coursed through Lilli's body. A pencil-thin band around her head tightened, and the blood rushed to her face.

"Anna! I was born here, too, wasn't I? 1929. My father took me away, took both of us away after I was born."

Anna's head dropped. She looked at Lilli without facing her. She nodded.

193

"And you knew her, too. My mother!" Lilli's brain was going into a spin. Every nerve in her body tightened.

"She was a beautiful young woman, then," said Anna, "about your own age, headstrong and terribly principled."

Lilli's voice was quiet and firm.

"Is that you, Anna?"

There was no reply. The warm, dead silence in the room throbbed into Lilli's head. A wave of nausea struck her.

"Anna, I want an answer," Lilli demanded in a rising voice. "Not a silent one. An open spoken answer, Anna. Are you my mother?"

Anna's deep jade green eyes were bright and feverish. "Mother?" the word was a question as though the meaning were unclear.

"Mother? Do you want a mother, now, Lilli? Is that what you want? You had a father, and you have Jesse. Now you want a mother, too. All right. Have a mother. I conceived you, carried you, bore you, nursed you for a very short time, and then never saw you again until yesterday. Do I have a right to call myself Lilli's mother? Do you have a right to ask me?"

"Why, Anna?" Lilli's voice was cracking. Her face was white, wracked by confusion.

Jesse stared grimly down at the floor. It was no time to interfere with his own questions.

Lilli exploded.

"Why, Anna? For God's sake, why?" Her voice sounded splintered. "I wanted a mother growing up. I want a mother now. My friends had mothers. Daddy told me I had no mother. My mother was dead. Jesse's mother was dead. What the hell went on here, Anna?—Oh, God, I'm sorry."

The two women stared at each other across the table. Anna's face was lined deeply around her mouth and in her forehead where the skin before had been only faintly etched. A light blue vein Lilli had not noticed before throbbed in her left temple where the hair was pulled back. In the course of a few moments of revelation, Anna had grown older.

Lilli cringed. She had been too cruel, she had brought those lines, that vein, that fretted look of pain to Anna's face. Yet Anna had already been troubled when she came in from her work. Lilli's words had only deepened the trouble.

Her voice softer, Lilli said, "What is it, Anna?"

Anna's figure was slightly bent. When she spoke, her voice

194

was vague, less directed to Lilli and Jesse than to something on her mind.

"We don't have a very great amount of time, I'm afraid. And . . ."

A mother and daughter had found each other after twenty-five years. And Anna seemed to be thinking of other things. Lilli interrupted.

"Why don't we have time, Anna? You've denied yourself to me for twenty-five years and yet you knew where I was, you've been in contact with my father. And now you're saying that you don't have enough time to talk about it." Her voice was not angry or accusing, but it was shot through with a plaintive kind of pleading.

"You are right to say what you want to," replied Anna, straightening a little, her voice less shaky than it had been a moment ago. "And to feel what you do. But your father and I did communicate during these years. If you can only hold back your judgment, Lilli, until you know what made everything turn out the way it did. You asked for an explanation a little while ago. And I hope to give you one. I mentioned the time because of Samuel. Something may be wrong."

"What do you mean?" The concern in Anna's voice had weakened Lilli's resentment.

"I have just called a friend on the outskirts of Jerusalem. Samuel should have been there by now. He wasn't. He hasn't arrived." She checked her plain wristwatch. "I asked that he call me as soon as he arrives. He's fifty minutes late. That's longer than a flat tire requires."

She drew a deep breath and released it as a sign of resignation. "He may decide to skip this stop and call me later. We'll wait and see."

"Is it the Mufti?" asked Jesse.

"These days it is always el-Husseini. We know what he wants. He hated your fathers and he hates you. Yet—if he could divert the Aleph Fund into his own pocket—he needs the money as badly as we do—he would have his revenge of another kind. That is why we have decided to keep you here until you leave the country."

Talk of leaving. A reuniting and now a leaving. Lilli started to reach out to touch this strange woman's hand. And she could not. She was afraid. What could she expect from Anna at that moment? Tears? Collapse? Pleas for forgiveness? Motherly love

195

and acceptance? Or perhaps rejection again? Not knowing what she wanted, Lilli dared not take the risk. Her hand stopped inches from Anna's.

Jesse felt Lilli's conflict, understood her hesitation. The air in the room had grown oppressive. Sounds from the outside seemed unreal, intrusive. Lilli remained hesitant, and Anna fell silent. Jesse broke the tension between the women himself. He wanted to ask about his own mother, but he did not. Anna would tell that part in her own good time. Instead he said:

"Anna, your relationship with Dad and Uncle Joe had some connection with the Mufti, is that right? Something to do with why they became such personal enemies?"

Anna looked relieved. "It had everything to do with him. But every Jew was el-Husseini's enemy."

"What about the first time you met my father and Joe?"

"We met in Cairo. I think I told you that. In 1920. The hot season was just gone. We did not meet in the jail but in a private place in another part of the city. It was Samuel's father who brought us all together—Sir Herbert Samuel."

Part 3

Chapter 1

Cairo, 1920

The three-man civil administrative court found the Quintana brothers guilty on all charges. The chief of the court adjusted his wig and read the sentence.

"The sentence for these crimes, Joseph and Michael Quintana, is eight years at hard labor in His Majesty's penal colony in the Sudan. However, the letters we have had from Colonel Lawrence and the note from General Allenby attesting to your contribution to the war effort in the desert—in addition to your praiseworthy war record with the Escadrille Lafayette in Europe—have made this court see fit to reduce your sentence to three years of hard labor at Khartoum. Prisoners to be removed at once for transfer within the month."

As Joseph and Michael were marched out of the spacious, cool courtroom, a guard whispered to them from the corner of his mouth. "You're bloody lucky, chaps. You'd never make eight years down there. If you behave yourselves, you'll get through three. It's bloody hell, but if you're healthy now, you'll make it, all right."

Back in their cell Joseph spoke buoyantly. "Well, Michael, what do you think? Are we lucky?"

"We're alive," said Michael lightly. "Probably shouldn't be, but we are. We'll get through this, too." He contemplated the bars on the window high above his head. "I guess we're both going to miss a woman as much as anything in that goddamn prison. Do you think they let some natives in?"

They laughed.

Michael said, "I suppose when we get out we'll take anything we can get. Three years. Jesus!"

"Three years isn't eight years and it isn't forever. But you're right, Michael. It's going to be damn boring."

Boredom *was* probably the greatest threat the Quintanas were facing. They talked about women, but it was as much the excitement of flying and the freedom to rove they were thinking about as well. Michael admitted he would rather be back fighting for el-Krim even if it meant killing Spaniards. Anything would be better than building a road to nowhere.

A week after their sentencing, the guard who had told them they would get through three years but not through eight brought them word that the prison ship had arrived. They would be boarding her in the morning to be taken back down the Nile to the Sudan, along with fifty-five other convicts.

"How are the accommodations aboard?" asked Michael.

"Do you see that slop bucket over there the two of you share? Well, on that ship, a couple of dozen boys will share one with you, a lot smaller. I'd plan for life to be bloody rotten, boys. Look, don't worry about them things now. I've got something to take your mind from them. Come on, we're going for a walk. Someone's waiting to see you, and he's not coming down here, not the likes of him in his white suit. We're going upstairs."

Unshaven, pale-faced, wearing cheap gray cotton prison suits that did not fit them, Michael and Joseph looked like a pair of crippled desert rats as they walked. Their legs were shackled two feet apart, and they moved clumsily, stumbling and cracking their bare ankle bones against the thick steel cuffs.

"Shuffle, shuffle," advised the guard in a helpful way. "You'll learn after a while how to move with them leg bracelets. Don't lift your feet off the ground more'n inch. Shuffle. Or you'll break an ankle. You won't get through three years down there on a broken ankle, I'll promise you that."

The Quintanas shuffled and slid their feet along the corridor floor. Climbing a flight of stairs was worse. They hopped and pulled on the railing. It was the first exercise they had had in a week. Their ankles ached and their shirts were stuck soaking in sweat to their bodies.

They were led to a room on the second floor. The door stood open. On either side in the hall were two dark-skinned men in civilian clothes. Inside, windows were open and the room was clean and airy.

A young well-dressed man in the white suit was seated at a long bare table. Another man in military shorts and shirt, whom Joseph recognized as a jailer of rank, was standing at his side. There was nothing else in the room.

The young man rose and handed a sheet of paper to the guard who had brought them. The officer said, "Take off their leg irons, Brown. These boys are going out with this young man on a twenty-four-hour custody pass."

The guard pursed his lips, winked at Michael, and signed the sheet. He handed it to his superior, who handed it to the young man, who signed it and handed it back to the officer. The guard unlocked the shackles with a thick square key and yanked them off. Almost at once Joseph and Michael moved their legs apart, raising them one at a time into the air, shaking them loose.

"Right," snapped the officer. "They're yours. Take good care." He raised a finger to his forehead in a polite salute to the young man and left the room. The guard behind him followed smartly, rattling the chains against his leg.

The young man spoke Arabic and the two men in the corridor came in and closed the door. The young man thrust out his hand to Michael first, then to Joseph.

"I'm Roger. From the office of the High Commissioner of Palestine." He spoke that almost as though he were apologizing. "Sir Herbert, Sir Herbert Samuel, that is, wishes to speak with you. You are Michael Quintana and Joseph Quintana, are you not? And you do fly?"

"Yes," Joseph said. "We are and we do."

"Good." The young man smiled in the friendliest way. His air of apology was gone. "Come along with me. We'll use this door." He walked to a door at the end of the room. "There's no need to go down through the cell areas. I'm certain you won't mind that."

He unlocked the door and led the way. Right outside was a flight of steps leading down to the street that ran by the side of the jail.

"By the way," said the young man, stopping halfway down the stairs, "the two men behind you are armed guards from the commissioner's staff. They have orders to shoot you if you try to escape."

"We won't," said Michael, looking over his shoulder. He nudged Joseph and shrugged his shoulders. Joseph made a face that said they should not look a gift horse in the mouth. Both of them were thinking of the twenty-four-hour custody. Twenty-four hours and they would miss the prison boat.

Parked at the foot of the stairs was a comfortable-looking Austin Vitesse heavy tourer with the top up. Roger took the wheel, Michael and Joseph sat beside him, and the guards took up part of the back seat. For the next twenty minutes Michael and Joseph enjoyed the ride across Cairo.

Cairo was nothing like Jerusalem. Jerusalem was a city that had survived from the past. It was ancient, its people were ancient, the languages they spoke ancient, the life and the flavor of the ity was ancient. Arab, Jew, Christian dressed in the garb of the past, kept one foot deep into the past and only a precarious toehold in the present. Physically, Jerusalem was an illogical network of footpaths, alleys, and roads—all noisy, all dense with people, shops, souks, tiny shacks and dwellings. The camel and the donkey were everywhere. The place smelled of dust and dung and incense.

In Cairo, it was the machine. The streets were paved and the machines were everywhere. Lorries, sedans, buses, taxis rolled and rumbled around in profusion. Cairo was on wheels and the smell of exhaust was in the air. And yet the traffic flowed in orderly fashion, thanks to the British, who demanded that it should.

The city itself had grown modern. New clean-lined buildings for offices and apartments, wide boulevards, sidewalks, electrified department stores and shops, open parks, sporting fields—for British officers—spacious hospitals, stately government buildings, movie houses, restaurants and theaters—all made Cairo a city to rival Boston.

Michael and Joseph would have preferred Boston, if they had been given a choice. But they were in Cairo now and happy to be out in the streets and curious about meeting a man who carried a title like High Commissioner of Palestine, who could send a handsome, well-dressed young man to unlock their prison door and carry them off like this.

It was late in the afternoon, with the sun still blazing in a clear western sky, when Roger, who had driven into the suburbs, stopped the tourer before a large white Georgian-style house set far back from the road.

A low iron rail fence ran along the front of the property. Beyond it, a green lawn spread right up to the house and was bordered along the wall and the house by a brilliant array of blossoming flowers. No plaque or sign indicated that the house was an official residence of someone in government. It was quite private.

Roger spoke to the guards, and they remained in the Austin when Joseph and Michael got out. Leading them toward the house, though, Roger managed to swing his suit coat open far enough to show them a big nickel-plated revolver holstered at his side.

"I'm not bringing the guards in," he explained, "because this is rather unofficial business the commissioner has in mind. The fewer people who know about it, the better it will be—for all involved. But I can use this revolver quite well, so please don't think of making a dash for it."

"We're not making a dash for anywhere," said Joseph. "Not in these rags. Besides, I suspect that the man inside here wants something from us that will keep us out of prison the easy way. And I don't have to guess he has the power to do that."

"Both of which," added Michael, "are very strong arguments for us to go in there and see how easy he's going to make it."

Chapter 2

Sir Herbert Samuel did offer the Quintanas an alternative to Khartoum, and he did have a commissioner's full pardon already made out for them, waiting for his signature to validate it. But before they found out what they would have to do to get that signature, there were a few preliminaries to suffer through.

They talked alone with Sir Herbert in a large library darkened by drapes and cooled by two overhead fans. Roger had made the introductions and left.

"Sit down, sit down," said Sir Herbert, motioning them to chairs. He remained standing in front of a small mahogany desk, bare except for some sheets of paper and a carved ivory box. He was a man of medium height about fifty-five years old, with a large, clean-shaven face, confident with the power of the practiced diplomat. His eyes were clear gray, intelligent, heavy-browed, and his hair was short, straight, combed flat, and parted on the left. He was wearing a dark blue linen suit, a high Edwardian collar, and dark tie.

In his hands he held a thin manila folder, which he never opened. He used it as a sort of pointer to emphasize his remarks.

When they were seated, he said, "Would you care to smoke? I don't think they allow you fellows that in the jail." He offered them English cigarettes from the ivory box on the desk.

When Joseph and Michael had lighted their cigarettes from a match Sir Herbert held for them, Sir Herbert began speaking.

"I've reviewed everything in this folder quite carefully. It's your dossier. Two separate reports but practically identical. Rather unusual, I should say, but not ineffective. Until this last piece of rotten luck you ran into at Beit Darras in Palestine. It's all here, your entire military record, a gap of two years that you have preferred to say nothing about, and then your arrest. Shot down by a British patrol right near the field you were planning to land at. The engines of the Handley Page were badly shot up. You were lucky."

"Only the starboard one, sir," corrected Michael. "But she could be brought in on only one. I hope it says in there that we didn't fire back although we could have."

"Yes, yes, to your advantage it does. But the old bird was ruined. A shame. It's all here." He tapped the dossier. "Your trial, sentence. Everything. Three years at Khartoum."

He paused. Joseph and Michael smoked and watched Sir Herbert contemplating them.

"Well," said Sir Herbert, waving the dossier before him, "you can forget those three years at Khartoum. I am going to spare you from them." He reached behind him and picked up the two sheets of paper lying there and handed them to Michael. "That's a pardon for the two of you. An original and a copy. When I sign them you will be free."

"I'd be happy if you signed it now," said Michael, checking with Joseph to find whether he agreed. Joseph nodded that anything would be better than Khartoum.

Sir Herbert's heavy eyebrows went up. "You have not asked what I want from you in return. That is not very politic of you both. It makes me suspect you will say yes to anything I ask and then run off somewhere when the first opportunity comes your way."

"We'll say yes to anything you ask, Sir Herbert," said Joseph seriously, leaning forward to hand the sheets back, "because we're prepared to do anything. You're the highest civil authority in this part of the world, above even the military. I don't know how wrong a thing could be that you'd ask us to do."

"You are quite right, Mr. Quintana," said Sir Herbert. He leaned over his desk, found a pen in a drawer, and signed the sheets. He handed the original to Michael.

"What you are going to do is actually quite decent. You might even say downright good. Your assignment will be beneficial to a great many people and some entire countries."

He had picked up the dossier again and tapped the folder with a finger.

A light knock at the door interrupted them.

"Come in."

A native servant entered carrying a tray of glasses and a whiskey decanter.

"As you requested, sir."

"Quite right, quite right," Sir Herbert replied abruptly. "But I asked that it be brought here earlier."

"I am sorry, sir," said the native. He placed the tray on the desk, bowed, and, looking at the ragged Quintanas, backed out of the room.

Sir Herbert didn't offer them a drink right away. He waited until the servant had gone and then addressed himself directly to the mission.

"You are going to fly a few people out of Cairo tomorrow morning and take them to that same little deserted airfield in Palestine where you brought the stolen bomber down. There you will find an automobile that you will use to drive these people to Jerusalem. That's all there is to it. It should be quite easy, but it could be difficult. The important need is to have these people safely in Jerusalem as soon as possible, this weekend at the latest."

Michael looked over at Joseph as though he wanted confirmation that he had heard what he thought he had heard. Joseph made a face that indicated he had heard it too. Then, as Michael was about to ask a question, Joseph signaled him to forget it. They were both stunned. They had left something in the old Handley Page that they'd like to get their hands on again. They had all but given it up. Now the sky demons—if they were behind the whole thing—were taking them right to the place they would have chosen themselves if they had been given a choice. And if the Handley Page had not been touched since they had left her weeks ago...

When neither Joseph nor Michael raised a question, Sir Herbert smiled without humor.

"Yes, yes, I see that look on your faces that says you think this is a bit odd. You could fly directly to Jerusalem tomorrow morning and be in Jerusalem before noon. Why need an automobile at all? Why am I not using our own people to carry out these procedures? Why bother with men like you? Why not put those people on a train right here in Cairo and send them on their way?" The humorless smile was gone.

"Those are the questions, all right," said Michael. "Don't get me wrong. We're grateful that you are bothering with us. We'll do the job if you have the aircraft and everything else. But we'd do it better if you did answer those questions."

There was more tapping on the envelope. "They'll all be answered in good time. But I'll answer one now that I can answer best. It's a rather complicated situation, from my position. You must understand, first of all, that my responsibility as High Commissioner is, most importantly, to carry out the policies created in Whitehall, our foreign office in London. I do that to the best of my ability. At the moment there is a policy developing in Whitehall that some members of one of my own bureaus oppose. That does happen, you know. In running a government, different departments very often disagree sharply over policies—and just as often it is the department on the scene that has the advantage, especially when its members are veteran administrators who have been on the scene for a long time." Sir Herbert finally placed the Quintana dossier on the desk behind him. He clasped his hands behind his back and stood taller and straighter.

"The people you are to escort to Jerusalem are—as I see it—instrumental in carrying out Whitehall policy."

Joseph immediately guessed what the commissioner was talking about. The Balfour Declaration. The document promising a Palestine homeland to the Jews of the world. Faisal had mentioned it. Suddenly a scene from the past crossed his mind. He recalled Lawrence's warning as he was walking away from their motorcycle outside the walls of Damascus the last time they saw him. Lawrence had turned and with a sad smile on his face had said, "You Quintana brothers—go back to Jerusalem and don't let the British take Palestine away from your Jewish people. You see, it's too late for my Arabs."

Sir Herbert was saying, ". . . but there are colonial officers in the Arab Bureau here in Cairo who would not want these people in Jerusalem this weekend. If they knew they were going there. And an open confrontation with my Arab Bureau will not help the people I need to help. Oh,"—he held up his hand—"I can stop the Arab Bureau for a while, I suppose—although an internal conflict within the colonial government would hurt us badly, and I am not sure I would win in the long run. But even if I stopped them now, I cannot stop the agents they may employ—I cannot stop the Mufti's men with British bullets." He shook his head slowly as though that thought should have been unthinkable. "The only alternative is to have these people taken to Jerusalem privately. And I'm hardly confident it can be done secretly. That servant, for example, who was just in here—I can't be certain that he works only for me or for the people at the Arab Bureau or the Mufti."

"Who's the Mufti?" asked Michael.

Sir Herbert's face glowered briefly at the question. "I think I will let Edouard Hirsch tell you the rest. After we have a spot of whiskey."

Chapter 3

Edouard Hirsch, with his wife and daughter, was waiting in another room in the house. Hirsch was fortyish, round-faced, ruddy-complected, balding through the middle of his head but with thick black hair on the sides. His hands were smooth and plump and yet strong in their clasp when he shook hands. He smiled easily and spoke energetically, but far too high in his throat to make him a good orator. He had a voice suited to private, intimate talks. He was openly affectionate toward his wife and daughter.

Mary Hirsch was as quietly sparkling in her face and manner as her husband. Only she smiled less with her mouth than in her large, deep green eyes. It was through the shining jubilance of her eyes and the warmth of her voice that the optimism and drive she shared with her husband appeared most visible. She was in her thirties, slim, olive-skinned, and pretty.

Their daughter Anna was seventeen. Unlike her parents, she had a somberness in her face as well as beauty, and her voice, when she said hello, was deeper than theirs. Her pace was slower, almost moody. She had her father's deep black hair and her mother's dark green eyes. Her nose was long and straight, and her chin was oval and slightly dimpled. Her skin was dark, like her mother's, and gleaming. She was taller than her mother, just as slender through the hips and waist, but fuller-bosomed in a higher, broader-chested shape. Unlike her mother, she had used a touch of red paint on her lips and a trace of antimony on her eyelids, like the Arab women of the city. The cosmetic lessened the somberness of her expression and accentuated her beauty.

For a moment after entering the Hirsches' room, Joseph and Michael caught themselves staring at the strange beauty of the young girl, who stared moodily right back at them. Joseph checked himself first and attended to the girl's parents. Michael's eyes kept shifting back to her, catching her eye and allowing himself a quick flashing smile. The girl did not smile back, nor did she lose her poise under Michael's open flirtation.

Sir Herbert made the introductions, and when the talking began, the girl faded from their attention. Michael began to apologize for their appearance.

Edouard Hirsch was quick to interrupt him. "What you look like, Mr. Quintana, hardly matters to us." His voice was cheerful and sincere. "What Sir Herbert tells us you have done and what you can do, does. Let me say that my family and I are very pleased to have you with us."

"They do look like desert rats," interjected Anna. She said it without condemnation in her voice or ridicule.

"More like desert birds," said Michael, giving her the wink. "We fly, we don't crawl." He smiled and added, "We'll get ourselves cleaned up a little and you'll find us more palatable."

"You're not impalatable at all," said Anna, suddenly smiling back. She spoke with a slight Continental accent that was not exactly French or German or Swiss. "Don't misunderstand me, please. But I do wonder if desert rats have ever done any thinking about Jews. What do you think about Jews, Mr. Quintana?" She flashed the question at Joseph, who was taken by surprise. He showed it in his face. Anna sat unblinking, as though she had asked the most natural question anyone could expect. There was no challenge or defensiveness in her voice. It was just a simple question.

"You really think, then, you should be asking that, Anna," said Mary Hirsch politely. "These men are being employed to protect us, not to accept our politics or to sympathize with our aims. Or even to understand them. As long as they get us to the meeting in Jerusalem in good time. If they do that, whatever feelings they have or don't have about our people will not count."

Sir Herbert laid his hand on Anna's arm and spoke to Hirsch. "I think that since Anna has brought up this question, they ought to know why you *are* going to Jerusalem. Then perhaps they may want to answer her—if it matters to them."

"Yes, of course," said Hirsch, as though he were somehow remiss. He leaned forward in his chair toward the Quintanas and folded his hands on his knees. His face had grown serious. "It is a meeting in Jerusalem that we are going to next Sunday in the Old City. A meeting of five Arabs who call themselves the High Moslem Council. It is most important for my people that I be there—for at that meeting those five men will be formulating an official Moslem policy in Palestine toward British plans to permit greater Jewish immigration into the country. And that policy can influence the mood of the entire Arab peasantry favorably or unfavorably toward a Jewish aim for a homeland."

"And you have friends on that committee," said Joseph.

"I wish I could say that, but the opposite is more like the truth. Its strongest member is a man named Haj Amin el-Husseini. He is the spiritual leader of the Moslems in Palestine. They call him the Mufti. Unfortunately, he is against us, and he intends to make that meeting a platform of his own to incite Arab opposition to the Balfour plan. Have you heard of the Balfour plan?"

"Yes, we have, as a matter of fact," Joseph said.

Anna's eyes widened its large jade-green ovals, but for the moment she kept silent as her father turned to her.

"You see, Anna, not much ignorance as you expected." Then he spoke to the Quintanas, who were sitting close to him, smoking more of Sir Herbert's cigarettes. "One other man on that committee completely supports the Mufti. But the other three—they are the ones important to us. Together they can overrule the Mufti. They are not beholden to him for anything. They are open-minded, and more important, they happen to be great admirers and supporters of the Emir Prince Faisal, who is sympathetic to our cause. If Faisal could only come to this meeting . . . Unfortunately, he is having his own trouble trying to secure a throne in Syria for himself. The French are blocking him."

Hirsch observed the look that passed between Joseph and Michael at the mention of Faisal's name.

"You have heard of him?" he asked, slightly surprised.

Sir Herbert said, "I haven't had the opportunity to tell the Hirsches about your desert service."

Michael was enjoying the way Anna suddenly glanced at him with interest. He said, "You could say that we know Prince Faisal. Joe and I met him with Lawrence when we were flying for them. Tell them, Joe."

"He's right. I took the prince up for a short flight in my Bristol once. He enjoyed it. And you might want to know that I heard him say something favorable about Palestinian Jews. It didn't mean much to me then."

Anna flushed in embarrassment over the way she had spoken to the Quintanas. An apology rose to her lips, but her father was speaking.

"This is all very strange and I hope prophetic of good things. You do understand the situation, then. I will be carrying with me letters of friendship between Prince Faisal and Chaim Weizmann, the Zionist leader. These are letters and agreements of mutual support between Arab and Jew. Faisal is a wise and understanding man. He has vision. He believes that a national homeland for Jews will be a great step toward Arab independence from France. If the Jews can create a free state, who will prevent the Arabs from following?

"If I can deliver these documents—written in the prince's own hand, I think those three members of the High Moslem Council can break el-Husseini's grip on the Moslems and weaken his opposition to a Jewish homeland."

Joseph was listening to Hirsch, but he was studying Anna. He got the feeling that her fascination with her father had now expanded to include Michael and him. They weren't the ignorant desert rats she suspected they might be. He watched her eyes move from her father's face to theirs and back to her father's. Once she caught Joseph staring at her, and this time she reddened. She turned away.

Hirsch was saying, "But the Mufti will use violence to stop us from delivering these papers. He would have us killed if he could." His voice became flinty, as though he were taking an oath. "I am going to Jerusalem to give some power to those Arabs who can break the Mufti, who can make clear to the Arabs what a Jewish homeland will mean to them. I am going as the emissary, you might say, of both Weizmann and Faisal."

Hirsch stopped as though he had finished a prepared speech. The silence that followed was like a vacuum waiting to be filled. Sir Herbert cleared his throat.

"What complicates these matters, Quintana, as I said before, is that people in my own Arab Bureau are supporting the Mufti. They are afraid that a Jewish homeland in Palestine will upset their own dreams of a great Arab nation dominated by British influence. It would be a world in which they would have tremendous importance. It has made them—some of them—virulent anti-Zionists. That is why I cannot use British personnel to escort the Hirsches to Jerusalem. My Arabists—Storrs, Waters, Calverson, and the rest—will get word of it. And the Hirsches, I am afraid, will not get there."

Sir Herbert stood up more grim-faced than before, clasped his arms behind him at the elbows, and paced back and forth before the Quintanas.

Michael glanced at Joseph from the corner of his eye. Joseph's expression said, "I don't understand this either."

211

The Hirsches, however, seemed to understand what was troubling Sir Herbert. They sat, avoided looking at him and said nothing.

Finally Sir Herbert stopped pacing and looked down at the Quintanas. "I feel a strong responsibility for the messy way these affairs have turned out, because it was I—" He snorted in a bit of self-disgust. "Yes, it was I, a year ago, who agreed to appoint the young el-Husseini as Mufti of Jerusalem, not knowing who or what he was. I must admit I was a piece of putty, then, in the hands of the old-timers at the Arab Bureau. I was the greenhorn. Now I am trying to make what amends I can."

Anna spoke to Joseph again, this time in a far less indifferent, much warmer tone. She had decided to concentrate on him for no better reason than that he seemed older, more serious, probably more thinking, and therefore more like herself and safer than the other brother called Michael, handsomer, more aggressive, but a womanizer. "Well, Mr. Quintana, do you think my question matters much? If my parents and I are going to place our lives in your hands, don't you think it matters that we know whether you ever think about Jews?"

She fixed Joseph with a bold, green-eyed stare, asking him for some reassurance. He pushed his brows together and brought lines into his forehead, puzzled by such a request from a girl who was not much more than a child. But then, he did not know Anna. He did not know that even at seventeen she knew exactly what the game was to be in her life. He already suspected her to be a child of her parents, but he did not know how completely she possessed their dream. For years—practically from her infancy, still nursing at her mother's breast—she had been with her parents attending meetings, lectures, rallies, all over the world, sitting up late beyond her bedtime, and, as soon as she was old enough to understand, listening to the talk, the arguments, the disputes among men—and a few women—whose chief and only concern always was the Return to Palestine. "Next year in Jerusalem." It was the thought that pervaded Anna's mind and heart even more than it had shaped her parents. For they had been swept into Zionism as young adults. Anna was born to it.

"Miss Hirsch, you and your mother and father can count on us," Joseph said. "We're getting a very good price for this job. It's also the kind of thing we like to do."

"That doesn't answer my question, Mr. Quintana," Anna insisted. Her green eyes were lovelier than ever as she held them unblinking on his. If Joseph hadn't understood her words, he would have thought she had asked him something far more personal.

"Anna, please," interjected her father coolly.

"No, don't stop her. That's all right," said Joseph. "I'm a Jew myself, Miss Hirsch." He said it looking into her eyes, not knowing why he was so anxious to impress her with the revelation.

That startled everyone in the room one way or another, except Michael. He stared at the ceiling, enjoying what he imagined would be Anna's embarrassment.

"Not a very good one," Joseph was saying, "by your standards, I suppose, but I am one. I hadn't thought about being one very much for a long time until recently, and it looks like I'm not going to be allowed to forget it too easily again. But you ought to know another thing before you say something that'll really embarrass you. Michael here is not really my brother, although we've never suffered anything letting people think we are. And he isn't Jewish. He's a defunct Roman Catholic, aren't you, Michael? But I don't think that means you can count on him any less."

The tension in the room suddenly broke. The Hirsches smiled and nodded their understanding. Sir Herbert unlocked his arms from behind his back and sat down. Michael winked at Anna again and almost chuckled.

Anna startled him by winking back and almost smiling. On her face was a look of deep satisfaction and no embarrassment at all.

"You see, Papa, we would not have found this out if I hadn't insisted. It does matter. Thank you, Mr. Quintana." She gave Joseph a brief but golden smile that caught him unprepared and made his pulse jump.

"I think I'll call you Joseph. I like that name. You both may call me Anna."

Chapter 4

Before dawn on the following morning, Roger, with his arms full, aroused the Quintanas from the best night's sleep they had had in weeks. They were in a comfortable upper-floor bedroom of Sir Herbert's house. The twin beds they had used were oversized and overstuffed. The sheets had been clean and fresh. The furniture was all oak, gleaming under the ceiling lights.

The night before, they had decided to keep everybody together from that time until they parted in Jerusalem. No one had objected.

While the Quintanas were in the bathroom, Roger gave a short report.

"The Hirsches are already up and dressed and waiting on you for breakfast. They've obviously done this kind of thing quite often before. I've brought you some fresh clothing I thought you would appreciate. The best I could do, considering. I hope things fit."

He dropped suits, shirts, socks, underclothes, belts, and even a pair of solid blue silk ties on the foot of their beds. They would have to wear their own rough shoes they had been wearing for weeks.

When Michael and Joseph emerged from the bathroom wrapped in towels, he said, "You chaps look better bathed and shaved, I must say. I heard she called you desert rats."

"How did you hear that?" asked Michael.

"Father told me. Sir Herbert is my father. I do this kind of thing for him now and then when he needs some secrecy. The boys at the Arab Bureau do give him one hell of a bloody time."

He picked up a leather case and placed it on the bed and opened it. Michael and Joseph looked over his shoulder as they were dressing. Michael, buttoning a shirt slightly too large, whistled in admiration. The case held two revolvers and two polished slabs of walnut, all nicely fitted in compartments lined in blue velvet.

"Yes, they are beautiful. I hope they'll do. I know you asked Sir Herbert if he could recover your Parabellums for you. Impossible. I don't even know where they are. These are automatic revolvers."

"Say that again," said Joseph, trying to get his tie right.

Roger took up one of the big revolvers.

"They cock by themselves after the first shot. Cock it by hand first. When it fires, the entire top section of the revolver recoils like this." He pointed the weapon toward the floor and pushed back on the barrel. "See. It cocks the hammer and rotates the cylinder to bring a fresh cartridge into battery. You can fire six shots rapidly and damn accurately. Then just push this lever, the weapon breaks open conventionally and ejects all six empty cases. Reload and you're armed. Very fast. Watch."

He demonstrated, ejecting live rounds onto the bed, fitting them back into the cylinder and closing the weapon with a crisp snap. "This wooden stock here fits to the butt like this,"—another demonstration with a curved flat piece of walnut taken from the case—"and the weapon is like a short rifle. Both revolvers are loaded and there's a full extra box of fifty here. These are two rapid reloaders." He held up two flat rubber discs with six holes cut around their edges. "Six rounds are held in this. When you've ejected the empties, just push the six rounds in this rubber clip into the cylinder and twist. The clip will come away and you're loaded. Very fast."

"They don't look very much like field pieces," remarked Joseph, admiring the finely checkered wooden grips, the deep plum-blue finish on the metal, and the highly grained walnut shoulder stocks.

"They're not," said Roger. "They're father's own fine target guns. But a good powerful caliber—.455. Webley-Fosberys they're called. He knew Colonel Fosbery himself. Take good care of them, will you? He's rather fond of them. So am I. It's all we could get in the short time we had. We didn't think of guns until you asked for them."

He snapped the case shut and escorted Michael and Joseph downstairs to a small dining room at the rear of the house, where the Hirsches, packed and anxious, were waiting breakfast for them.

Before they started to eat, Sir Herbert entered in a state of mild consternation. Joseph and Michael looked at each other uneasily. Their future might be taking another turn. Michael thought of the guns in the case at his knees.

But nothing happened right away. Sir Herbert greeted his guests politely and sat down. Breakfast was served by two servants who hurried in and out of the room with dishes and platters of food and pots of tea, and stood by when there was nothing for them to do.

The conversation drifted aimlessly from the weather to the food to some imaginary activity the Hirsches said they were looking forward to, like trekking out to the pyramids, and then back to the weather. Someone said it was going to be a perfect day for trekking. No one said anything about flying.

Outside, however, after breakfast, when they were on their way to the automobile, Sir Herbert took Hirsch aside and spoke to him briefly but intensely. Hirsch listened, nodded several times, and never changed his expression.

Michael was close to Joseph and Roger. "What do you think that's all about?" He and Joseph looked at Roger, who was to drive them to the airfield. Roger shrugged.

Finally the two men finished talking and shook hands. When they approached the automobile where the others were waiting, Sir Herbert was still worried, But Hirsch acted normally. Sir Herbert shook hands with everyone except Roger, wished them luck, accepted a gracious kiss from Anna, and walked briskly back to his house.

Roger drove easily through the early-morning streets. The sky was brightening and the air coming through partly opened windows smelled fresh and dry. Michael, who was sitting up front between Roger and Joseph, was growing impatient. He disliked the mystery that had developed outside the house and was about to ask for an explanation. Hirsch anticipated him and spoke first.

"We have had a change in plans."

Michael said, "We're not flying to Beit Darras?"

"Not directly," said Hirsch a little apologetically. "We never did expect to do that anyway. I'm sorry we've kept this back. Actually we were to fly to Port Said to pick up something that was being delivered there. Sir Herbert, however, received a call during the night. The package, instead, is coming to Suez by boat sometime in the next two days. Unfortunately there is reason to believe that the Arab Bureau has also gotten this piece of news. It has upset Sir Herbert, but there is nothing whatever we can do now. We have to go to Suez and wait. There is no choice in the matter."

He turned to his wife. "Nothing has changed, my dear, except
216

our route." Then, speaking to Michael and Joseph, he asked, "Will you young men have difficulty flying there and from there to Beit Darras? I have a map."

He handed a small rolled map across the backrest to Michael, who studied it briefly and passed it to Joseph.

"No," answered Michael flatly. "It won't be difficult. We've found more obscure places than Suez." He was annoyed, though. Hirsch should have confided in them last night. Suez would be easy, but he wondered what other surprises Hirsch might have for them.

Anna leaned forward and said, "I told Daddy you wouldn't need time to plan a route. I've looked at that map. If you fly northeast from Cairo you'll strike the Gulf of Suez. If you turn north you'd reach Port Said. Now, instead, all you have to do is turn south until we strike Suez. Am I right, Joseph? And the airfields are marked on the map."

A faint smile of satisfaction played at Anna's mouth.

"Well, Michael," said Joseph, nudging him with his elbow. "Out of the mouths of babes. We should let her fly navigator." They both were looking at her.

"Don't make fun of me," said Anna, making a face at Michael. Hirsch patted the air in front of his daughter. Roger twisted his head to see her. They smiled briefly at each other. Joseph was watching her, too. When Anna caught his glance she dropped her eyes briefly and then smiled up at him. He decided right then there was a difference in the way she smiled at him.

"There's just one other thing," put in Michael. "We need an aircraft that will carry us all. Have you noticed, Roger, that Joseph and I haven't yet asked you what you've got for this trip?"

"I've certainly noticed," Roger answered cheerfully. "And because you haven't asked, I've assumed you must have a motto— 'Fly one, fly them all.'"

"The hell you say," laughed Michael. "But you're right. Only I hope it's no four-engine monster."

"You'll see," said Roger. He fell silent after that and maneuvered the Austin through the ugly suburbs of the city and finally brought it onto a long, straight paved road. A mile down the road at its end, they could see the aerodrome of large hangars, a low observation tower, and a dozen unpaved landing strips. When they drove into the compound, only two or three laborers were in sight drifting toward the hangars. But the field in front of the hangars was crowded with aircraft of various designs and sizes, ranging

217

from a giant intercontinental Caproni to single-engine sports craft. Michael counted twenty machines lined up in perfect order.

When they passed by the four-engined Italian Caproni that dwarfed everything near it, Michael sighed, "I'm glad it's not that. We'd have trouble with that one."

Roger brought the Austin toward a much smaller plane parked in front of the farthest hangar. "She'll carry six people including the pilot," he explained. "She's rather new and very expensive. The best aircraft we could hire, and hire in a false name at that. She should be ready to go." He looked proud of the arrangements he had made. And he should have been. Joseph and Michael sat forward in their seats as Roger drove up and stopped.

"Holy Chirst!" Michael exclaimed.

It was not only the best aircraft Roger could hire. It was also one of the best aircraft in the world—a Dutch Fokker II, a single-engine high-wing monoplane with completely enclosed cabin, except for a single outside seat where the pilot sat between the big six cylinder in-line engine and the cabin. The Fokker had been painted a rich chocolate brown with silver lines and numbers. On its cowl were the silver letters BNEA, which Joseph guessed stood for British Near East Airlines. He envied the people who could own and charter such a ship.

Roger lingered near Anna and held her hand just long enough for Joseph to conclude he was in love with her. A touch of envy struck him when Roger kissed her cheek quietly as she stepped up along the side of the fuselage and bent to get into the cabin. She slipped a glance at Joseph to discover whether he had seen the kiss, was annoyed that he had, and then squeezed into the rattan seat next to the window on the starboard side.

Joseph went back to Michael with the air chart. The Hirsches were getting aboard. Roger was standing near the Austin on the far side of the plane to have a view of Anna through the window.

"Looks like he really likes her," observed Michael.

"That doesn't mean she feels the same, does it?" Joseph said.

"I think you like her, too," Michael said, unrolling the chart and holding it up with two hands. "I haven't seen you look at a woman like that too often."

"Let's forget it," said Joseph, annoyed that, at twenty-nine, he seemed to be letting a seventeen-year-old girl bother him by being friendly to another man. "We've got a job to do."

"Me," said Michael half-seriously, "I'd just as soon take the mother. Anna's all yours." He saw Mary Hirsch looking through the side window. He waved his hand at her and she smiled.

"Good luck," said Joseph. "I think all three of them are married to Zionism." Then he gave his full attention to the chart the Hirsches had supplied.

They made a few calculations, and Michael offered to fly the first leg to Suez. He climbed into the cockpit and checked the controls and gauges. Joseph used a short crank to wind the engine over. When it was running smoothly, he climbed into the cabin and, finding the Hirsches seated in front of Anna, he squeezed by them and pressed himself into the seat next to hers.

Almost at once Anna turned to wave to Roger and leaned slightly against him.

"Roger is a very nice boy," she said. "I like him."

"He's a fine fellow," Joseph agreed. "I like him, too. And it's easy to see how much he cares for you."

"Oh," she said and looked steadily at Joseph as though she expected him to say something else. He didn't. If Anna was disappointed that the subject of Roger was over, she didn't show it. Joseph kept looking at her, feeling a little foolish over the way she was beginning to attract him. When she took her eyes from his face, he paid attention to the takeoff and tried to get the feel of the aircraft as she moved on the ground. He would be flying it himself soon.

Michael opened the engine wider, and the Fokker rolled over the ground easily. He pushed the throttle all the way open. The aircraft lifted almost at once, rose high, dropped a few feet into a slight air pocket, making Mrs. Hirsch groan, and climbed quickly to five thousand feet.

The course they had set followed exactly the directions Anna had idly given. They headed northeast at 80 degrees, sighted the Gulf of Suez fifty minutes later, and turned south. When they landed without event at the turbulent port of Suez, the landscape was already steaming under the early sun.

Chapter 5

The airfield at Suez was hot and idle. A half-dozen hard-used small aircraft sat pegged to the ground in the open and another two or three were in open hangars where a mechanic or two tinkered with their engines. While Michael chocked the wheels of the Fokker and pegged a few lines from its wings to the ground in the fashion of the other planes, Joseph spoke to the airfield master, a middle-aged, sleepy Englishman, who took the field fees and accepted an extra two pounds for his own pocket to have the Fokker guarded.

From the airfield to the teeming street of hotels, warehouses, shops, and taverns fronting the Suez docks was a twenty-minute ride in an old, battered taxi. Despite the early hour, the waterfront swarmed with sailors and sea captains, white-suited managers and dock captains, and hundreds of dark-skinned laborers covered in rags or stripped to the waist and gleaming in sweat.

In the city, Hirsch assumed the leadership of the small group with a simple exertion of authority that seemed natural. He directed the native taxi driver to take them straight to the harbor master's office and went inside the white brick building that hung on the edge of a long wharf where it commanded a view of the gulf from both directions.

While he was gone, Anna began to point out places that interested her—a wharf crowded with men unloading a long Arab dhow, great winches working above the holds of a rusty steamer, a long row of low, dingy shops strung between hotels a few hundred yards away.

"Aren't they intriguing," she said, pointing to the shops. "Do you like to browse, Joseph?"

"When there's nothing better to do, I enjoy it," he said idly. "I've found some great junk in shops like those."

"Like that German motorcycle in Jerusalem, Joe," Michael said. "Do you know, Anna, he went out for a walk once and came back with this fantastic desert motorcycle he found in an auto-

220

mobile graveyard. We just had to take it out for a ride. You could never guess where we drove it."

Mary Hirsch, who had been watching for her husband, allowed herself to be distracted by the story. "Where did you drive it?" she asked.

Michael was pleased that she took an interest.

"To Damascus," he said, addressing her.

"All the way to Damascus?" It was Anna's voice, with a touch of wonder in it. "When was that?"

Michael and Joseph together filled in the details.

"And Lawrence knew you were Jewish, Joseph? Do you hear that, Mother. And he said that to you? 'Don't let the British take the land away from you Jews.' Oh, Joseph, I wish I had known that about him. We met him once not long ago, and I never talked to him—he seemed so . . . so aloof and cold." Anna had grown excited.

"We were probably wrong about him," said Mary Hirsch. "I'll have to tell your father."

At that moment Hirsch emerged from the brick building mopping his brow and climbed back into the crowded taxi.

"The Hotel Ixis," he told the driver in Arabic. The man nodded.

"Whew," sighed Hirsch, settling back against his wife. "It took some doing in there to get those people to work out a probable arrival for the ship. She won't be in until tomorrow. At least that's when she's expected."

The Hotel Ixis was as good a hotel as most of the places in Suez, and that meant not terribly good at all. By any standards it was third class, offering small stuffy rooms and nothing else to speak of, except a small bar on the ground floor. But the hotel was run by a Greek Jew named Kacandes who was friendly to the Zionists, although not a devoted Zionist himself. It was to his hotel that the package Hirsch wanted was to be delivered.

When Kacandes appeared from a back room there was a brief reunion with warm embraces and introductions. Hirsch had met him only once in Rome, but the two men acted like close friends. Kacandes was a short, dark, wiry man with a thick black moustache and a smile that stayed on his face. He expected the Hirsches, for he had received a wire the day before that they were coming.

Without much ado he showed them to his three best rooms on the second floor, explaining that they were his best rooms because they had thin scatter rugs on the wooden floors, two windows

221

each that allowed air to flow through, and white, ironed sheets and pillowcases on the beds.

"They will be fine," said Hirsch cheerfully, taking the room on the end. Mary Hirsch began to unpack a small bag and shake wrinkles out of some clothes.

Hirsch spoke to Anna and the Quintanas. "I'll be spending the rest of the day here. But you young people should get out in the air, look at the city, eat in a fine restaurant."

Anna looked expectantly at Joseph and Michael. Her deep green eyes sparkled. When neither Quintana jumped at the chance to join her on a little excursion, she said to her father, "I don't know that I'd care to right now, Daddy. I'll stay with you and Mother."

Joseph, giving Michael the wink, said, "We're not going to sit in that room over there, Michael, are we? Let's browse the city. And we'd better take Anna with us. She'll keep us out of trouble. At least we won't be able to pick up a lovely motorcycle."

"What do you say, Anna, come with us," teased Michael, as though he didn't know she was aching to go.

Anna glanced from one man to the other and then settled on Joseph. Her faced broke into a smile that showed she understood their little joke and accepted it. She slid one arm through Michael's and one through Joseph's.

"Joke all you want, the two of you, I'm ready to go right now."

Before they left, Hirsch privately offered Joseph some money.

"Thanks," Joseph said. "Sir Herbert was very generous. We don't need any."

Hirsch hugged Anna. "Take care of my girl, young men. She is my only one."

If the Quintanas thought they were taking Anna along with them, they soon found it was the other way around. She kept her arms hooked through theirs and led them to the places that had caught her eye. First they stopped for something to eat at one of the many wharf stands where greasy chunks of meat were dipped in a thick spicy sauce and grilled crisp over open braziers and served on thin wooden skewers. Flat baked bread, chewy and tasteless, went well with the sharp meat. Anna ate three sticks of meat and a whole flat bread before she moved on. Michael and Joseph could only manage two meats each and a single flat bread between them.

For the next hour, with the Quintanas in tow, Anna wandered from wharf to wharf, soaking in the sights of the dock workers, dark-skinned tough-looking men of many nationalities. She watched them unloading barges and dhows and cutters, jabbering and smoking and taking long pulls at small beer bottles. Everywhere Anna went she spoke at least a few words to the stevedores in a variety of languages—French, German, Italian, Arabic, English—a knowledge that awed the Quintanas, until she satisfied herself as to where the boats had come from and what they were carrying and who the workers themselves were. The stevedores eyed her body and spoke freely to her. The blacks spoke softly and answered her questions, but from the whites she got unexpected compliments and a few vulgar invitations. The presence of Joseph and Michael on either side of her inhibited very few of them. Often Anna understood their words and wondered what Joseph and Michael would do if they understood too. After awhile she found out. A few rough-looking workers who spoke Italian to her dropped their loads without warning and ambled over toward her, making their propositions physically vivid. Words weren't necessary to know what they meant. Michael and Joseph were spared a brawl only when Anna, making a joke in Italian that set the stevedores laughing, dragged her companions away.

Anna wondered aloud how all these homeless men from distant countries wound up here in the port of Suez, wearing their bodies and hearts out under the constant stream of orders mixed with curses flowing from the dock managers.

Neither Michael nor Joseph had any answers. The lighter side of Anna came as a revelation to them. For his part, Michael did not really care whether Anna came as a revelation to them. For his part, Michael did not really care whether Anna was a simple-minded idealist with limited interests or a complex woman of many tastes. The kind of woman she appeared to be now was more fun to be with. He enjoyed her. He thought Joseph was even more pleased to discover this different side of Anna.

For Joseph it meant a great deal. He had worried about getting entangled with a joyless woman dedicated to a cause—and nothing more. That wasn't the kind of woman he had ever dreamed about. And Anna had shown she wasn't that kind. Her smiles had hinted of a warmer person behind the somber face, but her devotion to her parents, their acceptance of her almost as their comrade, her background and upbringing—as little as Joseph knew of them— had warned him that she might really be no more than a dyed-in-the-wool Zionist. And as he had wondered how smart it was to fall for a girl like Anna, he had found now that it was going to be all right.

This exuberant side of Anna, quiet but strong, was a near balance to her sober moods. As he went along with her toward the row of grimy shops along the waterfront, he let his heart soar.

Before they went into the first shop that had its door open to the crowds on the street, Anna paused and looked toward the docks where the stevedores were all back to work. She had grown somber.

"Do you know that most of those men are not Egyptians. They have no homeland, their nationality has disappeared. They're just tolerated here for their cheap labor. They get washed from port to port like driftwood. To change that condition for our own people, Joseph, that's why my parents are going to Jerusalem. That is the work I shall have to do."

"Good," said Joseph, trying to keep things lighthearted for the time being. "But do you have to do it right now? I thought we were here to browse and enjoy ourselves."

"Come on," Anna said, smiling and entered the dark, musty shop. "I feel so good. I want to buy you both something you can remember me by."

They went from shop to shop, fingering their way through goods of quality and stuff that was junk, wares that came from all over the East—leather from Morocco, copper from Turkey, gold from South Africa, ivory from the Congo, wool from India, brass and silver from Egypt and Syria. In a hundred different forms from jewelry and cutlery to rugs and clothing—useful and decorative—the goods loaded the shelves and filled the cases and made all the shops seem alike.

Anna picked things up and put them down and found nothing to pause over more than a moment, until they were in the fourth shop. Smaller than the others, it displayed more silver and gold. She was moving slowly along a wall when she suddenly reached up and from a peg took a long necklace of hand-carved solid silver beads, each about the size of a large pea and no two exactly alike. A tiny hole had been drilled through each silver nugget and a fine but strong piece of catgut had been strung through them.

Anna ran her fingers over the beads and then spoke to the shopkeeper, an old, shriveled Syrian merchant who smiled toothlessly and almost simplemindedly at her throughout their brief bargaining. The figure they finally agreed on, fifteen pounds English, was exactly halfway between what the Syrian asked for and

Anna had offered. As soon as the sale was completed, Anna found two small soft leather pouches about the size of her palm and bought them the same way.

"May I have a knife," she asked the old man.

When he produced a sharp-edged dagger, she cleared a place on a table, cut the catgut, and spread the silver beads on the table. Then she cut the catgut into two pieces and counted some of the beads and carefully restrung them on a piece of the catgut, tied it, and placed the smaller necklace, more like a bracelet now, into one of the bags.

Joseph and Michael and the shopkeeper stood by curiously, watching her throughout the operation.

"What's it all about?" Michael asked.

"Shhh," said Anna, holding one finger to her lips as she began to count again. Out of the second group of beads she made another necklace for the second pouch. There were four beads left. She slipped them loose into her purse.

Outside the shop she handed each Quintana a pouch. "Inside are eighteen pieces of silver," she explained. "Eighteen in the Hebrew alphabet is *chai*, and *chai* means *life*. So it is an ancient custom with us Jews to give those we wish a long life eighteen pieces of . . . anything. Silver I thought was very nice. I was looking for ivory."

Touched deeply, Joseph tossed his pouch gently in his hand as though he were weighing the silver and the sentiment. Then he bent suddenly and kissed Anna's cheek. Michael followed his example, and under a sinking sun they started back to the Hotel Ixis.

Later that evening, after having observed his daughter at dinner, Hirsch turned to his wife in their room and said, "Anna seems unusually happy, did you notice?"

Mary Hirsch slipped out of her dress and climbed into bed. "It's happening, Edouard. She's reached the point in her life when it can come so easily. It happened like this to us—and I was younger. Joseph, isn't it?"

Hirsch got into bed and held his wife.

"Yes, I think it is Joseph. And I think he loves her, too. Have you noticed how he looks at her?"

"They're both quite nice. Michael has a better face. Do you think she is attracted to Joseph only because he is Jewish?"

"Partly. He's quieter, more serious. Much older than Anna."

"Anna needs an older man. She's like me."

225

Hirsch kissed his wife.

"I hope he finds out more about Anna before he gets too deep with her. There's Palestine in Anna's life, Mary."

"Yes," said Mary Hirsch, kissing her husband warmly and burying her face in his neck as he began to make love to her. "I know. But there is the love that can overcome everything. Palestine was in your life, too, when I met you. And I am still here."

Jesse murmured.

"What did you say, Jesse?" asked Anna.

"Just that I should have given them back. The silver beads. Dad gave me his pouch of beads when I went into the Air Corps. He told me to carry them whenever I flew. I thought they had something to do with the sky demons he and Uncle Joe used to joke about. Anyway, I carried them. I should have given them back when I came home."

"We both should have, Jesse," Lilli put in. "I begged Dad for his when Jesse got Michael's. I wore mine often, Anna . . ." She turned her face, filled with pain, toward her mother. "They might be alive yet if—"

"Nonsense, child," Anna said firmly. "That's nonsense. An old Jewish superstition. They save nobody."

Chapter 6

The *Il Capri* docked in the noonday heat opposite the outdoor café where Hirsch decided to wait. Among the passengers disembarking was a middle-aged bearded man who hurried across the road when Hirsch stood and waved. The man held onto his suitcase as he greeted Hirsch, but dropped a leather portfolio onto a chair. He embraced Hirsch and Mary warmly, kissed Anna's cheek, and shook hands with the Quintanas. Then, without further talk, he walked down the road away from them, carrying his suitcase and leaving the portfolio behind.

Hirsch picked up the portfolio, opened it to finger the contents, and said confidently, "We can go now. It's all here—the documents and the money. Teddy has never failed us." He circled his wife's waist with an arm, clutching the black portfolio with his other hand. "Tonight, Mary, we will be in Jerusalem."

"*Az m'vit leben,*" Mary Hirsch said.

Joseph smiled to himself at the sound of those words.

They wasted no time leaving Suez, and within an hour were climbing out of the same battered taxi in front of the Fokker airplane. In the early afternoon the airfield appeared listlessly inactive. The weather had grown very hot and dry and almost windless. A faint ground breeze stirred the dust on the landing strips. The mechanics who had been inside the hangar yesterday were now poking into the engine of a plane out in the open. They stopped the little they were doing to watch the Quintanas and the Hirsches.

A gang of half-naked Arab children were running around the aircraft parked near the hangars. Occasionally somebody chased them away by throwing a stone. A handful of people were waiting to climb aboard a large converted bomber that wasn't there yesterday, which would fly them somewhere far off. The only activity came from one or two small aircraft running their motors preparing to take off.

Quickly Michael and Joseph went over the Fokker, checking the engine, the controls, the landing gear. Nothing had been

227

touched. Michael noticed a small fresh oil spot in the dirt under the fuselage and checked the oil reservoir. It was full. He reexamined the engine gaskets and found them tight and dry. The airfield master was nowhere in sight. The mechanics across the field were still looking at him.

"Everything looks good," Michael said to Joseph, who was already at the controls. He cranked the engine and hoisted himself into the cabin and sat next to Anna. Joseph taxied the Fokker onto a landing strip. He rechecked his instruments, remarking to himself that the fuel gauge had not dropped at all during the short hop from Cairo, and gave his attention to the sweet hum of the in-line six.

A half hour later, flying over the Sinai, he regretted not having paid more attention to the fuel gauge. A plug began to go.

Almost imperceptibly it began to miss. It came as a faint flutter without loss of power. Joseph thought at first he was imagining it. Minutes later, though, he leaned forward and up into the wind blast and laid his head down onto the cowling. He heard it clearly.

He dropped the engine speed and then opened the throttle quickly to clear the plug.

It worsened. The spluttering grew clearer.

The windscreen behind him opened and Michael leaned over his shoulder.

"What?" he shouted.

"What did the fuel gauge read when we landed?"

"Slightly less than full," Michael shouted.

"Damn. It was full when we took off."

"Rotten. Listen. One plug is fouled. I think there's another one going."

They were shouting into each other's ear.

"Can you land her?"

"Find me a place."

Michael ducked back inside. "We're going to have to land. See those belts on your seats? Strap them over your hips as tight as you can."

He saw no panic in the faces of any of the Hirsches. There was hardly a sign of fear. The three of them fixed the belts across their laps, sat straight, and gripped the sides of the seats as though they had decided they were going to live through whatever happened.

Hirsch, tight-lipped and grim, asked simply, "What's happened?"

"Somebody back there sabotaged the engine."

Hirsch nodded. It was what he had expected. His face was tight with anger. He clutched the leather portfolio against his chest with one hand and embraced Mary Hirsch with the other.

Anna leaned foward. "Tell Joseph I know he can land us safely."

Michael thrust half his body through the open windscreen until he was practically at Joseph's side. The airstream pounded his face and made him squint. Joseph was wearing the only leather helmet and goggles they had taken.

"How are they?" Joseph shouted.

"Fine. None better. As though they had done this a dozen times. Either damned optimists or plain dumb. Anna knows you're going to land her safe. That's more than I know, unless we find a piece of level hard ground."

They were flying over the desert. Joseph was scanning the rough, rocky terrain to his left, Michael was searching to the right.

The third plug began to sputter and the Fokker lost altitude. The land below was broken and creviced. Whenever a flat stretch of ground appeared, it was freckled with too many rocks for a landing. Way off to the left Joseph sighted a tribe of Bedouin on the move. He did some fast thinking.

He had to take chances. One was that the Bedouins would not be unfriendly if he landed near them. Another was that they might be moving on easier, flatter ground than he had observed before or could see now. He might land without a crash. His final thought was that if they did flop badly, it would be better to do it where somebody could reach them. Either way—flop badly or land safely—they were going to be a long way from anywhere, and the Negev would be a furnace. They had no food and only a few small fresh-water bags Michael had stowed aboard. They were not very well prepared for any kind of desert trek.

His thoughts took as long as two bats of his eye.

"Michael, check that Bedouin." He pointed vigorously. "What do you think?"

The Fokker was dropping faster as the engine petered out.

Instantly, Michael reached the same decision.

"It's our best chance—if they're not just bandits."

The last cylinder began to sputter.

"It's our only chance. Here goes."

Joseph banked the aircraft to bring her around directly toward the distant travelers. They had a bit of luck as the engine caught for a few minutes in a burst, and the propeller revolutions increased and gave Joseph a chance to gain a few hundred feet of altitude Then as the cylinders failed badly, he cut the ignition and feathered the propeller to put the Fokker into a long, slow glide.

A lovely silence fell around the two men marred only by the low whistle of the wind slipping by them.

"Get into a seat, Michael," Joseph said. "I think I've got the spot."

Michael strapped himself in tightly next to Anna.

"It's going to be okay," he said. "There's a flat-bottom wadi down there I think we can reach."

That's what Joseph had sighted. The Bedouins were traveling on camel and horse, pushing their small herds of sheep and goats ahead of them along a wide dry river bottom. As Joseph dropped lower he could see that the floor was pimpled with small pebbles, marred here and there by a larger, deadly boulder.

A few yards beyond the lead sheep he thought the wadi was flatter and the pebbles smaller than anything else he could see.

He brought her in quietly over the heads of the Bedouins, who were gazing up at him unexcitedly. He passed a good twenty-five feet above them and dropped the Fokker twenty or thirty feet in front of the flock. The sheep stopped dead in their tracks and stared at what had fallen from the sky and was blocking their path.

The Fokker's wheels struck the river bottom, rolled for a few feet, jounced lightly over the small stones, and then got caught by the left tire in a shallow gully, twisting the plane to the left, swinging the right wheel sharply around. Directly in its path on that side was a boulder as large as the wheel itself.

There was a sharp jolt, a ripping screech, and the Fokker danced around its right wheel. The pneumatic tire collapsed, the landing strut snapped, and the Fokker came to a half-leaning stop over to the right like a crippled bird.

"They're on their way over," Joseph warned. "Everybody out the right side."

He climbed out quickly and slid off the fuselage where there were no steps to use. When everybody was out, he moved the Hirsches toward the rear of the fuselage where they were partly concealed from the Bedouins who were riding up.

Joseph already had the shoulder stock fixed to his Webley. He held it down against his side. Michael was carrying his weapon out of sight under his coat. He was out front of the Fokker near its engine.

Hirsch called to him. "Do you speak Arabic, Mr. Quintana? I do."

Hirsch joined Michael, without protest from anyone.

What appeared to be every male member of the tribe rode up through the scraggly herd of animals and formed a line across the wadi facing the Fokker. Behind the animals a few unmounted figures in full veils remained with a half-dozen baggage camels.

The tribe was very small. Michael's quick count was fourteen.

"Fifteen," Hirsch said. "There's one around to Joseph's side."

There was nothing friendly about them, but they kept their ancient muskets slung across their backs. That meant nothing, certainly not that they were amiable. Michael remembered how fast a Berber could unsling his weapon and fire it in one swift graceful move. He watched the man directly opposite him carefully.

Their face cloths covered them to the eyes and they glared sullenly at Michael and Hirsch, at the Fokker, and at Joseph and the two women. No one spoke. Some animals brayed and shifted their positions nervously and stirred up some dust.

Hirsch spoke first. He spoke in Arabic and at some length, addressing the men directly to his front. Whatever he said broke the staring match and the tension. The riders talked to each other and one of them tapped his camel's flank with his prod and the animal kneeled at once. The rider slid off and strode toward Hirsch. He spoke heartily to him and held out his hand. Soon the others were off their camels and horses and going up to the Fokker, poking around, touching it, peering inside, mumbling surprises when something moved.

"What did you tell them?" Michael asked.

"The truth. What kind of lie could I make up. I told him I come from Europe with letters of importance from Prince Faisal to the Moslem leaders in Jerusalem, Sheikh Jurallah, Sheikh Assal. I even mentioned el-Husseini and his supporter, Aref el-Aref. The chieftain—he's the one over there—look, he's just dropped his face cloth. He's got the gray beard. He was impressed. He's a Hashemite follower of Faisal, and my knowing those names tickled him."

Michael called to Joseph that things seemed to be all right. Joseph casually balanced the Webley over a shoulder, keeping his hand loosely on the butt, and led the Hirsch women out from behind the Fokker. The Bedouin men quieted as they saw the women.

Hirsch spoke again to the chieftain, straightforward as before, confident, amicable, dignified. The Bedouin men listened, grunted, seemed to lose interest in them, and, with the exception of the chieftain, who knew his manners, drifted back to their own women and children, watching a few hundred feet away. The chieftain spoke to Hirsch and gestured for them to follow him. Then he, too, went back to join his tribesmen.

"Come along," said Hirsch. "I think we can get them to help us. Can the machine be repaired?"

"Not by us," Joseph said. "We need clean fuel and a new landing gear."

"Then we certainly need their help," Hirsch said, leading the party through the small flock of sheep to where the Bedouins were gathered. "Now listen carefully and act accordingly. I told them that Mary and Anna are my wife and daughter. And, Michael, I must apologize to you, I did think up a lie. I told them you are my son and that Joseph"—he looked over at Anna, who nodded slightly—"is my son-in-law. I thought it wise to provide her with a husband." He shrugged his shoulders at Joseph. "If they turn out to be bandits, that won't matter, but I don't think they are. They will respect that she has a husband already in Joseph. That will keep them from trying to buy her from me. Right now we are invited to join the chieftain at his midday meal."

Joseph ambled over to Anna smiling, tossed an arm around her, and said, "I'd better act like a husband, then."

Small open tents had been set up for protection against the brutal sun. As the Hirsches and Quintanas prepared to set themselves on thick worn carpets, Hirsch said, "We had good luck earlier today and it seems mixed now. We'll see how far this sheikh—his name is el-Ayribi—will go."

Chapter 7

The Bedouin sheikh proved willing to go very far. At the risk of being impolite, Joseph and Michael spent part of their meal studying their chart to work out how much they could ask from him.

There were two choices.

"We're right here, eighty or ninety miles from Beit Darras," said Joseph, referring to the map. "And we're thirty-odd miles from El Arish. There's a railroad passing through there that could take us within five miles of Beit Darras."

"The railroad is run by the British," Hirsch said unhappily. "Can we take the chance that Storrs and his bunch have not got their Arab Bureau people watching the trains for us? They know we're here and suspect what we are carrying. I'm certain of it. Can we get on the train in the middle of nowhere without being noticed by one of their agents? Can we get off where we want to?"

Joseph asked a few questions about how well the Hirsches could ride horses. Fairly well, but not well enough to ride eighty miles in two days through empty rough terrain under a desert sun. Joseph and Michael were not sure whether they could do that either. That settled that.

The meal of lamb and rice was nearly finished.

Michael, nodding his head toward their Arab host, said, "We're not going any place without this fellow's help."

"All right," said Hirsch. "Let's see what I can do."

He spoke heatedly with Sheikh el-Ayribi, each man smiling and growing serious and smiling again. The two men rose and went outside and strolled toward the Fokker, talking energetically, using their hands, alternating between smiles and sober faces.

Watching them from the opening of the black tent, Anna said to Joseph and Michael standing behind her, "I think he has him. They're bargaining very congenially."

When they returned, Hirsch beamed. "He'll give us what we need—good horses, suitable clothing, food and water, and two

233

guides who know the country. Whichever route we take will not matter. And for tonight, he's offered us two tents." He glanced at Anna, who was leaning against Joseph. "I told him that for a single night one tent would be more than hospitable."

"That's fine, my dear," said Mary Hirsch in a voice that said she expected no less from him. "What did you give him?"

Hirsch looked at Joseph and Michael and shrugged.

"What else! I gave him the aeroplane."

Before daybreak the next morning, with two young Bedouin guides out in front, the Hirsches next, and Joseph and Michael in the rear, the small party of horsemen rode away from Sheikh el-Ayribi's camp. They were heading north to the rail line at El Arish.

Behind them in the dawn light, they could see the Bedouin men scrambling around the Fokker, rigging a rope to its tail, preparing to drag it off down the wadi behind a half-dozen camels harnessed to it. Michael and Joseph soon lost sight of the plane and its new owners, but they could hear someone cranking the starter that Michael had demonstrated for the sheikh the evening before. The engine coughed, caught, sputtered, and died. Again and again the starter was cranked and the sick sputtering sound flooded over the sands, until they had covered so much ground they could hear it no more.

Everybody was dressed for the difficult ride. Against saddle burns the women had been given men's baggy trousers to wear under their dresses. Over their dresses, covering their heads and bodies, they wore the same light, loose desert robes the men had been given to protect them from the sun. The horses they were riding were all well-broken Arabian mares.

When Joseph looked up toward the Hirsches thirty feet away he thought he was looking at three Arabs—until he compared their rather jerky seat in the saddle to the fine rhythm that blended the Bedouins and their animals into a single movement.

At first the Bedouins kept to a slow pace in consideration of the women. Their horses picked their way carefully across gray pebbley-strewn plains and rocky slopes and through soft stretches of whitened sand deserts. They kept single file and had little opportunity to talk. As the sun rose and the temperature soared, no one minded riding silently hidden in his own thoughts. The only noise in the air was the clatter of the horses' hooves on the flinty rock or their soft swish passing over shifting sand.

Two hours passed. The lead guide called out to the party. Hirsch dropped back to the Quintanas and translated.

"He wants us to keep watch for any riders. Last night el-Ayribi said that bandits have been very active up here in the northern Sinai. Raiders. Disappointed chieftains whom the French and English have betrayed—failed to restore their power when the Turk was driven out. They've taken to banditry and even slavery. He wants us to be careful."

When Hirsch went back to his wife, Michael dug out his Webley-Fosbery and fixed the shoulder stock to it. "Obliging with information, isn't he?" he said.

Joseph, who was thinking only of Anna, did not answer.

The Bedouin guides increased their speed, trotting their animals whenever the ground was right. No one fell back.

Joseph's attraction for Anna grew. He watched her adapt to the saddle, handling her horse smoothly, following every move of the Bedouins to her front. The earlier jerking movement in her posting faded as she caught the rhythm of the horse's gait. More and more she looked like a skillful Arab as the miles fell behind them.

Mary Hirsch was having a harder time, but she did not falter or ask for a rest. Her strong figure continued to jar out of harmony with her animal. Every now and then she pressed a hand to her lower back and stretched her body straight to ease the pain. If her husband, who was not doing much better, rode up to her solicitously, she waved him back and kicked her horse a little harder.

Michael and Joseph were holding out well. They had ridden considerably with el-Krim, and their general fitness had not been ruined by their weeks in jail. Michael was a little stronger, a little more flamboyant in his saddle, at times making his gray Arabian prance. Anna watched him from the corner of her eye and then glanced back at Joseph and knew which she preferred.

Joseph rode last. He admired Michael's flair, but he kept his horse steady. When he saw Anna twist around to look at him, he waved his hand. Anna waved back and kicked her horse forward.

Toward midmorning they struck a difficult stretch of sand desert that made their horses rear and twist to get through soft spots. The skills and strength of all riders were strained to control the animals. For what dragged on like hours—although it was more like thirty minutes—they navigated the low dunes and finally came down onto a flat, easy hard surface. Hirsch caught up to the lead Bedouin and spoke a few words. Then he dropped back to his wife, who showed signs of exhaustion.

"Not much farther, Mary. He says we've covered more than two-thirds the distance. But he won't rest. They're anxious to get us to the rail line and to return to their people."

"I'll be fine, Edouard." When she looked up the trail, she pointed. "Something's happened, Edouard. Look. They're stopping."

The Bedouin guides had dismounted and were walking off to the left.

"Get down and rest, Mary," said Hirsch, dismounting.

"I'm afraid I won't get back up if I do."

"Nonsense. Come, my dear," He reached up and helped her swing off. She sighed as her feet touched the ground and she took a few steps. Anna came up and dismounted easily and rubbed her buttocks and stretched her body.

Across the plain less than three hundred feet away the Bedouins were cautiously approaching several scattered clumps of rags that broke the flat surface of the ground. Joseph and Michael galloped up to the Hirsches and dismounted. The men watched the Bedouins crouch and examine whatever was lying out there.

Soon the Bedouins were racing back toward them. Excitedly, they ordered everyone to mount, using gestures to make Joseph and Michael understand them. As they waited nervously for Mary Hirsch to be helped up, they began to talk loudly to Hirsch, pointing to the rag bundles out on the plain, describing what they had seen.

Suddenly Hirsch held his hand up and spoke to them imploringly, shaking his head against what they were saying, waving his hand in front of him like a fan to repel their words. But the Bedouins continued to talk heatedly, making what seemed to the Quintanas to be obscene gestures.

"Oh, no, stop it!" cried Anna in English. Then, in the same tones of anguish, she was shouting at them in Arabic.

Mary Hirsch was shaken. She turned her head and, holding her saddle with one hand, bent sideways and threw up.

The guides became more excited. They pointed to the west, beyond the piles of rags they had examined, pointed to the north and again spoke urgently.

"Take some water, Mary," said Hirsch, offering his wife a small water goatskin. She rinsed her mouth out, gargled, spit, and then swallowed a second mouthful.

"Thank you, Edouard. That was very foolish of me. I'm all right now. We had better go or they'll leave us."

The guides were pacing their horses restlessly in circles a few feet away, as though they were making up their minds about which direction to go. When everybody was mounted, they struck off for the north.

Joseph rode beside Anna now, behind the Hirsches, feeling she needed him. But she said nothing and rode grimly, keeping her face straight ahead.

Michael was more curious than Joseph. Waiting to come up last, he galloped his horse over the plain toward the bundles of rags. The bundles turned out to be three dead Arabs fully clothed, sprawled on their backs. More curious than ever, Michael rode up closer. There was no blood on the clothes, no sign of violence on the bodies, yet their faces were twisted into terrible grins of death, lips curled back over the teeth and skins turning black under the sun. Flies crowded the air wherever flesh showed.

Around the bodies were the clear hoofprints of many horses. Michael circled the bodies and followed the prints until he could see they were leading away to the west. There was nothing out there to the horizon.

As he rode back to the party, one of the guides called out to him.

"What did he say, Anna?" Michael asked.

"Nothing. Something horrible. Please, let's not talk about it."

"Three dead men out there, Joe. Lots of horse signs. The ground's all trampled. But nothing else. Is that what makes your mother sick?"

"Forget it, Anna," said Joseph. "Whatever it is, don't think about it." He shook his head at Michael and shrugged. He did not understand what had happened any more than Michael.

For the next fifteen minutes a silence prevailed, more oppressive than it had been earlier. They rode in pairs now, the Bedouins farther up front than before, the Hirsches, Joseph and Anna, and then Michael. The Bedouins and the Hirsches seemed bent under the weight of thought. The pace the Bedouins set was faster.

Unexpectedly, Anna broke the silence and spoke swiftly and softly to Joseph.

"Mother is no weakling, Joseph," she began, looking across him from the corner of her eye. Then she fastened her eyes on the backs of the Bedouins who had grown smaller in the distance. "She has seen death before, we all have. Not what you've probably

237

seen, I know, but enough. Yet it was never so horrible as what those Bedouins described."

"Forget it, then," said Joseph. "Put it out of your mind."

"I can't. I've got to tell you. The way those Arabs were killed. A pistol barrel—inserted into their anuses and a bullet fired up into their bowels. Oh, God, what men can think of. The guide said some of the tribes do that to kill their victims without leaving a sign of violence. Oh, Joseph." A shudder of fear and revulsion shook Anna.

Joseph leaned over and squeezed her hand on the pommel. There was nothing to say.

Michael, who was riding to the rear, saw Joseph's gesture and was happy that his friend had found Anna. They both knew the time would come for settling down, and though they had postponed it, they had accepted its coming. Whenever they had been with women, they had talked of falling in love and what it would mean for the Quintana Brother Aces. They could not be certain, but they had once sworn an oath that it would mean little. But then again, Michael thought, they had been much younger. He rode after the pair of lovers silently.

Chapter 8

From two miles away they saw the black smoke of the train in El Arish. The Bedouins halted on a slight rise on the plain.

"We've got to hurry," cried Hirsch, waving his arm to those in the rear, "or we'll miss it." He spurred his horse forward, but one of the Bedouins drove his own horse to his front and blocked him. Startled, Hirsch's animal shied and came up off its front legs. Hirsch controlled him well.

Hirsch's round face looked hurt and puzzled. He exchanged some words with the Bedouins in a friendly but perplexed voice. The words grew louder. Hirsch's redness deepened. He spoke angrily. The Bedouin shook his head obstinately.

"This is as far as they will go," Hirsch said to Joseph, who had come to his side. "They want their horses now. Here. I don't intend to give them up. The train is down there. Will you please make yourself ready for trouble."

Hirsch seemed to relax. He reached under his robes and held out some coins to the Bedouins and spoke again. He kept glancing toward the column of black smoke in the distance. The Bedouin shook his head and spoke more harshly. Hirsch thrust his hand back under his robes. When he brought it out again it was clutching a tiny Mauser pistol. The sight of the weapon in Hirsch's hand startled the Quintanas. It was unexpected and strange. Hirsch pointed it at the Bedouin closer to him. He spoke again, curtly, in a way Joseph did not think him capable of.

The Bedouin smirked at the insignificant weapon, laughed, and started to swing his musket from behind his back. Before the strap cleared his head, Joseph's big Webley was sticking in his face. Michael was already covering the second Bedouin.

"Tell them to drop their muskets," said Michael.

When the muskets were on the ground and the intentions of the party understood, they all galloped toward the village and the train—the Bedouins again in front, Michael and Joseph right behind him, with their Webleys out, and the Hirsches in the rear.

Halfway to the village, they saw the steady column of black smoke change abruptly into large intermittent puffs.

"She's leaving!" shouted Hirsch. "Can we catch her?"

"Hold it," Joseph called out, drawing the reins of his horse. "Look."

The puffs were moving slowly to their left, to Egypt.

Almost simultaneously everyone, including the Bedouins, slowed their horses. The guides started to drift back to them. Joseph waved his revolver and they turned and continued toward the town.

El Arish was a small, bustling village growing out at both ends along the coast. Dozens of recently built, whitewashed mud-and-stone cottages were strung out parallel to the sea and the rail line. A cluster of older, badly weathered buildings and huts were jammed tightly around the rail stop, as though it were their source of nourishment to stay alive. Stockades facing the desert penned large herds of animals. Three great water towers rose above the rooftops of dilapidated buildings.

When the Hirsch party reached the outlying animal pens filled with sheep, goats, camels, and horses, Hirsch asked the Quintanas to put away their guns. He dismounted and quickly ran to help his wife, who sat dizzily in her saddle. The Bedouins sullenly remained on their horses. He spoke to them congenially, gave them the coins he had offered before, and with Michael's help gathered the five horses they had ridden. Anna and Mrs. Hirsch spoke their thanks, and Joseph and Michael held out their hands which they took after a moment of reluctance. Then, with their horses trailing behind them and smiling to show they had no bad feelings, the Bedouins slowly began their trek back into the waste land of the desert.

At the train stop, which consisted of nothing more than a wooden platform raised two feet above the ground opposite the water tanks, the Hirsches learned that the train east had been through for that day. Another eastbound was due midmorning on the next day.

They also learned there was only one Englishman in El Arish representing civil authority, and only one place to stay overnight. That was a solitary bistro in the town's main souk, called Cairo's Delight. It served as night club, restaurant, and bar, and had upstairs rooms, most of which were rented to ladies of the town.

When Hirsch heard this description from the villager who spoke

240

to them, he said to his wife, "I'm afraid, my dear, we're going to spend the night in a bawdy house."

Without batting an eye, Mary said, "We've spent nights in worse places, Edouard. You recall a fancy mansion in Zurich? It was filled with a fancy pack of liars. At least here the people may be honest."

Hirsch glowed and kissed his wife and embraced her with one arm. "Is it a wonder, Mary, why I love you as I do? What I make you put up with, and how you take it so well! With anybody else—who knows?"

Cairo's Delight was run by an Egyptian named Abd-el-Masri, a short, heavy, pleasant man, who gave them a warm welcome, a generous, surprisingly well-prepared meal of chicken stew and vegetables—and agreed beforehand to have the chicken's throat cut rather than wrung when it was to be killed. When Hirsch asked this favor, el-Masri took his hand and called them "fellow Semites." Better than the English.

The rooms he offered afterwards were what they had expected: crudely furnished, hot and insect-infested, and noisily located directly above the bistro with very thin partitioning walls. Good enough to sleep in, if you were thoroughly exhausted, but not the place to make first love to a girl you thought you were falling in love with, especially not when you found her a virgin.

That, anyway, was how Joseph felt later that night when he left Michael alone at their table downstairs, drinking and enjoying the town's two favorite belly dancers, and went upstairs to Anna's room.

Anna was awake, unable to sleep. The Hirsches were in the next room. Their voices and movements were coming clearly through the walls, competing with the music of the belly dancers downstairs.

Without a word, Anna rose and greeted Joseph by folding herself into his arms and kissing him warmly on the mouth. The kiss lingered, their lips clung together. When it ended, their embrace held. They kissed again and Anna consented. They whispered their love for each other, confessing things like their belief they had never felt this way toward anyone—he believing her for her innocence and youth, she not really believing him for his age and experience, but not really caring, knowing he loved her now. They clung to each other tightly.

Her consent was not in words but in the way she moved under

his caress. Joseph did not know how to love a woman without a caress. His movements were unpremeditated. He touched Anna's breasts instinctively, through her dress and then underneath.

As he caressed her standing against the wall, they could hear her parents in the next room as though no wall were there at all. The noises they heard were unmistakable, the bed going, the sighs and light moans.

"I don't mind that," whispered Anna against Joseph's ear. "They love each other more than any other people I know. They make love every chance they have. I've heard them often. It's beautiful, isn't it. The Talmud says they should. I've grown up in the same room with them and they know I know. And there is no shame in it." She circled his neck with her arm and tightened their embrace.

She opened her legs a bit when his hand moved up under the hem of her garment. Her underclothes were gone, her body was moist. At his touch her heart thudded, her legs shook, almost buckling under her. When she stifled a groan at his finger's first gentle probe proving a vigin's tightness, he knew with some shame that he had let himself be deceived about her age by the force of her character and the ripeness of her figure. She was seventeen, untouched, still a girl-child. And yet ...

He took his hand away. The love and desire were still there, flowing from her to him and back again. The room was musty, unhealthy. It was all right for the Hirsches, who had prepared her well for this moment. But tonight—it was no place for Anna.

"Come outside?" he asked.

Under a black sky shot full of millions of stars, Anna and Joseph undressed near the darkened edge of the village and became lovers. The air had grown chilly, even here at the side of the warm Mediterranean, but in each other's arms Joseph and Anna found warmth enough.

For these few precious minutes that can come only once in a girl's life when she takes her first lover, the world around Anna faded into oblivion. The chilly air, the hard damp ground, the yesterday of Cairo, Suez, and the plane crash, the desert trek of today, and tomorrow—a train ride to an automobile and then a dash to Jerusalem—yes, all of it, even Anna's cause, sank out of her mind beneath the passion of their love.

With each touch Joseph grew more tender and selfless than he had ever been. His concern was only for her. The women he had known before Anna had given him fleeting experiences, moments

242

of pleasure, hours of friendship, hardly more than weeks of acquaintance. He had liked them all, been good to every one, loved a few. Although some may have loved him in return, none had drawn anything like what he was feeling for Anna. None had been this young, none had been a virgin, none had relied so fully on his care.

For Anna now in the pale light of the stars, he controlled his passion. He delayed. He sought to make her ready. He kissed her wherever his hands had been, seeking through the kiss, the oral caress, a sweeter surer way to Anna's happiness. From the inside of her thigh to the nape of her neck Joseph missed nothing, tasted everything, felt Anna's responses, savored them, salty, warm, and growing ready. Patiently he waited for her readiness, for readiness, he knew, was everything.

When she cried for him softly and took him, she spanning, he diving, she felt no pain, he no guilt. He entered gliding, without force, sailing and soaring, climbing home, then diving once again. Beneath him Anna felt the rapture of being loved. She grew complete through the loss of her innocence. Deflowered, she blossomed. She came. In her mind she gripped Joseph. She came again, like nothing she had ever known by herself. Then, suddenly, he was leaving her, going, flying in fear of concern for her, then gone, leaving her empty. She felt his own warmth splash on her skin across her belly and her thigh.

The scene had flowed through Anna's mind in all the vividness of reliving the mind can evoke. As she told it, however, to Jesse and her daughter Lilli, the words were simpler and the scene veiled. She said it all in a little line.

"It was in that little nondescript Arab village of El Arish near the Mediterranean that Joseph and I, that evening, first became lovers and that I felt myself grown up into a woman. A little young, you think, having just reached seventeen?"

Lilli thought of her own delays and hesitations and shook her head.

"He was good to you, then?" she asked.

"As good as a man could ever be to a woman, my dear daughter," answered Anna. "And never changed for as long as I knew him. I never regretted not waiting. There was too much happening in those days to wait."

Chapter 9

In the early morning darkness Joseph, restless with joy, left Anna sleeping in her room and strolled alone out into the desert behind the town.

On the plains of the Near East, although darkness comes fast, it seldom comes under a sky cover of clouds than can blacken the land as it can, say at an aerodrome in France or on a field outside of Boston. Sometimes in those places you really cannot see the hand held out before the face.

Over the deserts of the world there are always the stars, and when the moon is in phase, the land below is no darker than a bleak day in some wetter climate. Tonight the moon was only a thin silver crescent. Forty feet away a person could be seen as something of a blur, but he could be seen.

Before he had gone more than a hundred yards, he heard someone behind him, and then a voice carried over the sand.

"Joseph, a word with you, please." It was Edouard Hirsch.

"Sure," said Joseph, stopping for him, thinking of what he would say if Anna's father spoke about them. *You must understand, Mr. Hirsch, my intentions are honorable. I mean no harm to your daughter. I know she's terribly young, and I'm much older, but that should not matter to a girl like Anna.*

It sounded foolish to him.

"It is about Anna," Hirsch began.

"Yes, I thought it would be," Joseph replied too quickly. "I love her, you see, it may..."

"That is not the point at all, Joseph," Hirsch interrupted gently but firmly. "I can see that you love *each other,* and I know how these things can be. It happened so with Anna's mother and me."

The two men commenced to urinate back to back.

"It is not really Anna alone that concerns me. It is you, my friend, who concerns me more. You do not know my daughter as I do."

They finished and Hirsch waited to face Joseph before he went on. They could see each other clearly.

"Anna is a zealot and her cause is Zionism. You are an adventurer, and your cause is—you can better describe for yourself what your cause is. It is this warning, therefore, that I wish you to remember. You must listen and bear it in mind. Do not ever bring yourself to make Anna choose between Palestine and you. For, no matter what she should decide, she will become a wretched person, and so will you. If you truly love her, do not do this. As for me, I give you both my blessings—and hope that you will be discreet."

Joseph listened and absorbed each word. Hirsch was no foolish father. He said, "What you've said about Anna I know to be true. And you're almost right about me. I am not a Zionist. I never even heard about Jews and homelands until two years ago. Even then I didn't think much about the subject. Yet, somewhere inside me, I feel Jewish, and although I may be the adventurer you've described, what you and Anna believe in is a kind of adventure, too, isn't it? These past few days have been your doing, Mr. Hirsch, not mine, and they've hardly been boring. Then, who knows? Your adventure could become mine."

"Joseph, Joseph, do not mistake us. These are temporary things. The real course of Zionism leads to physical labor, to farming, building, irrigating, working with one's hands, with plows, not guns. Our ideas of adventure, I am afraid, are far apart."

Joseph understood Edouard Hirsch clearly. He was possibly right, but he wanted Hirsch as an advocate, not as an obstacle. He said, "As long as there are people like the Mufti around, you Zionists are going to need people like Michael and me."

Hirsch shrugged and left Joseph alone.

When Joseph returned to Anna, she woke and asked him where he had been. He told her of his meeting with her father.

"He warned me that you would leave me for Zionism if you were forced to make a choice."

Anna, lying on top of him, laughed softly into his ear. "You'll never leave me, will you, my dear Joseph, even if I did choose the dream?"

"I'll never leave you," Joseph promised. "You'll have to send me away." He raised his head to kiss her and felt her body close down over him.

"Never," Anna swore, "will that day come."

And, making love, she bent her head to seal those words with a long soft kiss.

245

Chapter 10

Friday morning was an anxious time for the Hirsches. The Beirut train—with the name *Empress of the Coast, Cairo–Beirut* painted on her steel boiler shields—did not arrive until after ten o'clock. The Hirsches had been ready at seven-thirty. They took a first-class compartment where the seats were upholstered, the floor carpeted, the air circulated by ceiling fans running continuously. At opposite ends of the carriage were two toilets for men, two for women, marked in English. That convenience itself was luxury.

Just before the train began to move, a message was handed through the door by someone asking for the Americans. Michael took it.

It was from the bistro-keeper.

Fellow Semites:

Your business is not my concern. Mr. Stanford Miles, civil manager of the district, has made it his. He has inquired of you at *Cairo's Delight*. Your names he has—may they not be your real ones. Your destination he has not. His curiosity extends to your religion. He takes you for Jews. I informed him you are not. Take heed. He has sent wires to his masters. We Semites must unite against these English. Allah escort you.

ABD EL MASRI

Michael handed the note to Joseph, who read it and passed it to Hirsch opposite him. Anna read it over her father's shoulder.

A gloom settled over the compartment. Hirsch made a few self-recriminating remarks, and Mary made a few encouraging ones. Then Michael took the map out and traced his finger along the train route.

"I think we're going to be all right," he said with genuine optimism. "Look, there's nothing between us and Ashquelon, where we're getting off, except Gaza. If we get through Gaza without trouble, we're going to make it."

246

Approaching Gaza, they took as many precautions as they could. They hid the portfolio in the seats. Anna went to a toilet room and locked herself in. Joseph and Michael were given the address in Jerusalem where the portfolio was to be brought. (The Quintanas by now were enlisted in Hirsches' mission and would see it fulfilled if the Hirsches were detained.) Then Joseph and Michael made their way separately to other parts of the train and waited.

When the *Empress of the Coast* pulled into the dusty open square in the village, the only people there to greet her were a handful of shabby peasants carrying crated livestock in their arms for the markets up north. Michael watched the traffic carefully from a perch between two cars. Nobody looking like trouble for them boarded the train, and a few minutes later they were all back in the compartment, laughing and congratulating themselves and watching the town of Gaza shrink in the distance. As the Hirsches hugged each other, Anna kissed Michael on the cheek and Joseph on the lips.

In Ashquelon, too, there was nobody to greet them. It was hardly a town at all and had no wireless connection with other major stops on the rail line. That was a relief. But the Hirsches had trouble hiring horses for the trip to Beit Darras, for there were almost as few animals in the town as people. Finally, in desperation, Hirsch offered the leader of a small caravan passing through an outrageous sum of money to detour on his way to Jaffa to take them to Beit Darras. The merchant haggled and haggled, recognizing Hirsch's dilemma, and squeezed another few pounds out of him. In return Hirsch demanded they leave immediately and travel at the fastest speed the caravan could reach.

As ruthless a bargainer as the merchant was, once the bargain was made, he stuck to it scrupulously and deposited the Hirsches and the Quintanas, heat-stricken and shaken, a few hundred yards east of Beit Darras at two-thirty under a white-hot sun.

The airstrip was there as they had left it, and so was the crippled bomber. Nothing had been touched in three weeks. The Quintanas scouted the whole base quickly and found it deserted. In one of the small hangars, under a heavy tarpaulin, they found the automobile Sir Herbert promised would be there. It was a closed six-passenger Vauxhall, carrying two spare tires on the running boards and one behind the trunk. It looked like the kind of car that had once borne important dignitaries in its faded luxurious

247

interior. But the years had left their marks on its surface. The paint was mostly gone, leaving a fine red rust everywhere, the nickel on the heavy bumpers was peeling, the once fancy grillwork was perforated where it shouldn't have been, and not one fender lacked a good-sized ding or two.

But the metal was sound, the chassis strong, the rubber good, and the glass intact throughout. And when Michael kicked the engine over, he knew he could trust the machine to take them to Bombay and back, if it had to.

Hirsch and his wife started to climb into the rear of the Vauxhall just as Michael switched the engine off and got out.

"I need a few minutes, just a few," he said.

Michael drifted over to the Handley Page. One engine had lost its propeller and sagged loose from its mounting. Anna was awestruck by the craft. It was more than twice the size of the Fokker in every direction. The Hirsches stood close to the car and watched him.

Michael ambled about a bit and finally said to Joseph, "What do you think?"

"Go ahead, who knows? It doesn't look as though it's been touched except for the guns. They're gone."

Michael climbed up easily into the second seat. Hirsch and his wife grew curious. They were impatient to leave for Jerusalem, but they held in their protest.

Michael bent out of sight in the cockpit. Joseph and Anna had drawn closer to the bomber and could hear some scraping around and cursing from inside the fuselage. Then came a cry of satisfaction.

"Goddamn! Got them!"

Michael's head appeared and then an arm, holding a small cloth bundle. He tossed the bundle over the side to Joseph and crawled back into the hole behind the gunner's seat. When he came out he had another bundle. Both were handkerchiefs tied by the four corners to form a bag.

The Quintanas brought the bags into the shade of the bomber's wings and untied them on the ground. The Hirsches came over to see a small pile of gold coins and jewelry sitting in the middle of each handkerchief like parts of a pirate's treasure.

"The small rewards of a dubious past," Michael laughed. "The police found the other half before we could hide it with this. But this is ours. We earned it."

Anna picked up several trinkets, made comments, and put them

248

down again. Joseph knelt beside her and said, "Pick one you like, Anna, please. Any one."

Anna demurred and shook her head. She could not. Joseph said, "You gave Michael and me something a lot richer than anything here. Take something from us."

"If they want you to have something, Anna," advised her mother, "it is not very good manners to refuse. Choose, Anna, and let us go."

Anna looked up at her mother and then at Joseph. She started to reach for a plain gold ring and then changed her mind and took a thin gold bangle and worked it onto her wrist. Joseph found another just like it, took her hand, and slid it on.

Michael then found a fine lady's ring with a small red stone in it and a larger man's ring carved into a scarabus. He handed the rings to Mary Hirsch and Edouard.

"What's this?" asked Hirsch, taken slightly aback.

Michael was already knotting one small bundle and Joseph was working on the other. Michael said, "Mr. Hirsch, do you know where Joe and I would be right now if you and your family had no urgent business in Jerusalem?"

Hirsch said no more, found a finger that the ring fit, admired it on his hand, and helped his wife up into the car. Anna sat in front between Joseph and Michael, who, with a final silent look at the Handley Page, drove off.

With Michael at the wheel driving the flamboyant way he flew, the Vauxhall danced around rocks, pirouetted by potholes, slid smoothly through bends, its engine running at peak torque, never straining, never overrevving, hardly changing its pitch except for those short seconds when the clutch engaged at a low gear.

The forty miles of dirt road to Jerusalem sped painlessly by, and minutes before dusk the ancient city of domes and spires rose slowly above the darkening horizon.

Chapter 11

Beit Darras—1954

The outside telephone bell rang loud and harsh. It jarred Lilli's mind out of its trance. She saw the gleam of hope come and go in Anna's eyes and the painfully anxious look that replaced it.

"We have only one telephone there," Anna said, rising. She looked drawn. "It's in another building."

A voice in the road shouted, "Anna."

Anna headed for the door quickly.

"May I come along with you, Anna?" asked Lilli, under the compulsion of an almost childlike instinct not to let go of her mother even for a few minutes.

"Of course, Lilli," Anna said, taking Lilli's outstretched hand. The women remained close, body to body, for a brief moment, and then Anna, her strong hand clasping Lilli's, led her out toward a large building across and down the dirt road.

People they passed were all wearing worn and faded work clothes. They nodded to Anna and spoke a few serious words, but no one stopped her, and no one talked long enough to ask about the young stranger with her.

She went into the building with Lilli. Inside was a barracks lined with beds on both walls, a lavatory at one end, a small desk with a telephone on it close to the entrance. The receiver was unhooked from its cradle.

Anna picked up the phone and spoke briefly. Lilli could tell nothing from Anna's face. Then Anna made a call and talked with someone at length. Her face grew more haggard. She hung up slowly and tried and failed to smile.

"He hasn't arrived at any of the places expecting him," she said. Then she breathed deeply without shuddering. "But come, my dear. We can do nothing but wait. There are good people looking for him right now. I can only pray they find him well."

Outside, Lilli asked, "You married him, then, Samuel, is that it, Anna? You never married my father."

"No, my dear daughter, I married your father and never married Samuel. Not even when our children were born."

250

Again they walked close together toward Anna's quarters. This time Lilli threw a comforting arm around Anna.

Jesse, watching them through the window, thought they looked like schoolgirls, sisters, arm in arm, unashamed of their affection. They were two beautiful women. But their faces were somber, and he expected the news to be bad.

Anna was saying, "Roger took the name Samuel—Samuel Lev—when he decided to stay here instead of returning to England with his father. That was 1923 or 4. He was so young then, not much older than I. He loved me knowing I loved Joseph, but he was also growing to love the country."

Jesse was outside striding toward them. Anna gave him the news, and they went back inside.

Seated in her own room surrounded by familiar things, Anna said she wanted to go on talking. She kept her voice up, her spirits high, letting the words, the memories, the presence of Lilli and Jesse help divert her mind. The two young people sitting so tangibly opposite her, found so suddenly, reminded her deeply of Joseph and herself.

"Joseph and I never divorced. He did not wish it and I did not wish it. And Samuel did not care when I accepted him still married to your father. By then your father had been gone for a long time. I took Samuel's name when I came to live with him, and we loved each other as I have always loved your father. You see, Lilli, you must understand—your father and I parted lovingly. We loved each other, but two people do not make up a world by themselves. There was Michael and there were the Jews of Palestine and there were my murdered parents."

"Murdered? Your parents were murdered?" Lilli's voice trembled, her emotions were twisting into confusion again. She was beginning to feel lost and helpless amid the maze of revelations.

"Yes, Lilli, we share that, too. The loss of our parents. That's what it all came to for them. We did get to Jerusalem in good time that Friday. Singing, too. We were all singing 'Yerusholayim, Yerusholayim.' Your father and Michael repeated the words we gave them. My father, your grandfather, was happy not to break the Sabbath. And it was good that we did not. It turned out to be his last."

Chapter 12

Jerusalem—1920

They went into the Old City through the Zion Gate in the south and shortly were safe in the Jewish Quarter. Everywhere people were hurrying home for the Sabbath eve. Shops were closing down, market stalls emptying, streets deserted by animals and machines. Small crowds of black-robed men gathered near synagogues. Women in head shawls, their arms filled with twisted breads, fled toward their flats.

The people who were expecting the Hirsches had rooms two streets away from the Arab Quarter and next door to an ancient Crusader church. Their building was old, neatly kept, and dim. The rooms were the same. Present were three middle-aged Jews, two of whom had fought for Britain in the Jewish Brigade, and a fourth young man. The younger man seemed to be the leader. Besides Anna and her mother there were no other women evident in the building.

The Palestinians were expecting only three people, but Anna refused to let Michael and Joseph be housed elsewhere. One of the men left the room and returned in five minutes to say that two beds on the same floor had been made available for them.

Before the Sabbath prayers and after some expression of gratitude was made to the Quintanas, there was a stream of talk in Hebrew. For fifteen minutes Joseph and Michael sat as bored spectators, picking up a thought or two through Anna's translation. Finally they got up and said they were going for a walk.

The young man shot some words at Hirsch.

"He says you cannot. In the streets there is trouble. The Mufti has been agitating, and there have already been assaults on people in this neighborhood. Nothing very serious. No one has been injured, but they are keeping all our people off the streets as much as possible this weekend. Most of the women and children in these buildings have gone for a few days."

"There's still a police force here, isn't there?" asked Joseph.

Through Anna's translation the young man replied, "The police are doing nothing. There have been appeals, but nothing has been

252

done. Our own Jewish police have been transferred out of this quarter and confined to the Allenby barracks outside of the city. We have tried to reach the High Commissioner in Cairo, but we can't get through to him. His own people have isolated him from us."

Hirsch said, "Until the Moslem Council meets and expresses its views, the Mufti is having his way with the people. It is not safe for any of us to go out."

"If that's so, how is that portfolio there getting to the right Arabs?" asked Michael, not only out of curiosity but as though an investment of his were at stake.

"We are working that out right now," said Hirsch, drawing his lips between his teeth. The talk continued. Joseph and Michael were left out, as though they were no longer there.

They said good night and went to sleep in the room that had been made ready for them.

At two in the morning Anna woke them. "It's done," she said. There were shadows beneath her eyes, but her eyes were bright with happiness and her voice was excited. "The business is over. Daddy just got back from a meeting with Sheikh Jurralah of the Moslem Council. The sheikh has read the correspondence between Prince Faisal and Weizmann. He sympathizes with the Prince's views. He told Daddy that the council will oppose the Mufti. Oh, Joseph,"—she clasped her hands together—"he believes the council can be swayed to proclaim support for Jewish immigration and put an end to the trouble between our peoples. Daddy and Mother are delirious. Come on. They want you to drink wine with them right now. Everybody is waiting."

Joseph covered her clasped hands with both of his and smiled gently into her tired, happy face. She stood on bare tiptoe and reached up to kiss him. Michael, smiling his own sense of gratification, embraced the two of them with both his arms.

When they were all gathered in the room down the hall, the four Palestinians, the Hirsches, the Quintanas, toasts were made. The glasses were small, the toasts numerous, the wine bitter.

"To Edouard Hirsch and his wife Mary."

"To Prince Faisal."

"To the Quintanas, without whose help this night could not have come."

"Hear. Hear."

"To *Yerusholayim.* Tomorrow has come. *Az m'vit leben.*"

"To the defeat of el-Husseini. The Mufti. May his soul rot like an onion, with his feet in heaven and his head in hell."

"Amen. Amen."

"Hear, hear."

The toasts were sincere and hearty, but they were not heard where they most would count. The defeat of the Mufti came too late for the Hirsches.

Chapter 13

While the Supreme Moslem Council were squaring off on Sunday morning to forge their policy toward a Palestinian home for the Jews, Arab mobs were already flowing in the streets and marketplaces of villages and cities, howling for Jewish blood. The Mufti's agents had finally penetrated and destroyed the lethargy of the peasants by proclaiming "The government is with us. No police interference." From the mosques and the souks and alleys the mobs, incited at last by the promise of loot and the blessings of Allah and the British government, poured out of the Arab quarters of the country into the Jewish sectors.

At the first sounds of cries in the street, the crash of glass, and the screams of fear, Edouard Hirsch ran white-faced downstairs with his wife at his side to turn the mob back. He ran more like a man flying *from* something he dreaded than *to* something he feared. He could not allow a wound to be inflicted in the body of either people that might fester for years to come. Success was too agonizingly close. His mind reeled as the same words spun around his brain, again and again—"If they only knew, if they only knew, if they only knew."

Joseph, Michael, and Anna, who had gone back to their bedrooms, followed too late to stop the Hirsches.

A ragged mob armed with knives and clubs had just flooded the head of their street. Shouting slogans of death and justice, they smashed through store windows and doors and raced up into buildings. Some filled their arms with whatever they could carry, others dragged people down into the streets and beat them. A few stunned Jewish residents came out of their flats to find out what was happening and were seized, mauled, stabbed, and thrown into alleys. The screams of the mob drowned out the screams of the victims.

The two British policemen who had replaced the Jewish guards in the street were gone. The mob howled in glee and the shouting grew obscene.

Hirsch, dressed in business suit and tie, staggered alone disbelieving, into the street twenty or thirty yards from the first wa of young thugs. Mary, at first stricken with fear, had stopped the edge of the walk. Down the street, half sprawled in the alle and half on the walks, were the beaten—unconscious, perha dead victims of the mob's first taste of blood.

Hirsch was possessed by a fine madness. As though he cou turn the mob back with his own body, he raised both hands abo his head and ran toward them down the center of the street. F a short, sickening moment the peasants, idlers, thugs, and bulli that are the core of every mob were surprised motionless at t sight of this lone, well-dressed lunatic calling to them in the own language, throwing his arms up, palm toward them, as if push them back out of the Jewish street, back into the Ar Quarter.

They paused, listened, watched him jog toward them, mouthi words like "Faisal," "brotherhood," "comradeship," "unity." A then there was a woman running after him, catching him, teari at his arm futilely, and finally joining him to speak to them.

Mary and Edouard Hirsch, linked by their arms, changed the pace and walked slowly toward the growing mass of Arabs choki the street. They held out their free hands toward the mob in a pl palms up, and Edouard pleaded in the hushness. He pleaded n for mercy, as Anna later told Joseph, but for friendship. He talk and talked and walked toward the white robes that shimmered the morning sunlight.

Joseph, Michael, and Anna had just come onto the street. T mob stirred, grew listless, jostled each other.

And then when Mary and Edouard seemed about to reach o to touch the front ranks of Arabs to offer them their hands, heavy club rose into the air. Above the voice of Edouard Hirs soared the words clear and loud, *"A' dowlah ma' ana,"* the go ernment is with us.

The club slapped down across Edouard Hirsch's skull, and crack that shivered the air resounded the length of the stree Hirsch's frame collapsed toward the ground.

Anna screamed.

Instantly another club arched above the heads of the mob, a before Hirsch's body had stopped twitching, Mary Hirsch w crushed to the ground like a dead weight next to her husband.

Before Joseph or Michael could do anything, the bodies of t Hirsches disappeared under a swirling blur of forms hammeri away at them as though the mob was bent on pulverizing the tw dies into the ground. The arms went up and down, up and own.

Anna was still screaming.

Joseph and Michael, who had grabbed their revolvers on their ay to the street, began to fire steadily into the heart of the swarm. omebody behind and above was shooting also. A single figure aggered from the mob and collapsed. Two other men fell as they ammered. Finally, at the eighth or ninth shot, four bodies were the ground, a fifth man was crawling away, and the frenzy of e mob collapsed like a punctured boil. Knowledge seeped into e mind of the mob. They were being shot down.

The howl of glee changed into a wail of terror. The mob sintegrated into splinters and flew in every direction. Some thugs linded by fear ran straight toward the men who were shooting em.

Joseph and Michael watched the panicked murderers approach em. They had dropped their clubs and ran empty-handed for fety.

"Forbearance," Hirsch had once said.

Joseph did not fire. He lowered his pistol and touched Mi- ael's raised gun hand and went back to where Anna stood, aralyzed and sobbing.

The man firing from a window higher up did not forebear. As e fleeing Arabs came by, he shot twice and dropped two men, ot many feet from where Joseph was holding Anna.

When the street was quiet and empty of the living, the British olice appeared in force and collected bodies and conducted in- uiries, interrogations, and searches. Six Arabs had been shot ead and six Jews had been clubbed or stabbed to death. The olice looked for guns and the shooters, but they found nothing nd learned nothing.

The next day Anna's parents were buried in the Jewish cem- tery on the Mount of Olives.

A few days later the High Moslem Council announced a softer ough not a completely friendly attitude toward the prospect of Jewish home in Palestine.

The Mufti publicly issued a cold statement of his concurrence ith the council and regret for the deaths, but privately he let it e known that the Jews would never build a nation in his part of e world while he still lived. And to some select friends he

257

complained bitterly that of the five people who had defeated him on this occasion, only two had been properly repaid. He would not, he swore aloud, forget the other three.

Chapter 14

Two weeks after the riots Joseph and Anna were married. There was no honeymoon. With Michael as a third partner, they had purchased from Arab villagers the entire acreage of Beit Darras, including the old abandoned airstrip and buildings the Quintanas had used so often. From the British they had also bought the Handley Page as scrap. The small bags of gold trinkets and coins had turned into more cash than they had hoped.

From the wedding ceremony in a rabbi's study, Joseph and Anna drove the Vauxhall to Beit Darras. Michael followed in a heavy lorry loaded with enough supplies and tools to get them into the business of converting the empty land into a settlement.

Since none of them knew a thing about farming, their first objective was to bring in people who did. Anna did the recruiting. Each day she drove as far as she could through the countryside visiting other settlements, talking with farmers, pleading, arguing, cajoling, bribing, until she persuaded three experienced men to leave their families for a short while to throw in with the new settlement at Beit Darras. The recruiting took three weeks. Then she spent days in the ports of Jaffa and Haifa talking to the immigrants who were trickling in from Europe. Without distorting the prospects of her settlement, she was barely able to convince three or four families to accept her offer. She transported the people herself in the lorry and spent long hours getting them settled into routines. She was up at dawn and back at dusk in time to eat with Joseph and Michael. They each took turns with the cooking.

While Anna was busy recruiting, Michael and Joseph worked on the buildings, putting up partitions to create rooms, fixing roofs, installing screens and windows, getting old wells to give up some water. Michael picked up a secondhand gasoline generator in Jaffa when he was there getting windows and screens, and restored the electricity in the buildings. He fitted the three wells with small electric pumps and discovered that the British had sunk one well so deep that its water supply alone far surpassed the settlement's personal needs. The surplus from the other wells could irrigate a good-sized piece of land, but just how much he didn't know. It was Michael's discovery of sufficient water that finally gave Anna the persuasive power to bring experienced farmers to the settlement. When the farmers heard about the wells they agreed to come, and the settlement really got under way.

It was not all work without play. Anna and Joseph had each other. Their love grew deeper even as they spent less time with each other. Joseph was learning how to share Anna with Palestine.

As for Michael, he sought his own pleasure by driving into Jerusalem or Jaffa on Saturday evenings and coming back Sunday after dark. He never spoke about what he did there except privately to Joseph, but everyone understood that he was the only unmarried adult in the settlement, and he never showed the worse for not having a wife. Each week Anna expected him to bring back a girl. But Michael never did.

Six months after their arrival at Beit Darras, the settlement had fourteen residents including three children and one on the way. But the unborn child was not Anna's. One night in bed early in their marriage when Joseph in a moment of passion was on the verge of ignoring contraception, Anna held him back.

"No, no, my darling," she whispered. "We mustn't. We don't want a baby until we're both ready, do we? There's too much work here to be done—and you know I've been asked to help out at the Jewish Agency in Jerusalem. I'm young, Joseph. We're both young. There's time for children yet. Unless you really want a child now." She drew his head down to her breast. "Do you want a child, Joseph, even if it comes by chance?"

"No, my sweet apricot Anna, not until you say so. Children can wait. I didn't mean to just now. Sometimes I can't wait, my darling. I'm glad one of us has a little sense."

And so they agreed that for the time being there would be no children.

Anna began to spend two days a week at the office of the Jewish Agency working for the Land Bank, whose sole purpose was to handle funds for the purchase of land. She became part of a campaign to raise money from Jews the world over. She catalogued and counted the gifts of hundred of thousands of *push kies*—little tin boxes with slots in their covers through which coins were dropped by Jewish families. The monies were small, but the stream of coins steady. The Land Bank did not grow much, for it funneled the money out for land purchase as fast as it came in.

Anna was spirited and optimistic. She grew more beautiful and loving to Joseph as the months passed, and Joseph's happiness deepened.

One late Friday afternoon, when Anna had been to Jerusalem, she came home with a dark-haired, brown-eyed slip of a girl she had grown friendly with at the Agency. The two girls found the Quintanas in sweaty undershirts, drinking a cold beer in the kitchen before washing for supper.

"Joseph and Michael, this is Hannah. I've invited her to spend a weekend with us here on the settlement. Hannah's a *sabra*, born here, but she's a city girl."

"I've been on farms," Hannah protested shyly, shaking hands first with Michael. She wore a simple, straight brown dress with a white lace collar, and her shoes had small silver buckles on them. "Anna has been telling me such wonderful things about Beit Darras that I couldn't resist meeting her American husband and her friend who have become such Zionists."

Michael, holding onto her hand, said, "I'm the friend. And I welcome you to this place of blossoming earth." He made a deep bow and swept the air with his hand to show her the roughly furnished interior of the room. "You're lucky it's Sabbath, Hannah, or Anna would find something for you to do. Mmmmm. Hannah—Anna. We're going to have trouble with your names, do you know that?"

"You love the place as much as we do, Michael," Anna laughed, challenging him to deny it. "He does more than all of us around here. I'm sure he'll show you his handiwork tomorrow." She slipped her arm through Joseph's. "And this is Joseph, Hannah."

Joseph pressed Hannah's hand warmly, wondering if she would be a girl good for Michael. Then, laughing at himself for thinking like a matchmaker, went off with Michael for fresh water and soap and clean clothes. While they were gone, the two girls gossiped about them a little and prepared a traditional Friday supper of soup, chicken, and noodles.

At the table, Michael was quieter than he had been. He had found something about Hannah that reminded him of Mary Hirsch, especially the way her eyes shone with life while her face seldom broke into a smile. Hannah's voice was soft and content like Mary's, and her figure was slim as well.

Michael had been attracted to Anna's mother but had never showed it. When he and Joseph had met the Hirsches, he had said to Joseph jokingly that Joseph could have the daughter. He pre-

261

ferred the mother. Only Michael ever knew that he had meant it
In the short week that he knew Mary Hirsch, he began to imagine
that she could be the kind of woman who could settle him down
During that week, however, he kept his distance, respecting her
devotion to her husband. Not once did he feel an impulse to do
anything more than think of her. He treated her as a friend the
way he treated Edouard. He labeled his feelings an infatuation,
and they probably would have remained nothing more than that
but Mary Hirsch's death changed him.

In the street where she was killed, he nearly lost his control
and would have gone on shooting her murderers if Joseph had not
been there. At her funeral he repressed his grief or expressed it
only through sympathy for Anna. Privately, he took the loss of
Mary Hirsch hard. It was for her sake, as well as for Joseph's,
that he had first given his heart to the settlement of Beit Darras.
Making the farm a success, he believed, would give some meaning
to her death and her husband's.

But Michael was young and by nature sanguine. The more time
and energy he sank into the experiment of the farm, the deeper
he found himself involved for its own sake. The months of labor
and sweat, problems and solutions, little failures and larger suc-
cesses, had gradually faded the memory of the woman into a faint,
idealized image. He had stopped thinking of her as a woman he
could have loved and thought of her as Anna's mother, Edouard
Hirsch's wife.

Now, sitting across from him in the glow of Sabbath candles
was the Palestinian girl Hannah, who had made him think of Mary
Hirsch again. But as the talk went on through the evening, he
found Hannah quite different from Anna's mother.

Hannah was twenty and came from a family that had lived in
Jerusalem for as long as anyone could remember.

"There are books in my father's library that have dates in them
written by family members in 1700," said Hannah, answering a
question from Michael. "And there are gravestones that go back
further."

"Joe's family is buried in Barcelona. Mine came from Madrid.
We got a chance to go down to Barcelona once during the war
and found some Quintanas in a cemetery. Stars of David and all,
dating from the 1700s too."

Hannah stopped eating. "Anna told me that you were not Jewish. And yet you are like Joseph's brother. I can understand that.
I have an Arab sister. Yes, and Arab brothers, too. The whole
262

Majaj family is my family. We have grown up next door to each door, and I know what it means to choose a sister and a brother."

The talk turned back to the Quintanas, and Michael and Joseph enjoyed themselves taking turns to describe their friendship, reliving the experiences that had brought them together in Boston and kept them brothers through the war. Anna, hearing much of the story for the first time herself, listened as fascinated as Hannah.

The four young people talked through the late night, and Joseph again began to think that something might grow between Michael and Hannah. When he and Anna were alone in their bedroom, he said, "What do you think, Anna? Does she like Michael? Do you think anything can come of this?"

Anna smiled as she slipped out of her clothes and embraced her husband. "You old romantic *bobbeh*," she said. "Do you think I brought Hannah down here just for Michael to look her over?"

"Yes, I do." He stroked Anna's back.

"Well. I don't want Michael to become restless. These Saturday night escapades of his—don't you get jealous when he tells you about them?"

Joseph kissed her fiercely. "What could make me jealous when I have you?"

They were lying down now.

"Just the same," Anna whispered as Joseph leaned over her, "think of how good things would be if Michael found someone like Hannah and really settled down."

Chapter 15

The next day Michael spent a few hours alone with Hannah, showing her around the settlement. Hannah let Michael do most of the talking. He explained the routines, the problems, the immediate and long-range goals of the settlers, especially the aspirations of people like Anna. Hannah knew them all, naturally, but listened attentively as though she were hearing new words.

Finally she asked, "Are you hoping, too, that someday Palestine will become a Jewish country, Michael?"

Michael paused over the tractor engine that he had begun to repair yesterday. "Listening to Anna these past months, I guess you'd say, has converted me. It certainly makes everything we do more definite." He tinkered with the engine as he talked. "I thought a lot of Anna's mother, although I only knew her for a week. And her father. You couldn't help liking, even loving both of them—and what they were doing seemed pretty right to me. Joe thinks so. And that's important. We both like it here, we like what we're doing. We did a lot of things before—when we were flying, I mean—we didn't tell you everything. But it was wild. Maybe this quiet life is good for us, I don't know. Sometimes I think it's too peaceful."

Michael stood up, wiped his hands on a clean rag lying near the engine, and took Hannah's hand. "Come on back here. I'd like to show you something."

He brought Hannah to the rear of their living quarters, where he and Joseph had towed the Handley Page to its final resting place. They had begun to build a shed over the great aircraft to protect it from the sand and wind that wanted to bury it.

"That's what we flew for a long time. Thousands of miles."

Hannah only said, "It's frightening to think about." She seemed very tiny next to the bomber.

"Would you fly if you had the chance?"

"I don't know. I don't think so. I don't like heights. I once went up to the top of the King David and looked out. It's not terribly high, but I was frightened."

"You get used to it," said Michael, walking with Hannah away from the shed.

"I don't think I would," said Hannah seriously.

"Well," Michael said as they reached the top of a knoll from which they could see almost the whole settlement of buildings, fields under cultivation, a windmill that supplemented their electric power, a watchtower the British had put up. "What do you think of Beit Darras? We've been here little more than half a year."

"It's wonderful," said Hannah warmly. She shaded her eyes with her hand. "But I like the city. I'll stay in Jerusalem. The city makes me feel secure."

Michael thought of the Hirsches dying in the city's streets. But he said, "It's your home." Then he led her down to where Anna and Joseph were waiting so that the four of them could set out for a picnic in a grove of mimosa trees a half mile away.

That evening before supper Michael shook Hannah's hand. "It's been very nice meeting you, Hannah. I hope you can do this again." Then, turning to Joseph and Anna, "See you tomorrow night." He climbed into the Vauxhall and drove off into the falling darkness and did not return until the following evening long after Anna and Joseph had driven Hannah back to Jerusalem.

Chapter 16

Over two months passed before Hannah came to spend anoth
weekend at Beit Darras. But before then Anna brought anoth
surprise visitor from Jerusalem.

Roger Samuel had appeared at the Jewish Agency to say hel
and good-bye. He was leaving the Near East for England. An
insisted that, since he was not sailing for two weeks, he cor
down to see what the Quintanas and she and a dozen people we
doing at Beit Darras.

When Roger stepped out of the car, Joseph and Michael rush
over to greet him warmly and immediately took him on a tour
the settlement.

"You've really got it quite under way," Roger said later
they headed toward the house. "I've been traveling all over t
country here. There aren't many places as progressive as this or
You could help a lot of people—especially with the way you'
put in power to work for you. That well system is beautiful. Eve
settlement should use it."

During supper Joseph asked, "What's happening in Cairo
politically?"

"Since the riots, things have quieted," Roger said. "But I do
trust the Mufti. Dad's leaving in a few months. He's going hor
for good. I'm going too, although I don't think that's what I real
want to do. Political career. Maybe Parliament. It doesn't see
the kind of life I'm terribly looking forward to."

"Stay here, Roger, with us," said Joseph. He put his knife a
fork down and looked dead seriously at the young Englishma
"I mean stay here at Beit Darras. We need every hand we can g
out to the other settlements with some of our ideas. And if you'
right about the Mufti, something should be done to organize t
settlements to protect themselves. And you don't sign a contra
here, you know. You can go home to London any time you like

Anna touched Roger's hand. "Stay, Roger. At least until y
know what kind of life you really want. We need you."

Roger looked at Anna strangely.

"That would be a great idea," Michael said. "And Joseph is right. We've talked about defending ourselves, but I don't think there's more than a few odd rifles or pistols on any of the settlements. There's nothing much more. Maybe you have connections that could help us." Michael got up from the table. "That reminds me." He went into his small bedroom at the end of the main room and returned with the cased Webley-Fosberys. He opened the lid.

"Just the way your father gave them to us six months ago. They've been used a little, but there's not a scratch on them. They're beautiful. Thank your father for them."

He pushed the case across the table to Roger, who ran his hand over the walnut shoulder stocks. He closed the case and handed it back to Michael.

"They're yours to keep. Dad said that if I ran in to you fellows I should tell you that they're a gift now, from him to you."

"Hey, that's great!" Michael cried. He raised his glass of wine. "A toast to Sir Herbert."

"To Sir Herbert," said Joseph.

When they had all drunk, Roger, slightly flushed, said, "Do you really think I'd fit in here?"

In unison the three Quintanas boisterously cried yes.

"I'll give it a try, then," said Roger.

Roger gave it a good try. Within a year he had changed his name to Samuel Lev and had become an integral part of the movement to transform Palestine into a homeland for the Jews. For several months he stayed mainly at Beit Darras, working alongside Joseph and Michael, planting, building, harvesting. Gradually he began to concentrate on creating a small defensive force to protect the settlement. As Michael had hoped, Samuel had contacts through which he acquired modern arms. In short order he mastered them all and trained everyone on the settlement to use them.

Roger's feelings for Anna had never changed, and Michael, Joseph, and Anna herself knew it, but he made no one uncomfortable. He kept his feelings perfectly to himself and was quietly busier than everybody.

After a while his work kept him on the move throughout the country, building the nucleus for a secret army of defense against the Mufti's threat. On the surface of things a lethargy fell over the land. Arab and Jew lived together with little conflict. The British kept a low profile. The Mufti suffered broodingly on his estate in Jerusalem. Jews continued to trickle into Palestine, and almost imperceptibly the balance of population between majority Arab and minority Jew began to change. Samuel had to remind everyone occasionally that the Mufti was still the Arab power in Palestine, and to think that he would let things continue as they were would be foolish.

He mentioned el-Husseini one night when Hannah was there. Throughout the meal she sat quietly and listened to the talk flowing around her, talk of settlement, of immigration, of defense strategies. She had little to contribute, but she did not feel ignored. Michael looked at her whenever he spoke, and Anna asked her opinions and she gave them. She was not a committed Zionist like Anna, although like her she worked for the Jewish Agency. Palestine, she said once, was her home, and she did not care greatly if it became anyone else's. She loved all Palestinians, Jews and Arabs alike, and she loved the land. Her voice betrayed a touch of possessiveness that seemed to say the land was hers, and she was uncertain how happy it made her to think of its becoming the home of many others. In her mind she knew clearly that the work of the Agency was right, and she supported it, but deep in her heart a grain of jealousy ruffled the smoothness of her life.

When she listened to Samuel's remark about the Mufti, she nodded her head. "Oh, that's very true. I hear the same thing from my friend Ninira. She's a teacher in an Arab school, and she says that the Mufti's bad feelings about us are being forced into her work. She's afraid for me because everyone listens to el-Husseini."

Michael said, "You told us once that Jerusalem made you feel safe. You might be safer out here." He spoke casually, without suggesting that he cared one way or another where she felt safe.

"No, I'm afraid not," she said. "I'm still a city girl."

That weekend Michael kept to his routine and left Beit Darras and stayed away until Sunday evening late.

Hannah returned three weeks later and spent all day Saturday watching Michael service the engines of the settlement's two tractors. It was a day of rest for the Jews, but the tractors needed work badly. Hannah stayed by his side, not talking much, handing him a tool now and then, eating lunch under the wing of the Handley Page, listening to his tales of flying in Morocco and in the desert. He got Hannah to climb into the cockpit and showed her how the controls worked and made her shiver, describing takeoff and landing and what the ground looked like from a few thousand feet up.

"Will you want to fly again some day?" Hannah asked when they were safely back on the ground. She asked as though she were inquiring the time of day, only out of idleness and not because it was important.

Michael looked at her curiously, wondering what answer would please her. He hedged. "Maybe, maybe not," he said, and continued to watch her. There was so much attractive about her and so much that worried him. The resemblance to Mary Hirsch no longer seemed as strong as before. He had thought at different moments that he would like to kiss her, that she wanted to be kissed. But right now a kiss would make his life complicated. Hannah was too innocent and vulnerable, definitely not the kind of girl he could kiss and leave behind to visit the girls he had been seeing in Jaffa or Jerusalem.

Michael thought of girls as deep or shallow. Anna, young as she was, was deep. She had a power flowing within her, not to be easily redirected once its course had been set. Zionism was its name for Anna. That was depth. Hannah was deep, too. But not from an involvement with ideals. Hannah would give herself completely to a person, not to a cause. The warm shade in her eye, the set of her mouth, the gentleness of her voice told him that Hannah's commitment to a man would be total. Whether or not she would need the same devotion in return was what worried Michael.

No, he thought, as he took another cup of tea she had poured for him, whatever the answer was to that question, a kiss with Hannah could not be casual. And there was something else that bothered him. He was a little afraid of her timidity. What would he want with a girl so fixed against flying and perhaps fixed against his flying? At twenty-five, he did not think his flying days were really over, although the prospects just then—as he looked around the settlement—were pretty damn slim.

Michael finished his tea and went back to work on the tractor engine. As Hannah watched him dismantle parts of the engine with a marvelous finesse, she began to wonder if he was not really an important part of the reason she liked her weekends here at the settlement. She tried not to believe that Michael had so little interest in her visits that although he spent time with her as he was doing right now, she did not stop him from going off to spend the night with some woman.

But that was not her business. It should not annoy her. Yet it did. Sundays were not as enjoyable as Saturdays. She could not deny that to herself. But she tried.

Looking at him bent over the engine, she saw that he was too different from her to be even a close friend. He was an American, a Christian, a lover of excitement, and a man too experienced with women. Nothing disturbed her as much as that last thought. She had always thought she would find a man as little experienced that way as she was, or not very much more. Michael was not that man. She would not think of him this way again.

Yet that night when Michael said good night and drove off, she could not suppress a quiver of jealousy, and she promised herself that she would not visit Beit Darras again too soon.

Chapter 17

Hannah changed her mind two weeks later when Anna invited her to spend her entire week's vacation at Beit Darras. She accepted almost at once.

On Monday morning, Michael, who had returned very late Sunday night from his weekend jaunt, asked her to come along with him when he left for the day.

"I can't," she said. "I promised Anna I would stay with her to learn what a woman can do around here besides cooking for her men."

On Tuesday he asked again, and again she looked him innocently in the face and shook her head. "Anna needs me to help her with some seedlings she's planting. If you want, though, I'll go with you tomorrow."

Wednesday, Michael took Hannah with him to a settlement forty miles to the east where he was helping farmers install a well pump and irrigation pipes. When he had difficulty talking to the settlers, who spoke a mixture of Hebrew and Yiddish, Hannah translated and suddenly found herself more than a spectator. Michael's interest in her grew.

The remainder of the week Hannah divided between doing odd chores for Anna around the settlement and assisting Michael by translating for him or teaching him Hebrew when they were alone. It was a working agreement that brought them close but not too close. Never once did he try to kiss her, and she began to wonder why. She did not think a kiss too much to ask, but she knew it was too much for her to give without his asking. She never could make the first gesture.

By Saturday, though, they were willing to admit to themselves that their friendship had deepened into something like a stronger comradeship. Neither dared think of the word love.

But not everything changed. Saturday evening came and Michael, following his routine, put on fresh clothes and left once again. Hannah's spirit fell again, but not too low this time. She had seen a different look in his eye during their supper, and this was the first time he had not left until after he had eaten. And there was an obvious reluctance to say good-bye. What he might be doing tonight bothered her little, perhaps because she did not have the imagination to picture it.

When Joseph and Anna were busy, Hannah stepped outside under a curtain of stars to be alone for a while and wonder what an involvement with Michael could be like. If she let it happen, he would be her first, and Hannah's imagination could not include the possibility that there could be others afterward. Her idea of love consisted of a single fixed idea: a man and a woman joined to each other forever.

"Is it happening between the two of you?"

Hannah turned. Anna had followed her outside.

"I don't know. We like each other, I suppose. I don't think I really mean anything to him. And I don't know what I feel myself. Oh, Anna, does it have to happen quickly to be real?"

"It happened quickly with Joseph and me. But it doesn't have to. We were in a hurry. You and Michael have time. It could be wonderful, couldn't it, the Quintana Brother Aces and their two Jewish girls?"

Hannah did not answer.

Michael returned the next day much earlier than he used to and drove Hannah to Jerusalem. Anna found several excuses to let them go alone. Through the entire trip Michael sat as though something heavy was on his mind. He brooded and made brief unimportant remarks about the Gaza Road they were driving on or about the land around them or about some problem they had shared together during the week. Hannah did not help him make conversation. She nodded, spoke little, and kept a space on the seat between them. Once Michael threw the Vauxhall through a sharp turn that should have brought Hannah hard against him. But she caught a door handle and kept herself from falling sideways. Michael grumbled.

Darkness had already fallen over Jerusalem as she directed him to a small house set on a hill a few yards above the street. He climbed out and held the door open for her. Hannah stepped down and found Michael blocking her path. He had her suitcase in his hand.

"Michael." She started to say something.

"Christ!" Michael said, and leaned into her to kiss her lips lightly. Hannah did not move. Her heart beat faster, but she did not kiss back. When he took his lips away she turned her head, ook her suitcase, and walked around him. He stayed by the door of the car and watched her shadow disappear into the darkness.

From the gloom of her doorway she called down to him quietly.

"Michael, do you want me to come again?"

"Do what you want to," he said, a little angry with himself, not with her. Then he said, "I could use more Hebrew lessons if I'm going to get anything done in this country."

Another year passed before Hannah allowed Michael to become her lover. From that night in Jerusalem, whenever they parted they parted with a kiss. Hannah's visits to Beit Darras, however, were erratic, sometimes occurring two or three times a month, sometimes only once. And Michael's trips to Jaffa on Saturday nights grew just as irregular—until they stopped altogether. That happened after he finally admitted to himself that he loved this quiet, thin slip of a girl who had grown up overprotected and sheltered from the rough edges of the life in this country of so many rough edges.

To get Michael to confess his love to Hannah took an extraordinary circumstance.

Michael and Joseph were traveling frequently in their second year at Beit Darras to help establish new settlements like their own. They had developed skills in farming techniques, irrigation projects, communications, and organizational structures useful to the new immigrants. For men who had bred themselves to adventure, however, the work was plain fare. But they found the way to spice their life.

An American businessman traveling in the Near East visited their settlement late in 1922 and was surprised by its prosperity. He asked the Quintanas what they could use most to increase their success and extend their influence. Joseph began to talk of trucks and farm machinery when Michael chimed in.

"An airplane. We need an aircraft to get around. We're pilots, you know. And the old girl back there doesn't fly any more." He pointed in the direction of the shed protecting the Handley Page. Michael spoke in jest and everyone laughed, including the American.

Two months later two great lorries rumbled into the settlement and dropped a dozen wooden crates on the road in front of their barracks. They contained a dismantled surplus Curtiss Jenny, complete and nearly new.

Within a month Samuel had thought of the best use for the aircraft. At his urging the Quintana Brother Aces secretly began to teach young Jews how to fly. Each week they took time off to fly to some remote settlement or to bring young Jewish students or clerks from the cities down to their own Beit Darras and train them in the Jenny. They were not exactly sure why they were turning these willing volunteers into pilots, except they couldn't think of a reason why they shouldn't. There was the Jenny asking to be flown, and to Samuel especially, it did not seem such a bad idea to have a core of men in the country with skills like flying. Samuel would have liked to have the Quintanas train them with machine guns too, but there were no machine guns for Jews to have. The most Michael and Joseph could do was to manufacture a homemade bomb that could be dropped by a contraption camouflaged to look like a part of the landing gear. They stockpiled the bombs, but at Samuel's request kept a half dozen aboard along with some hand grenades that had been smuggled into the country.

The Jenny injected excitement into the wearing routines of settlement life. But more important, it also brought to a head Michael's private dilemma.

Within two weeks of the Jenny's first flight, Hannah arrived at Beit Darras in the late afternoon as Michael was practicing simple maneuvers above the airstrip. When he saw the Vauxhall, he made a final turn around the settlement at two hundred feet, waving his helmet to Hannah as he passed over her.

Though Hannah knew about the airplane from Anna, she trembled at the sight of Michael swooping by over her head. Whether it was fear or thrill that struck her she couldn't tell. Her heart continued to pound even after Michael landed the Jenny in a large easy glide and taxied over almost at an idle to where Hannah stood. Without cutting his engine he climbed down to greet her. His face was flushed. Hers was pale and drawn, but her eyes glowed with a mixture of love and disapproval.

"It's a beauty, isn't it!" Michael exclaimed over the putter of the engine.

Hannah caught the excitement in Michael's words. She saw in his face the love of the craft and the act of flying it.

Slowly, her breath feeling harsh in her throat, her breast rising and falling in nervous pants, she looked away from Michael and fixed her stare on the aircraft. "Will you take me up with you, Michael?" she asked. Then she repeated the request louder.

"In the Jenny? Sure. Whenever you want. Next week. This summer. We'll get you used to her on the ground first."

"No, I mean right now. I want to go up with you right now. This minute. Before I change my mind."

Michael said nothing. He handed her his leather helmet and, seizing her by the waist, helped her into the second cockpit.

At five hundred feet he twisted around to ask her by pointing whether she wanted to go down. She shook her head hard with her lips tightly clenched and pointed to the Mediterannean. They stayed in the air for an hour, flying in any direction Hannah indicated.

Joseph and Anna were standing a few yards from where Michael brought the Jenny to a halt. They watched him help Hannah down and saw her fall forward into his arms. He held her tightly for a few moments until she pulled the helmet from her head and shook her hair loose. She was still in Michael's arms, looking up into his face. Finally they kissed in a long hard embrace.

Anna swung onto Joseph's arm. "It has happened!" she cried happily.

"Not like the way with us," Joseph said, circling his wife's waist tightly.

He was right, of course. He and Anna had loved at first sight, slept together in two days, sworn fealty to each other in four, and married within three weeks. Their courtship was framed by violence and sealed in bloodshed. It was nurtured under the shadow of Zionism.

Michael and Hannah's union grew slowly, cultivated in peace and nourished with work. The shadow of Zionism fell on them more faintly. The process took three years, and the love was as strong as Joseph and Anna's, but strangely, much more possessive.

The four of them all labored for the cause, but none with the passion of Anna. Joseph shared much of Anna with Palestine. Michael, on the other hand, found that Hannah wanted little else but him. Yet even as his own love for her deepened to displace almost everything else, his friendship with Joseph was as strong as ever.

The two men continued flying the Jenny and training young pioneers to fly. But Michael, who had always shown a more vigorous love for his freedom than Joseph, was the first to accept the restrictions of parenthood and family. His and Hannah's baby boy was born within a year of their marriage, while Anna and Joseph went on postponing having a child of their own.

The Mufti continued to sit in the Arab Quarter of Jerusalem, preaching against the Jews. There were no more organized riots, however, no more public attacks, and at the same time immigration fell off. Most of the land was barren, the heat was terrible, and the future under the British mandate was uncertain, to say the least. Yet the Quintanas stayed and made their settlement a model for others. They lived in harmony with the country and each other. They said it was a good life to lead, and for a while they believed it.

As for the dream of the Hirsches? Very early at Beit Darras the Quintanas learned that the dream could move toward realization only on rails greased by money. Money was the one essential, irreplaceable by manpower, will, or prayer. Money to buy, to hire, to repair, to transport, to replace, to bribe. Money to breed money to continue the process.

It was never money for itself they wanted, never money for a luxury. But it was money they had to have.

Chapter 18

"Then it was money that made them come back to America?" asked Lilli, pushing aside her half-empty plate at a meal no one had much of an appetite for.

Anna had been able to relate the scene of her parents' death with little pain. Time and experience had healed her. But Lilli had suffered a hurt inside that continued to ache even as Anna had gone on to describe Michael and Hannah's courtship.

Jesse had been listening solemnly and silently to the story of his mother, Hannah. Finally he broke his silence, responding to Lilli's question. "It wasn't money, Lilli, was it, Anna? If it had only been money, they would have come back when they made it. It was more than money. It had to do with something else, didn't it? It's why, for all these years, they never talked about the whole Palestine thing."

"Yes, Jesse, that's right," said Anna, her dark green penetrating eyes staring into Jesse's as though she were searching there for his character. "It was not money that broke the families up and sent your fathers off. It was the Mufti."

It was always el-Husseini.

It was el-Husseini in 1920 and it was el-Husseini in 1929.

That was the year of Lilli's birth, which happened the way it should have happened with lovers like Anna and Joseph. After eight years of caution, they threw caution to the dark wind one night in an orange grove, and the baby was conceived, unplanned, under the stars, as spontaneously as the love that had sprung between its parents.

And it was three months from the day of Lilli's birth that the Mufti cried havoc again and loosed his thugs on the Jews of Palestine.

The attacks were carefully synchronized. Again in the cities they were the mobs from the souks. Out in the country they were squads of irregulars armed with rifles and machine guns. They struck at dawn at a dozen places, from one end of the land to the other.

When the attack began at Beit Darras, Michael and Joseph were fifty miles away at a settlement on the Dead Sea. They had flown the Jenny there the evening before, planning a training session that morning for three promising young settlers who had shown a fine knack for flying. Young Jesse, three years old, had flown with them.

Left behind at Beit Darras were Samuel, Hannah, Anna, and the baby, Lilli, and sixteen other permanent residents of the settlement, including nine men and three women. There were four children, not counting the new baby.

Their total defense arsenal consisted of five rifles, one shotgun, and a few pistols, all hidden in the barracklike buildings where everybody lived.

It was not much of a force to face twenty men armed with good rifles and two light machine guns.

The first shot opening the attack killed the lone sentinel, whose post had been manned every night for years without having its peace interrupted once, even by a desert dog. The sentinel, a middle-aged Jew from Austria, had seen the Arab approaching him in the early dawn and had waved his rifle in welcome when the bullet broke through his chest and left the settlement with nine men and four rifles to fight off the attack.

The surprise attack shocked everyone. The Arabs had set up their machine guns at each end of the compound and raked the buildings as the people in their first moments of sleep-ridden bewilderment ran into the road. Three men were killed instantly. Those who escaped the barrage found their rifles and the shotgun and took up positions at windows and doorways out of the line of fire of the machine guns.

The only break the settlers were given was through the inexperience of the attackers. They were as untrained as their victims. They made mistakes. Their main force, consisting of fourteen men, rushed into the middle of the compound, expecting little resistance and hoping to overwhelm the settlement in the first assault. They stopped to shoot, kneeling to take aim, jubilant to watch a man topple through a window. But their position forced their machine guns to suspend their fire.

Suddenly there was heavy gunfire coming from both sides of the road, and Arabs were groaning and dropping to the ground.

278

Three Arabs were hit and slightly wounded by a shotgun blast from the left, and another was killed by rifle fire from the right.

The Arab leader screamed for a withdrawal. His men fell back to a storehouse, losing another irregular to the Jewish gunfire. There they took stock of their situation. The settlers had not surrendered as they had expected. They were even shooting back. The leader was shocked that they were resisting. The Mufti's agents who had recruited, organized, and armed them had promised them no resistance. The slaughter would be simple and rewards ample. There were animals to be had in the settlement, and machinery, and women. His Arab peasants would have them all. Now there was trouble. The Arab leader sent word to have his machine guns brought down to his position.

Before the first assault was over and the Arabs were driven toward the supply house, Samuel had fought his way around the perimeter of the compound to Anna's barracks. He found her and Hannah, both armed, near a window. Anna, crouching, was holding Joseph's revolver. Hannah, slimmer and more delicately built than Anna, was firing a heavy rifle from a standing position. They both had learned to shoot from their husbands. But the situation was hopeless.

"Get the baby, Anna," Samuel ordered across the room.

When she did not respond, he went to her and dragged her by her arm away from the window.

"Listen to me, Anna. This is very bad. You've got to save yourself for the baby. Both of you can be saved."

"I'm not leaving Hannah," Anna cried.

"Go, Anna, listen to him," said Hannah. She looked up and down the road and then hurried to Anna's side and held her. Her face was white and she looked shaken. But she spoke softly, pleadingly. "If the baby can be saved, you've got to save her. . . . These Arabs . . . Anna, please. If Jesse were here I would go to save him. Now he's going to need you. The children, Anna."

One of the machine guns was firing again down the road. When it stopped, an Arab speaking Hebrew called for the Jews to give up. A shotgun blasted from across the road. The shouted obscenities that came from the attackers described clearly what the women could expect. One very clear voice said, *"Jehudi*, listen— Allah has set my member up and only a Jewish slit will get it down. Surrender, *Jehudi*, and see what real men are like." Laughter broke out. Another voice cried out, "How do you Jewish girls

279

like it—up the front or up the back? We will have you both ways, like it or not."

A settler across the road in another barracks screamed his own curses in Arabic, fired his weapon, and kept firing. You could tell it was the same man by the rhythm of the shots.

Anna's mind reeled in conflict. Across the room she could see her infant beginning to stir from sleep.

"For Lilli's sake, Anna, try," begged Hannah, clutching Anna's arm hard enough to hurt her.

Anna decided. She scooped her baby out of its crib and looked at Hannah.

"Good-bye, Hannah. I love you as my sister."

"God guard you, Anna," Hannah said. She was trembling badly and there were tears in her eyes. "Tell Michael I love him and—comfort him, Anna. He will suffer so." She spun away and went to the window.

Anna whispered to Samuel. "There is one place that may be safe. Can we get to it unseen?"

"Where?"

"The shed. The Handley Page."

Samuel scowled, thought for a moment, and then nodded his head. He could not suggest anything better. He ran to the rear of the building. A window there faced the shed that stood fifty yards away, beyond a knoll outside of the rectangular compound. He tried to place the Arab positions in his mind. Could they see anyone moving from the rear of the barracks straight back to the shed? There was only one way to find out. He yanked the window open and jumped down. He kept his pistol ready.

The storehouse where the raiders had gathered after the first assault was a hundred feet away on the other side of the road. The machine gun at this end of the compound was too far to the right to cover the shed's entrance, although the gunner might have the side of the shed under observation. Samuel was not certain where the other machine gunner was sitting. He crouched, took a breath, and ran crookedly toward the shed, reached it, and raced straight back to the window.

Anna handed the infant through the window and climbed down, then took back the baby. With her pistol in one hand and her infant girl clutched against her body in the other, she followed Samuel across the open land toward the shed.

Halfway there the baby cried. The cry started as a cough and then burst into a wail. Anna crushed the infant's face against her

280

bosom to smother the sound. She broke into a fast run. Samuel dropped behind her, watching both ends of the barracks.

Anna reached the opening to the shed. An Arab dashed around the corner of the shed and saw both of them. The dawn light was brightening into day.

Samuel and the Arab fired at the same time, the Arab instinctively dropping to his knees to aim. Anna whirled in the entrance in time to see Samuel crumbling to the ground. Coolly, Anna raised the big Webley and, still hugging the baby against her body, shot the Arab three times. Samuel lay on the ground, wounded, supporting himself on one hand. He waved Anna on and began to crawl back toward the barracks.

Inside the shed, Anna glared down at her baby and repressed a scream. The little face had begun to turn blue. For the next terrible ten seconds Anna prayed and patted its back. The baby sputtered and choked and breathed and started to squawl. Quickly Anna tore her dress open and offered her breast. The infant clamped onto it tightly and quietly sucked.

With the child nursing at her breast and with the pistol tucked under the arm holding her, Anna climbed onto the wing of the Handley Page, up into the second cockpit, and somehow worked herself and her baby into the hole that was concealed by a flap behind the gunner's seat.

For the next thirty minutes Anna lay huddled in the fuselage of the bomber, terrified by the gunfire that wracked the settlement. The machine guns made her body shudder as though she were afflicted by a severe fever and chill. Her baby ate and slept, ate and slept. She did not cry again.

Finally the gunfire stopped. Anna could hear Arabs outside the shed, coming in, searching, poking into the Handley Page. Someone called them out, and she imagined she could hear screaming, a woman's high-pitched screaming, two women screaming. She pressed her hands over her ears and began to cry softly to the screams inside her own mind.

Joseph found her there an hour later, physically numb, no longer crying, steeling herself, through her love for her husband and the dream of a Jewish homeland, recalling the words of her father and his colleagues—"Blood may have to dampen the ground, before the ground can be called ours."—steeling herself for whatever lay outside the shed.

It was worse than she imagined.

All the children were dead. Except her own Lilli. And Jesse held in Joseph's arms when he came to the shed to get her.

Five men were dead. Among the living but badly wounded was Samuel, who had crawled under the building, where Joseph had found him half conscious.

The women were all dead.

Anna handed Lilli to Joseph, who watched helplessly as she ran through the compound to find Hannah.

Hannah was out in front of the barracks that she, Michael, Joseph, and Anna had lived in. She lay dead in Michael's arms naked, partially disemboweled, her blood mingling with the sperm of her rapists.

Michael went crazy. Not openly, visibly crazy, not raging crying, cursing crazy, and not rampaging crazy like a wounded animal. But quietly, methodically, a crazed mood settled over his brain and, two days after Hannah's burial, he set out to liquidate the Arab population of Palestine. He did it with deliberation and malice and cunning.

Each morning he left the settlement and went to Jerusalem or Gaza or Haifa or Bethlehem. He carried his Webley and a dagger and on some occasions he took along small vials of poison that could contaminate a water well.

And each night he returned he cut a mark on the walnut butt of the revolver as he had read gunfighters in the old West had done. He never brought himself to use the poison, but on two nights he came home with bloodstains on his knife. And he added two lines on the butt of the Webley parallel to those already there.

Each night he came into Joseph and Anna's room as they lay in the dark, and in the dark he whispered aloud the details of that day's killing. After the second night Anna slipped out of the room and went away when Michael came in.

Only the two men, then, shared the secrets of Michael's revenge. Joseph made no effort to stop him. On the seventh day when Anna said she was going to Jerusalem for a doctor, Joseph shook his head and flatly forbid her.

When the fifteenth cut was made on the Webley butt, the crazy lifted from Michael's mind, and the following morning he did not leave the settlement. That day the news reached them that the Mufti had gone into hiding with his bodyguard because of the mysterious, unpatterned killings of Arabs in the country. The British had responded by doubling their personnel in all Arab quarters throughout the Mandate.

When Michael appeared on that morning, the cold glint that had glazed his eyes for weeks was gone. It was as though a fever had broken and the old friendly Michael had returned. Anna and Joseph were at breakfast with the children. Jesse was at the table, and Joseph was holding Lilli.

Michael sat down, put his arm around his son, and looked across at his friend. "It's all over, Joseph. I can feel the pressure gone from here." He pressed a thumb and finger against his eyes. "I feel the weight lifted. But"—he hesitated for the blink of an eye—"I'm leaving."

Joseph's deeply tanned face showed only faint surprise. His eyes shifted his glance at Anna and then back to his friend. The announcement was not unexpected, but Michael's making it so casually in front of Anna was.

"The country? The whole thing?" he asked.

Anna paled and felt herself shiver. She tried not to stare so hard at Michael, but could not help herself. She sensed the nearness of another disaster. She caught her breath and unconsciously held it, waiting for his reply.

"Everything, Joe," Michael said, and leaned over the table and paid some attention to Anna's baby, tickling Lilli under her chin with a finger and making her gurgle.

"I'm taking Jesse to America. You come, too, with Anna and Lilli. Give your daughter a chance to grow up. It won't be running away or giving up the country. There's money to be made in America by a team like us, Joe, and what's needed here is money now. Not any more of our blood."

Anna started to reach out for Joseph's hand, but stopped herself. It was Joseph's choice, Joseph's dilemma, not hers. She had no choice. She would not, could not waver a fraction away from the course she had followed since childhood any more than she could voluntarily stop herself from breathing. Watching Joseph now begin a struggle in his mind, holding the infant Lilli, who was clinging to his arm, she felt a wave of estrangement toward both of them sweep through her and then pass on. She looked at Lilli and her heart began to ache.

Joseph spoke to Michael without consulting Anna with a word or another glance.

"Are you asking me, Michael?" asked Joseph. He was remembering Morocco nearly ten years ago, remembering the promise he had made when Michael had agreed to fight for el-Krim on Joseph's account. It was a debt Joseph had incurred and never

forgotten. Just as important as the debt, though, Joseph agree
with him now. Michael was right. Lilli wanted a better chanc
to live than the four children had had, or Hannah.

Hannah. Anything to spare his little beautiful Lilli that.

Michael looked at him. "I'm not asking you—yet, Joe." H
left the baby alone and sat up straight. "But I might. I don't know
how good I'd be at anything without you. Together—well, w
know what we can do together."

Joseph finally turned to Anna. "Is he right, Anna, about goin
to America?"

Anna stared at Lilli, pressed tightly against Joseph's chest.

"He's probably right about himself, Joseph. And he might b
right about you. But he's not right about me." She wanted to g
on and say "and he's not right about our daughter," but she coul
not say it. She did not really know what was right for Lilli
Edouard and Mary Hirsch had known without question what wa
right for their infant girl Anna, but they had never exposed he
to enemies with guns and the hate to use them.

For the next two weeks Joseph and Anna discussed Michael'
intentions with growing despair as their own intentions clarifie
in their minds and toward each other.

Joseph was inclined to go. Anna was bound by every nerv
and fiber in her body to stay. Haunting both of them were th
words of her father that Joseph had heard and repeated that nigh
in the desert:

"Do not ever bring yourself to make Anna choose betwee
Palestine and you. If you truly love her, do not do this. For n
matter what she should decide, she will become a wretched perso
and so will you."

When Anna saw Joseph's mind bending toward Michael, sh
recalled her father's words aloud. But Joseph only shook his head
It was too late to listen to them now.

Although Michael had never mentioned the Moroccan deb
after that first discussion, Joseph had made up his mind to go
knowing his decision was partly on Michael's account, but partl
on Lilli's, too. Which one weighed more heavily in his mind h
never could tell.

Chapter 19

Beit Darras—1954

"The friendship between your fathers was a rare thing," said Anna. "They were truly brothers." She was looking very tired, and her voice had fallen hoarse and solemn. She reached out on either side of her for a hand from Jesse and a hand from Lilli. She clasped their hands tightly. "Now, my dear children, I can see in your faces, in your eyes, the image of your own fathers. There's a friendship between you, I think, like that between them. And there's more than that, no? You're smiling, yes, you're smiling, and I can see it's true. You've had the friendship and you've found love. You've got them both. How lucky you are, my two newly found children! How lucky!"

She released their hands and circled their necks and drew Lilli and Jesse close to her bosom, their heads touching. She held them but an instant.

"Oh, well, it has been a long two days. And so much talk. I am tired." She rose.

"Wait, please," said Lilli.

"Yes?" asked Anna.

"You gave me up to Daddy just like that?"

"No, Lilli, not just like that. Not like that at all. I went back to work at the Jewish Agency in Jerusalem and came home one day to find them all gone. Michael, Jesse, Joseph, and you. I knew Joseph was leaving soon. We had said our good-byes many times. But not you. We had not decided about you. He took you. I was frantic and helpless and—but what need is there to describe that? I loved you. Perhaps, though, deep inside me I was glad you had gone to where you would be safe. I don't know. They flew to Athens in that Jenny and sold it and sailed to America.

"Letters came, promises that you would come back when the money was good. Then money came, and some pictures of you and Jesse, but none of your father. You were growing beautiful. You looked happy. Then there was trouble about running whiskey, and the letters stopped for a while. And then started again. And the money increased—until one day, three years later a man came

285

to us and said he was from the Quinn brothers. The Aleph-Palestine Fund began. By then Samuel and I were living together. And our lives, Joseph's and yours and Samuel's and mine, seemed parted for good. There was more trouble with the Mufti in the middle thirties and your father wrote he could never send you back. You had become a little American girl, growing healthy and happy and rich. By then Samuel and I had our own two children to replace the one I lost. Our letters grew infrequent, and then with the troubles in Europe, they stopped altogether. But the A Fund continued. Your fathers never forgot."

Chapter 20

At eleven o'clock at night the call came in from the Mufti's headquarters in the northern quarter of the Old City. Jesse and Lilli sat up in bed as they heard the outside telephone bell jangle and then stop. Feet crunched on the gravel outside, a knuckle rapped on the door, and someone spoke with Anna, who seemed not to have gone to bed. Anna went out.

She returned a few minutes later. Jesse and Lilli were dressed, waiting for her in the sitting room.

Anna came in slowly, dragging her feet like an old woman who had suffered one blow too many. She sank into a chair opposite the Quinns and held her head with both hands. Over her nightdress she wore a thin dark cotton robe whose shapelessness added to the despair in her face.

"The Mufti has Samuel," she said, taking her hands from her face and straightening up. Then expelling her breath in a long sigh and gripping her knees, she said, "So."

Lilli covered her mouth with her hand.

Jesse grasped her arm.

"He's all right," Anna said. "I spoke with him. The Mufti will release him unharmed if we meet his conditions." She released her knees and clasped her hands together, locking her fingers.

"What are they?" Jesse asked when Anna did not offer to say.

"What you would expect and what we can not give him. He says he wants the Aleph Fund, not revenge."

"But he tried to kill all of us yesterday," said Lilli, forcing herself not to think of Powell's body outside of Barclay's. "He killed our fathers only a few weeks ago."

"Yes, I know," Anna said, shrugging. "He says he wants money. Things have changed at the bank. He knows all of the details about the fund. Now he wants us all alive, at least until he gets our signatures. I believe that much. Since the '48 war he has lost much power. He still has his followers. But he needs money."

"Then we'll give it to him," said Jesse. "It's only money. We'll give it to him as we would pay a ransom and then we'll stop the whole thing when Samuel's out. The most he'll get is a single payment or two."

"You think he doesn't know that?" said Anna grimly. "He's very cunning. He wants the two of you to meet him personally and sign over the fund to him—you'll bring my signature with you. And he has Samuel. Once he has all four signatures, he can kill any one of us and delay the collapse of the fund for months, maybe years. I know what the entanglements are. It's too dangerous. We can't risk giving him such money. And I won't put three of you into his hands."

"What's the alternative?" asked Jesse. He thought of what the Mufti could do to Samuel to force Anna to give in. "Can Israeli police go in there after him?"

Anna shook her head. "Politically impossible. The Mufti is alive today because of politics."

"Listen, Anna," Jesse said, trying not to sound melodramatic, "you and Samuel have been taking all the risks for Lilli and me. Our coming here in the first place caused a lot of this. My father and Lilli's took their risks, too. It's our turn now, do you understand? Do you think we can just climb aboard a plane and go home? Or wait around here for . . ." He refused to put into words the thought that had entered his mind. "I've got the documents. You and Lilli will sign them. Samuel will sign them when we're sure he's out of their hands, and I'll take them to the Mufti myself."

Anna stared at Jesse gravely. "He said there would be no meeting unless you both go."

Jesse did not need to look at Lilli. She was pressed against his side. He knew what she would say if he asked.

"How do we make the arrangements?" Jesse's voice was flat and serious.

Anna shook her head again and stopped biting on her lip. Her eyes were cold jade green. "Lilli cannot go. I will not permit it. I lost her once. I am not going to lose her again. Not even for Samuel."

"You won't lose her, Anna," said Jesse emphatically. He was thinking of three bodies lying on cold stainless-steel tables in the Ipswich hospital. There was a chilly deadness in his own chest. "We'll have a plan."

At the moment Jesse had no plan. He had been trained in the Air-Corps, but never for anything like this. What kind of plan could someone with his inexperience devise that would have even a faint chance of succeeding? In spite of the doubts, he spoke confidently. "We'll go in there with a plan, Anna, a good one."

Lilli held Anna by the arms and spoke with a determination to match Jesse's. "I couldn't let Jesse go alone, Anna. It is my decision to be with him, not yours. We're a team, like our fathers. You said so yourself."

After a brief silence, Lilli continued: "How does Jesse make the arrangements?"

Before Anna answered she looked into Lilli's face intensely then into Jesse's.

"I have a telephone number. They've set up a telephone connection that crosses the barrier. That's how I could speak with Samuel."

Vague ideas that were more reckless than clever began to tumble through Jesse's mind. "Do you have a street map of Jerusalem?" he asked.

Anna rummaged through some papers in a drawer and came up with a detailed map of the entire city. Jesse bent over it for ten minutes, asking Anna questions. Finally he asked, "Can I get three or four armed men to work with me?"

"Samuel's people are on the way here right now to bring me to Jerusalem. I called them right after I spoke with Samuel."

"Fine," said Jesse. "Let's go talk with the Mufti's people. I hope one of them speaks something besides Arabic and Hebrew."

Chapter 21

Mohammed Said Haj Amin el-Husseini bent courteously over
the low table to pour a thickish coffee for his three visitors. The
service he used was of solid silver, the cups of Dresden porcelain
prewar, the coffee a fine blend of Turkish-Brazilian bean with
Madagascan mocha added to mellow the flavor. The sugar was
unrefined brown. No one took cream.

Two of the guests had been frequent visitors to the Mufti's
spacious villa on El Omarz Road. They were his keystone henchmen, who carried his orders to a third level of leadership, through
which the orders were passed on to those who carried them out.
Each of these two men had comfortable villas of their own in
other parts of the Old City, where they did the entertaining for
men of the third rank. Both were richly dressed in fine business
suits, silk shirts, imported English shoes of the softest leather
and silk ties. They were still paid well from the Mufti's private
coffers that had been nicely filled years ago by his German hosts
when he had been forced to flee Palestine. He had been made a
welcome guest in Berlin by Hitler himself. He and the Nazis
shared opinions about Jews.

But the Mufti's treasury was running low, and the contributions
from the Arabs of Palestine had shrunk to a level below that of
the Mufti's expenses. He had began to deplete what was left of
his German funds. Power, the Mufti had learned from the British
when he was a favorite of theirs, began in the capacity to distribute
rewards to a select group. Beyond that inner circle of supporters
fear was as effective as money. His power was diminishing.

The Mufti, however, never lost an inch of his dignity or an
ounce of his sophistication. From the top of his flat, spotlessly
white bowl-shaped hat to the manicured nails on his toes protruding from polished leather sandals, el-Husseini was immaculately the gentleman. His eyes were light blue, frosty and obser-
vant, his nose long and straight, his lips curved in long feminine
lines, his reddish beard perfectly trimmed, his hands soft and
delicate.

He moved his hands gracefully to serve his guests, the fingers caressing the cups, the little finger spread, the silver coffeepot tilted with both hands, not spilling a drop and then the hand lifting the cup by the edges of the handle, carrying it steadily over the table and setting it delicately onto a saucer without making a sound of glass brushing against glass.

And there was always a smile on his lips. It was not a grin or an inscrutable smile meant to intimidate. It was the smile of the congenial mind at peace with itself, the smile of the man who intended that his friendship be left in no doubt to those in his company. It was the smile of self-assurance, consciously intended to convey all these things.

Yet when the Mufti bent to serve his coffee, his cocoa-brown *abiyah* that was draped across his chest billowed open a trifle more than it should have, and the Mufti's third guest, who was sitting crosslegged directly opposite, saw the twilled beige covering of a bulletproof vest.

This third guest was dressed Eastern style, in a snow-white burnoose and carefully wound dark turban. When he observed what the Mufti's offer of friendship and trust really amounted to, he repressed his own smile and kept his remarks to himself. Like the Mufti, he too had suffered reverses in his past, and he too retained in his own country a following of the faithful he had once ruled. But unlike the Mufti, he had given up his dream and lived now as peacefully as he could in exile.

For thirty years he had not been to his homeland, and he had no hopes of ever returning. Twenty of these years he had spent in exile on a small French island in the Indian Ocean, where he had cultivated true serenity of mind. And when the French had allowed him to change his place of exile to France, he had escaped his escort in Athens and made his way to Cairo, where he had settled down among his own Moslems.

He sat tall and slim and sleek-faced, and studied the Mufti suspiciously through hot dark-brown eyes that made the Mufti's seem ice-cold by contrast. He had never liked the Mufti, and he did not like the Mufti now. He did not like the Mufti's coffee, and he scorned the man for not caring that a Moroccan would have vastly preferred tea flavored strongly with crushed mint.

In his sash, Mohammed Abd-el-Krim retained a long knife that the Mufti's bodyguards had let him keep. On his arrival at the villa they had searched him insultingly for guns just before the

291

Mufti entered to greet him. El-Husseini affected displeasure with his bodyguards for having humiliated his guest. He spoke his apologies profusely and then quietly chastised his guards for in discrimination. But the fact did not escape el-Krim that the Mufti had not appeared to greet him until after the search had been completed.

He wondered why he had accepted el-Husseini's invitation to be his guest in Jerusalem for the week. Why, indeed? They did not like each other. And the greeting he had received hardly reflected trust.

"To heal wounds, Abd-el-Krim, to mend breaches," murmured el-Husseini, as though he had been reading the mind of the former Riffian leader. "I cannot believe your sedentary life in Cairo makes you very happy. You are a true believer and a great warrior, and you and I are not old. We are not young, but we are not old. There are things to do—here in Palestine and there in Morocco. And you and I have the power to do them."

He tasted his coffee with great satisfaction. His henchmen sipped at theirs.

"It is a Jewish problem, Abd-el-Krim," continued the Mufti "here and in Morocco, just as it was in Germany and Europe."

For the next three hours Haj Amin el-Husseini explained to the Riffian leader why the Arab problem was a Jewish problem. He outlined in fine detail what the solution was, how it was to be reached, and what the role of two such charismatic leaders as themselves would be.

As he spoke he kept wetting his lips, and his mouth moved as though he were tasting the words. The night wore on while Abd-el-Krim listened politely and grew increasingly convinced that the Mufti was mad. The two men in elegant business suits however, nodded their heads and added their approval whenever their leader paused.

As the hour for sleep approached, el-Husseini poured a final cup of coffee.

"You, my friend, will not be alone with me in this movement of the *Jihad Maquades*, Strugglers of the Holy War. You are only the first of many whom I shall invite to join me. There is Ghory in Jordan, and Rousan in Syria, and Tell in Egypt, and Majali in Beirut, and Azzam in Iraq. A general staff with members like these will take care of those Wailing Wall Jews, el-Krim. What do you say?"

El-Krim said nothing more than that he was tired and would give Husseini's proposals serious thought.

The Mufti rose and took el-Krim by the arm.

"How inconsiderate of me to have kept you up so late on your first evening here. Forgive me, my good friend."

Before they parted for different parts of the villa, a message was handed to the Mufti. His smile widened as he read it. His eyes grew brighter, bluer. His feelings were high, but when he spoke, the refinements in his tone and manner were as pronounced as ever.

"We have an auspicious commencement to our program, el-Krim. The acquisition of money, as I've told you, is an absolute necessity to raise the *jihad*. And the payment of old debts is almost as important. If I can impose on you to rise early tomorrow morning, you will have the opportunity to witness a happy conjunction of the two in one short meeting, which I am about to arrange with an interesting young couple of foreigners."

Chapter 22

The gray Chrysler was parked a few yards from the Mandelbaum Gate on the Israeli side. The ruined skeleton of the Mandelbaum mansion stuck out against the early gunmetal sky like a spectre in a bad dream. Only a single arching wall of the grand building remained, still supporting a balcony along its side. The rubble around its base had never been cleared away. At the intersection of St. George Street and Shmuel Hanovi Avenue stood the Mandelbaum Gate, which controlled any and all traffic between Arab and Jew in Jerusalem.

The gate was a seven-foot steel door that swung open against a half-demolished wall. It was covered with rolls of barbed-wire barriers, sandbag shelters, and gun emplacements. Up and down the streets dividing Israel from Trans-Jordan, the barbed wire was strewn in even greater masses, supported across big double wooden crosses lying upright. The war had been over for six years, but you could never tell from the scene here.

Two soldiers armed with Uzis lounged at the gate, which stood open wide enough to admit two people walking abreast. On this side of the gate nothing moved, not a dog or a hungry bird. On the other side, through the opening, the outlines of two or three people were visible.

In the rear of the Chrysler, Jesse and Lilli were waiting for 5:30 to appear on their watches. The location for the exchange was Jesse's demand. The early-dawn appointment was the Mufti's. These arrangements were simple and had been agreed on easily. Time and place, movements for exchange, guarantees of noninterference and safety—there was hardly any discussion on these. The Mufti's agents had been amiable and pliant on the phone.

The difficulties were in two other demands, one from either side. Jesse would hand the signed paper to no one but the Mufti himself. The Mufti agreed only if the American woman came over first.

294

After a brief heated argument with Lilli, Jesse had agreed to the Mufti's demand.

On the ride to Jerusalem during the night, Jesse had ridden in a separate car from Anna and Lilli. Three other unidentified men were in the car with him. They talked over hastily-made plans to free Lev and get Jesse and Lilli out safely. The discussion was heated and sometimes angry. A big rawboned man sitting next to Jesse in the back seat spoke English in the deep guttural accents of an uneducated man.

"Anna tells me you are carrying a pistol on your body, a tiny one that belonged to her father. You expect to use it to get you out of there once you're in?"

"Is there another way? A direct attack by your people, maybe? No one seems to want that. If you have some people in there already where I've suggested, to give me some help if I need it, my chances may be very good. What do you say?"

"They'll find the pistol before they let you see him," the man growled. "You'll have no chance at all then."

"Back at Anna's," Jesse argued, "I asked one of your men to show me how he would search someone for a weapon. He searched me, and I was carrying it then. He didn't find it."

"I would," the man said. "The Mufti's men will. Then where will you be? I've got something a little better they won't find. And I'm going to give it to you on one condition."

"There were no conditions back there," Jesse said. He had the uncomfortable feeling that his own simple plan was about to be challenged, and he did not even know who these men were or how great their experience was.

"There is one," came the harsh voice in the darkness. "If you want us to go along with you, you'll have to go along with us." He waited for Jesse's reply.

"I'm listening." Jesse had no choice.

"We want el-Husseini. We have wanted him for a long time. You are going to kill him for us."

"Kill him for you?" Jesse looked up sideways, his forehead drawn tight, his eyes narrowed.

"Yes, with this." He handed Jesse a small flat case two inches wide and six inches long and turned a flashlight on it. "Open it."

Jesse pried the lid up. Inside was an ordinary-looking fountain-pen-and-pencil set. Jesse did not touch it.

"They both work fine," the man said. "You can write all morning with either one. But the top half of the pen is filled with *plastique* and has a tiny detonator packed into it. The pencil will explode the detonator from twenty-five yards, no more. You just slide the clip on the pencil down as far as it will go and it'll detonate enough *plastique* to kill a man carrying it without hurting anyone else seriously more than a few feet away. We've tried it a dozen times, not on real people yet. It always works. But until now we've never had a chance to get it to the Mufti."

"And I'm supposed to give it to him, is that it?" Jesse asked quietly.

The voice of the rawboned man rasped away in the darkness.

"You're going to sign papers, aren't you? Right in front of him. That's your arrangement, right? We couldn't have set this up better ourselves. What would be more natural than to get him to sign the papers too, step away a few feet—and—*pfff*. He's gone. At that moment, and—listen to me—only at that moment will our people move and get you out."

Jesse started to give the case back. It was too complicated. His own plan was simpler. The rawboned man, however, thrust a big hand in front of the case and forced Jesse to keep it on his lap.

"If you don't take it along, you're a fool. You'll go in there with your cousin alone. You can't count on our help until that little device goes off in the Mufti's hand."

"I thought your government didn't go in for this kind of thing. I thought it was considered politically unwise."

"Do not think for the government, Mr. Quinn. The government has nothing to say about it. This is not a chance we're passing over. You will agree to use the pen or this whole affair is off. We'll go in after Lev our own way—and people will be hurt. Maybe Lev will be hurt, maybe not. But we will go in to teach them they cannot do this sort of thing with impunity. Listen. Keep your little gun. But use the *plastique*. It is much more effective."

Jesse reached down and touched the tiny automatic he had pushed inside his sock into his shoe. The pistol was smaller than a package of cigarettes and thinner. It cramped his instep a bit, but he managed to walk in a natural gait without calling attention to himself.

Jesse did not reply to the threat from the rawboned man until they reached the Mandelbaum Gate in the dark. Kill the Mufti in cold blood? The thought had been preying heavily on Jesse's mind for hours before the man with the harsh voice hung the heavier weight of a command onto it.

Could he do it? Earlier in the evening he had thought so. But as the thought grew closer to the act, he realized it was not so easy. He had certainly killed before—in his fighter plane. He had killed the Messerschmidt pilots and bomber crews he had shot down, but they had died hundreds of yards away, faceless, obscured, hardly victims of his guns at all. He had killed airplanes, really, seldom feeling the shock of taking a human life until he was forced to make a conscious effort to think about it back at the base during the debriefing sessions. He was unsure of himself now. And what about Lilli? She would be very close by. Jesse wanted to talk with Anna. He waited for her to leave the second car and then called to her. She ignored him to talk to another man. He called again, but she acted as though she did not want to hear him. He came to her side and waited for the man to join his companions. Lilli was detained by another man in the car.

"Anna, listen, they're asking me to kill him, the Mufti. With this deadly little gadget." He opened his suit coat and showed her the harmless looking pen and pencil he had reluctantly tucked into the inside pocket.

Anna nodded her head. "I know all about that deadly piece. Samuel helped in its design several years ago. It's never been used."

"Are these people the government?" Jesse asked.

Anna looked at him strangely, her green eyes the color of dark jade in the breaking but gloomy light. After a moment in which he could see her making up her mind, she spoke to him as to one she was confiding a secret that really was no secret at all to everybody else.

"No, Jesse. The government would never send you in there. They would never let a foreigner do this—especially an American. This is an Israeli affair. The government pledged never to bring an American into an Israeli affair of danger. And there are good political reasons why. They would let Samuel die for those reasons."

"Who are these men, then?"

"Irgun," she said, wondering whether the name meant anything to him. "Or what's left of the Irgun. Samuel was once a member, a founder. So was I. We were terrorists. We were Jabotinski's people. The organization is gone now, unneeded. But we still have these friends and old comrades and old scores to settle. When I heard from Samuel tonight and what the Mufti was demanding, I called *them*, not the police. Samuel gave me a signal to do it.

A dozen or more like these men are already inside the Old City to protect you."

Jesse started back toward the dark Chrysler where Lilli's white face was staring from the window. He felt worse than he had all night long. Now that he had been given a quasi-license to kill and an instrument to do it with, he should have felt resolved. But his first thoughts were for Lilli. Whatever developed on the other side of the wire, Lilli's safety had to come first, not the Mufti's death. He would make a move against el-Husseini only when he was certain that Lilli was out of harm's way. The hell with the Irgun.

Anna caught up to him, seized him, hugged him tightly, and echoing his own thought, whispered hoarsely into his ear.

"Save Lilli, Jesse. Whatever you have to do to save her, do it."

"I will, Anna. It's all right." He patted her back gently and tried to give her a reassuring smile, but he could not imagine what his face looked like. He climbed back into the car.

He told Lilli nothing about what he was ordered to do. She had anxiety enough. They sat quietly holding hands until 5:30 and then left the car. Jesse walked to the steel gate. The guards were gone. The gate was ajar.

Lilli waited.

Through the gate a light from the other side of the wall flashed on, clearly visible in the fading night, winked off, on and off, and stayed off.

"That's it," said Jesse. "I'll be with you in a few minutes." He squeezed her arms hard and let her go.

Alone, Lilli began to shake inside as though she were suddenly very cold, but she walked erect and quickly through the gate, past rolls of barbed wire, into a deserted street. She could still feel Jesse's final hard clasp on her arms. Her courage rose. Her heels clicked sharply on the stone like a formal announcement of her approach. She walked boldly in the dim light.

Directly across from the gate were three figures near a building. One figure advanced toward her, flashed a light into her face, and said something in Arabic. She answered in French. The man put his face up close to hers and replied in French.

"Follow me." His breath smelled sour.

He led her down the street toward a corner. The other two men fell in behind her. The three men were wearing hard leather heels, and the footsteps of the four of them sounded outrageously loud to her.

The men wore Western business suits, open shirts, no ties, checkered headcloths. The man leading had on a blue one, the others wore different shades of red. Their dress made her feel less nervous than she would if they had been in burnooses. In their suits they seemed civilized. She knew, however, that the difference between civilization and brutality was certainly not the difference between a Western business suit and an Eastern robe. That kind of comfort was irrational. But she welcomed it anyway, for it made her fear easier to control.

At the corner the man in front stopped. The two men behind came up to her side and took her roughly by the arms. She almost screamed. They went through her handbag and found the envelope containing the crucial Aleph-Palestine Fund papers. That brought grunts of satisfaction to their throats. They handed the envelope to the man in the blue headdress. Then quickly, rudely, more erotically than necessary, they ran their hands over her body, under her dress, under her underclothes, into her body. Her skin crawled. She protested. The searchers laughed in a way that confirmed that they had not really been looking for anything other than the thrill of abusing her.

The man in the blue headdress checked the papers in the envelope and handed them back to Lilli, apologizing for the treatment. He led her around the corner to a large sedan of familiar make parked close to a building.

Inside, with a small bandage plastered to the right side of his face, was Samuel.

"Be careful," cried Samuel the moment he saw her.

It was a strange remark, considering their positions. The man next to him struck him across his arm with a pistol and ordered him in Arabic to be silent.

"The papers, please, at once," the man demanded. He thrust his hand through the open window. Lilli placed the envelope in it. She looked into the front seat. Sitting there with his hands tied behind him, was the little man from Barclay's, Paul Martin.

Lilli leaned against the car. "I'm very sorry about this, Mr. Martin," she said.

The little man whose eyes had feasted on Lilli in the bank looked at her again. He shrugged as if to tell her that she could not help it.

The man in the back seat removed the papers from the envelope and held them under Martin's face.

"Are they good?" he asked.

299

Martin read through the contents as the Arab turned the pages. He finally raised his head and nodded.

"Is that Anna Lev's signature there?" the man asked. Martin nodded again.

The man drew a fountain pen from an inside pocket and unscrewed the top.

He spoke to Samuel. "Sign your name next to your wife's."

Samuel raised his eyes to Lilli, who was bending slightly to watch.

"Please sign it, Samuel," she said. "That's what we've decided to do." The chill that had been shaking her body left. Seeing Samuel alive, close enough to touch, and knowing Jesse would be coming to her soon to help her face the Mufti, Lilli felt calmer, though she knew she was not at all safe.

Samuel signed the papers. The man opened the door, got out, and ordered Samuel from the car. This fourth man's suit, a knubbysilk affair, was more elegant than those of the other three. He wore a tie and went hatless. His thick black hair was combed into a wave rising above his forehead. Stuck in his lapel was a small red pin shaped in a crescent with a white star inside its arc.

The pin drew Lilli's complete attention. As she glared at it, it increased in size, growing closer and closer to her eye, until it was all she could see of the man. Finally he moved and the illusion broke. The man motioned with his head to his three henchmen. The Arab in the blue headdress tapped Samuel on the shoulder. The street was growing quite light with the pinkening of the overhead sky. The air was still cool and dry and scented with the smell of jasmine.

"We walk back to the gate now," the man in the blue headdress said in French.

Samuel's face was puzzled as he looked at Lilli.

"You're coming, too, Lilli." He spoke half-questioningly.

"No, Samuel, they're waiting for you out there. Everything is arranged. Jesse's coming to get me. You'd better go. It'll be all right."

Samuel started to protest. The man in the blue headdress seized his arm and physically forced him along the street. Samuel pulled his arm away, walked, looked back at Lilli over his shoulder, and disappeared around the corner.

Lilli stared again at the red crescent pin. She pointed at it.

"That has a meaning?" she asked.

"Jihad Maquades," Ahmud Darwish said, smiling at her.

300

"What does that mean?"

"You will find out one day, Jewish lady."

Jewish lady. Lilli Quinn. Daughter of Anna and Joseph Quintana. Palestinian and American Jews.

She thought of her Beverly club, the polo crowd, the tennis gang, the trap buffs, the whole North Shore. Few Jews there. Could it ever be home again? How much easier to be there with Jesse instead of waiting to meet the murderer of their fathers!

Shortly before her feelings had the chance to sort themselves out, Jesse arrived. How cool and confident he looked! She didn't know he had just been roughly searched by the same two henchmen who had abused her. One of them had felt under his arms, picked into his pockets and jacket, and squeezed the lining of his coat. He had glanced at the pen and pencil and not touched them. The other man simultaneously had felt into Jesse's crotch, circled his thigh with his hands and slipped them down his leg. Jesse's breath had stopped, but the man had not probed below Jesse's ankle.

Jesse came immediately over to Lilli. "Are you all right?"

She nodded without looking at him. Her face was somber.

He went up to the man with the tie. His voice was hard and blunt. "Can we get this over with? You need two more signatures on those papers you're holding. And we're not putting them on there except in the Mufti's presence. He wants it that way and so do I."

"Please, then, as you wish," said the well-dressed man. He opened the door of the sedan. It was a late-model Buick Roadmaster, upholstered in dark red leather. He ushered them in with his hand.

Lilli started forward, but Jesse, ignoring her and deliberately forgetting his manners, stepped in first and moved to the far side of the seat. Lilli climbed in after him, blocking Jesse from the view of the well-dressed man, who followed her.

When they had settled back and the order given to the driver, Jesse considered their chances of getting out of there alive much better. Resting in his jacket pocket in his right hand was the small Mauser pistol that had cramped his foot a few seconds ago. He wiggled his foot inside his shoe.

As the Buick pulled away into the street, Jesse felt the unusually heavy ride, the engine laboring harder than it should, the wheels rumbling too firmly over the cobblestones, the car riding flat. He studied the windows, all of which were rolled up. The air was stuffy and smelled. Jesse tried to lower the one on his side. It would not budge. He tapped it. It was thick and immovable. He noticed the slight distortion of both the front windshield and the rear window.

Bulletproofed. The Buick was a heavily armored bulletproof machine. Whoever owned it had set a high value on his life.

Gradually, the driver got the heavy car to move a bit faster, and then it rolled easily under the impetus of its own weight like a small locomotive.

"The Mufti has good taste in cars," said Jesse.

"Yes? You think so? It was custom-built for him in your own country."

They sped down a wide, empty street for over a quarter of a mile, skidding at last through the Damascus Gate into the Arab Quarter of the walled Old City. If you did not know where you were heading, you found out as soon as you passed through that gate. On every street, in any direction, white-domed mosques flanked by slender minarets stood high above the surrounding buildings. Street and shop signs were in Arabic, and the few people who were beginning to appear on the streets were in robes and *kaffiyehs*. If the thick windows of the Buick had been down, Jesse and Lilli would have heard the shrill call of muezzin summoning the faithful to early prayer. And they would have smelled the heavy scent of fresh-killed lamb already basting on the spits in the markets.

A few minutes into the quarter brought them past the startling golden Dome of the Rock, rising massively from the top of its purple, green, and white mosque and dominating everything else in sight by its size and splendor. The huge dome glittered under the first direct rays of the sun cresting over the Mount of Olives.

Jesse and Lilli almost forgot what they were facing as they stared in awe at the flashing gold they had only seen previously from their balconies at the King David. There the dome had been no bigger than a yellow tennis ball. Now its immensity seemed to reflect the pondering greatness of the Moslem spirit, of the power of the spiritual leader of the Moslem community, of el-Husseini, Mufti of Jerusalem.

Yet these thoughts intimidated neither Quinn. Lilli looked straight ahead and sat erect, shifting just a bit to keep her hip from rubbing against the body of the well-dressed Moslem when he changed his position and moved closer to her. She forced her mind to dwell on Anna and Samuel, safe together, and on strong imperturbable Jesse, staring aimlessly out of the window next to her, almost pleasantly taking in the sights of the Arab Quarter.

Jesse was actually searching the walks, the doorways, the roof-tops for signs of life. At times he thought he saw a shadow or two move back from the edge of a rooftop or fade deeper into a doorway. But whether they were Mufti men or Irgun killers, or phantoms of his own mind, he could not even guess.

He glanced sideways at Lilli, who seemed composed and confident. For a fraction of a moment he had the impulse to take command of the car, turn it around, and make a run for it. But the man near Lilli might not let that happen without a fight. Jesse had seen a gun in a shoulder holster under his jacket. With Lilli in between them, he could not take the chance.

And there was the Mufti, waiting for them. Jesse felt an unreasonable compulsion to meet el-Husseini face to face. Leaving now would make it almost impossible to believe in the man's existence. Michael's and Joseph's deaths would always seem the work of phantoms. No. Jesse resolved to see the man in the flesh.

Three minutes past the Dome of the Rock, the heavily armor-plated Buick slowed to a faintly lurching stop at the end of the ancient wall.

To Jesse and Lilli, when they stepped out next to it, the Wall was more awesome than the Dome. It rose fifty feet above their heads and stretched more than several hundred feet across an empty courtyard toward some dark buildings to the north. This had been the western wall of a temple destroyed long ago and was its only surviving structure.

Without the glitter and gold of the Dome, and perhaps because of its beckoning grays and blacks, the Wall drew Jesse and Lilli across the few feet to its base. There they touched the stone as though it were Chinese porcelain. Moss grew above their heads to the top of the wall, but from the ground to as high as a man could reach, the smooth stone was disfigured in chalk and paint with the scrawl of Arabic words.

The southern end of the Wall, where the Buick was standing, was attached to nothing. It stood there as its own complete edifice, holding nothing up and walling nothing in or out. The far end of the Wall, however, abutted a stone building that seemed as ancient as the Wall itself. The building and wall joined at right angles, the building rising a few feet higher. Along the top of the building was a low wooden railing of lattice, and behind the building, towering over everything, was a square minaret topped by a small dome.

Down the side of the building a half-dozen or more empty openings like windows stared vacantly onto the courtyard. From any one of the openings a man could have a completely clear view of the dusty rectangle of ground half formed by the building and wall. At the base of the building, almost where it joined the Wall, was an entrance leading down into a grottolike basement. It appeared to be the only entrance to the building on that side.

On this morning no one prayed at the Wall, and there had been no one praying there for the last six years, since the city had been cut in half and the Wall had fallen into the half controlled by the Arabs. The air was cool and breezeless, and the thick dust lay quietly undisturbed on the ground. The well-dressed Arab wearing the red crescent pin pointed down the Wall toward the building at its end.

"Come," he ordered. He started to walk toward the building, keeping well within the deep shadow of the Wall.

Jesse and Lilli followed. They were both acutely aware that they were walking through this courtyard dust in the shadow of this old wall only because of a dream their parents had had and which, almost without their knowing it, had been passed on to them. They had thought at first they were going to Israel to uncover a money problem, but instead they had to come to discover some part of themselves, their fathers, their mothers, the land of their birth.

Less than halfway to the shaded building, Jesse stopped. He could just make out the shapes of several figures under a small awning at the building's entrance.

The well-dressed Arab was impatient. "Well, he is waiting for you over there."

"Tell him we'll sign his papers right here," said Jesse.

"But Mr. Quinn . . ."

Ignoring him, Jesse called out in German to the figures near the building.

"Haj Amin el-Husseini!" The name seemed to reverberate ominously along the ancient stones. "We are both here as you wished, my cousin and I. The papers are here, also. With two signatures on them. You have released Samuel Lev and kept your word. We will sign the third and fourth signatures right here, where I am standing—in your presence."

Two figures separated themselves from the darkness at the foot of the building. Talking to each other, they strolled almost casually toward Jesse and Lilli and the Arab who had brought them. The

wo figures were draped in long Arab robes, one in a burnoose
ith hood down and wearing a light turban, the other in a white
biyah folded from one shoulder down across the chest to the
opposite hip. This man wore a stiff white pillbox hat that widened
ward the top into the shape of a saucer. He walked with short,
hoppy strides, as though his legs were shackled or something
as binding him at the crotch.

As the two men approached, Jesse could see that the man with
he funny walk was wearing a short-clipped beard which, in the
hadow of the Wall, appeared to be gray. When they were close
hough for the bearded man to offer a limp hand in a gesture of
ourtesy, Jesse saw what he was looking for. The beard *was* a
lvery gray, but it was mottled with fading red. "The red-haired
astard," Simon had called him. Watching the limp hand rise
oward him, Jesse was not even casually aware of the second man.

The second man, however, whose face had caught Lilli's eye
nd frozen her attention to it, was staring back, not at her, but
t Jesse. The Mufti had just finished telling him about these cous-
ns Quinn from America who were going to finance his plans and
epay an old debt for their fathers. Now the phrases struck him
ith the suddenness of a flash mountain flood. The Quinn fathers!
Quinn cousins. Brothers!

"Quintana?" asked Abd-el-Krim, addressing Jesse.

Jesse didn't hear him. He was thinking of other things.

The Mufti's extended hand waited patiently for Jesse to take
. How easy it would be to kill him right now. He was so close
hat he could press the muzzle of the little Mauser against the
Mufti's left breast and fire one shot into his heart. But there was
he man next to the Mufti—a bodyguard, although a little too old
or that—and the man with the cresent pin in his lapel a few yards
way. And there was Lilli—in the middle.

Jesse took the Mufti's hand but could not control a shock of
ausea that struck the pit of his stomach and rose into his chest.
he Mufti's hand was cool and dry and not like the clammy hand
e expected it to be.

Lilli was talking in Spanish to the man with the Mufti, but
esse's own thoughts about his next step blocked out everything
lse around him. He extended the document to el-Husseini, almost
hrusting it into his hands.

"You must sign this first," he said, speaking German. "Then
ve'll sign and clear out. It'll be all yours." He unscrewed the top

305

from the fountain pen he had removed from his breast pocket an capped it on the bottom and held it out. "Well?"

The Mufti offered a trifling smile that did not break across ha his lips.

"Ah, no, Mr. Quinn. Allow the lady to sign first. Please." H German was soft and cultured and came from the front of h mouth and not from this throat.

Jesse looked over at Lilli and fought against hesitating. Lil stopped talking to the second man and said something to Jess that sounded like the name el-Krim. Jesse's eyes glanced at th man. Was this el-Krim? What was he doing here? Now? Ther was no time to surmise answers.

He shifted his gaze back to Lilli. Her face came into focus It was strangely relaxed, almost beaming. Did she know wha kind of trouble they were in? Even if this other man turned ou to be the man their fathers had flown for, that was thirty yea ago. What could he do for them? Why would he do anything? H was with the Mufti now.

"The young Miss Quinn first," the Mufti repeated.

Lilli took the document from the Mufti and held out her han for the pen Jesse was still holding lightly in his fingers. At th second he wanted to throw it as far as he could. But with a grea exertion of will, he forced himself to pass the pen to her. In hi breast pocket the pencil suddenly acquired bulk and sensitivity Jesse held himself motionless, almost suspending his breath s as not to jar the pencil a fraction.

Lilli scrawled her name quickly at the bottom of the document looked at her signature beneath those of Anna and Samuel, an offered the pen and paper to the Mufti. Again the smile crosse el-Husseini's face fleetingly.

"No, no. Mr. Quinn must sign it. And I will accept it." Hi hands remained limply at his side.

A frown marred el-Krim's face as he watched the maneuver of el-Husseini. He had seen the dark shadows of men outside th grotto while they were waiting for the Americans to arrive. A least one of them had been cradling a submachine gun.

Jesse was writing his signature now. When he finished, el Husseini took the document in both hands. Jesse was holding th fountain pen out toward him. El-Husseini read the document an smiled in complete satisfaction and reached out for the pen. A Jesse watched, immobile, the Mufti removed the cap from the en of the pen, screwed it on over the point, and dropped the pe omewhere inside the folds of his *abiyah*. He folded the document nd said, "Our business is almost finished, Mr. Quinn, Miss Quinn. I shall add my signature later, at a more opportune time. ut now . . ."

Jesse reached inside his coat and clamped his hand over the encil.

Suddenly el-Krim spoke almost bitterly to Jesse in Spanish. You are a fool, Quintana. He's not going to permit you to walk way alive." The Mufti, not understanding, looked sideways at is companion, puzzled. "You are a fool," repeated el-Krim. "Not ke your father at all."

The Mufti began to raise his hand.

El-Krim moved with the agility of a young man. He took two uick steps away from the side of the Mufti, and in a blur of notion snaked out his short curved sword. Within the same move- nent his arm thrust out to its full length to press the point of the word into the Mufti's throat without drawing blood. He spoke arshly to the Mufti in Arabic. The Moslem leader lowered his rm and remained deathly still.

Lilli gripped Jesse's arm badly confused. "It *is* el-Krim, Jesse."

The Mufti stood motionless. His face had gone white, yet not muscle or nerve quivered. His composure was so much a part f his being that even the needle point of the sword about to break he skin in his neck did not disturb his outward calm. Hate, owever, stood bright in his eyes as they shifted from el-Krim to esse and back to el-Krim.

El-Krim continued to talk, his words spurting rapidly between ips almost compressed. When he finished, the Mufti muttered a ew words. El-Krim increased the pressure at the tip of his sword nd a drop of blood appeared on the blade.

The Mufti spoke louder, and the man with the blue headdress nd the red crescent pin backed away, drawing a big pistol from is shoulder holster and holding it on el-Krim.

"Jesse!" Lilli cried. "Look down there. There are others."

Two figures had emerged from the shadows of the building at he north end of the Wall. When they stepped out into the daylight, esse could discern one carrying a machine gun. The other held revolver.

"Stalemate." The Mufti strained to get the word out in German.

Jesse was thinking as fast and clearly as he could. The blade t the Mufti's throat did not frighten the man enough. He acted s though he could escape it easily. There was the fountain pen

307

in the Mufti's robe, but to threaten him with that would soun
like a ridiculous bluff. For the moment no one moved. It *was*
stalemate.

Then the Mufti began to talk to el-Krim. El-Krim shook hi
head. The old Riff chieftain switched to Spanish. "Quintana, tak
your cousin and get down to the automobile. Now, at once. Gc
His men will not dare to stop you as long as the point of my swor
is in his throat."

Lilli gripped Jesse's arm harder. "No, Jesse, we can't. W
can't leave him to be killed. Our fathers would never do it. Never.

Jesse didn't answer. He drew Lilli behind him and backed he
against the Wall so that they were behind the Mufti. Then hi
hand came out of the pocket, holding the Mauser pistol. His lef
arm circled the Mufti's neck, knocking aside el-Krim's sword
The point tore a light gash in the flesh and made el-Husseini cr
out in pain. Jesse locked his forearm on the Mufti's windpipe an
pressed the pistol tight into his temple. He backed into the Wa
next to Lilli, dragging the Mufti with him. He had no trouble. H
was taller, heavier, stronger than this man who had given so man
orders in his lifetime for so many people to die. Jesse had to figh
the urge to squeeze the trigger. Only Lilli's presence next to hin
strengthened his self-control. When he finally spoke a threat i
German into the ear of the Mufti, his voice was strained an
harsh. He hardly recognized it as his own.

"One shot, just one shot or one wrong move from any of you
people out there, and you'll be shot in the brain. Do you under
stand, Husseini, shot in the brain." To emphasize the threat, Jess
fired a shot into the ground a few feet away and immediately du
the pistol barrel harder into the Mufti's temple, forcing his hea
over to the side. "Maybe you weren't afraid of the sword at you
throat, but there's no way you'll avoid a bullet in your brain. Nov
tell that to those men out there. All of them. Your life depend
on them."

Jesse did not know that he had struck the single weakness i
el-Husseini's defenses. The man did not fear death, especially a
honorable death that comes through a blade. But he had a morbid
consuming fear of dying violently at the hands of an assassin
close up, facing him with a pistol. Throughout his life he ha
taken every precaution imaginable to preserve himself from as
sassination by gunshot, the form of death he had doled out t
hundreds. He wore the vest, his cars were bulletproof, his body

uards numerous, his schedules erratic, his patterns and routines
ndefinable.

Now, confronted with his greatest fear, he obeyed instantly.
Ie did not cringe or cower. He kept his poise and control. But
he threat of the bullet in the brain placed his mind completely
t the will of the man holding the gun at his head.

The moment he understood that it was no longer el-Krim threat-
ning him but these American Jews who had good reasons to kill
iim, he called out his orders to the man nearby with the crescent
in, to the bodyguards approaching from the northern end of the
ourt, and to the driver of the Buick, who was heading toward
hem with a gun in his hand.

"He gave the right commands, young Quintana," said Abd-el-
Krim in Spanish.

Lilli, stunned by what Jesse had done, was breathing hard, her
eart thumping badly in her chest. "Should we start for the car?"
he asked in a shaky voice. "What do we do, Jesse?"

Jesse heard her words, but his mind was on el-Husseini, press-
ng against his body, and on Lilli, who was exposed to the court-
ard. She had expected none of this, and he had to depend on her
ow as he never had before.

The Buick was sixty or seventy feet away. The southern exit
rom the Old City was not more than three or four hundred yards
eyond that. Then the barrier between the Jews and the Arabs in
ront of St. Peter's on a road whose name he only half remem-
ered—Malk . . . And—if they were lucky—home. His mind ig-
ored thoughts of the Irgun's command. Kill the Mufti. Getting
o the Buick was all that mattered.

"Lilli, listen carefully. Move along the Wall as fast as you can,
ut don't move away from me. Keep close between el-Krim and
ne." He spoke without looking at her. "All right, el-Krim. It's
our move."

The Mufti spoke without loss of dignity. "Be calm, Herr Quinn.
Do not squeeze the trigger by mistake. It will kill us all if you
lo. Keep me alive and you keep yourselves alive."

"As long as nobody tries to stop us," growled Jesse into his
ar.

They shuffled along the Wall toward the Buick, el-Krim lead-
ng, Lilli sticking close to him, Jesse coming last, dragging the
Mufti. The dust was stirring toward their knees as they moved

their feet one at a time, left foot, sidestep, right foot drawn up, left foot, sidestep again.

The Mufti's bodyguards inched slowly along with them on a line parallel to the Wall, carefully avoiding drawing closer.

"Keep moving, Lilli, keep moving, el-Krim," said Jesse Spanish.

"Yes, my dear girl," el-Krim muttered. "Keep close to me. He has men all over the area. We are safe as long as we keep close to each other."

Lilli nodded.

"Hold onto him, young Quintana," advised el-Krim. "He's frightened of the death you are offering him, although he does not show it. But he is frightened of the gun more than of the sword."

The distance between them and the Buick shrank.

The cords in the Mufti's neck bulged like thick steel wire beneath the skin. Jesse could smell a faint sweet cologne in the man's beard. He spoke again straight into the man's ear.

"Tell your driver to open the doors on this side of the car and to get in, start the engine, and get out."

El-Husseini's voice was hoarse from the pressure of Jesse's arm.

Lilli looked questioningly at el-Krim, her forehead wrinkled in light lines.

El-Krim translated into Spanish. "He ordered the driver to start the motor, open the doors on your side, and get out of there."

Lilli's feet were moving along the wall at the same time, her hands spread behind her, gliding along the stone. The surface of each block was smooth, felt almost polished to her touch, yet when she glanced up over her shoulder, she could see the stones above her head were rough-hewn and gritty. How many hands had caressed the stones her hands were caressing now? How many hearts had prayed right here as hers was praying now, in a way so different?

She shifted her glance from the Buick to Jesse. The car was standing with its doors open, its engine running. Jesse was tight-lipped, perspiring lightly, breathing a little heavier than usual. She stared at the back of el-Husseini's neck, at the tiny red and gray hairs that had been freshly barbered and ran in neatly increasing lengths up the back of his head and flattened where his white hat was pulled down tight.

They reached the car.

"Lilli," Jesse spoke without looking at her. He had not looked at her once, moving along the Wall. He spotted more dark figures slipping away from the building and flattening themselves against the Wall. The driver had drifted out into the middle of the courtyard and stood there forlornly, uncertain of what to do with his hands.

El-Krim moved closer to the front right side of the Buick a few feet away from Jesse and el-Husseini. Both men showed deep strain in their faces. The Mufti's face was reddish, his lips tightly drawn back over his teeth in a sickly smile of terror. Jesse's face was seamed with lines of sweat trickling down toward his chin. The expression in their eyes was unmistakable, one man's filled with fear, the other's with anger.

When Jesse spoke to Lilli, however, he was cool and unhurried.

"Lilli, you'll have to drive. O.K.? I think it's an automatic. You can handle it."

She bent away from the Wall and leaned inside through the front door.

"It is automatic. But, Jesse, I'm not sure—"

Before Lilli could finish, Jesse, without taking his eyes from the Mufti's men across the court, asked, "El-Krim, can you drive it?"

"I'm afraid not, young Quintana. You will have to drive it yourself."

"Lilli, get in the front," Jesse ordered. "El-Krim, in the back."

The Mufti's bodyguards began to move slowly toward them. When Lilli and el-Krim were inside the Buick, Jesse said to the Mufti, "Order them to stay where they are."

The Mufti shouted to his men. They stopped in their tracks. Jesse started to drag the Mufti toward the open rear door of the Buick. Suddenly, with an unexpected surge of strength, el-Husseini twisted savagely away from Jesse and broke loose. He did not run but stood four or five feet from the open door. In a moment he had recomposed himself. He grew aloof, dignified, unafraid, staring blankly into the tiny bore of Jesse's Mauser.

"Shoot me now, Quinn. I will never get into that machine to become the prisoner of Jews. Shoot me."

"Jesse, get in, they're coming!" It was Lilli.

Swinging the rear door closed, Jesse crawled behind the wheel and dropped the gear lever into drive. The door opposite him slammed shut as the Buick shot forward jerkily. The car was facing north, and Jesse had to cover fifteen yards before he could

311

swing the heavy machine around in a tight U-turn. A small dus storm rose up behind him as he drove back along the Wall.

"You can still kill him," el-Krim urged, leaning forward int the front seat. "Kill him. For your fathers. He told me all abou them." The Mauser pistol was on the seat next to Jesse. He wa drawing abreast of the Mufti. The man had not moved. He re mained in the spot as though he had been fixed there. Somethin had drawn the Mufti's attention from the escape of the Quinns t the top of the Western Wall.

Jesse slowed the Buick and tried the crank of the window b his side. It was locked like the others. The Mufti now was glarin straight at Jesse through cold blue eyes. Nothing was in th bearded, long-nosed face but pure seasoned hatred. Jesse wante to smash the face, grind out the hatred.

The Mufti's hand was raising.

"Kill the Mufti," the coarse voice had said to him in the dark ness of the car on their way here, "Kill the Mufti or you'll be ou there alone." El-Krim had said. "Kill him for your fathers."

"Kill the Mufti," a voice within Jesse's own brain was saying "Lilli is safe. Lilli came first and is safe in this car."

The Buick was now past the Mufti. Twenty feet, thirty feet forty feet, still crawling toward the outer range of the plastiqu in the fountain pen.

Jesse pulled out the pencil. Someone outside had begun firing Jesse could hear the bullets rattling against the body of the Buick Lilli screamed once.

In the rear-view mirror Jesse could see the Mufti looking u at the Wall. Jesse reached for the clip on the pencil with hi thumb. He braked the Buick hard and felt the car nosedive forwar under its extra weight. Had he passed the twenty-five yard limit His thumb was on the top of the clip. He felt the metal beginnin to give under pressure.

Suddenly he heard a muffled explosion and watched in surpris as the Mufti was thrown backward against the Wall a few fee behind him. The front of his *abiyah*, where he had placed th document and the fountain pen, blew outward away from hi body, shredded into rags. The great saucer-shaped white hat tha the Mufti loved floated from his head and settled in the dust. Wit outstretched hands, el-Husseini clawed at the smoothness of th stone wall as he slid slowly toward the ground.

The pencil was still in Jesse's hand, the clip in its origina position. His thumb had hardly moved it. Had they tricked hin

312

about what would explode the device? Or had someone else exploded it from somewhere else? Goddamn them.

Jesse dropped the pencil on the seat next to the Mauser, pushed the gear lever into low, and stomped on the accelerator. The Buick's rear wheels spun, gripped, and, as Jesse eased off the throttle, the car roared away. Lilli and el-Krim were shouting, but he paid no attention to what they were saying. He had seen what there was to see, but unlike them, he knew what had happened.

Several machine guns were clattering dimly behind him, and the bullets were striking the rear of the Buick, making sounds like *kerchunk, kerchunk, kerchunk.* The rear window developed spiderweb cracks but nothing shattered, not a bullet penetrated the interior. As the Buick sped by the end of the Wall and the feel of the ride did not change a trifle, Jesse knew the car had been fitted with solid-rubber tires. There would be no flats. He sat back in his seat and gripped the wheel. He felt as though he were driving a tank. A small, repressed joy started to make its way up from his stomach toward his mind, reminding him of the feeling he used to get when he shot down an enemy plane.

In the rear-view mirror through a swirl of rising dust he caught sight of the Mufti lying on the ground surrounded by a half-dozen men. Other men were scattering out in the courtyard firing their machine guns wildly. They were no longer firing at the Buick, but up at the Wailing Wall and at the rooftop of the building behind them. Two men picked the Mufti up by an arm and leg and were carrying him like a sack along the Wall toward shelter at the north end. All over the courtyard little chains of dusty geysers were racing around chasing one Arab gunman or another. Jesse never saw whether any Arab gunman lost a race. But somewhere from up high, old members of the Irgun were trying hard to catch them.

Jesse left the Old City through a low gap in the wall called the Dung Gate. A few minutes later, following a map he had memorized at Anna's, he reached the square of St. Peter's Church.

El-Krim was sitting on the edge of his seat, leaning forward, grinning. "I saw it. I saw it and did not believe it. It was *plastique*, no? How did you do it?"

Jesse said, "The fountain pen. But I don't think I touched it off. Somebody else did it."

"Is he dead?" Lilli asked. "What was it?"

"Maybe," el-Krim answered her first question. "Maybe not. Do you know, Quintana, he was wearing a bulletproof vest. He

313

may survive yet. But you have hurt him badly—oh, very badly
How sweet as honey is the taste of revenge. Your fathers, may
Allah bless them, are blessed with children such as you. My own
sons threw in with the enemy."

At that thought el-Krim grew somber and sat back in his seat

As they entered the square of St. Peter's Church, they heard
guns going off up before them. Jesse had no choice except to head
straight for them. Three loud explosions to their front sent vibrations right up through the Buick. Lilli clutched the armrest on her
right and thrust herself back against the seat, braced for whatever
was going to happen.

Dead ahead of them, cutting across the road, was a high, heavy
barbed-wire barrier raised over short steel spikes and low concrete
pylons embedded in the ground. The barrier had been set up to
stop everything but a heavy tank.

Right in the center, however, under debris and smoke that was
just settling, was a shallow crater ten feet long and three feet deep
and five or six feet wide. Samuel's people had done what they
said they would do, but they had taken a good piece of the road
with it.

Jesse crossed the square at forty miles an hour. An Arab sentry
jumped out from behind a sandbag emplacement and waved him
down. El-Krim leaned forward and waved back to confuse him.

Jesse roared right by. A machine gun off to the right raked the
car from end to end. Lilli said, "Oh, Christ," and jumped away
from the door and held on to Jesse without hampering his driving
El-Krim sat upright in the back seat, cursing quietly in Arabic and
watching the fighting around him.

From the other side of the barbed wire two men were shooting
automatic weapons into the square. One raised his arm and waved
Jesse on frantically. Rifles were going off from both directions.
Inside the sealed Buick the explosions sounded dull and impotent.

Jesse aimed the Buick for the gap, dropped his speed, and
lifted himself over the wheel to measure how deep the crater had
been blown. Then he drove into it. The heavy car rumbled downward, sounding as though its bottom would drop out. It crossed
a few feet of rubble and accelerated toward the opposite incline.

It rocked and jounced and started to climb. The rear wheels
spun and gripped and then, with the car fishtailing slightly, pushed
the overweight chassis up the slope, edging the front wheels over
the rim farther and farther. When they were half over the edge,
the rear wheels lost contact with the ground and spun helplessly

in the air as the bottom of the heavy sedan hung up fast on the asphalt.

Three men dashed into the street in front of them and began shooting across the barrier.

"Out," yelled Jesse. "We're stuck."

"Wait," said el-Krim. "Precaution, precaution."

He threw open the rear doors. The gunfire crackled sharply now. First one gun would fire and another would answer on a different note. The air was filling with guns speaking to one another.

"Go now," shouted el-Krim.

Jesse seized Lilli's hand and dragged her across the seat after him, jumping into the road. A few yards away was a small bunker of sandbags and concrete blocks. A man stood there, waving them on.

Jesse pushed Lilli in front of him and they ran crouching toward safety. Bullets were thudding into the Buick or whistling over their heads. Before them the three men were firing continuously. Shielded by the Buick standing with its doors spread like guardian hands, they reached the bunker and dropped to the ground on their knees. Jesse immediately crawled to the side and peered around a sand bag.

El-Krim was crawling over the back seat into the front. Then, following the track of Jesse and Lilli, the old Moroccan chief trotted almost casually over the ground and arrived at the bunker, smiling broadly at the welcome he received. Politely, he accepted the compulsive hug Lilli threw around him and with a corner of his burnoose dabbed at the tears of happiness and relief streaming down her face. Jesse laid a hand gently on the back of each one, wondering how a great old warrior chieftain of the Riffs could feel about such informality from the son of an old infidel friend.

Within thirty minutes a happy, exhausted Lilli and a quietly exuberant Jesse were reunited somewhat tearfully with Anna and Samuel. And with el-Krim along as a welcome guest, the five people drove back along the Gaza Road toward the settlement at Beit Darras.

Chapter 23

News of the incident at the Western Wall never leaked out of the
Arab Quarter. No mention was ever made of the Mufti, and the
fate of el-Husseini remained an uncertainty. The members of the
Irgun faded back into the populace and the Israeli press reported
the bombing of the border barrier at St. Peter's as an unfortunate
mysterious mistake. El-Krim spent three days at Beit Darras and
then returned to obscurity in Cairo.

A week later, on the morning of their departure from Israel,
Jesse stomped on a wine glass wrapped in a towel and he and Lilli
were married in a simple ancient ceremony performed at Beit
Darras. A small group of people gathered for the occasion before
the entrance of the long open shed that had been decorated with
plants and desert flowers according to tradition.

Anna and Samuel, with their own three children by their side,
looked on with faces as close to beaming as they had been for
years. Just inside the shed, the rabbi, facing the opening, gave
the final blessing.

Jesse and Lilli, their heads slightly bowed, held hands tightly
and raised their eyes toward the magnificent ruin of the Handley
Page. Just then, in the few rays of sunlight leaking through the
roof, the great phantom of an aircraft seemed aglow with the
spirits of the Quintana Brother Aces, Michael and Joseph, who
had flown her so well and whom she had saved so often that they
might live to father and to shape the lives of these cousins Quinn.

About the Author

Elliot Tokson was born and raised in the environs of Boston, Massachusetts, and went to school at Boston University and Harvard, from which he holds several degrees. He also has a Ph.D. in English from Columbia. Mr. Tokson has traveled extensively in eastern and western Europe. He is a crapshooter and a collector of old English revolvers. He lives in Armonk, New York, with his wife, her two children, two Doberman pinschers, and an orange cat named Ace.

THRILLS * CHILLS * MYSTERY
from FAWCETT BOOKS

Great Adventures in Reading

EAST OF JAMAICA   14309 $2.50
by Kaye Wilson Klem

    She was a titian-haired New Englander who had fled to the lush, volcanic island of Martinique. She never dreamed she would be forced to become a pleasure toy for the island's women-hungry planters.

THE EMERALD EMBRACE   14316 $2.50
by Diane du Pont

    Beautiful Liberty Moore sought refuge at sea in the arms of a handsome stranger, unaware that he was the naval hero Stephen Delaplane, unaware that she would be taken from him and forced to become the bride of the most powerful ruler in the East.

KINGSLEY'S EMPIRE   14324 $2.50
by Michael Jahn

    Here is the story of a great shipping dynasty built on the ashes of a shore pirate's wiles and with the fire of an heiress's beauty.

FAWCETT GOLD MEDAL BOOKS

Great Adventures in Reading

THE GREEN RIPPER   14345 $2.50
by John D. MacDonald
  Gretel, the one girl the hard-boiled Travis McGee had actually
fallen for—dead of a "mysterious illness." McGee calls it murder.
This time he's out for blood.

SCANDAL OF FALCONHURST   14334 $2.50
by Ashley Carter
  Ellen, the lovely mustee, through a trick of fate marries into the
wealthiest family in New Orleans. But she must somehow free the
man she really loves, the son of a white plantation owner, sold to die
as a slave. In the exciting tradition of MANDINGO.

WINGED PRIESTESS   14329 $2.50
by Joyce Verrette
  The slave: Ilbaya, of noble birth, in love with his master's concu-
bine. He risks death with each encounter. The Queen: beautiful Nef-
rytatanen. To keep the love of her husband she must undergo the
dangerous ritual that will make her the "winged" priestess—or destroy her! An epic of ancient Egypt.

FAWCETT GOLD MEDAL BOOKS

Buy them at your local bookstore or use this handy coupon for ordering.

COLUMBIA BOOK SERVICE (a CBS Publications Co.)
32275 Mally Road, P.O. Box FB, Madison Heights, MI 48071

Please send me the books I have checked above. Orders for less than 5 books
must include 75¢ for the first book and 25¢ for each additional book to cover
postage and handling. Orders for 5 books or more postage is FREE. Send check
or money order only.

Cost $_____   Name _____
Postage_____   Address _____
Sales tax*_____   City _____
Total $_____   State _____ Zip _____
*The government requires us to collect sales tax in all states except AK, DE,
MT, NH and OR.

This offer expires 1 April 81   8100-2